'The Wayward Spy' by Roger Croft is not your James Bond type of spy thriller. Croft is more the John Le Carre-type writer with a heavy mix of Graham Greene. International intrigue, twisted plots and spy craft all make for an interesting read....Michael Vaux is a very likeable character that readers are pulling for from the start—and there is just enough humor to keep this book a fun read.

Portland Book Review

Croft deserves credit for building his story line on an unusual foundation.

Publishers Weekly

Our protagonist Michael Vaux is not a career intelligence officer—he's a retired journalist, independent-minded and seemingly never without a drink in his hand....The plot is elaborate and takes the reader down countless blind alleys. But the reader would be hard-pressed to foresee the final outcome.

Pete Willows in The Egyptian Gazette / Mail, Cairo

'The Wayward Spy' takes the best of spy novels from the likes of Le Carre and kicks it up a notch....Wayward this spy might be, but I found I couldn't put the book down.

San Francisco Book Review

At the heart of this espionage story is the brewing nuclear arms build-up that could disrupt the balance of power in the Mideast....Syria is preparing to complete a multi-billion dollar arms deal with Russia—and Michael Vaux's old college friend is Syria's top arms negotiator.

Rudd Review

Croft's book is cynical and bleak but also thought-provoking.... The prose is intricate and deeply textured...In the end (Vaux) is torn between betraying his friends or betraying his country.

John D. Trudel, author of 'God's House'.

Fun read, like the great spy novels, but with added humor.

The descriptions and details in the novel are as sharp as daggers...the plot is full of winding curves.

The Wayward Spy

Roger Croft

To my sister Margaret Horner
In memory

Other books by Roger Croft

Swindle!
Bent Triangle

Cassio Books International

In one respect indeed, our employment may be reckoned dishonest, because like great statesmen, we encourage those who betray their friends.

– John Gay 1685-1732

You can't go home again.

– Thomas Wolfe 1900-1938

PART ONE

England, 1992

Vaux hated flying. The danger of sudden, violent death—
or worse, spiraling earthward with time to contemplate the
final impact—was a recurring fear he probably shared with
most people. But Vaux had two additional phobias: to be seated
next to a talkative, cheerful bore or an exquisitely elegant and
attractive woman of a certain age. When he had traveled on
assignments, he traveled first class—thanks to the pervasive
myth among editors that the possibility of meeting a showbiz
celebrity or high-profile corporate executive (even an influential politician) was high.

'Contacts' are the holy grail of competitive journalism.
But in the comfort of the first-class cabin, he was securely
cocooned within a wide, deep seat and didn't feel inclined to
be sociable. In any case, he had observed that moneyed people
usually ignore their anonymous traveling companions—hence
the editorial myth. What's more, after a few drinks and a passable meal, he usually fell asleep, oblivious of the nebulous dangers that swirled around the sleek metal tube soaring through
the ether.

So perhaps it was only half an ill omen that on this, his final return to England, he was placed in the middle seat (economy class) between a good-looking boy-next-door type, and a
slim peroxide blonde in super-tight jeans and billowy blouse
whose lined, tanned face betrayed her 'mature' years. Young
men hadn't lived long enough to become boring and in any

case, equipped with headphones and a Walkman, were usually preoccupied in some silent music heaven of their own. He was glad he had packed his whisky flask in the inside pocket of the blazer that hung from the back of the seat in front of him. He'd have the two pre-meal free drinks the air- line customarily allowed and then augment the alcoholic fix as the night wore on. The drinks would break the ice and ease the way to what he saw as the inevitable opening conversational gambits between him and the worldly lady who sat so close but traveled alone.

Suddenly he realized someone was talking to him. It was the flight attendant—a rather portly matron who in the Dark Ages would have been retired years ago. She was telling him that the last of the steak had been taken by his blonde compan- ion and that therefore he had no choice but to take the fish. The steak lady smiled in apology: 'I do hope you don't mind. But I'll be having fish for the next few weeks as a steady diet, so I fancied the steak.'

'Oh, not at all,' Vaux lied. 'Sounds as if you're going on a fishing holiday.'

'Not really. My son lives in Aberdeen, and he and his wife both believe in taking advantage of the fresh fish they can buy every day at the market. Caught the same day, you see. He's in oil, by the way, not the fisheries.'

Vaux gave a sidelong glance at the young man who was al- ready bent over his meal, scooping up the remains of some Jell- O-like dessert. His eyes were half-closed and unseeing as his head nodded metronomically to the rhythms of his private music collection. Vaux was relieved. After the dried-up bluefish with desiccated button mushrooms, he fell asleep—thankful that nei- ther of his obligatory traveling companions was too demanding.

* * *

The rented Audi Cabriolet from Heathrow took him smoothly and relatively quickly—despite a couple of episodes of grinding gears, stalled engine, and angry honking from drivers piling up behind him—to his first destination, an unprepossessing b&b on what, before the M1 was built, was the major highway to London. The old building had been recently painted white (he remembered it as gray) with the familiar well-proportioned window frames now painted a high-gloss black. Even though it had the appearance of once being a small farm house, he had always thought that the basic design of the pub—for that's what it was—owed a lot to Georgian architecture.

Which could not be said of the houses and bungalows in the nearby maze of roads and lanes that had sprouted in the speculative building boom of the long-ago 1930s. These suburban dwellings represented a mish-mash of architectural styles from mock-Tudor and ersatz Elizabethan to rococo Italianate and phony Mies van der Rohe. But this was home. And as usual on such visits, he would down a pint of bitter and eat a cold sausage while inquiring about a room.

* * *

The fat and bald fellow who was here four years ago had been replaced by two men whose mannerisms and tenor of voice indicated the mutation of the Pig & Whistle to gay ownership. How times change, thought Vaux. Dear old Florrie, who ran the pub in the turbulent war years, must be turning in her grave, not to mention Uncle Aubrey, who had spent most of his leaves from the Royal Navy ensconced in the Pig & Whistle's now enlarged saloon bar.

'Front or back, sir. You have a choice,' said the younger of the couple. His highlighted blond hair was cut short with a little quiff. He had blue eyes and full lips. His partner was tall and scrawny with a bald spot crowning his short salt and pepper hair.

'Any difference in price?' asked Vaux.

'The front goes for sixty pounds, the rear for fifty,' he said as he skimmed some froth off the pint of Watney's.

'Knowing Watford Lane, I guess the front's kind of noisy,' said Vaux, who didn't care about traffic noise but just wanted to sound conversational and maybe make clear he was no stranger to these parts.

'Day time, yeah. But not at night, really.' He smiled as he put the beer down on the old oak bar.

* * *

When the newspaper laid off most of its senior writers, Vaux took it philosophically. It was a bolt from the blue, and few staffers had any inkling of the tough measures the paper's management deemed vital to boost the proprietor's return on his mega-buck investment. And since his cohort of seasoned journalists had reached an inevitable seniority and could claim fatter paychecks than their younger colleagues, economic necessity demanded the old hands be sacrificed on the altar of higher profits. Vaux was not an economic illiterate, and so he understood the logic of the market place even if it hurt him personally. Softening the impact of the pink slips were surprisingly generous cash payouts coupled with a guaranteed lifetime pension which, though only a fraction of his salary, he figured was probably enough to live on.

But what to do? Freelance perhaps. Or should he take the opportunity to do something he had been dreaming about for some time: go back to England. Specifically, see if that bungalow opposite his mother's home was still for sale. Unlike many who had left home for North America, Vaux had not developed a love-hate relationship with his mother country. With him it was all love. He knew that ultimately he would go back. Was it nostalgia? Partly. But also an unwavering conviction that this was where his roots had sunk too deep to let go.

* * *

A 'For Sale' sign was posted on the thick trunk of the large willow that dominated the front garden. He used to climb that tree with John, Mrs. Goodchild's only son and his constant companion until they both parted ways for different schools. Old Mrs. Kingston (she had seemed forever old) had lived opposite them for more than two decades, all through the war and until her bedridden mother finally died on VE day. But the whitewashed stucco bungalow had had several tenants since those far-off days and most of them had known his mother. So here it was—finally vacant and beckoning. He had already put in a bid, and Susan Appleby, the local estate agent who kept in touch with him, would be waiting for his telephone call. Yes, here it was, his unremarkable dream house—with two large bedrooms, a box room, and two living rooms.

The big, old-fashioned kitchen looked on to the rear lawn and beyond. And *the beyond* held the key to Vaux's fascination and obsession with No. 32 Willow Drive. For beyond the tall wood fence at the end of the back garden lay the rolling verdant hills, spotted with clusters of oak and beech and scattered copses of silver birch and elm, that formed the inviolable green belt, the legislated vast swath of farm and parkland that separated the southern outreaches of Hertfordshire from the amorphous conurbation of London. For years, Vaux had marveled at the fact that there would be no man-made obstacle— except maybe a haystack or tractor—to mar his view of England's green and pleasant land (he was sentimental).

Beyond his long-planned terrace outside the french windows of the rear lounge (a feature of all Willow Drive's identical bungalows) would stretch acres of pasture, hedgerows, and woodlands. The long garden swept down to a farmer's field—used mainly now by a horse-riding school—and if he wanted, there was space for a swimming pool. In his mind, this was the most overlooked, under-rated vista within miles. It meant that the value of No. 32 was about 30 percent

more than his mother's bungalow—directly opposite—
that had no view and a postage stamp of a backyard. Real-
istically, he thought the bungalows on the south side of the
street, those with an uninterrupted view of the green belt,
should fetch double the price of the same dwellings across the
road. Thus No. 32 was a veritable bargain and he had convinced himself that he could be happy here for many years.

* * *

'Oh, Mr. Vaucks? A Susan Appleby phoned—from the estate agents.' This from the young man with blond highlights
who was tending the bar alone.

'V-a-u-x,' spelled Vaux. 'Pronounced veau, as in French
for veal.'

'Ah, sorry, mate. I'll remember next time,' said the young
man cheerfully as he wiped some knives and forks. 'Like a
beer, would you?'

'No. I think it's late enough for a whisky,' said Vaux. 'A
Cutty if you have it.'

'Nah, sorry, mate. But we've got Dewar's or Haig. Glen-
fiddich in the malts.'

'Make it a Dewar's then, please.' Vaux saw a white phone
at the corner of the bar. It was just past 5 p.m. and there was
no one around. He thought he'd better be a little more sociable since the boy and his presumed lover were going to be his
hosts for a few weeks.

'Can I use that phone? What's your name, by the way?'

'I'm Pete, and you can use it any time—for local calls,
mind.'

Vaux fished his diary out of his pocket, looked up
Ms. Appleby's number, and dialed.

'Michael! How are you?' She was her usual gushing self,
thought Vaux. He decided not to ask her to the Pig & Whistle

for a drink until tomorrow. Jet-lagged and tired, he'd have an early night.

'I'm just fine. But tired from the trip.'

'Of course you are, my dear. We'll get together tomorrow, if that's convenient.'

It was. 'Any news?'

'Yes. I'm afraid someone's put in a higher bid.'

'For the house?'

'What a silly question, Michael. You *must* be exhausted.'

'Sorry. Just a little shocked. After all these weeks with no one else showing any interest, I thought it was in the bag.'

'Unfortunately not, my dear. The latest offer is for £20,000 more than the asking price—or your bid,' said Susan with more enthusiasm than Vaux thought appropriate. No doubt salivating over the fatter commission in the offing.

'Oh hell. Well, that's a disappointment.' They both said nothing for what seemed to Vaux like two or three minutes. Clearly Susan was waiting patiently for him to up his bid and clinch the deal. God, how he hated haggling over money.

'Let me sleep on it,' he said finally.

Efforts at small-talk with Pete were frustrated by the pub's ultra-high decibel sound system. He had three double scotches and a cold beef sandwich before mounting the creaky narrow staircase to his small room overlooking Watford Lane.

2

Susan Appleby nibbled at a croissant while holding the clunky new Motorola mobile phone to her ear. It was the usual breakfast call from Betty, who apparently found it difficult to face the working day without first touching base with her best friend. Betty looked upon her more as an elder sister, Susan told herself, though the difference in ages was more like aunt and niece. The topics discussed in these early morning gossips varied from men to real estate sales and back to men.

Betty had asked what the new stranger in their midst looked like.

'Well, I've never actually met him face to face. We've talked a lot on the phone, of course. But Jean, my predecessor, says he's tall, quite handsome, and single,' said Susan. 'Knocked around a bit, I shouldn't wonder. But, you know, an older man.'

'Sounds like you may at last have found your Mr. Right. You could be on the verge of a big, romantic adventure, Sue,' said Betty, her tone enthusiastic though betraying a dash of skepticism.

'Betty, please. You know that's not my style. Never mix business with pleasure. I've told you that a million times.'

'There's fat chance of that in my job, don't worry.' Betty was a family doctor's receptionist, stuck behind a desk eight hours a day. 'So he's single, is he. Divorced, widowed, or confirmed bachelor?'

'He mentioned an ex once—supposed to be living in California. He said that he'd considered going to California at first but finally decided to "go home," as he put it.'

'Funny buying a place on Willow Drive, though.'

'He was brought up there. His mother lived at No. 23 for years and died about twelve years ago. But he wanted one of the places opposite—with the "superb, southerly view," said Susan, quoting directly from No. 32's sales sheet. 'Anyway, darling, I must go. Maybe we'll have a quick lunch later in the week.'

She had arranged to meet Vaux in the lobby of the newly built Hilton that marked the turn-off from the M1 into the sprawl of suburban development that had spread willy-nilly from Watford and its satellites.

Vaux had agreed mainly because he didn't particularly want to talk business in the saloon bar of the Pig & Whistle where Pete and his partner would probably eavesdrop, if only for momentary entertainment. What's more, it was quite possible, to his suspicious mind, that they knew the competition—the would-be buyer who had outbid him. He found the hotel without much difficulty and sat himself down in one of the over-stuffed armchairs with its back to the main entrance. At 11:30 a.m. precisely he heard the rapid click of high heels on the travertine floor. He turned and guessed it was Susan. He got up and smiled a welcome.

'Mr. Vaux, I presume.' She shouted across the lobby as though determined to beat him to the draw. He was holding against his chest a *Daily Telegraph*, a simple ploy he said he would use to ensure instant recognition.

She was better looking than he had imagined. Slim, mid-thirties, blonde hair pushed back into a ponytail, retrousse nose, lips rather thin, probably blue eyes behind the dark metal-framed sunglasses. She was wearing a narrow-fitting sheath dress with, for that time of day, a deep décolletage. And the same posh English accent.

'Yes, indeed. Nice finally to meet you, Susan.'

She sat down in the chair opposite him. His eyes instantly locked on to her now exposed and thinnish thighs as she opened her Prada brief case. She produced a sheaf of papers which she began to sort through.

'Ah, here we are. Their formal offer. As you see it's for £200,000.' She handed over the photocopy of a letter. Vaux saw it was from a firm of solicitors (Abel, Bates, Collins & Dalfen) with no indication who was making the offer.

They sat in silence while he read and re-read the letter.

'Well, okay. I've been thinking about it, of course. And I'll top his offer by £5,000. I don't want to get into a sort of auction here. But the other point I wanted to raise was this: do you think that if I were to meet the sellers it might do any good? I mean, if it's some old lady moving into a nursing home or something, maybe she'd prefer to sell it to someone who was brought up in the area.' Vaux always had faith, misplaced or not, in his own powers of persuasion.

Susan's eyes widened. 'Well, for starters it's not some old lady. A woman died there six months or so ago and her two sons want to sell it. I can assure you that the only thing that matters to them is the money. They have their own lives and live in London. At least one does, the other's in Australia.'

Was she on his side or was she being deliberately blunt and a little cold? It was nearly midday and he decided to make the move he had planned as he sipped the strong tea and nibbled at the greasy margarined toast that had been brought up at 8 a.m. by Mrs. Caldwell, the pub's cook and general help.

'Look, how about some lunch. We can talk the whole thing over and then visit No. 32. What's the restaurant here like?'

'Oh this place is the pits. It's new and I don't think they've found a proper chef yet. But have no fear, Michael, I know a nice little spot in town.'

* * *

He wished she had told him it was an Italian restaurant. Pasta and rich Italian sauces always seemed too heavy for lunch. But she made clear from the outset that the meal was 'on her' so he voiced no objection. For Watford, a dreary and quiet dormitory town only twenty miles northwest of the English capital, it was quite a spiffy place: art deco furnishings, white on white color scheme, and a super-charged espresso machine that hissed and wheezed spasmodically. He chose the non-pasta special—*nodino di vitello*—and Susan opted for the grilled tiger shrimp. She ordered a vintage (1983) red wine called *Amarone Masi*, which Vaux noted, cost an alarming £130. The conversation centered on the health of the property market (booming, as usual) and Mrs. Thatcher's drive in the late '80s to sell council houses at rock-bottom prices to sitting tenants to encourage what she called 'a property-owning democracy.' The net result so far had been that most of the council tenants had said thank you very much and then turned around to sell the houses at three or four times what they had paid to buy them. Another case of mispriced privatization, suggested Vaux.

During the meal Susan spoke enthusiastically about her annual trip to a small farmer's cottage in Tuscany and how her knowledge of Italian wines had increased 'exponentially' since she fell in love with the country. Vaux, who had a delicate stomach, had always been indifferent to wine. He was relieved that she was happy doing most of the talking. She poured the last two glasses for herself, sensing perhaps that Vaux wanted to keep a clear head. Two demitasses of espresso arrived.

By now, Vaux had decided that in a brassy sort of way, Susan was an attractive woman and probably not unamenable to a fling, should he opt to plunge into a British relationship this early in the game. No, he thought. Better to wait until he'd bought the bloody house. Mustn't let what little wine he'd had go to his head. Finally he raised the question that had been hovering throughout the meal.

'Who is, or are, my adversaries?' he asked bluntly.

Again the widening of the eyes—which had turned out
to be a deep azure blue, accentuated by a generous application
of mascara. 'I'm not at liberty to say as of this moment, Michael.
But I think you'd better know that the party has ample resources
and I frankly don't doubt that he'll trump your increased bid.
By how much I don't know. But he seems to want the house
badly.'

So it was a 'he.' 'Um. Well, we'll have to see.' He knew
that he too could go higher. But it could mean cutting into his
retirement payout that he would have preferred not to touch.

No. 32 was in a terrible state. Mrs. Kingston, who had
lived there for fifty years or so, had done nothing in the way
of decorating or modernization. Faded and stained wallpaper,
worn-out linoleum in the hallways, wood floors that in some
places sagged with the onslaught of dry rot, ominous cobwebs
that hung from tobacco-stained ceilings, chipped paintwork.
It was a depressing sight—though not unexpected. Susan
had warned Vaux that the place needed a complete makeover
and he had included refurbishing and some minor structural
changes (he wanted to pull down the odd wall) plus the expense of an up-to-date kitchen with shiny stainless steel appliances in his estimate of the total costs including the purchase
price. Of course, now it seemed he'd have to throw those calculations out the window.

He walked from the kitchen, where Susan was running tap water in the sink to wash down a few bewildered
earwigs and wood lice, and walked through the narrow
corridor to the rear living room. Yes, the french windows were intact, though boasting perhaps two years of
grime and what looked like peeling scotch tape where the
warped wooden frames left a narrow gap. Mrs. Kingston
must have been a practical woman: she had found a cheap
and effective way to block an English winter's cold and
chilly drafts.

He pulled the tarnished brass door handle down and pushed gently to see if the doors were still working. They creaked and moaned but finally gave way. He stepped down to a small flagstone terrace with dandelions and crabgrass and assorted weeds sprouting between the stones. Then he raised his eyes, and there it was: the reason for all this effort and expense—the long and broad vista of green, lush countryside stretching as far as the eye could see. That made everything else worthwhile. But Vaux's sudden burst of elation sank as he thought of the bidding war that seemed now inevitable.

The garden itself looked neglected but wild in an attractive kind of way. The overgrown lawn hadn't been cut since the previous summer and the haphazard flowerbeds, planted to no apparent overall landscaped design, looked as if a good week's work by a skilled gardener could put things to rights. Bright yellow daffodils and crocuses were pushing up for daylight above the overgrown grass, and a few straggly rose bushes looked sad and neglected. He heard Susan's unmistakable footfalls and stepped back into the room.

'I was thinking of pulling that wall down and making an even larger living room,' said Vaux, optimistic again, simply not believing that all his plans and dreams could be easily shattered by some greedy speculator who saw the same possibilities and attractions of the property as he did. He was gesturing toward the wall that separated the rear lounge from what the sale sheet had called the second bedroom.

'Yes, I think that's brilliant,' said Susan with some unexpected enthusiasm. 'Then perhaps you could install another pair of french windows to open up on a much wider terrace.'

'That's exactly what I had in mind. Wider and much deeper, like the patios one sometimes sees in America. This is about the size of a postage stamp. Funny how the English don't seem very keen on outdoor living, barbecues and that sort of thing, isn't it.'

'Michael: thirty years' absence has helped you forget. The weather, remember? I mean, we've had some beautiful summers recently. But very often they can be wet and soggy.'

'Ah yes,' conceded Vaux. 'But that view will be something like a Turner, or more accurately perhaps, a Constable, on a wet and cloudy evanescent summer day,' said Vaux dreamily. Today, he had to admit, it was a rather gray scene with low, dark, billowy clouds scudding south to London and a chilly northerly wind that rocked the big trees and ruffled the hedgerows.

Susan looked at Vaux with some amazement. She would have to remember that reference to Turner. It would resonate in some future sales pitch for a 'modern desirable residence with splendid view.'

On a final look-around, Vaux made note of the semi-tiled bathroom and ancient fixtures—1930s vintage, stained and cracked. The toilet boasted a vaulted water tank that nearly touched the ceiling and a long pull chain to release what was still an impressive flood. New fixtures would be a must, but he might be able to do something with the lion-pawed old bathtub. He recalled reading somewhere that they were all the rage again. That's if he finally moved in.

Vaux sat gloomily over his whisky in the saloon bar of the Pig & Whistle. It had been a long day, but an illuminating one. No. 32 had been just as imagined: the layout of the only floor—the ground floor—had of course been identical to his mother's house opposite. The original spec builder's only concessions to variety were small modifications to the facades of each bungalow—some had wooden, Tudoresque gables, while here and there would be an unexpected bank of red brick or an inlaid slate to prettify a wall. The other variation the builder figured might attract buyers was the thick frosted glass in the solid wooden front doors: some were round, some square, and there was even the odd stained multicolored diamond window.

The universal porch had now succumbed to a new wave
of fashion: Vaux remembered them as identical from one end
of the street to the other. But now it seemed that every other
owner or occupier had enclosed the porch—no doubt another
attempt to keep the chilly winds of winter at bay. Mrs. Kingston hadn't bothered with this excrescence, and he was thankful for small mercies. But why was he thankful? He didn't even
know if he would ever move in. This explained the existential
gloom. Plus the darkness and a wet late-April evening.

'Excuse me, old chap, did I see you with the beautiful Ms.
Appleby today? She's my estate agent as it happens. Looking
around the neighborhood then?' The speaker was a big man
in every sense: over six feet tall, heavily built with handlebar
mustache, red face, and large, flattish nose. He reminded Vaux
of an RAF pilot in a film about WWII.

'Yes, as a matter of fact. Yes to both questions,' said Vaux,
forcefully trying to lift himself out of the gloom. He told himself that being sociable to the neighbors was essential if he
were ever to live here. After getting to know them he could
go through a sort of triage to eliminate those he didn't care if
he saw again.

'I live just across the road. You'll like it here. Can I get you
a drink—scotch, isn't it?'

'Oh thank you. A Dewar's.'

3

Arthur Davis slumped down in his deep, leather armchair, reached over for the red secure phone, and dialed a London number. It rang several times—longer than usual; his fingers started tapping on his knees out of impatience.

'One-oh-three.'

'Albert here. I think I may have something for you. Name of Michael Vaux. Late fifties. Left U.K. in his early thirties after working on several Fleet Street papers. Posted to North America where he decided to stay. Worked for *Time* and various newspapers. Now retired. Went to Bristol University, studied economics and law. Look 'im up.'

Davis put the phone back in the drawer and looked through the leaded windows. The tall pine trees filtered the view of the main road. The Pig & Whistle was as usual floodlit, and its ground-floor windows projected bright beams of light onto the road. Suddenly he saw an upper floor window light up. A man's figure loomed through the glass and heaved the sash window open. It was Vaux.

Davis hoped he would get a good night's rest. He got up and went through to the kitchen. Mrs. Fletcher, his housekeeper, had left him a casserole of what looked like her expert rabbit stew. All he had to do, as she always said, was put it in the microwave. He didn't really feel that hungry, so he opened a cupboard next to the fridge and extracted a large bottle of Glenmorangie 18. A clean tumbler stood on the counter and he filled it to the brim, wondering why a discerning man like Vaux would prefer blended whisky. He moved back to the lounge, sat in the leather chair, looked up a number in the back of his diary and picked up the regular black phone. An answering machine came on as soon as he dialed. 'Hello. This is Susan Appleby.' The recording was cut off and he heard instead Susan's live and unmistakable voice. 'Hello?' She sounded out of breath. Perhaps he had called at an awkward time.

'Oh hello, Susan—it's Arthur, old girl. Got a minute?'

'Always for you, darling. What's up?'

'You sound a bit out of breath.'

'Oh I've just got in, that's all. Nothing else, I assure you.' She knew him well enough to know what his dirty mind was thinking.

'I met Michael Vaux in the pub tonight. Seems a nice kind of chap. Says there's a competing bid for that shitty bungalow he seems to want to buy.'

'Arthur! Don't be unkind. It's where his mother used to live—or at least just opposite. He likes the view and he plans to do it up if he succeeds in buying it.'

'So I gather. I know you can't say who else is bidding, but I wonder, Susan, if you could do me a favor.'

'It may cost you a dinner and late-night drinkies, dar-ling.'

'That would indeed be a pleasure. Like old times. Do you think I don't yearn for them to return?'

'Don't let's get too much off the point, Arthur.'

'Okay. I'd just appreciate it if you could let me know when and if the other party's offer is withdrawn. I can't see a bidding war without limit. One of them will end up paying more than the damn property is worth, anyway.'

'Do I take it you are interested too, my dear?'

'I'll fill you in when we get together. How about tomor-row week, around 7 p.m.'

'I'm not too sure about that. The market's wild just now and I often have to accommodate would-be buyers in the eve-nings. I'll call you early next week, darling, to confirm.' Susan

wondered what the old sod was up to. But that was him—
devious and totally selfish. She remembered the fling—it
lasted about a year—and how he began to take things for
granted. She was glad she'd ended it, no matter how much
money he had. The house alone was worth about a million, an
old stockbroker mock-Tudor pile that abutted Watford Lane
and was built eighty years ago when the surrounding area was
still farmland. She found herself feeling somewhat empty. He
was always a satisfying fuck. And it was God knows how long
since she'd had a good lay.

* * *

Pete heard the rattle of cups and plates and smelled the
homely fragrance of frying bacon and sausages coming from
the kitchen below. He looked at the alarm clock on his tiny
bedside table. *God! Eight o'clock already.* He moved to get out
of bed when an arm twirled around his waist to tug him back.
Moments later Pete heard Harry's familiar gasp, waited a few
seconds, and then sprang out of bed.

'Do you want Mrs. Caldwell to bring you up some breakfast or are you going to have it downstairs?' he asked.

Harry replied with a groan and pulled the sheet over his
head.

He'd be dead for another hour, thought Pete. He slung on
a pair of jeans and a white t-shirt and made for the bathroom.
On the narrow landing he passed Vaux in underpants and
shirt gripping his sponge bag as if it contained all his worldly
goods.

'Good morning!' greeted Vaux.

'Oh hello, sir. Sleep all right, I hope?'

'Yes, very well as a matter of fact.' He passed the boys'
room whose door had been left ajar. He allowed himself a
quick peep and saw the recumbent body of Harry under a pile
of sheets and blankets, his feet and shapely calves exposed at

the bottom of the bed. His head faced the window. Vaux heard Mrs. Caldwell coming slowly up the stairs, breathing rather heavily, the rattle of china and cutlery presaging delivery of his breakfast. He opened his door for her and she laid the tray down on the narrow walnut dressing table by the window.

'A full English breakfast today, sir,' she said with some pride. 'We always do this on weekends. Hope you like your eggs scrambled.'

'Yes, Mrs. Caldwell. I like eggs any way you care to cook them. Thanks very much.'

'And that's Sainsbury's best Cumberland sausage, that is.'

'Absolutely marvelous. Haven't had a good English sausage for years,' he lied.

He pulled a straight-backed wicker chair up to the dressing table, but it was too low. So he rested the tray on his knees. If there was one thing the English knew how to cook it was breakfast, thought Vaux as he tucked into the sort of bacon rarely found in the States; the sausages too—which he had to admit were probably an acquired taste since there was no demand for them in any other country he knew of. No doubt too much cholesterol, but once a week wouldn't kill him. Yes, he was coming back to all this! And he surely wasn't sorry to say goodbye to the hot dog, the hamburger, and those oversized, glutinous marbled steaks. On the other hand he mustn't be too critical. He liked the odd hotdog, and hamburgers were bloody ubiquitous. He would bet his last dollar that there was a McDonald's within a five-mile radius.

He felt the gloom of the previous evening lift. He would now think positively about the house. He *would* buy it, goddammit. There had to be a limit to what the other guy would pay. And thanks to his lump-sum pension payout, he had ample ammunition with which to fight the son of a bitch. Meanwhile, as Mrs. Caldwell had reminded him, it was Saturday, and he'd better make a plan for the day. But he couldn't go far (to London?) because he had rashly accepted that airline pilot chap's invitation to dinner at his house across the road. He had always

liked that rambling old timbered house since he was a small
boy cavorting and bicycling around the area with his friend
John Goodchild. Even back then, they instinctively knew it
was a rich man's residence. So if they were out scrumping
for crab apples or otherwise violating private property, they
would always avoid the imposing pile.

Which led to Vaux wondering how a retired airline pilot (that's what the man said he was) could afford the place.
Perhaps he had married into money, a stratagem he had often
pondered when earlier in his career he felt the constraints of
not having any real wealth. But for better or for worse—and
in his case it was for worse—he had married a pauper, albeit
a very pretty pauper. Poor Joan. He really had led her a bit of
a dance. It had been an amicable divorce, though. And thank
God for Jonathon, whom she had met in her despair and who
would be a much better husband for her. They were the same
age for one thing—he was twenty years older—and Jon had
a successful dental practice in Los Angeles. Hence the 50-50
divorce agreement, which, thank God, excluded his pension
and final payout from the newspaper.

And then there was the beautiful and lissome Sylvia
Blackburn. She had obsessed him, probably because he was
so young at the time and it was his first real adult love. He
met her when he worked at *Time's* Cairo bureau. She was a librarian at the British embassy, the nineteen-year-old daughter
of a Foreign Service officer who was stationed there. He had
always known that Sylvia's father disapproved of him; was it
because he was an upstart Englishman who'd arrived in Cairo
as a journalist for an American publication? Or was it perhaps
that his social antics or solecisms caused some raised eyebrows
among the Foreign Service elite?

He sighed at the twin memories of Joan and Sylvia. It was
water under the bridge, he told himself, but very deep water.
Made all the more poignant by Sylvia's untimely death a few
years later in a car crash in Greece where her father had just
been posted.

He pulled his socks on, got into a navy blue blazer and khaki corduroys, put on a pair of loafers, and went downstairs. All was quiet, and he decided not to visit the bar since to be observed hovering in the saloon at this time of the morning might suggest he was in dire need of a drink. He went out. The wind was brisk, but there was that unmistakable resinous country tang to the air that reminded him of his childhood.

He got into the Audi, parked on a side street near the pub, and drove first to Willow Drive to have another look at the bungalow, then on down to the local railway station. Nothing had changed there: the old clock tower atop the Victorian gothic building still told the correct time, the incongruous grasshopper weather vane perched above it still functioning. But what had changed were the surrounding houses. They were the typical working-class cottages of the early twentieth century: two rooms, one up, one down, and maybe a closet of a kitchen. Lavatory and washhouse out back in the small yard.

Now to his amazement these small, seedy, terraced dwellings had morphed into smart 'bijou' residences with tiny paved front yards where straggly grass and perhaps the odd primrose or crocus used to grow. Middle-class commuters had clearly decided that the area, forty minutes by train to Euston, would be a gold mine once gentrification took hold. The result was a sort of ribboned patchwork, some houses freshly painted with big new bay windows and built-on porches, others holding out, refusing to modernize or beautify.

No doubt Mrs. Thatcher's late '80s privatization plan was having its desired effect—even if lower-income families had to find somewhere else to live. But where did they go? wondered Vaux. Perhaps he was just out of touch. Maybe the really poor, the poor as he remembered them—farm laborers, coal deliverymen, bus drivers, charwomen—simply didn't exist in post-Thatcher Britain. Maybe years of working abroad had made him more out of touch than he thought. And, horrible thought, maybe the other party that wanted No. 32 had a lot more cash at his disposal than he had calculated.

He felt somewhat queasy now, so he parked the car and walked into the Railway Arms. At least this place was unchanged. A dingy, small public house that sold only beer and wine, handily located for commuters to have a quick one before going home to the wife. His mother had told him that even his father, parched after a day's work in the hot, sticky City, would pop in here 'for a restorative beverage.' If he understood his long-absent father at all, it would more likely have been a double whisky at the Pig & Whistle.

* * *

Vaux arrived at 'The Cedars,' the Davis residence, at exactly 7:30 p.m., the time Davis had specified. He was shown in by Mrs. Fletcher, a matronly type with gray hair pinned back in a bun, thick solid legs, and a no-nonsense air about her. Davis got up from his armchair and asked what Vaux's particular poison would be tonight—whisky presumably. Vaux said he thought that would be fine and Mrs. Fletcher went through to the kitchen where she found a newly bought bottle of Cutty Sark. (Davis had remembered Vaux saying it was his preference.)

'Take a pew, take a pew, old man,' said Davis. Vaux duly chose to sit on the wide sofa with its back to the large leaded windows. Before he turned to sit, he observed a crowd of young men and girls milling round the Pig & Whistle, some with tankards of beer in their hands, the girls with flute glasses. Backs were being slapped, smiles and laughter all round.

'Looks like some sort of celebration over there,' observed Vaux as he sat down.

'Oh, the usual Saturday night overflow. Thank God the pubs still close at eleven, otherwise I'd never get any sleep.'

'Handy, though, a pub just a walk through the garden.'

'Yes. The old place was there long before this house was built, of course. One of the old coaching inns, I suppose, on the way to London Town.'

There was a silence while both men took long pulls on their drinks. Vaux noted the oak paneled walls, the tall bookcase at the other end of the long room, the oak beams across the ceiling. The fireplace was of the sort he'd seen in East Anglia (you could almost sit in it) with large, glistening fire irons hanging from a brass crucifix and logs stacked up on either side. On the walls, gilt-framed faded canvas scenes of the foxhunt intermingled with what looked like seascapes from the era of Nelson. Somehow Vaux had expected pictures of Boeing 707s and the old VC 10s—but he looked in vain.

They both heard commotion in the hall, female voices raised in greetings, shared laughter.

'Just a few guests I thought you might like to meet, old chap. Neighbors, that sort of thing.'

Vaux was introduced to Ann Whitely and Peggy Brown, both middle-aged, Ann quite slender and tall, Peggy plump and shortish. Davis looked at his watch and said that he expected the last guest to show up any minute. Then the phone in the hallway ran. They heard Mrs. Fletcher express commiserations and sympathy then put the phone down.

'Mr. Goodchild can't make it. Says he has a terrible late-spring cold.'

'Very well, Mrs. Fletcher. Ten minutes?'

'Right you are, sir. I trust you all like roast Aylesbury duck,' she inquired without smiling.

There seemed to be unanimous agreement, and Davis got up to dispense more drinks before they all went in to dinner.

The dining room, dominated by a long rosewood table and a wide mahogany sideboard, looked out to a well-manicured garden with beech and laburnum trees mixed with pines and cedars. It was getting dark now, but Vaux could see what looked like a hay field beyond the garden fence and then the wooded copse that screened Willow Drive from the main highway. Conversation picked up slowly as they ate their shrimp cocktails and roast duck with new potatoes and fresh peas. Mrs. Fletcher was a traditional English cook, and once again Vaux felt that his decision to come home was vindicated in the small things: the pint of Watney's, the steak and kidney pudding he'd had for lunch at the Railway Arms, the tolerant ambience of the clientele at the pub where he was staying, the vast array of serious and tabloid Sunday papers he was looking forward to in the morning.

Mini-biographies were exchanged. Ann worked for a firm of chartered accountants in the City. She took a train up every day. Her husband was a doctor with *Médecins sans Frontières* and was currently in Ethiopia. She had long, light brown shoulder-length hair, wore a dark blue jersey suit with pearl necklace and earrings. She'd been to the local grammar school for girls—the twin of the boys' school Vaux had attended probably some twenty years earlier. The grammar schools, she told him with some pride, had recently retrieved their traditional name after several years as 'comprehensive schools,' so-called after the Labor government deemed the grammar schools fostered class distinctions and snobbery. She informed Vaux, as if he didn't already know, that the 'public' schools, expensive private schools that educated the sons of the rich and powerful, were left alone in this attempt at reforming England's education system to promote equality. Vaux listened sympathetically.

Peggy Brown was a jovial housewife who worked part-time at the local Tesco supermarket. Her husband, a mechanic with his own repair shop close to the railway station, had been invited to the dinner but excused himself with the same ailment as Goodchild. Vaux thought spring flu was probably the diplomatic illness *du jour*. Peggy had short black hair with bangs and wore a white blouse and brown woolen slacks. They had three kids, all at various local schools, aged from six to fifteen.

She talked with a familiar local accent, Vaux noted, a sort of mixture of rustic Hertfordshire and London cockney.

Vaux gave his usual short bio.

'That sounds a very interesting life,' said Ann. 'You mean you actually interviewed Carter and Trudeau?'

'Well, it's all in a journalist's day's work really,' said Vaux, hoping not to sound too falsely modest. 'I even interviewed Mr. Heath but never got round to Mrs. Thatcher.'

'Didn't miss much there probably,' said Peggy gloomily.

'Not your type?' asked Vaux.

'Nah. My husband liked her, but I couldn't stand the woman. That fake upper-class accent and all.'

Davis intervened. 'That was the result of elocution lessons, my dear. Not some sort of phoniness.'

'What's that then—taking elocution classes indeed. Did Kinnock bother with that sort of thing?'

'Ah, but the Welsh lilt has always been more acceptable than a London accent,' rebutted Davis who, Vaux suspected, tried to hide his own Home Counties accent with the sort of upper-class drawl adopted by so many of his fellow middle-class countrymen.

But Davis had said little all evening. He watched Vaux intently, joked with his female guests, and clearly chose not to exchange any more detailed personal biography than he'd given Vaux when they had met. He avoided the conversation when it got political—except to say that, unlike Peggy, he had a lot of confidence in the current Conservative government of the young John Major.

* * *

The ladies had left after the coffee and brandy, and Vaux sat on the couch again opposite Davis. He felt uncomfortably bloated—the effect of the wine—but in no mood to relieve his host of his presence. Davis for his part had seemed to enjoy the evening and was now quietly smoking a big Havana cigar.

'You mentioned a Mr. Goodchild, or at least Mrs. Fletcher did. He was invited to dinner. That wouldn't be a John Goodchild, would it?' asked Vaux.

'Yes, old chap, it would. Known 'im donkeys' years, as a matter of fact. Odd jobs around the house, that sort of thing. Why, do you think you know him?'

Vaux hesitated. Did he really want to know John again—if it really was his old buddy? Nearly forty years was an awful long time. He would be unrecognizable. And it didn't sound as if his life had been too successful. 'Well, I knew a John Goodchild as a boy—we were mates, you know—same age and same tendency for mischief. Got into a lot of trouble together. We both lived on the same street.'

Davis exhaled a large blue-gray cloud of smoke. 'That must be the same man, old boy. Still lives on Willow Drive. His old father passed the house on to him. Plus a bit of money. Since then he hasn't worked much. Comes over to see if he can earn a bob or two.'

'Extraordinary,' said Vaux. 'Is he married?'

'I'll say. Three boys—all tearaways as far as I can gather. Eldest's about twenty. Didn't get married till he was about forty, you know. If you take my advice, I'd avoid him like the plague—if you move here, that is.'

'Oh, I'm moving in all right. Have no doubt about that.'

Davis didn't reply. He got up and refilled their balloon glasses. Vaux thought this was as good a time as any to put to him the question that he had planned all evening. 'Talking of which, do you have any idea who the other punter could be? They've upped their bid, you know.'

'Yes. So I gather. No, I really don't. Probably a local developer. Sees the place as a teardown. Build some monstrosity in its place and make a bomb. But I couldn't say for sure.'

'Um. So this could become a serious bidding war…'

'Be prepared for anything, old boy. Keep your powder dry. When you think he's made a final offer, then you top his bid.'

'Sounds simple. But how will I know when it is his final offer?'

'Keep in touch. I know everyone around these parts. I'll do all I can to help, Michael.'

4

On the Monday following the dinner party, Davis got up at 6 a.m., went down to the kitchen, and poured himself a tomato juice. He took some Hovis out of a wrapper and put two slices in the white Dualit toaster. Mrs. Fletcher had left the butter dish out on the big square kitchen table so he didn't have to wait for the butter to soften. He wouldn't bother with coffee this morning; he wanted to hit the M25 early to avoid the traffic. He'd have the early lunch with Sir Walter Mason then return home before the evening rush hour. He could have taken the train to London but at his age he preferred the smooth ride of the Bentley Turbo as well as the isolation from other commuters. Besides, after some thirty-five years of taking the 8:20 a.m. to Euston (and back usually on the 6:35 p.m.), the thought of paying homage to the old routine filled him with something like disgust.

Davis had worked in the Middle and Near East section of MI6 since his national service with the Royal Air Force. He had trained as a fighter pilot and had seen action in the Suez campaign when Prime Minister Anthony Eden, in the last throes of the British Empire, decided to punish Egypt for the audacity of nationalizing the Suez Canal, then owned jointly by France and the U.K. He'd downed two Egyptian MIGs over Alexandria and joined the Israelis and French, both allies, in several dog fights over Sinai. The adventure was a fiasco, with the anti-colonialist Americans insisting on withdrawal and the U.N. demanding recognition of Egyptian sovereignty.

Later, at Cranwell, the RAF staff college, he had studied aeronautics and general science. He had signed on for a five-year stint and then (he saw it as a miracle) he was recruited by the Foreign Service and seconded temporarily to the intelligence division, a rich source of recruits for Britain's Secret Intelligence Service. Over the years he had the odd foreign assignment, but looking back, he knew that most people who imagined a career in intelligence as exciting would be surprised at just how routine and tedious it could all be. Running agents from London's HQ had its cloak and dagger moments—and its emotional upheavals—but the amount of sheer deskwork was at times staggering.

But he'd enjoyed it. They had given him a good pension (based more on *ad hoc* calculations than any contributions made over the years), which supplemented the tidy sum left him by Donna, his wife, who died in her late thirties when he was forty-five. She had inherited The Cedars from her father, a successful architect and widower, who had collapsed and died on his way through the garden for a pint at the Pig & Whistle. He still missed Donna; she was an attractive and elegant woman (before the cancer took its toll), a great hostess who clearly helped him in his career, and she never should have died so young.

* * *

They had agreed to meet at Mason's favorite Greek restaurant, the Olympus in Jermyn Street, a small, inexpensive place despite its upscale location. Davis assumed his old boss liked it because it wasn't far from the offices of the *Economist*, where he regularly attended board meetings as an outside director and—probably more likely—because his favorite holiday destination had been Greece and its islands for as long as Davis could recall.

He parked the Bentley in a garage close to Leicester Square and walked from there to his bank and then on to his club on Pall Mall. He had invited Mason there for lunch, but Mason had declined with the odd assertion that the Olympus was more secure. By which he presumably meant that they wouldn't be seen chatting by anyone who knew (however vaguely) their business.

The usual mid-morning cronies were in the lounge, some sunk so low in their over-stuffed leather-buttoned armchairs that only their silver or bald heads emerged. Others were harder to recognize because their faces were concealed behind either *The Times* or the *Daily Telegraph*. Davis sank down in one of the few vacant armchairs and looked up at Sir Robert Peel, Britain's youngest ever prime minister. The portrait, yellowed by the tobacco smoke of two centuries, hung over the wide marble fireplace that now housed a flickering metal contraption that purported to represent a glowing fire but gave out no heat. The young waiter came over and he ordered a sherry. He mustn't drink too much though he knew Mason would be pushing dry martinis on him throughout the lunch. He would resist, pleading the drive back to Hertfordshire.

He picked up an outdated edition of *Time*, turned to the Britain section, and read that Neil Kinnock had resigned. And a bloody good thing too, thought Davis. He couldn't fathom whom the Labour Party would choose as their new leader. Probably another left-wing radical like that old dolt Michael Foot who had had his chance and, thank God, blown it. He flipped through the dog-eared weekly and confirmed his life-long impression: never liked it—too damn slick and glossy. But Vaux had said they paid well, which was more than could be said for those poor buggers at the *Economist* where, according to Mason, the writers were paid a pittance because of the prestige of just working there.

* * *

'No, love, he didn't say. Why—do you think we should give him a discount for a long stay?' Pete was responding to Harry's question about how long Vaux planned to stay at the Pig & Whistle.

'Don't know really. The summer's coming and we should be able to rent all the rooms at full price—especially with the series of ads in the *Gay Times*. If it was dead in the middle of winter, it would be different, wouldn't it? We're lucky if we rent any rooms in Jan. and Feb. But anyway, ask him when you see him. Is he in now?'

'No, he went out. And anyway, babe, I still don't understand why you blew all that money on trying to get a gay crowd down here. What in the name of God is there for gays to do around these parts?'

'Come on, Pete, think for a change. It's the couples we want—romantic weekends, that sort of thing. We're not aiming for the cruising crowd. That's the last thing we need—to turn this place into a gay bar.'

'You said it, not me.'

* * *

Vaux had decided to visit the cemetery at St. Michael's parish church where his mother and father were buried. He left the Audi in a parking lot in front of the local Conservative Club. The sprawling, low white building had been there since he was a boy. Little else had changed in the parish. The gray flint church, with its Romanesque tower, dominated the narrow High Street, now lined with small, terraced cottages whose lower floors had been converted into shops and boutiques.

The cemetery, unlike those in North America, looked neglected. Grass cutting was the only gesture made toward any kind of landscaping. But this, Vaux supposed, was how the English liked it. Some graves were attended to regularly by relatives and friends of the dead, others totally neglected. His parents' grave fell into the last category. He had brought a pair of sturdy leather gloves along to protect his hands from the stinging nettles he knew (because of bi-annual visits) would have overgrown the site. It was a modest grave. A low marble wall marked the rectangle, and the square tombstone simply carried his parents' names and lifespans. He pulled at the roots of the nettles, the crabgrass, and yellow cowslip, and uprighted the collapsed lower section of the marble surround. A big black bird, perhaps a raven, cawed loudly from the top branches of a tree. His mission was depressing but, as usual, he was uplifted by the bosky charm of the churchyard—the yew trees, the big old beeches and planes, and a massive oak that was reputedly three hundred years old. Wild bluebells and daffodils sprouted in haphazard clusters. Moss and lichen covered high stone crypts.

Just beyond the old, decrepit lych gate he had noticed a flower stall. He bought several bunches of potted primroses, his mother's favorite, and took them back to place on the grave. They'd last about a week, but unlike previous fleeting visits, he could now come back fairly often.

Susan Appleby's office was less than five minutes away up the High Street, past the small duck pond toward what was known as The Heath. A mallard was leading three ducklings in single file on a tour of the old and dank water hole, now clogged with duckweed and water lilies and bordered by tall bulrushes. Vaux thought he'd go in and see if Susan had any news about the rival bidder for No. 32. He passed a variety of shops—a family butcher, a hardware store, and a chemist.

In the front display window of Appleby, Frost & Lewis were photographs and accompanying sales sheets of at least fifty houses for sale in the vicinity—including No. 32. He was shocked at first, but realized she had been quite right not to withdraw the 'For Sale' status since the bloody bungalow hadn't yet been sold. Things were not going according to plan, he told himself. And something had to be done. He decided to take an aggressive approach—more for his own satisfaction than any hope that it would affect the final outcome. The outer office was unimpressive. No doubt formerly the front parlor of the small cottage. A young girl (Vaux figured about sixteen) sat at a desk and looked up from her typing as he entered. He asked for Susan Appleby and gave his name.

'Do you have an appointment?'

'No, but is she in?'

She was not too young to give reproving looks. She picked up the phone and pressed the intercom button. She said, 'A Mr. Vo is here to see you. Are you free right now? Or shall I tell him to make an appointment?' She held the phone closely to her ear for what seemed a long time for such a simple decision to be made.

'She'll be with you in a few minutes,' said the girl finally with a brief smile. She had short, dark blonde hair, a small, upturned nose, and rosebud lips. She went on with her slow typing. Vaux looked for somewhere to sit and found a low armchair in the corner beside a glass coffee table. A continuous roar of traffic shook the old building as a stream of cars, lorries, and busses sped up and down the High Street. If a by-pass had been built for this small Hertfordshire village, it looked like no one was bothering to use it.

He heard a door open, some voices, and then Susan's greeting.

'Michael, how are you, my dear. So nice to see you. Couldn't have come at a better time, as a matter of fact. I was about to call you at the Pig.' Vaux heard the young receptionist give a sort of chuckle.

'Oh? Well, let's talk then.'

'Of course. Come right in.' He saw a tall man (presumably Mr. Frost or Mr. Lewis) quickly leave the premises after whispering something in the girl's ear.

Susan sat down at her large oval leather-topped desk. Besides a computer and a phone, there was nothing else to clutter the matted surface. Behind her was a long credenza on which files and papers and some real estate magazines had been stacked. She opened a drawer and took out a notebook. She looked at it for a few seconds. 'I have to tell you, Michael, that a new offer for No. 32 has been made for £215,000. That's ten grand more than your last official offer.'

Vaux felt like someone had punched him in the solar plexus.

* * *

Arthur Davis was not a very introspective man. But since his retirement he'd had lots of time to think about his life, his role in the SIS, and his performance as a case officer. In particular, he wondered why he had never been made head of his particular section despite long and loyal service and no real fuck-ups along the way. There had been no moles discovered under his watch, no double agents, no defectors. He had weathered the great spy scandals of the '50s and '60s when traitors like Burgess and Maclean and later Philby had become household names in Britain. All through the years he had watched for disloyalty, guarded against bolshies like Blake and that homo at the Admiralty—Vassar. Yet the boys at the top withheld the final accolade—chief of Section B3, the specialist sub-sub group of MI6's Near and Mideast desk.

He had retired as one of three assistants to the chief. He often felt, too, that his higher than expected pension was partly a conscience payment on behalf of the director-general and his staff. When he pondered the injustice of it all, he reluctantly came to one rather bolshie conclusion: his background did not measure up to what was required.

Sir Walter Mason, head of Section B3, was the stereotypical Establishment product: Eton and Sandhurst, the Guards, retirement as brigadier-general, then a parachute into the Secret Service. He could never claim such an impeccable pedigree, bolstered by Sir Walter's early, opportune marriage to the daughter of a wealthy duke who owned countless acres in Dorset.

But such rebellious thoughts were soon banished. He loved his queen and his country and he was satisfied he had done his duty. He had been given opportunities hardly dreamed of when he was a trainee pilot at Cranwell. There must be no self-pity, no negativism. And he was happy that the service still wanted his occasional input. Michael Vaux would very probably be one more feather in his hat. For he was sure that it was about Vaux that Sir Walter wanted to talk.

* * *

'You are looking rudely fit,' declared Mason as he studied the menu.

'Can't think why, Walter. Get damn all exercise these days.' *Now then,* thought Davis, *don't start sounding negative.*

'Good Lord, Davis—with all that spare time? I'm surprised.'

'Actually, I have got in the odd game of tennis recently. I think I shall make that my summer exercise. That and bowls— I've just joined the local bowling club.'

'Good show. Ride horses, by any chance?' Davis knew that one of Sir Walter's passions was to preside over the west Dorset foxhunt. Maybe the old man had forgotten that Sybil, his wife (umpteen Christmases ago), had given him those foxhunt etchings that now hung on the walls of his living room. She had said that maybe they would persuade him to take up the hunt.

'No.'

Davis ordered the same as Mason—braised lamb, rice, and roast potatoes. For starters they both had Greek salad.

Two bottles of Mythos beer were ordered. Sir Walter, thought
Davis, must have forsaken the dry martinis. George the Greek,
the owner, fussed over the checkered tablecloth and repeated
the order to a flustered young white-coated waiter. The beer
arrived.

Mason took a long draw from the glass without waiting
for the head to subside. 'Well, exercise or not, you haven't
lost your touch, Arthur. You were always one of our best talent
spotters. Clearly retirement hasn't in any way blunted your
instincts.'

'I take it you refer to our Mr. Vaux?'

'Yes, old boy. Looks like you've hit the jackpot. We've
done our homework. If he's not an excellent candidate for
a short-term engagement, I'm a Dutchman. The only thing
we are missing is the tipping point, if you know what I
mean.'

'You mean an irresistible incentive, sir.'

'Quite. I'm confident you can think of something. But
just let me say that before you go the money route, let's see
if he'll do something for us out of sheer gratitude or loyalty
to queen and country. Don't forget he went to Bristol on a
Herts County Council grant, financed by Her Majesty's government. And then, after national service, he takes off for the
U.S.—or was it Canada? Anyway, he just may feel he owes
Britain something. He's had a successful career as a journalist, after all. And he may feel it's time to pay something
back.'

'You say he did national service. I missed that. What was
he in?'

'RASC. Posted to Essen. British Army of the Rhine in the
late '50s. Demobbed as a second lieutenant.'

The lamb shanks arrived, and Mason immediately shoveled the rice onto a side plate.

'You like I take away?' asked George.

'Too much carbohydrate, George.'

'Sorry, Sir Walter. Some steamed vegetables perhaps?'

'No, thank you. This is just fine.'

Davis was about to outline what he thought was his brilliant idea to help Vaux come round when Mason chose to announce his own impending retirement.

'Later this year, old boy. Along with the director-general. We'll both be joining the eminent ranks of the retired and revered. They'll soon be saying "what a sad and irreplaceable loss"—as they say about everyone. All of which is phooey, what? Nobody, but nobody, is irreplaceable.'

'Who's on the short-list to replace the D-G? Any idea?' asked Davis.

'As a matter of fact, yes. Entre-nous, of course. Believe it or not, it may well be a woman. The prime minister's office is rooting for Stella Rimington. Times they are a-changing, Davis. She has a tremendous record. Been with the service over twenty years. I think she'll ring some pretty radical changes.'

They exchanged some office and personal gossip and reminisced about past triumphs and a few fiascos, some comical, some that ended tragically for their operatives. Sir Walter paid the bill with a credit card and left some cash for a tip. As Davis got out of his chair, his ex-chief hit his forehead and threw down his napkin. 'Oh my God, Arthur, I forgot the most important thing…'

Davis thought the gesture a bit theatrical. He sat down again. Surely Vaux was the only purpose of the meeting—unless it was to pass on the news about the new C.

'On a more personal note, old chap. There's good news and bad news.'

Davis's mind raced. But he couldn't fathom what the old boy meant.

'First the good news: you're going to get your gong—Companion of the Order St. Michael and St. George—C.M.G. Let me be the first to congratulate you. I know you were disappointed you didn't get anything on retirement, but sometimes it takes one or two years to filter through the higher echelons.'

'Well, thank you, anyway. I am greatly honored,' said Davis, making a mental note to get some new business cards printed with the revered letters after his name. It wasn't a knighthood. But after a long career in the service of HM government, it was a welcome (and, he thought, well deserved) gesture. He steeled himself for the bad news.

Sir Walter took a deep breath. He slowly slid his horn-rimmed glasses into a pouch that was then deposited in the inside pocket of his tweed jacket. 'As you've no doubt read, Arthur, the Major government has been clamping down on spending like there was no tomorrow. The Treasury told the D-G he had to do his part in reining in government expenditures. All sorts of cuts are to be made, and I'm very much afraid the service itself will suffer if some of the cuts are not reinstated.

'Anyway as part of the service's spending review, obviously some personnel costs had to be cut. Unfortunately, the Treasury's auditors couldn't fathom how your ultimate pension was calculated. They assumed that some sort of *ad hoc* decision had been made by the D-G or his advisers to give you almost double what you were entitled to according to the actuarial tables. I'm sure you deserved it at the time. But we live in a different age, Arthur. Perhaps a more egalitarian age. And the thinking now is that your total annual compensation is out of whack with the rest of the service. In short, our finance masters don't think it's fair to other ex-staffers in the same grade to plod along with half what you're getting.'

Davis was shocked. It wasn't the money—bless Donna for that. It was the principle. And he felt that the C.M.G. had lost a little of its gloss.

* * *

51

lter walked back to his office on Gower Street,
ript building squeezed between a hospital and an
He skipped up a narrow staircase to his office and
imbleby, his portly, middle-aged secretary, that he
wanted to see Craw, the man who two years ago had replaced
Davis.

Craw sat down in a high-backed chair opposite his boss.
Mason was scribbling something on a notepad and did not
look up for a while. Craw got out a packet of Player's and lit
up. Mason smoked occasionally himself, so he knew the old
man wasn't about to object.

Mason looked up. 'Well, got that over. The hard bit was
about the pension. But he seemed to take it pretty well.'

'I guess the C.M.G. helped.'

'Probably thought it was a sop.'

'How did you explain the cut?'

'Told him the Whitehall was slashing expenses all round.
We weren't exempt from Major's economy drive.'

'Only half true.'

'We deal in half-truths.'

Craw opened the manila file that had been resting on his
lap. 'How much did you tell him about Operation Helvetia?'

'Hardly anything, of course. Simply that we'd looked into
Vaux's files and found the chap an excellent potential candidate. Said nothing about why or for what plan. On a need-to-
know basis, Davis's briefing is finished. But we still need him
to bring Vaux in. Therefore I want you to liaise with Davis on
strategy. See what it's going to take. And I want you to tell me
what you honestly think: are you the man to work on Vaux or
shall we leave it, at least initially, to Davis?'

'So Davis knows absolutely nothing about the key reason
for wanting Vaux?'

'I told you. He knows only that in our view he has struck
gold. He knows enough about our *modus operandi* not to probe
any further.'

Mason got up and walked over to the grimy sash window that overlooked a white-tiled internal well. A month or so ago, he'd decided to recheck the title of the shell company they had chosen to front for Section B3. Engraved on a small brass nameplate at the entrance of the building he read: Acme Global Consultants Ltd. He checked the shingles of his fellow tenants in this rundown office block. He could see them now, below and opposite him—the accountants, the scrap steel dealers, the tea merchants, the secretaries and typists.

These, Sir Walter reassured himself, were the people who made the whole damned system tick over. He turned to look at Craw, who was still perusing the file. He was all right; a bit too fond of office politics, highly strung, no family money, but young, lean, and ambitious, a first-class degree in PPE from Oxford—the new breed.

Mason said, 'I still want more than we've got on this Ahmed Abdul Kadri character. I'd like more background details. All I know so far is that he worked for the Syrian central bank after leaving Bristol University where he and Vaux seemed to be very close. Is there any hint of a homosexual relationship between the two? They were both young students—and we know that Vaux's married life wasn't all that successful. The more we know about Vaux before we confront him, the better. Then there's the fact that three years ago Kadri gets transferred to the Syrian Defense Ministry—to do what, exactly? He's an economist. What's he doing at Defense?'

'First, on the queer angle—I doubt it,' said Craw. 'He had a very heterosexual fling with Sylvia Blackburn, daughter of a middle-rung Foreign Service diplomat when he worked for *Time* in Cairo. She died later in a car accident. As to why Kadri got transferred: he was appointed head of the purchasing section, import division. He's expected to negotiate with arms suppliers and get the best possible deal for the country. They say Assad is a stickler for getting value for money. So I suppose they reckon that an ex-central banker will have enough financial sense not to be taken for a ride by corrupt and greedy arms dealers. Hence Kadri's Geneva assignment.'

'To horse trade with the bloody Russians—who under Yeltsin are as capable of mischief and breaking international arms agreements as they ever were under the old guard,' declared Mason.

5

Patrick Goodchild was nineteen and a drifter. As soon as he left school, his father had got him fixed up as an apprentice with a master plumber. That lasted six months. Patrick had said he couldn't face the thought of training for five years at the same place with the same old man. His boss was forty and he was glad to see the last of him—what with never getting to work on time, taking two hours for lunch, and quitting early every day to link up with his current girlfriend. His father, John, then asked him what he wanted to do—did he want to learn another trade, go back to school, or just hang around the house and be a bloody nuisance. The boy asked for time. It was an important career decision, after all.

While the young man was contemplating his future he discovered that the pocket money his dad gave him didn't stretch to what he wanted to spend on a night out with the boys, let alone give his girl friend a good time. So he opted for casual jobs—an assistant at a local newsagent's shop, bus boy at the Pig & Whistle, helping his dad with odd jobs and gardening around the neighborhood. John chalked it all up to experience; Patrick was the oldest of his three boys and maybe he was expecting too much to hope he'd settle down in his late teens to a serious occupation. After all, he himself had never done much of anything until his early forties. Like father like son. What the hell.

'What's for lunch?' asked John Goodchild. 'If you're good for nothing else, I'll give you this: you make a hell of a good sandwich. And that chicken casserole last night was

brilliant.' They were in the kitchen alone together. His wife
was staying with her sister in Brighton for a few days and the
two younger boys were both at school. Pat had his back to
his father, busily cutting slices off a large loaf of crisp white
bread.
   'Newly baked this morning, Dad. You'll love it. Fancy
tuna?'
   'I suppose so, and make sure there's lots of salad cream.'
   'For this concoction I use real mayonnaise, Dad. Much
better.'
   'Whatever. But when you're done will you please turn
your attentions to the washing up. Those bloody plates have
been sitting in the sink for friggin' days. They'll be walking
out the door soon.'
   'Keep your 'air on, Dad. Will do.' Pat's compliant and cooperative attitude led his father to the inevitable conclusion
that the boy planned to go out later and that he would need
some dosh. Thank God there was still a bit of cash left from
his father's legacy. Not a hell of a lot, but enough to make a
difference. Then there's this business he'd heard about where a
bank will lend you money on the value of your house provided
you own it in full. Well, thanks to his old man, he did. So he
planned to go see his bank manager next week on just that
very subject. Pat sat opposite him and between them placed a
large oval plate of thick triangular sandwiches.
   'Oh, very neat, very elegant, my boy. You know something—maybe this is what you should do. Take a cookery
course. Become a chef. I hear they can make over fifty thousand quid a year these days.'
   As usual, all suggestions of some meaningful employment
fell on deaf ears. Pat was preoccupied munching away at his
sandwich. He gulped down some milk and swallowed loudly.
'Guess what I heard today, Dad. You know you always talked
about that friend of yours when you were both nippers, like.
Michael whatsis name. Well, he's moving back—right here, in
this very street.'

John Goodchild's tuna sandwich stopped in mid-air. He looked at his son in disbelief. 'How would you know a thing like that then?'

'Mrs. Parker.'

'That old gossip.'

'She may be an old gossip, but she's often right on the ball. You must admit that.'

Mrs. Parker, who lived at No. 19 Willow Drive, was a lively widow, an octogenarian who spoke to everyone who knew anything about the goings and comings in the neighborhood. Even Group Captain Arthur Davis had not felt it beneath him to offer her a lift when he saw her at the bus stop weighed down with several bulging plastic shopping bags. He found her an impeccable source of local information and occasionally traded his own harmless tidbits for hers. But quite how Mrs. Parker had learned of Michael Vaux's intentions would challenge even Arthur Davis's intelligence-gathering talents.

* * *

Davis got back in good time that afternoon. He parked the Bentley outside a small variety store that stocked some good wines and his favorite champagne. He bought two bottles of Pol Roger and stocked up on some dinner wines. Then he made a call from the public phone just around the corner.

'Turquand, Wolfson.'

'Mrs. Whitely, please.'

'I'll see if she's available.'

'Ann Whitely.'

'Ann. Arthur. How are you?'

'Arthur! Thank you for the nice dinner. I enjoyed meeting your new friend.'

'Yes, he's an interesting man. I've just returned from London—it's been quite a day, actually. And I've got something to celebrate. Can I come round later?'

'I wanted to stay with you Saturday night but thought it diplomatic to leave with Peggy.'

'You could have come back after dumping her.'

'It was late. Anyway, do come round. I should be home by seven.'

Davis put the two bottles of champagne in the fridge, undressed as he climbed the wide staircase, and had a hot shower. Mrs. Fletcher had left the place immaculate, fresh towels in the bathroom, his cologne and toilet accessories placed on a fluffy white face cloth on the side of the wash basin. London always charged him up—the activity, the bustle, knowing that despite retirement he was still needed. Or used. What difference did it make? And the rewards were real despite the cut in pension. It was mean and niggardly of them, but then he'd heard worse stories. Men who had devoted their whole lives to public service who'd ended up with a pittance in their old age. The honor counted for something too. If it had come down to a choice between the bigger pension and the C.M.G., he had to admit he was enough of a snob to choose the honorific.

Ann Whitely lived in a large house on the outskirts of Watford. It was one of those double-fronted suburban dwellings with bay windows and netted curtains, four bedrooms, and two 'reception rooms.' A large kitchen looked on to a back garden that was fenced for privacy. Brian, her doctor husband, spent many months of the year away in places she often had to look up in an atlas. She was a healthy woman in her late thirties, slim and attractive—and she enjoyed sex.

About six months ago, Davis had made a pass in the privacy of his study (other guests were in the dining room); she became interested, but delayed a final decision for some weeks. Davis would not threaten her marriage to Brian—he was too old and too committed to his widower life. He had told her that and she accepted it. He wasn't unattractive despite his years. A bear of a man, really. And he'd told her that he'd had a successful career as a BA pilot flying around the world.

She worked in the City at a prestigious accounting firm that over the years had resisted being merged into one of what they called the 'big five.' She hadn't been made a partner yet, but she was confident she'd make that milestone within a few years.

* * *

Arthur Davis strode through the hall to the kitchen. He knew the place as well as his own. He reached up for some tall flute glasses and uncorked the first bottle. The golden sparkling liquid formed a small, fizzy head and he raised his glass to hers. 'We are celebrating, my dear—the final and official recognition of my services to crown and country.'

'What are you talking about, Arthur?' The one thing that rather rankled her about Davis was his periodic flights of pomposity. 'Don't tell me they've given you a "K." Will we have to call you *Sir* Arthur now?'

'Not quite that grand, my dear. But the next best thing— Companion of St. Michael and St. George, a C.M.G. It'll be in the Queen's Birthday Honors list. And I'm not joking.'

He refilled the glasses. They still stood opposite one another in the kitchen. He leant forward and they kissed gently. He could see her calculating. She seemed skeptical. 'Darling, that's simply marvelous. But isn't it sort of unusual for an airline pilot?'

'They take everything, one's whole life, into consideration. My service in the Suez campaign probably played a role—'

'But that was ages ago, surely.'

Davis asked himself why he always went for intelligent women. Why couldn't she just accept the good news and chalk one up for her lover? 'I told you. They take the whole gamut of one's career. And British Airways, don't forget, was a nationalized outfit for many, many years. We were public servants, really.' Where, he asked himself, did that one come from? It sounded pretty plausible.

'Well, yes. I can see that.' She took his hand and they climbed the stairs, glasses in hand.

* * *

Betty decided to give Susan Appleby a brief call. She was in a hurry this morning since she got in late last night and never heard her mother's wake-up call. She just wanted to tell Susan how happy she was at last and she knew Susan would welcome the news.

'Susan? Betty. I'm in a bit of a rush. My own fault. But I just had to tell you. I met this bloke last night called Patrick and I know you're going to laugh, but this time I think it's for real. He's so cute, and nice with it. Seems quite intelligent, though I forget what he said he did for a living. But we had a smashing time. He borrowed his old man's car and went up to the West End. Drank too much, but he really knew his way around. We finished up in this private club in Soho where he seems to be very popular. They all knew him, anyway.'

Susan tried to get a word in edge-ways. 'I thought you said you were in a rush, Bet. Look, I'm delighted for you. But don't let one night decide the rest of your life, luv. I have made that mistake once too often...'

'Funny, I knew you'd put a damper on things.'

'Not at all. I'm sure he's a charming young man—by the way, you didn't tell me his age.'

'Oh, about twenty, I imagine. So it's not as if he's trying to take advantage.' Betty was eighteen.

'No, of course not. Look, you'd better put the phone down and get to work. Dr. Stevens won't be too happy if you're not there when his first patient arrives.'

'Bye. Love you, Su.'

6

Vaux sat at the bar of the Pig & Whistle nursing a tumbler of Cutty Sark—the boys had got in a crate especially for their long-term guest. Harry had confronted him over the weekend about how long he planned to stay. It was unusual for guests to stay longer than a few days, and despite what Harry had told Pete, he was considering lowering the rate to £50 a night, the same as he would pay for one of the back bedrooms.

Vaux had told him that he still didn't know exactly when he'd be able to leave, but it probably wouldn't be for a few weeks. Vaux wondered just how long this shadow auction was going to go on for. It did cross his mind that it could be a so-called Dutch auction where a mysterious punter would bid up the price just to get the party who really wanted to buy to pay an ever-higher price. But Susan had assured him that this was not the case, and she clearly resented the implication since she would be the first to put a stop to such an unethical practice.

He had of course increased his offer. It now stood at £225,000, thirty grand above the original asking price and, in what seemed those far-off non-competitive days, his sole bid. But Susan was still being tight-lipped about his rival. He tried to think about a sensible strategy. Apart from the fact that he was prepared to go higher if necessary, it would surely help if he knew whom he was up against. Despite Susan's seeming opposition, perhaps a shrewd move would be to get to know the sellers. The son of Mrs. Kingston, who had owned the place, was supposedly in London somewhere. Vaux figured that if he was up against some amorphous corporation who wanted to tear down the place (as Davis had suggested), then Mrs. Kingston's son could be more sympathetic to his own plan to do the place up. In a way (Vaux, the sentimentalist) it would, under his guardianship, always stand as a memorial to the two boys' dear mother. This had possibilities. He had to penetrate Susan Appleby's wall of silence.

Pete emerged from the kitchen with an over-sized packet of potato crisps and proceeded to fill various bowls dotted around the bar.

'Nice evening, Mr. Vaux.'

'It is. And thanks for getting my favorite scotch.'

'All in the service, mate. Fancy some crisps?'

'Thanks. Tell me, Pete, do you know a good restaurant where I could just walk to?' The pub only served sandwiches and cold meat pies in the evenings.

'Nah, not really. We're in the boondocks here. Nearest place is three miles away. Most of the regulars come in here for a few drinks then go home to supper. Then the real boozers come back for long nightcaps.' Pete snorted at his own candor.

'Steady business, though, I should think.'

'Yeah, it is really. But I just work here. Harry's the boss. He holds the license.' Pete smiled to himself as he wiped the bar and took some glasses out of the dishwasher. A serene sort of guy, thought Vaux. Not a care in the world. But there was plenty of time for that—he was only in his early twenties.

'Ever get away—you know, holidays, that sort of thing?'

'We close up for two weeks in August and go to Mykonos. Harry's got a friend there who runs a small hotel. Only costs us the air fare.'

They seemed to have their lives pretty well organized. Pete disappeared into the kitchen and Vaux moved to the phone at the end of the bar. He dialed Davis's number.

* * *

Davis opened the door. Susan smiled and gave him the wrapped bottle of cognac he'd asked her to pick up. She wore white cotton slacks, a navy blue shirt, and the minimal high-heeled sandals she liked to wear. Her toenails were ruby red. 'Thank you, my sweet,' said Davis. She offered her cheek and he kissed each cheek twice. 'Mrs. Fletcher left us roast pork and all the works. Are you hungry?'

'Let's relax a little.' She walked over to the big leaded windows and looked out onto the now floodlit Pig & Whistle. It was a mild evening and still quite light out. Davis looked at her rounded bottom and was pleasurably aroused. He liked a real woman's arse, none of those slim boy-like melons for him. Though he had to admit that Ann Whitely was the super-slim type with virtually a boy's figure. Even her tits were minimal. The trouble with him, he told himself, was that he liked anything in a skirt. Susan turned and he could see the ample bulge of her breasts, the open shirt showing just enough cleavage to drive a man mad. He went through to the kitchen where he poured her a large vodka and tonic and himself a malt.

Davis knew the drill. They would have a few cocktails, he'd check the meal in the oven then he'd join her on the leather couch. A bit of teenage smooching and then upstairs for a quickie. He knew she liked it that way. She was a little inhibited and gasped and sighed a lot but he often wondered whether she faked the orgasm.

He had his hand around one bare breast when the phone rang. He went over to the side table by the armchair and answered. Susan heard him tell someone that he'd be delighted to see him and that Susan was right here but could he come in about an hour.

Susan had cleared the kitchen table—they both preferred to eat in the kitchen when he wasn't entertaining guests—and was putting plates and cutlery in the dishwasher when the doorbell rang. It was Vaux in a polo-neck black sweater and blue jeans. Davis guessed it was only a social visit, so he would just listen to what Vaux had to say. He was bound to learn something useful. They nursed more drinks and talked about the weather, how Vaux liked the area, how he passed the time. Finally Vaux broached the subject that had all along been on his mind.

'Arthur. Any news about my rival bidder?'

Susan looked sharply at Vaux and he felt like he had said the unmentionable. But Davis felt expansive.

'Look, you're sitting here with the horse's mouth, if you'll excuse the expression, Susan. She can tell you all about it, isn't that right, my dear?' Stir things up a bit, he thought.

'Well,' said Susan doubtfully, 'I'm still not at liberty to divulge the other party, I'm afraid. But I was going to call you tomorrow morning, Michael. I'm afraid they've topped your latest offer. Now they're bidding £240,000.'

'God almighty,' said Vaux. The evening's scotch, undiluted by any nourishing food, began to take its toll. His heart was beating faster and he felt he had to trump the latest bid there and then. Maybe it would impress Susan and maybe he could finally get some information out of her.

'Okay. I'm putting £250,000 on the table, that's fifty-five grand more than I thought I'd have to pay...'

'The market's strong,' said Susan.

Now Vaux was getting annoyed. Whose side was she on? 'It's got nothing to do with the market. I'm in an auction here and the price is going skywards. Do you really think that run-down bungalow is worth a quarter of a million pounds, Susan?'

Susan looked at Davis for support, but his face wore the mark of a non-combatant. She said, 'It's worth what it can fetch, Michael. Do I take it that that's an official offer you just made?'

'Yes, you can take it to the bank.' Susan's thin lips betrayed some amusement. Vaux thought, quite accurately, that she was thinking of the swelling commission. 'I'll be frank,' he said. 'It would help me if I knew whether I was up against a big developer or a private individual. It could also help me if I could talk to this son of Mrs. Kingston. Would he really want his mother's old house to be demolished?' He knew he was being emotional, but he needed all the ammunition he could get.

Susan relented. 'I can tell you that it's not a corporation or a developer. It's someone who like you is retiring and loves the place. He's a local and quite rich. He and his wife are empty-nesters. Their kids are now grown up and they want to sell their big house on Hampstead Lane and move into a smallish bungalow with a good view.' Susan downed her last drink for the evening, felt she'd said her piece (she had planned to give Davis the information anyway), and hoped to have crushed Vaux's illusion that she was batting for him or anybody else. As far as she was concerned, the bloody shitty bungalow would go to the highest bidder.

Vaux said: 'So why all this cloak-and-dagger stuff? Why can't they come up front about it?' Davis coughed quietly, his last gulp having gone down the wrong way.

'They wanted it that way. I have to respect their wishes,' said Susan.

Vaux reluctantly got the message. But at least he knew now that appealing to Mrs. Kingston's son was a non-starter.

He was told by Davis to stay put and have a final nightcap. Davis followed Susan to her magenta Jaguar XJS parked in the driveway. 'Okay, now we're alone again, Sue, you can tell me who the other punter is.' He knew that Susan sometimes appreciated a direct approach.

'For your ears only. It's Mr. Johnson, until the end of last year headmaster and major shareholder of Lincoln College, that private boys' school in Berkhamsted. It's got a very good reputation. He's done very well for himself and he seems determined to move into the place.'

'Ah, I see. Keep me posted if either of them withdraw from the battle, won't you, dear?'

* * *

Vaux was just in time to buy a cellophane-wrapped ham and pickle sandwich at the bar. It was busy, and a blue-gray miasma of tobacco smoke floated in mid-air. He decided he wouldn't have another drink. He noticed that Pete was doing most of the bar-tending while toward the back of the saloon Harry played host to a bevy of young men. They were standing in front of the open sliding doors that gave on to the small, flagged patio where on warm evenings customers sat at marble-topped bistro tables.

He climbed the narrow staircase wearily. He was not in the best of moods. In bed, his mind wouldn't shut down to let him sleep. He told himself he would go to £300,000 if necessary. He hadn't come all this way, physically and metaphorically, to be denied his dream home. What's more, if it looked like he would eventually have to use up a big wad of his retirement payout, so be it. He'd get a job. London was full of newspapers. He used to be a sub-editor in his early career. He could offer his services once again. He wasn't sixty yet and he was pretty sure that with his *curriculum vitae* he'd land a Fleet Street job. Then he remembered that the dailies, broadsheets, and tabloids had moved to the East End. So what. He'd go by train up to Queen's Park and get the Bakerloo Line that as far as he could remember went to London's docklands. His last thoughts were of the tube, rattling and shaking, as the crowded train took him and his mum toward the bright lights of the West End.

7

'Was that the guy from the States?' asked Patrick Goodchild as he delivered a tray of dirty glasses to the countertop. Pete unloaded them one by one and put them in the dishwasher.

'Yeah, actually. Why?'

'Just wondered, that's all. My old man used to know him—years ago, when they were kids.'

Pete knew that Pat's father was a regular with a dicey reputation among the other customers in the area. His social instincts told him to be discreet.

'Will he be here around lunchtime?' asked Pat.

'Never can tell. He comes and goes a lot, keeps to himself, really.' Pete turned away to pull a pint for a customer. Not for the first time, Patrick felt Pete was kind of standoffish.

When he got home, Patrick told his father that he'd probably find Vaux in the pub around lunchtime but couldn't guarantee it. John Goodchild sat at the kitchen table with a can of beer. His grunt signaled that he'd heard the message.

* * *

At noon, Vaux came into the saloon bar, feeling that he should plan the day. He would probably call Susan to confirm his latest offer, just in case she had dismissed it as the drink talking. Then he would call his bank in New York to ask about the transfer of funds to Westminster Bank in Watford.

He didn't know if there would be taxes to pay and he hadn't
yet decided whether he wanted them to transfer the money in
dollars or in pounds. He'd buy a newspaper and look up the
current exchange rate.

Mrs. Caldwell was behind the bar substituting for the
boys, who didn't seem to be around. 'Special today is fish and
chips, luv. Halibut—fresh from this morning's market,' she
declared as she put down the pint of Watney's.

'It's a bit early for me, Mrs. Caldwell. But I'll think about
it,' said Vaux. She turned to serve a short, stout man who had
just entered the bar. He was bald with a cropped crescent of
salt and pepper hair from ear to ear and a small gray mustache.
He looked about sixty with heavy eyelids and parallel creases
down both cheeks.

'Bass please, love.' He looked over to Vaux as he ordered
and gave an unsmiling nod of acknowledgement. He took a
long draw from his glass, stared with small, beady brown eyes
at him and then said: 'You're Michael Vaux, aren't you?'

Vaux knew immediately who it was, more by instinct than
recognition. 'That's right, though I don't think we've met,' he
lied.

'Oh, yes we have, mate. My name's John Goodchild and
we used to be great friends many years ago…'

There was no avoiding the man, even if he wanted to,
which he probably didn't. 'God, yes! Of course. John. Jesus, I
hate to think how many years it's been!'

Goodchild walked round the bar to shake hands with
Vaux. He was wearing baggy old gray worsted trousers, a
blue aertex shirt, and dirty white trainers. 'Never thought I'd
see you again, mate. Went to the States, they said. Or was it
Canada?'

'I've lived in both places, but most of the time in the U.S.'

'Newspapers, they said.'

Vaux wondered who 'they' were. 'Yes, you seem to be
well informed, I'll say that. And you, John, how's life been
treating you—well, I hope.'

Goodchild, who hadn't smiled yet, looked slightly amused at the question. 'Oh, this and that. Married with three kids. Did you ever get married?'

'Yes. But I'm divorced.'

'No kids?'

'No, unfortunately.'

'Blimey, you've got to be joking. They've given me no end of trouble, my kids.'

Silence as both men drained their drinks. Mrs. Caldwell refilled Vaux's pint. 'I'll get that for you,' offered John.

'That's very nice of you, John.'

Both bought each other a few more rounds and John wrote out his address and telephone number so that they could get together and reminisce about old times. As he gave the piece of paper to Vaux he said: 'Look, why don't you come round now? The house is empty and we can have a good old chinwag.'

Vaux was taken by surprise and knew he was stuttering for an answer. He supposed he could put off that call to Susan and the bank business. So he surrendered. Mrs. Caldwell warned him that the fish and chips special wouldn't last long with the expected lunch crowd. Vaux shrugged and threw up his arms as if to say it was now out of his hands. They walked to No. 7 Willow Drive.

* * *

No. 7 reminded Vaux of No. 32. Same 1930s fixtures, the big sink in the kitchen, the ancient separate W.C., the stained lion-pawed bath with the gas-fired brass geyser for hot water. Rusting metal-framed windows, cheap wooden doors that the rising damp had warped so that they couldn't properly close.

Goodchild ushered him through the back door and into the kitchen. The table was strewn with dirty plates and glasses, some of which he gathered up and placed on the draining board beside the sink. He went into a small pantry and came out with a six-pack of Heineken. Without saying anything he opened two bottles, passed one over to Vaux, and raised his glass. 'Cheers, mate. Nice to see you after all these years.'

Vaux raised his glass to tap Goodchild's. 'Cheers. Yes, it seems incredible. Though I thought it quite possible that you might have stayed here in Willow Drive. Perhaps our paths were destined to cross again,' said Vaux cheerfully. He was feeling a little uncomfortable at Goodchild's seeming inability to smile. Did the long, serious face portend something? His unhappiness at the way his life has turned out—two old friends whose lives had perhaps been so dissimilar?

They engaged in small talk and the exchange of potted versions of their respective careers or, in Goodchild's case, the lack of one. He seems to have drifted, thought Vaux, from one blind-alley job to another. His excuse for immobility—physical as well as social—seemed to have been having to put up with his sickly father as much as the mundane need to feed a growing family and a wife who took long absences, thanks to a big family with sisters in far-flung towns like Birmingham, Liverpool, and Brighton. Goodchild's father, it seemed, had run a small but successful grocery store that had, by the time he got sick, grown to the optimum size that the big supermarket chains found attractive. A firm called Waitrose bought him out and set him up for a comfortable retirement.

'Didn't leave much by the time he had the last heart attack. Used to spend it all on cigs and booze. If he couldn't be found at meal times, my missus used to send one of the boys to the Pig & Whistle to fetch him. Either there or the Royal Oak at the bottom of Farlands Lane,' said Goodchild, thus disabusing Vaux of any hope that his childhood friend could have been left enough cash to be comfortable.

'So anyway, you know what I'd like to know?'

'What?' asked Vaux. They were now well into the second six-pack. Despite an earlier promise to make a sandwich, no food had yet appeared. They sat at the kitchen table slowly drinking themselves into a sort of maudlin, nostalgic oblivion. There was a long silence as Goodchild lit up another cigarette and offered one to Vaux, who shook his head. 'I'll have another beer while you work on the big question,' said Vaux. He opened another bottle.

'What fucking big question?' said Goodchild, who was annoyed at Vaux's attempt at a little light-heartedness. 'What I'd like to bloody well know is why the hell you want to come back and live here.' His words slurred together but Vaux understood the question.

'The view. The great view you get when you live round the bend,' laughed Vaux, realizing the double meaning of his answer. He was referring to the right-angled bend at the bottom of Willow Drive, which gave the few bungalows on the south side of the street the view that he so treasured.

'Round the bloody bend is right, mate. That's what you must be, to want to come back to that dump,' said Goodchild dismissively. He staggered over to the welsh dresser—another fixture in common with No. 32—and opened a big cake tin. He extracted an iced fruitcake, cut a few slices, and brought them over to the table. Vaux snapped up a slice. They both ate silently. It was beginning to dawn on Vaux that he had better go while he was able to walk. He looked at his watch and muttered something about having to make a few phone calls.

Goodchild waved his arm in front of him, shook his head, and said, 'No fuckin' way, man. We're just getting started, aren't we?' He got up and opened the bottom cupboard of the welsh dresser and pulled out a bottle of Dawson's whisky. Vaux didn't know the brand but welcomed the change. He was feeling uncomfortably bloated. Goodchild found two thick tumblers in the sink, rinsed them under a tap, and poured two large drinks. He sat down opposite Vaux again.

'You know something? I often think of what you led me into doing when we were those two happy little eleven-year-olds. You know, general fuckin' mischief—like smashing greenhouse windows, smoking fags in your mum's garage, and that competition we 'ad with that older kid, Peter from Peckham, to see who could shoot the farthest after we wanked off.'

Vaux shook his head in remembrance. Yes, he did remember all that kid stuff. 'We sound like we were the original juvenile delinquents, don't we. Boy, so long ago.'

'You were the leader, all right. You led me down the wrong path more than once. I was real mixed up when we sort of went our own ways, like. Always seemed to be missing a mate after you left for that bloody grammar school.'

'I was still living here, John.'

'Yeah, but it was different, wasn't it? Something came between us. Probably your mother. She was a bit of a stickler, if I remember right. Kept you at your bloody books and that.'

Vaux tried to change the subject. 'Whatever happened to Angela—the girl who lived at No. 3? She was a bit younger than us, and even at that age I remember we both fancied her.'

'Oh yeah—blonde and curly hair. She was quite a looker. Moved back to London with her parents, didn't she.'

Silence fell on the two old friends. Vaux pushed back his chair.

Goodchild seemed preoccupied in the search of lost times. He stared morosely at the oilcloth that covered the kitchen table. Then he looked up at Vaux, his eyes now glassy, his face still grim.

'Got to go, old thing,' said Vaux cheerfully. 'I've got your phone number now, so I'll give you a tinkle and let you know if I do finally buy the house.' He had told Goodchild of the bidding war.

'See you,' said Goodchild, his eyes fixed on the checkered pattern of the tablecloth.

* * *

Several days went by. The bidding war for No. 32 Willow Drive between Vaux and Paul Johnson, retired headmaster of Lincoln College for Boys, picked up momentum. Each trumped the other's latest offer within twenty-four hours. The price jumped by quantum leaps, and Susan Appleby dispensed with insisting on formal written bids and just sat back to take the succession of phone calls. Anger was running high and neither contestant could believe the other's relentless determination. The latest bid came from the headmaster for £335,000 compared with the original asking price (and the price Vaux had initially thought he'd have to pay) of £195,000. Vaux could often be seen at the bar furiously punching at his pocket calculator. In the financial pages of the newspaper he discovered one tiny crumb of comfort: since his official retirement in January, the dollar had strengthened against the pound sterling. It now cost $1.74 to buy one pound against $1.83 a few weeks ago.

* * *

Davis heard the low buzz of his scrambler phone. He pulled out the drawer of the sidetable where it was discreetly housed.

'Craw here. Any progress?' The sharp, efficient tone of voice irritated Davis, though he realized it was wrong to let emotions run away at the seeming officiousness of the new generation. If anything, he wanted to show them that casualness and insouciance were more effective in their line of work. 'There's always progress, Craw. But sometimes one needs a little patience. The first round's not yet over. I'm awaiting some developments, and they can't be forced. I'm optimistic that it'll be a matter of days now when we'll know one way or the other.'

'You mean there's a possibility that we won't get him?' Craw sounded incredulous.

'He's not a bloody criminal, is he? No, what I mean is that I'm waiting for certain events to transpire, events that will give me the ultimate trump card that should clinch the deal. I'm confident he'll be cooperative, but until certain things have come to pass, as it were, I don't want to make a move. It would be premature. Fools rush in and all that.'

Davis's long-winded excuse for not having definitively secured Vaux's services irritated Craw. He said, 'It's just that Sir Walter is anxious to get started—the briefing etcetera. I sense he wants to take the measure of the man before presenting him to the D-G.'

'I understand.'

'Time is of the essence.'

'I'll be in touch.'

Davis put the red secure phone down and closed the drawer. Then he picked up the black phone on top of the table and dialed.

'Susan Appleby's office,' said a young female voice.

Davis recognized Jane's voice. He could hear the accompanying click and suck of a gum-chewer. In the old days she'd be sacked on the spot. 'Is she there, my pet?'

Jane hated that sort of patronizing familiarity. 'Hold on,' she said abruptly. Davis couldn't understand why the young girl couldn't bring herself to obey the basic laws of courtesy and just say please.

'Hello, Arthur dear. What's up?'

'The usual. Any more news re No. 32?'

'Yes, as a matter of fact. Vaux has just increased his offer to £350,000. Sounds very confident that this will prove the winning bid, but I have my doubts. Old Johnson seems absolutely resolute. What's made him even more determined is that he thinks his rival is an American. What right have the Yankees got to come over here and push up property prices and all that.'

'And I suppose you didn't disillusion him.'

'I'm just the referee between these two maniacs. I daren't take sides. That would hardly be fair.'

It suited Davis, so he said nothing. And he figured that Vaux must be near the breaking point.

8

He would remember that morning for a long time. Vaux had wiped the last of the shaving cream from his face. He'd had a shower in the cramped bathroom at the Pig & Whistle and he was feeling rather hung over. The evening before, he'd been drinking heavily with John Goodchild, who had apologized for his morose (though he didn't use the word) behavior at their first meeting and who had then quickly asked for a 'short-term' loan of £2,000. Vaux had prevaricated and told him he'd let him know once his own finances took on a more transparent look. He still didn't know how much he would eventually have to fork out for No. 32.

Pete had knocked on the bathroom door. Vaux opened it. 'Phone, sir. Susan Appleby. Says it's urgent and would you phone her back immediately.'

'For Christ's sake,' murmured Vaux as he made his way to his room. He'd had to increase his offer to £380,000 after his contender had topped his previous bid by £10,000. This was beginning to look like madness. He dressed quickly and went downstairs to the bar. He called Susan.

'Don't tell me—he's topped my latest offer yet again.'

'No, Michael, not at all. I heard last night. Mr. Johnson had a bad stroke. He was rushed to the Victoria hospital but died during the night. Mr. Johnson, by the way, was your rival's name.'

A long pause ensued. Vaux didn't know whether to feel good about the demise of his antagonist or, as far as humanly possible, sorry for a complete stranger's sudden death.

Susan's suggestion was sensitive and sensible. 'Look, why don't we get together later and discuss where you go from here. I'm too shocked to think right now, as I'm sure you are.'

'Yes, of course,' said Vaux. They arranged to meet at her office at 11 a.m.

* * *

Davis had taken the Bentley to a sprawling shopping mall just outside of town. He liked the supermarket there and wasn't surprised to meet Peggy Brown behind the fresh fish counter. She could always be found either there or at one of the checkout stations.

'Hello, love,' said Davis. 'I want a word with you.'

She leant over the glass counter and looked downright conspiratorial. 'Before you say anything, Arthur, I've got some real nice cod steaks just in. I'll cut 'em nice and thick like. You always said Mrs. Fletcher was good at grilling fish.'

'Give me eight. If they're really fresh, I'll freeze some of them,' said Davis. 'Here's the thing, Peggy. Could your husband take in my car today? I've got a problem with the petrol gauge and there's a funny sort of rattle coming from the exhaust pipe. Shouldn't take long, but you know how I like it back the same day.'

Peggy said she'd give her husband a ring as soon as she'd finished cutting the cod steaks. She went into the back, came out with eight wrapped cod steaks, and said she'd called Tom and he'd be waiting for him. Davis then went to the Epicerie Charles, an unlikely but good little delicatessen that sold an array of French gourmet products including his favorite pâté de foie gras. Then he went to the tobacco kiosk where he bought a box of Montecristo No. 3s.

He drove slowly, cursing the petrol gauge for showing EMPTY when he was pretty sure he'd filled the tank after the

London trip. He hadn't used the car much since. About a mile from the garage where Peggy's husband ran his repair shop, Davis noticed Mrs. Parker, loaded with plastic shopping bags, making heavy progress as she climbed the hill to the station. She wore a blue and white floral tent dress and tennis shoes. He drew up beside her. She nodded in acknowledgement and he leant over to open the door for her.

'Ever so nice of you,' she said. 'Whew! What a morning. Quite warm for this time of year, isn't it, Mr. Davis.'

'Yes it is, Mrs. Parker. Look, I'm only going to the garage near the station. Something's wrong with the old jalopy.' He produced a five- pound note from the top pocket of his suede bomber jacket. 'Here, my dear, take this. Get a taxi at the station. You can't walk all the way home with all that shopping.'

'Oh, Mr. Davis, I couldn't.' She took the fiver and stuffed it in one of the plastic bags. 'Did you hear about that Mr. Johnson, then?'

'No, what about him?' Davis seemed to think he should know the name but couldn't recall exactly why.

'He died, didn't he. Last night. Brain 'emorrhage, they said. He was the other one trying to buy No. 32, you know. Used to be headmaster of that posh private school on Hampstead Road. Just retired too. You never know, do you?'

Now Davis remembered. Hells bells, he'd have to phone Susan from the garage.

* * *

Vaux entered Susan's office. She had her hand on the phone as he walked in, but removed it to shuffle some papers that lay on the desk. Vaux sat down on a chrome and leather chair opposite her.

'What next?' he asked.

'I would say the ball's in your court, Michael. You can now go ahead and buy the property.'

'Yes, but at what price? Now the auction's over, do I have the right to lower my bid to a more sane level?'

'I don't know what the legal ramifications are. None of your recent offers have been in writing. And even if they were, you never made a final and legally binding contract. Anyway, I'll call Toby Kingston and feel him out. If you want to revise your last bid, and assuming no one else is interested in No. 32, I should imagine you're in the driver's seat. After all, if you're now the sole bidder, you're in a buyer's market. Quite a turn-around in your fortunes, isn't it?'

Vaux had a dark thought. 'What about the wife, the widow. Would she want to go ahead, do you think? Maybe she's determined to buy the home her late husband dreamed of retiring to. You never know.'

'I'll be calling Mrs. Johnson this morning. Then I'll talk to Toby. I tried earlier, but he wasn't in.' The phone rang. Unguardedly, Susan cried, 'Oh hello, Arthur! Er, no. No, I haven't any news on that. I'll try calling you later.'

At The Cedars, Davis put down the phone. He guessed she couldn't talk.

Later that morning, Susan called Toby Kingston. He said he'd have to talk to his elder brother in Sydney. But he supposed Vaux was in his rights to lower his offer. If no one else wanted the house, then they'd be forced to sell to Vaux. They definitely wanted to get rid of it.

Then she called Mrs. Johnson, who, not surprisingly, didn't want to come to the phone. Her son, a landscape architect who had drawn up elaborate designs for No. 32's large garden, told Susan that unfortunately his mother had made it quite clear that she wanted no part of the bungalow now that his father had passed away. There was a sister in Portsmouth, also a widow, who had told him earlier that morning that she and his mother had always had an understanding that they would, if necessary, live their lives out together.

Susan also called Davis. She was surprised to hear he had already learned of Johnson's death and couldn't fathom where that old bat Mrs. Parker got her information.

* * *

Vaux was walking on air. He'd always felt he had been lucky throughout most of his life (with the exception—his hasty marriage to Joan—proving the rule) and now this: the man who could have cost him a fortune now suddenly and literally overnight, was out of the running. Something told him it would be ungentlemanly to go back to his original price of £195,000—even though that was the price on the books when the bungalow was put up for sale. It would seem mean and indecent. So he decided to come back with an offer of £205,000, reminding the vendors that a lot had to be done and spent on the property. He was almost delirious with delight. His half-a-million-dollar lump-sum payment wouldn't have to be touched after all. The interest on that sum would boost his regular pension by a tidy bit, and his worries were over. He would be in possession of the house of his dreams, and Lady Luck had once again rescued him from a tricky situation.

* * *

'How far is C prepared to go on this?' Davis asked Craw.

'He's leaving it to Sir Walter. The secret contingency fund will be used. And as you probably know, there aren't too many constraints on what we pay freelancers so long as the job gets done,' said Craw.

'Um. Well, I think it's best that Sir Walter knows it won't be less than £200,000. I can't go into the whys and wherefores now, but a full explanation will be forthcoming as and when requested,' said Davis, wondering why Mason couldn't

call him personally on such a sensitive matter. 'Where is Sir
Walter these days anyway?' he asked.

'Fishing trip —Scotland. Should be back next week,' said
Craw.

Davis picked up the regular phone and dialed Susan's
number. 'You know I told you to stand fast, my dear. Well,
here's the situation. I'm afraid the old bidding war is about
to resume. I've just heard from Abel, Bates, Collin and Dalfen—same law firm as Johnson used. Seems another interested party has appeared on the scene. A builder, apparently.
They're writing a formal offer now of somewhere in the region of £400,000. The chap thinks the property's worth that
and plans to build a super-modern American-type ranch house
after tearing the old bungalow down.'

Susan seemed unimpressed. *She's a hard bitch,* thought
Davis.

'Very good, Arthur. I'll pass on the good news to Vaux.'

Davis then phoned the Pig & Whistle. Vaux was out, so he
left a message to call him. He asked Harry to tell Vaux that it
was urgent.

9

'Thanks for that, Craw. Better you speak to him than me. He's liable to gripe about the lower pension—he looks upon me as a friend rather than as a former boss and I can't really be bothered,' said Sir Walter Mason.

'What do I say, sir, if he raises the question with me?'

'Tell him you'll take it up with housekeeping. He'll know what you mean.'

Mason picked up the folders that had been placed in front of him. He opened the Vaux file. 'An ideal candidate as you say, Craw. But one or two regrettable blemishes: at Bristol he joined the Socialist Party of Great Britain, which in those days was left of the British Labour Party—quite a bit left. He also joined the students' union, then dominated by radical left-wing sympathizers, especially at the provincial universities. Then there's his membership of the union's Film Club in the late '50s. That was another hotbed of lefties. They used to show those Italian productions that highlighted the extreme poverty of the Ities just after the war. All the filmmakers in those days were either far-left socialists or communists.'

'You're not suggesting, sir, a potential Maclean or Burgess in our midst?' asked Craw, half joking.

'Good God no, man. But it needs checking into. He's worked all his life for pretty conservative newspapers, and certainly *Time* is a faithful disciple of free enterprise and the American way.' Mason put the Vaux folder to the side and picked up the Kadri file.

'Our friend Kadri is a full-fledged member of the Baath Party and, I suspect, kow-tows with no hesitation to kindly President Hafiz Al-Assad. But that's what you have to do if you want to make a living in Syria. Kadri got a first in economics, by the way, so he did better than Vaux, who got a second. Also, he's married and has three children—all grown by now. So I think my earlier theory about a possible youthful homosexual fling between Vaux and Kadri is now nugatory, non-valid. Pity, really. The chummier these two are when they meet, the better it will be.' Craw nodded in agreement.

'One last thing: one summer they both went together to France. Kadri speaks fluent French like all educated Syrians and Vaux was taking French as a subsidiary subject. They had digs at the Cité Universitaire in Paris and then went south to Nice where, like all poverty-stricken students, they stayed at a youth hostel. What interests me, however, is that Kadri, along with Vaux, went to the Syrian embassy in Paris. What was that all about, I wonder.'

'A visa renewal perhaps?' hazarded Craw.

'Look into it,' said Mason curtly. His tone indicated end of meeting. But then he had another thought.

'Oh, before you go. Did you ever ask housekeeping to change that silly nameplate downstairs—Acme Global Consultants Ltd? Bloody unoriginal and unimaginative. I asked you to see about it last year, didn't I?'

Craw had turned around at the door. 'Yes sir, you did. But they said they had other more urgent priorities. They'd let me know the new title as soon as they'd thought one up.'

'I see. Well all right, Craw.'

* * *

The euphoria evaporated as quickly as early morning mist on a warm spring day. Susan had informed Vaux of a new, anonymous offer for No. 32. She read from the solicitor's letter: the formal bid was for £400,000. Vaux felt that sinister dark forces were again gathering to sabotage his dream, so closely within reach just hours ago. Was there oil, or perhaps coal, under No. 32? he asked, semi-seriously. If he entered the latest bidding war, he'd see his lump-sum pension payment evaporate. He would be back to square one—worrying about making ends meet like he used to when he was young and struggling.

But once again, he told himself, he was not over the hill—just yet. He was still young enough to get another job, even as a lowly sub-editor. Then once they had taken his measure and recognized his writing talents, why, he could end his working life as a lofty leader writer or even a political pundit. He'd commute from Willow Drive. It would be like the old days when he still lived with his mother and went up by train to Fleet Street every morning—reading his own pieces in the morning paper.

Davis had invited him for drinks and a quiet dinner of Mrs. Fletcher's cold roast beef and potato salad. He felt like drinking that night and had three double whiskies before crossing Watford Lane to The Cedars. It was a dark night, but the gentle wind carried a warm touch of spring.

Vaux told Davis of the latest developments. Davis decided to tap his best thespian talents. The occasion deserved his finest efforts. He had always had dreams about acting before he joined the RAF, and this evening presented itself as an opportunity to practice his undeveloped gifts.

'Incredible, absolutely incredible, dear boy. Somebody's obviously willing to pay way over the top for that little bungalow. This time I'm convinced it has to be a developer. Either that or some big company pension fund trying to diversify into property.'

Vaux shuddered at the thought of doing battle with a big, amorphous corporation bent on maximizing profits. He signaled with his empty old-fashioned that he'd like another drink. Davis poured him a smallish whisky and half a finger of malt for himself. He wanted to keep a clear head and he didn't want Vaux to forget the crucial conversation they were about to have when he woke up tomorrow morning.

'But here's the thing, old boy. I have a proposition which could just solve your problem with No. 32.'

Vaux had the surprised look of a drowning man at the unexpected appearance of a lifeline.

Davis proceeded to tell Vaux that as a globe-trotting British Airways captain he had from time to time done 'special work' for the British government. Hush-hush stuff for queen and country, that sort of thing. Sometimes acting as a courier, sometimes doing the odd drop-off to secret agents friendly toward the West, etcetera. Sometimes even helping an agent in trouble to do a bunk. This of course was the Cold War.

'Now it just so happens, Michael, that I have been advised by my people that they're now looking urgently for someone to do just the sort of one-off assignment that I used to do— only now of course I'm retired.'

'But so am I,' protested Vaux.

'You're a good six or seven years younger than I, old man. And your background is ideal—far better than mine ever was.'

Vaux looked doubtful, bewildered, even mystified. Davis then delivered, as casually as he could muster, the clincher. 'Of course, this particular assignment is top priority, and as such, the operative, whoever he is, will be well compensated. I'm talking serious money—a hundred grand plus.' Davis raised his glass and looked over the rim to see if the information had penetrated.

Vaux said: 'Tell me more.'

* * *

He had noticed her one evening and here she was again. An incongruous, exotic young creature to appear in a time-worn local watering hole in the suburbs. She sat at one of the small tables at the rear of the saloon bar. She was alone and she seemed preoccupied. Her handbag sat open on the tabletop, as she seemed to be fishing for something. She found what she was looking for, a blue packet of Gauloise cigarettes. She lit up and exhaled a powerful cloud of blue-gray smoke. She glanced up and smiled at him, a shy sort of smile but, he thought, encouraging. He had probably had too many drinks with old Davis—especially after it sank in that he might be able to afford No. 32 after all. Feeling somewhat reassured, he felt no hesitation in walking over with his whisky to where she was sitting. The bar wasn't crowded and Vaux recognized a few familiar faces.

'Do you mind if I join you?' he asked, careful not to slur his words.

'Not at all. I think I saw you here the other night.'

'Probably. I'm billeted here—upstairs. For a month or so, probably. My name's Michael, Michael Vaux, pronounced veau—as in the French for veal.'

She laughed, her perfect white teeth contrasting strongly with her olive skin and the dark red lipstick that she wore. She had full lips, hazel eyes, and long black hair. He could see she was a tall woman, probably six feet, a fraction taller than he was.

'Do you always say that to people you have just met?' she said.

'The silent "x" doesn't come easily to an English tongue.'

'I suppose not,' she said. 'I'm Veronica Belmont.'

Vaux had sat down and looked at her half-empty wine glass. 'Please let me get you a drink,' he said. She said she was drinking the house red and Vaux looked in vain for Harry or Pete. 'I'll get it at the bar,' he said, smiling and determined to walk with a steady pace. The barman was a burly stranger called Bill. He said he worked sometimes to give the lads a night off.

Veronica Belmont told Vaux that she was doing some research into the early Roman settlements in and around Verulamium—now known as St. Albans, about forty minutes drive from the Pig & Whistle. She said the study would be published eventually with several other monographs about the Roman influence in Britain.

'So you're an academic, I take it,' said Vaux, delighted to find a well-educated young woman who was sexy too. He was amused to think how rare a commodity that seemed to be in the neighborhood he'd chosen to live the rest of his life. She opened her handbag again and took out a business card. She had a PhD after her name and worked for an outfit called the Imperial Historical Institute.

Vaux in turn told her about his intentions of moving here for good and about the house he had set his mind on. He didn't go into the problems he was having once again with a rival bidder because he didn't have the time. She had got up, put a dark blue silk scarf around her neck, and declared that she really must be going since it was almost closing time.

'Back to London, then?' asked Vaux.

'No. I'm staying at the Watford Hilton.'

'May I call you there—perhaps dinner if you're still here?'

'Oh, I'll be here for several days. Yes, do ring. I'd love to.'

10

Davis called the next day to tell him that a meeting had been arranged. 'You will travel tomorrow morning by the 8:20 a.m. to Euston where I shall meet you at the main taxi rank just outside the station. Bring a change of clothes since you will probably stay overnight,' said Davis, thoroughly businesslike.

Vaux wondered why he had to meet Davis in London instead of them both driving there in Davis's luxurious Bentley. He supposed they had their reasons. He should, he told himself, adopt a modest, eager-to-learn pose since he didn't want to get off on the wrong foot. He'd had a rough night, tossing and turning, thinking first of Veronica (he surprised himself by how keen he was to see her again) and then of the project Davis had, in only the barest of details, outlined to him. But did he really want to get mixed up with this sort of thing at his age? He was looking forward to a carefree retirement, perhaps some odd freelance work, going up to the West End to the art galleries, to see the latest plays—do things his career had never given him enough time to do.

But necessity dictated certain actions, he supposed. If he didn't feel he needed the sort of money Davis told him would be forthcoming, things might be different. But the renewed war over No. 32 had changed the situation. With the extra cash, he could contemplate the real possibility that he had a good chance of being the eventual victor—and move in. Without some sort of windfall, he would be facing at best a sort of non-retirement, almost a regression, a return to the life of his twenties. He dressed that morning in the only dark suit he now possessed (charcoal gray) and wore a paisley tie with a white shirt. He resolved to call Veronica Belmont from London—perhaps they'd have dinner when he got back.

* * *

Davis, in a trilby and trench coat, was standing a few feet from the long queue of people who were waiting for a taxi. The black cabs drove up rapidly and the line-up seemed to be moving quickly. Davis waved him over to where he was standing as though to suggest they wouldn't be joining the queue after all.

'Take this,' he said, handing Vaux a small piece of paper on which he saw an address. 'It's a hotel in Swiss Cottage. Just ask the cab driver, he'll know it. There'll be someone looking out for you there. You're booked in for tonight, by the way. Don't bother about identification or payment—it's all been taken care of.'

'You're not coming?' asked Vaux, a little confused.

'No. I've done my job. Good luck, old boy. Give me a ring when you get back, if you like. Oh, by the way, you're Mr. Sanders as far as the hotel is concerned.' He disappeared behind a stout stone column before Vaux could ask any more questions.

As he looked in the direction he thought Davis had taken, he caught sight of a tall young woman with a striking resemblance to Veronica. She was striding through the teeming masses of commuters that thronged the big station's concourse and appeared to be headed for the tube entrance.

'I reckon that's the old Finchley Hotel, guv,' said the taxi driver, looking at the small piece of paper Vaux had handed him through the glass partition. 'Number 45, Hendon Avenue, yeah, that's the old Finchley. Don't know the new name but it must be the same place.'

The hotel was one of those big terraced houses built in the nineteenth century for the up and coming rich commercial classes—four stories high with basement and porticoed front entrance. Those houses that hadn't been turned into luxury boutique hotels had been transformed into small flats or bed-sitters with eight or nine tiny nameplates displayed to guide visitors and postmen.

A uniformed man with a gray top hat opened the taxi door as Vaux scrambled out clutching his overnight bag. 'Welcome to the Monet, sir,' said the doorman.

Vaux saw that the small lobby was festooned with the great impressionist's prints along with those of his contemporaries—Manet, Pissarro, and Renoir. At a low office-like desk sat a shiny-haired, dark-suited young man whom Vaux observed nodding to someone behind him as if to signal that all formalities would be waived. Then he felt something or somebody touch his arm. 'You must be Sanders. Mr. Silverstein is waiting for you. Can I carry your bag?' The speaker was a tall, lean man in his early forties, pinstriped suit, white shirt, and black and gold college tie. They made their way to a small elevator, which creaked and groaned until it stopped with a jolt on the fourth floor.

Craw ushered him into what the hotel called its penthouse suite. The first thing he saw was a big print of Pissaro's *Church and Farm at Eragny*. In the far corner of the room was a large desk at which a distinguished-looking gentleman sat reading what looked like *The Times*. 'This is Mr. Silverstein,' said Craw. They had agreed to use aliases because Vaux had come in from the cold—and because he had not yet been briefed on the Official Secrets Act. 'And my name's Kelly.'

Vaux noticed that Mr. Kelly had taken his overnight bag into another room, presumably the bedroom.

Sir Walter Mason offered him a drink, which Vaux declined on account of the time of day. 'Some coffee, perhaps?' said Mason.

The briefing commenced. Operation Helvetia was to be conducted by MI6 operatives who were to report directly to Section B3, the Near and Middle East desk. Vaux, if he came aboard, was to report to Alan Kelly, Mr. Silverstein's deputy in the Helvetia project. Before outlining the purpose of the exercise, said Sir Walter, he would like to tell Vaux that they were familiar with his background, were impressed with his career, and considered him an excellent candidate for the job.

Vaux listened intently. It was a bit Alice in Wonderland, he thought irreverently. What on earth had he really done to impress these spooks? A hint came in Sir Walter's next comment.

'We are aware that you spent three years in Cairo in the mid-'60s where you agreed to do some undercover work for the Central Intelligence Agency— '

'That's not true,' said Vaux quickly. If this was the quality of their intelligence, he was not impressed. He remembered the stories in the American press, and in *Time* for that matter, about the incompetence and amateurism of Britain's intelligence establishment. Deep penetration by Soviet agents into the inner sanctums of the SIS—he even recalled rumors that the head of MI5 was under suspicion at one point—had made sensational headlines and stories at the time.

Sir Walter smiled and put his hand up, the heavily lined palm facing Vaux. 'That puts that matter to rest. I accept your denial. May I continue?'

The bombshell exploded after the coffee was brought, along with a plate of chocolate digestives. Craw was removing the tray when Mason, having lit up a Dunhill, pushed his chair back, stood up, and turned to look out of the tall window. 'The key to all this, Vaux, is your acquaintance with one Ahmed Abdul Kadri, a Syrian national whom you befriended in your years at Bristol University. You were classmates, I understand.'

The impact was numbing. Vaux was momentarily speechless. They *had,* after all, done their homework. Sir Walter had turned around to observe Vaux's reaction. His expression suggested he could wait while Vaux composed his reply.

'Yes, we were friends. A long time ago. I haven't been in touch with him for some years. I doubt if I'd even recognize him now. But how does he come into this?'

Sir Walter opened a folder that *The Times* had been concealing. 'Ahmed Kadri is now working for the Syrian Ministry of Defense. He heads the purchasing department and he's responsible for the procurement of weapons and armaments and other military equipment—from tanks and trucks to cruise missiles and rifles.' Mason paused.

Vaux's eyebrows rose as he digested the information. 'When I last heard from him he was working at the central bank in Damascus—Bank of Syria, I suppose. He was an economist there and I think he headed up the statistics department, such as it was in those days. He used to joke about how primitive the state of the art was among the Arab countries. He was coming over to Washington to take a course given by the World Bank in statistics and data systems and the like, specially designed for third-world central bankers. I remember he said he'd call me when he was in Washington. I was then in Ottawa, but quite prepared to fly down and see him, of course.'

Mason and Craw exchanged glances. 'And did you eventually get together?'

'No—there was some sort of hitch at the last minute. After that, well, you know how it is. We got on with our lives. He was having some trouble with his marriage at that point and my own marriage was pretty much on the rocks. In that sense we still had a lot in common. We had a good laugh about that.'

Mason continued: 'In the summer of '59 you went together to France, stayed in Paris at the Cité Universitaire complex. Is that correct?'

Vaux recalled that idyllic summer. Six weeks with Ahmed,
drifting around France, getting drunk on cheap red wine, discovering French food, his French improving by the day (Kadri
had insisted they speak to each other only in French), and
Ahmed's surprise success with the girls. Vaux figured they
liked his olive skin, his dark, hooded eyes, his slight build, and
probably his Arab-accented French. But there was no rivalry
between them.

'Yes. I remember it well—with apologies to Maurice
Chevalier.'

The attempt at humor was ignored. 'And you both vis-
ited the Syrian embassy before heading south—presumably to
Nice. Can you tell me why you went to the embassy on the
Rue Vaneau in the Seventh Arrondissement?'

God almighty, thought Vaux. This seemed like an official
interrogation. *What the hell am I doing here?*

'It was so long ago, I can't recall.' Put that in your pipe,
thought Vaux, happy perhaps to have scored a point for himself—and Ahmed.

The session went on. Dinner was brought up by room
service—club sandwiches and some beer. A Foreign Office
lawyer visited and apprised Vaux of the main thrust of the Official Secrets Act. He left a thick paper-backed volume of the
legislation for bedtime reading.

Vaux was left alone at about 11:30. He put on the television and saw some late-night news. The House of Commons
had elected its first woman speaker, Mrs. Betty Boothroyd,
who seemed to Vaux to be kindlier and gentler than the U.K.'s
first woman PM, Maggie Thatcher, now kicked upstairs to the
House of Lords. He was told not to use the phone in the penthouse, so he thought he'd call Veronica in the morning from a
call box.

* * *

In the taxi that took them northwest across London from
Century House, MI6's headquarters in Lambeth, to the Monet
Hotel in Swiss Cottage, Mason asked Craw whether there had
been any developments overnight.
'No. Silence all evening, except a few sighs, shuffling of
newspapers—oh and the late-night news.'
'Phone?'
'Nothing.'
'What do you think?'
'About Vaux?' asked Craw.
Mason nodded.
'I think he'll be all right. A bit of a cynic, but aren't all
journalists?'
'Did you believe what he said about his politics?'
'Since his days as a paid-up member of the Socialist Party
of Great Britain? Yes, absolutely. He's been too busy making
a living. And the more he made headway in the world, the
less he was actively interested in politics. He may prefer the
Democrats to the Republicans, but so what?'
'So, rock solid?'
'I'd say so—with a little supervision.'
'Which you will provide.'
Sir Walter looked out at the forlorn old newspaper build-
ings as they raced up Fleet Street toward Trafalgar Square, so
he never saw Craw's smirk of self-satisfaction.

* * *

Vaux had showered and shaved and had breakfast downstairs in the hotel's restaurant. It was a buffet affair and he ate
too many sausages. He thought he'd phone Veronica when he
got back to the Pig & Whistle. He returned to the penthouse

to discover his new employers had already let themselves in.
Kelly seemed to be leaning over the desk phone, no doubt
checking if he'd used it overnight.

'Ah, Vaux. Well, we seem to be almost through,' said Mason. 'Sit you down.' Vaux sat in the chair opposite Sir Walter.
Kelly seemed to be doing something in the bathroom.

'To recap: Operation Helvetia will yield vital information
regarding the Soviet Union's—sorry, Russia's—planned clandestine arms deal with the Republic of Syria. This is probably
the biggest arms sale by the Russians since their infamous deal
with Egypt's Nasser in the '50s. It's vital that we know just
what's involved, not so much the final cost to Syria in terms
of foreign currency—we suspect they'll be paying for some of
it with Saudi oil—but the details of the supplies. How many
new tanks, troop carriers, gun batteries, etcetera. Particularly
whether the Russians are selling them certain types of guided
missiles. And even though we doubt it, if they have agreed to
help them on nuclear research—thin end of the wedge, leading perhaps to the development of nuclear weapons or, God
forbid, the bomb.'

'I understand,' said Vaux. He seemed to hesitate. He was
wondering how Ahmed would react to his back-slapping, old-
mates-reunited approach when they 'bumped into' each other.
The man had surely changed after thirty-plus years in Syria.
He had been forced to work with what was there—a totalitar-
ian regime which, as Silverstein had reminded him so forcefully, had been guilty of human rights abuses, in particular the
massacre of women and children in a town called Hamah.

It was in '82, the town had been taken over by the extrem-
ist Moslem Brotherhood, and Assad had gone in with tanks,
artillery, and bomber aircraft. Silverstein had mentioned that
Amnesty International estimated that twenty thousand civilians had lost their lives. Had Ahmed become a hardened
Baathist? Was his life so comfortable that he had persuaded
himself that the cause was just? Vaux couldn't answer that—
but he did know that the West, too, had a lot to answer for.

Was he now prepared to aid and assist the former colonial powers in another piece of meddling in internal Arab affairs? He heard Mason's raised voice.

'Are you still with us?' asked Sir Walter amiably. Vaux smiled and gave a slight nod.

'Housekeeping—the money and expenses plus the technical assistance you will need will be looked after by Mr. Kelly,' said Mason. 'I wish you luck.' He got up, stretched out his arm, and they shook hands.

Kelly sat down. They heard the door close as Mason left. Kelly then told Vaux that a first deposit of £50,000 would be made in two days' time. The account number would be given him on his next visit. The money would be deposited with Credit Suisse in Geneva, and since Operation Helvetia was centered on Geneva, it made sense for Vaux to have the account there. The name of the account holder would be Derek Westropp, which would also be the name on his new U.K. passport. He would be calling Vaux within five days via Davis's scrambled phone. Davis would simply be the messenger—he didn't have to be told any details of the operation. He'd have to come up to London again for a two-day crash course in security (basic tradecraft) and technical training—mainly, it seemed, instruction on how to use a miniature micro-Minox camera for document copying.

II

As Vaux approached the Pig & Whistle—he had walked there from the station—he saw what looked like an overweight, balding man in dirty jeans and battered tweed jacket who resembled John Goodchild. The man waved as he got closer and confirmed his first impression.

'Hi, Michael! Didn't know you'd gone away. Trying to find out where you'd got to but nobody in there knows nothing.'

Vaux thought this was all he needed right now. He looked at his watch and it was just past 11a.m., so the bar was open. He ushered John in and bought two pints of Watney's. Mrs. Caldwell, in a blue cotton apron that had seen better days, was polishing glasses at the bar.

'I told 'im you was away, Mr. Vaux, but he didn't take a blind bit of notice,' she said sternly. Vaux assumed that Goodchild got most working souls' backs up. The local layabout. He steered John away to the back of the bar. The doors were open on to the small patio and they could hear excited birdsong while a warm spring breeze wafted in to dissipate the smell of stale tobacco.

Vaux said, 'I had to go up to town on some business, that's all, John.

'Oh, well, I wondered, you know, if you'd done a bunk or something—'

'Why should I do that? I'm still negotiating for the house. I'll probably stay here until the deal's done.'

'You reckon you'll get it then now that old Johnson's snuffed it.'

'You're not up to date. Another buyer or would-be buyer's come forward. Whoever it is, they seem to want it as badly as Johnson ever did. I'm going to have to pay through the nose to get that bloody house.'

'Oh Christ, I had no idea.' Goodchild drank his beer. 'I'll get another,' he said, not waiting for a reply. Vaux thought he should phone Veronica before noon and he knew he didn't want to get bogged down in another afternoon drinking bout with Goodchild. He heard no conversation between Mrs. Caldwell and Goodchild. She had pulled two pints, grabbed the money, and run the till.

'I wanted to ask you back, Mike. Come for lunch. My son's roasting a chicken. If there's one thing he's good at it's cooking. I'll say that for the lazy bugger.'

'No, I can't today, John. I've a lunch appointment. Perhaps later in the week.'

Goodchild put on his long face. 'Look, I'm sorry I raised old skeletons that time we had a good chinwag. I didn't mean to imply that I resented or regretted our childhood friendship. I didn't mean to be rude or unsociable.'

'I know you didn't. We've been over all that and you've apologized once already. Let's just forget it.'

'I wish it was that easy,' said Goodchild enigmatically. There was a long silence, punctuated by Goodchild's elaborate display on how to strike a light on a damp book of matches and successfully fire up a Rothmans. They both heard the chattering of the sparrows and the chaffinches and the starlings. A gray pigeon waddled toward them, jerkily picking up minute crumbs left by yesterday's lunch crowd.

'Look, mate,' said Goodchild finally, 'have you thought any more about what I asked you last time we saw each other?'

'You mean the two grand?'

Goodchild studied the pigeon that now seemed to be looking him straight in the eye. Vaux thought it was an accusing look.

'Yeah. You see, I really need it. The missus is still away and I had to send her money because she can't just live off her sisters, can she. Then I had to fork out six hundred bloody quid for my second son's summer camp—Jason.'

Vaux observed the facial expression of a man who had been betrayed by the world, a man who despite his best efforts never seemed able to gain traction. Then he thought of the money that was about to land in his own lap. An unexpected windfall for a dubious assignment. There would be no turning back. He wondered if he'd ever be able to put it behind him. He feared that, in the end, in his soul, there would always be a touch of corruption.

Vaux drained his glass. As if to assuage any nascent guilt about the temporary but clandestine job he had agreed to take on, he decided to be unreservedly generous. 'Okay, John. Give me until tomorrow afternoon. Two grand. I'll give you a check.'

Goodchild was elated. 'You'll get it back, Mike. I swear.'

* * *

'Sir Walter didn't try the old debt to queen and country caper then,' said Davis. Craw had phoned him at the request of Mason, as a matter of courtesy.

'No sir. C told him not to bother with that line of approach. He considers it old hat in this day and age. Money speaks louder than patriotism. If Vaux was of the landed gentry and owned a Chatsworth it might be different. Besides, after thirty years out of the country, loyalty to the crown probably wears a bit thin.'

'I think C is probably right. There's not much more for me to do then.'

'You've done an admirable job, sir.'

'Did you arrange for a watcher just in case our lad decides not to stick around after laying hands on the booty?'

'It's taken care of. And we're paying him on an install-
ment basis, just as a precaution. The final sum on completion
of the operation.'

Davis put the phone back in the drawer. His job, of course,
hadn't been done. He must call Alec Abel of Abel, Bates, Collin & Dalfen, solicitors and commissioners of oaths, to make
sure he was on top of Vaux's latest bid and to up the ante by another £5,000. There's no better producer than a hungry man.

* * *

They had dinner at the nearby Hilton. Vaux found the
food moderately good. Veronica had said she was too tired to
go hunting for restaurants and in any case the Dover sole here
was excellent. She looked beautiful, tired but relaxed, her
black hair draping her bare shoulders. The cut-glass pendant
earrings sparkled like diamonds and threw into relief her olive
skin.

'So you saw the bishop today?' asked Vaux.

'No, just the dean—he's head of the business side of
St. Albans.'

'I haven't been there since I was a kid. Mother used to
take me for picnics on the grounds and the usual guided tour
of the cathedral. When I got old enough to drive her car I used
to go to The Cock, that old pub in the cathedral's hallowed
grounds. Drank myself silly.'

'The oldest pub in Britain, so they say. But I couldn't
believe how busy the poor man was. Every five minutes we
were interrupted by the canon or one of the sub-deans or by
some young seminarian. Then the builders came in, asking
him about the restoration work. It was a circus. Finally he told
his male secretary to bar all visitors until he'd finished with
me. A remarkable man. He's going to let me have a peek at
some archives that haven't seen the light of day since about
1750.'

She looked very pleased with her obvious coup. Vaux wondered if there was a story here for some enterprising ecclesiastical reporter. 'Did that take some persuasion?' he asked.

'I suppose I convinced him of the importance of scholarship and the pointlessness of keeping these particular papers under wraps. They related to Alban's martyrdom. The Romans executed him in the mid-third century for harboring a priest. When I said I saw a parallel between the Romans eventually giving in to Christianity and the Communists in Eastern Europe finally surrendering to democracy, he seemed to see the light. He became totally enthusiastic.'

Vaux had never looked at the crumbling of the Iron Curtain in quite that light. But he supposed she had a point. Now, though, he wasn't so sure about Mother Russia. Later, he asked her if she had gone up to town on Monday. He could have sworn he saw her in the crowds at Euston. No, she said, she had spent the day at St. Albans.

They went into the small bar off the restaurant for coffee and cognacs. Vaux wanted to be quite bold and ask if he could take her up to her room. But his courage withered along with the conversation. She had given him little encouragement: when he looked intently into her eyes she looked away. And when he made light of the eternal war of the sexes, she changed the subject. A challenge had always intrigued him—and here he was again, fascinated and dazzled by what he couldn't have. They shook hands in the lobby and Vaux headed back to his small room at the Pig & Whistle.

* * *

It was past midnight and Vaux found the pub's door locked. It was a simple Yale lock and he'd been given a spare key but he'd left it on his dressing table. He saw a bell button that he'd never noticed before and within thirty seconds the door sprung open. Pete, his face flushed and his eyes glazed over, greeted Vaux like a long-lost uncle. He shouted something, hugged him, and led him by the hand to the saloon bar. The jukebox was at full volume, playing an oldie that he instantly recognized: the youthful voice of Sir Cliff Richard celebrating his possession all those years ago of a *Walkin', talkin', livin' doll.* Clustered around the bar were six or seven men all, thought Vaux, feeling even less pain than he was.

'This is darling Mr. Vaux, chaps. And I'm going to pour him a large, a very large Cutty Sark—his favorite. Isn't that right, Mr. Vaux?'

Vaux was embarrassed, but he tried to rise to the occasion.

'That will be very welcome, though I thought it was closing time.' Everyone laughed and went back to whatever they were talking about to one another before Vaux's entrance.

Pete said, 'Nah, don't worry about that, love. This is a private gathering—some old friends I'd like you to meet.' Introductions were made all round. Vaux realized suddenly that they were all under thirty—except perhaps for Harry, who was at the back of the bar with a young man. They were sitting at one of the round marble-topped tables near the open doors.

Pete handed him a big old-fashioned, filled to the brim with one ice cube floating forlornly on the surface. 'Sorry, love, we're out of ice. Harry! Where's that fuckin' bucket of ice you were supposed to be fetching?' he shouted across the room. Harry's answer was an incomprehensible muttering followed by a screech as he slid his chair against the old tiled floor in an effort to get up.

'It doesn't matter,' said Vaux.

'Yes, it does matter,' said Pete emphatically. 'You're not the only one who likes ice with their drink, you know. Now Mr. Vaux, I want you to meet a dear friend of mine. We were at school together—Harrow. Not where Churchill went, dear, Harrow Secondary Modern. Justin! Come over here! Meet my friend.'

Vaux said, 'I wish you'd call me Michael.'

'Mike it is,' said Pete, laughing. 'Anyway, this is Justin. Justin, Mike.' They nodded to each other. Then Pete made a gesture, which suggested that to be heard properly over the loud music, Vaux should bend his ear closer to Pete's mouth. 'Justin likes older men,' he whispered.

Vaux smiled. If he was surprised at Pete's forwardness, it was only because he was an old fuddy-duddy. He must take all this in the spirit in which it was meant.

'Oh, well, that's wonderful. I don't feel such an outsider now.'

Justin, who was tall and lean, had shoulder-length light brown hair and wore a nose stud, took Vaux's hand and led him farther down into the bar. Vaux saw Harry get up and give his companion a brief peck on the cheek.

'Is the party in aid of anything special?' asked Vaux, cooler than he'd meant to sound. Then suddenly he realized who Harry's temporary paramour was: John's son, Patrick Goodchild, for God's sake, the bus boy who picked up a bit of extra cash by helping out at the Pig.

'No, not really. They often have private parties on weekends. Doesn't do any harm and it's not illegal,' said Justin.

'No, of course not.'

'I live fifteen minutes away—on The Heath. Have you got a car?'

Vaux was trying to think of an exit strategy, and this would do just fine. They left together, all eyes—except Harry's and Patrick's—on the newly met couple. He didn't like what he was about to do, but sometimes a tactical withdrawal came at the cost of popularity. They drove to The Heath and Justin pointed to a small terraced house by the side of a narrow footpath. Justin got out. But Vaux stayed behind the steering wheel. Justin then lowered his head to look through the car door's open window.

'Sorry, Justin. I'm dog tired. Some other time,' said Vaux.

Justin looked disappointed but not defeated. 'Not to worry, mate. See you at the bar. Bye now.'

* * *

Earlier, Arthur Davis had enjoyed the late-night movie. He'd seen *Mrs. Miniver* for the umpteenth time. He switched off the TV and walked over to the long, leaded windows. The Pig & Whistle was now in darkness. Davis yawned. The revelers had all gone home. Then suddenly the front door swung open and two men staggered out, holding each other for support. He looked closer. My God! It was Vaux with some long-haired hippie in t-shirt and jeans. They made their halting way to the side lane where the pub's clientele parked their cars. Then he saw the Audi speed away as though Vaux had no time to lose.

12

Sir Walter said: 'Our man in Damascus says Kadri and his team will arrive in Geneva five days before the actual Middle East conference is due to open. Nothing exceptional about that except of course it will present a window of opportunity for Kadri to get together with the Russian negotiators to hammer out an arms deal. The Syrians have booked in at the Beau Rivage. I suggest Vaux and the watchers get rooms at the Hotel de la Paix, which is close by on the Quai du Mont Blanc.'

'Cheaper, too, sir,' said Craw. 'Four stars against five for the Beau.'

'If it was the other way round, Treasury would nag us like an old fish wife,' agreed Mason.

They were at Sir Walter Mason's cramped offices at Gower Street. Sir Walter had invited Alan Craw down to his sprawling estate in Dorset for the weekend. They had agreed not to talk shop. Mason had put in a lot of horse riding while Craw, who didn't ride, caught up on a couple of novels he'd been meaning to read—Len Deighton's *Berlin Game* and Alan Furst's *Night Soldiers*. One of the firm's staff cars had brought them back to London and the first order of business was Operation Helvetia.

'Sir John called me Saturday evening after dinner.' Mason referred to Sir John Blakeley, the aging director-general and top man at Britain's Secret Intelligence Service. 'There's a lot riding on the success of this bloody deal. I just hope our Mr. Vaux doesn't somehow goof up. Anyway, you'll have to give him a full briefing later on this week and then get him moving. I'd like to see him installed in Geneva within seven days.

'I scribbled some notes after talking with C,' continued Sir Walter, employing the ideogram insiders used to refer to the D-G. 'Hard to read because I was jolly tired.'

Craw got out his little notebook and unscrewed the top of his old Conway Stewart fountain pen, now poised to write.

'Ah yes. Well, it seems that Yeltsin may have resigned from membership of the Communist Party, but he bloody well hasn't changed his stripes when it comes to foreign policy. First off, Sir John reminded me that in 1980, Syria and the Soviets signed a top-secret treaty of "friendship and cooperation." It was to run for twenty years and, as far as we know, hasn't been abrogated. Our friend Boris, it seems, is keen to boost friendly ties with Syria as part of Russia's chess game in the Mideast. Assad, for his part, has played a clever game—never completely giving in to all demands the Russians make in terms of military and naval bases or in terms of relaxing its policy on suppressing the Syrian Communist Party.

'Russia feels compelled to help Syria build up its armed forces for two basic reasons: as a counterpoint to U.S. and Israeli pressure on Syria and to give a much-needed boost to its overall Middle East policy which calls for a comprehensive Arab-Israeli peace guaranteed by the United Nations, backed by the military might of the international community—meaning a joint U.S.-Russian peace-keeping force. With me so far?'

'An excellent backgrounder, sir.'

'I hope you're taking it all in, Craw. Vaux has to know that what he's doing is in the interest of peace, perhaps even eventually a satisfactory Middle East settlement. I may not be a psychiatrist, but I do know people. That man has to be motivated by more than money. If he feels like a mercenary, he won't maximize his performance. It's essential that we have him totally on side—and not as a sort of quasi-journalist interloper.'

Craw could see that Sir Walter's patriotism was rising to the surface once again. Long weekends at a magnificent country estate, his wife's impeccable hospitality, two or three good horse rides in the bucolic splendor of the Dorset countryside—that was enough in itself to make him an ardent patriot. But what really helped stir the brew was being reminded that his day job could only further the political and economic interests of Great Britain and, of course, the American cousins.

'I quite see your point, sir.'

'Now where was I? Ah yes.' Mason turned the envelope on which he had scribbled the highlights of C's policy analysis. 'In the last few years, Syria's combat strength has deteriorated markedly, much of its equipment obsolescent and poorly maintained. Hence Syria's desire for a big arms deal and military aid of one sort or another. The army is in dire need of new battle tanks, armored personnel carriers, reconnaissance vehicles, artillery, self-propelled rocket launchers, etcetera, etcetera. The Syrian air force is only 50 percent operational. They need new fighter planes and spare parts and maintenance supplies for the four hundred MIGs now out of service.'

Sir Walter now turned the envelope sideways. 'And this is the most crucial point,' he read. 'Syria's missile command is impressive. We think Assad's trying to enhance the capabilities of its Scud missiles and the Russian-built Frog-7 missiles. According to Sir John, whose staff of course is in constant contact with our field agents, some 150 warheads have been modified for WMD (weapons of mass destruction) and they want to increase that number tenfold. Of course, most of the ballistic missiles are aimed at Israel—particularly its nuclear facility at Dimona.'

Craw wanted to get up and dictate his own notes into his Sony tape recorder. If he couldn't read his own writing, he'd have to rely on his memory. 'Can I expect more formal briefing papers, sir?' he asked hopefully.

'You could get on to those ivory tower Arabists at the Foreign Office, if you like. God knows what the hell they do

over there since we lost Egypt and Iraq—and the Gulf states,
for that matter. But I suppose that's ancient history. And they
certainly didn't tell anyone Saddam Hussein was planning to
march into Kuwait a couple of years ago. Anyway, that's it for
now, Craw. Bottom line: this deal between Russia and Syria, I
don't have to tell you, will upset the whole military balance in
the Middle East. Our friends in Washington are totally against
any Russian influence in the area and certainly oppose any
joint action to guarantee Israel's borders. They're quite happy
to do that unilaterally. We have to know what the final deal is
and what it entails. Then diplomatic pressures can come into
play to hopefully reduce the impact. You're his case officer, so
go to it, Craw. And get Vaux up here a.s.a.p. and fill him in.'

* * *

It was about 3 a.m. when Patrick Goodchild got back to
his home on Willow Drive. He was surprised to see the light
on in his dad's bedroom and the hall light's pale glow through
the stained glass oval window of the front door. He quietly let
himself in and then heard his father call him.

'Where the 'ell have you been? I thought the pubs closed
at eleven,' he said. He was lying in bed, propped up on pillows
and reading the racing section in the sports pages of the *Daily
Mail.*

'I had to clean all the glasses, didn't I? Plus general clean-
ing up and that,' said Patrick.

His father continued to study form. 'Mrs. Smith's been
round here all evening. Know who Mrs. Smith is?'

'Betty's mother,' said Patrick, visibly surprised. 'What she
want?'

'Only to tell me her daughter's pregnant and you're the
bloody father.' Now he looked up from the paper to see the
reaction. Patrick sat down on the bed, put his face in his hands,
and shook his head in denial.

'That's impossible, Dad. I always, well, I was always careful. She's bloody lying. I know for a fact that Betty's been going
around with some other guy for some time.' He looked hopefully at his father.
'It'll have to be got rid of, mate, whoever's the father.'
Patrick got up. 'You can't say that, Dad. She might want
it. I'll get it sorted tomorrow, all right?'
'And if it is yours? What the 'ell are you going to do about it?'
'I dunno. Maybe marry her.' He gave a little, nervous
laugh.
'Well, in that case, my son, I think you'd better get your
little act together. Get a full-time job, for example. Earn some
real money, 'cause you're going to need it. Blimey, wait till
your mother hears about this.'
Patrick left the room. He couldn't guess that his father's
true feelings were an odd mixture of hope and annoyance. The
silver lining, his father told himself, was that this could be what
the lazy drifter needed. A brand new, cute little human being
often turned bums into breadwinners. Patrick might finally
get off his father's back. He heard the bath running, planned
his bets for tomorrow's races, turned the bedside lamp off,
and slept better than for many a night.

* * *

At promptly 11a.m. the next morning Mrs. Parker,
her thin hair newly curled and blue-rinsed, entered the Pig
& Whistle for her daily tonic: a pint of Guinness, as recommended by her G.P., Dr. Paul Lewis, employer of Betty Smith,
Patrick Goodchild's girl friend. Harry was behind the bar,
mopping the counter and tidying up. She had observed that
boy Patrick in the backyard. He was kneeling and seemed to
be painting the cast-iron tables and benches.
'You'd better give him a full-time job,' said Mrs. Parker.
'He'll be needing it.'

Harry's ears pricked up. 'Pat? Why, what's he gone and done now?'

'I hear he's put his girl in the family way. And he's not got two pennies to rub together—much like his old man.'

Vaux came in after paying another visit to No. 32. He ordered a pint of bitter. He could feel Mrs. Parker's eyes burning into him. So he looked toward her and nodded. 'Good morning,' he said.

'And you must be Mr. Vaux who's going to move into Mrs. Kingston's old place—'

Harry had disappeared. Vaux said, 'Yes, that's right.'

'I'm Mary Parker. I knew your mother.'

'Oh really, that's interesting' said Vaux.

'That place will be as damp as a swamp after the winter we've had. No heating and all,' said Mrs. Parker.

Harry reemerged. He caught the gist of the conversation. 'Every house around here is damp. It's what they call the London clay—the rain can't drain away so foundations get waterlogged,' said Harry.

'That's why you've got to keep the places heated. Mind you, those bungalows on Willow Drive are worse than most places. I should know—I've lived there most of me married life. Jerry-built from the start, they were.'

'Yes, there's a lot of work to be done if I ever move in,' sighed Vaux. Mrs. Parker gave him a curious look and was about to ask him what he meant (her network of informers had let her down—she didn't know the bidding war had resumed) when Harry came unexpectedly to the rescue.

'Call for you, by the way. About an hour ago. Please ring Group Captain Davis. You can use the phone in the kitchen if you want privacy,' suggested Harry.

Vaux took his pint into the large back kitchen where Mrs. Caldwell was busy cutting sandwiches. The phone had a long lead and he was able to go out of the kitchen door into the pub's backyard. He saw Patrick Goodchild busily sandpapering rusty table legs in preparation for a glossy black paint job. He wondered if the young man had a hangover from the previous night's debauchery. They smiled at each other as Vaux heard Davis's authoritative voice.

* * *

Davis had given the matter a great deal of thought. What on earth was his golden boy up to on Saturday night? Vaux and his companion seemed to be hugging each other like old friends as they left the pub. Presumably Vaux gave the boy a lift—and then what? Surely to God he wasn't one of *them*? If Vaux turned out to be queer it could be catastrophic—a blot on his own escutcheon for misjudging an otherwise promising recruit and possibly a reason to scuttle the whole mission.

Davis was totally opposed to homosexuals working for the government in any capacity. They were obvious security risks, open to blackmail, and when all was said and done, completely unreliable. Most of the queers he'd known turned out badly. Look at those two lover boys Maclean and Burgess. And then there was Vassal, the little jerk of an Admiralty clerk who financed a high lifestyle thanks to selling navy secrets to the Soviets. And that wretched, over-cultured creep Anthony Blunt, the Commie who became the queen's art adviser, for God's sakes.

No, the security and intelligence services couldn't and shouldn't take the risk of hiring these misfits. He'd often wondered about that Pete and his partner; a bit flighty with quite effeminate gestures surfacing at times—mostly when they were talking to customers their own age. He'd have to ask some of the regulars what they thought. Damn all this tolerance and understanding he kept reading about—these nancy boys didn't fit in and neither should they.

After pondering any potential action on his part, Davis came to one very English conclusion: he decided to let sleeping dogs lie. He wouldn't say anything to Vaux, let alone hint at anything dubious to the team at B3. He would hope for the best and put trust in his original judgment. After all, maybe Vaux really was just giving the young man a lift. It seemed an odd time of night, though. Why didn't the boy get a taxi—or walk?

Vaux had been invited over to The Cedars for a light lunch. Mrs. Fletcher ushered him through the kitchen and out into the garden where Davis lay on a hammock-like sun lounger. He was reading a paperback book.

'Ah, Vaux, my boy. Nice to see you. Have a drink. Mrs. Fletcher makes an excellent Pimms No. 6—just the thing for a warm morning like this.' He put aside Agatha Christie's *They Came to Baghdad.*

'Yes, that'll be fine, Mrs. Fletcher,' said Vaux. He sat down on a yellow and white striped deckchair and looked out to the long, deep spinney that bordered on Willow Drive. Through the gaps in the serried trees and the thick bramble and bracken he could see the backs of the bungalows and wondered if a solitary figure going to and fro apparently mowing grass was John Goodchild. He also wondered if he'd gone through the two grand yet.

'Heard you had a good session with the boys,' said Davis.

'I suppose so,' said Vaux unenthusiastically. His mind these days was more on the relentless bidding for No. 32 than for the vague job they called Operation Helvetia.

'Keen as ever?' Davis had noticed the lack of enthusiasm.

'Oh yes,' said Vaux. 'It looks like I'll need the extra cash. Which reminds me, I'm supposed to call Susan this afternoon.'

'You can do it from here, old boy.'

Mrs. Fletcher came out with a big jug of pale, golden Pimms. Ice rattled as she poured slowly into a tall glass, topping off the careful procedure with the deft insertion of a straw. 'Lunch in fifteen minutes, Mr. Davis?'

'Rather, old girl. We'll have it out here.' Mrs. Fletcher
left the jug of Pimm's on a low rattan table and retreated to
the kitchen.

Davis said, 'I've been told to inform you that things are
developing fast. You have to go up for a two-day briefing later
this week, and a day or so later you'll have to go to Geneva.
Your cover is that you will be representing or writing for the
Evening Standard as a Mr. Derek Westropp and your task is to
cover the Mideast Peace Conference. 'Course, the conference
won't get anyone anywhere. It's just a platform for the U.S. to
tell Russia to butt out and for the Israelis to say no progress
is possible so long as the Palestinians condone terrorism. The
Palestinian Liberation Organization will say the cause of terrorism is continued Israeli occupation of Gaza and the West
Bank. So deadlock.

'However, it gives you great subterfuge for carrying out
whatever they have in mind for you to do. You must realize
that I don't know the specifics of your mission—and I don't
want or need to know. To finalize your arrangements you can
call Craw later on my secure phone.'

'Craw?' asked Vaux, mystified.

'I mean Kelly. Yes, you'd better call him Kelly until he decides to throw away his alias. It was just a preliminary precaution. But don't let on I made a slip.'

'First they decide to call me Sanders and now I'm Derek
Westropp. A bit confusing, really. Perhaps they'll come up
with a third choice before I leave for Geneva.'

Davis considered the remark needlessly flippant and
somewhat disrespectful and wondered again whether the real
Vaux was the same Vaux as he portrayed himself to the world.
They ate a light lunch of cold chicken and salad. Davis lit up a
Montecristo and indicated to Vaux that he could now use the
phone. Mrs. Fletcher would show him where to find it.

PART TWO

13

Vaux looked out onto Lake Geneva and saw in the fore-
ground a shimmering, hovering rainbow as the soaring *jet d'eau*,
the landmark man-made waterspout, reflected the setting sun.
To the left, he could see snow-capped Mont Blanc. Just below
him, pleasure steamers and myriad small yachts were moored
at the quayside. He was standing at the tall french windows
of his hotel room after a short flight from Heathrow. He had
checked in to Room 302 with a British passport bearing the
name of Derek Westropp. On the hotel's official guest form he
had described his occupation as journalist.

He thought he heard voices through the connecting door
to the next room (usually the two rooms would have been let as
a suite) and surmised that the hotel was probably full. The Conference on the Middle East was due to start in five days. The
confab was to take place at the Palais des Nations, originally
built for the ill-starred League of Nations whose unaccom-
plished aim was to guarantee the peace after World War I. To
get to the Palais, Vaux had just to walk a few minutes, turning
left out of his hotel, which had also been constructed in those
heady post-war days and aptly called the Hotel de la Paix.

If he turned left out of the hotel and walked a few minutes, he would come to the Beau Rivage where Ahmed Abdul
Kadri and the Syrian delegation had booked several suites.
Both hotels, like every other hostelry in Geneva, were teeming with Arabs in white, flowing, gold-embroidered *dish-
dashas,* some wearing the distinctive *keffiyeh* of the Palestinians. There were also hordes of men with close-cropped hair,

button-down white shirts, charcoal gray Brooks Bros. business
suits, and wing-tips—the American contingent. Beefy, solid
types with baggy suits and equally short haircuts comprised
the Russian representatives while the Israelis chose to wear
super-casual attire that disdained neckties and showed a penchant for socks and sandals.

In London, Craw had told him that he'd be on his own.
Back-up would be there but invisible. If he ever got into 'an
unfortunate' situation, which no one expected, the phantom
team of helpers would materialize. It all sounded rather nebulous to Vaux's ears, and in the final analysis he felt that the only
person he could rely on was himself. After all, the strategy was
simple enough: meet his old friend 'by accident,' renew the
friendship, socialize—and somehow gain access to top secret
information that would clearly be under the tightest security
and safe-keeping procedures.

'Easy as taking candy...' sighed Vaux. He picked up his
blazer and felt for the subminiature Minox, what the technicians in London had called his secret weapon. The tiny lightweight camera used films a quarter the size of the standard
35mm with fifty frames per cassette. The phone rang. He sat
down on the bed and lifted the receiver.

'Hello,' said a refined female voice that he thought he recognized. 'It's Veronica, Michael.'

'Good God, how did you know where to find me?' If this
was security, he didn't think much of it.

'You told me the other night that you'd landed a freelance
job for the Evening Standard, remember?'

Vaux vaguely remembered. They'd gotten pretty plastered
that evening. She had agreed to come to the Pig & Whistle after
a long day researching brittle 350-year-old parchment records
in St. Albans Cathedral's vast and chilly vaults. He had thought
there was probably no harm in telling her that he'd be away for
a few weeks on an assignment. But how did she know that he'd
be in Geneva? He didn't recall telling her his itinerary.

'Oh yes. But how did you track me down?'

'Called the *Standard's* news editor, Nigel Nutting,' said Veronica. 'Seems a nice man.'

'Oh absolutely,' said Vaux, who had never met the man and cursed him for his complete lack of discretion. Even more worrisome, it seemed that the man hadn't been briefed about Vaux's true mission.

But Vaux was wrong there. Unbeknownst to him, Nutting had sent one of his star reporters as a back-up. She would cover the conference while this totally unknown quantity would be left to do his thing—some confidential mission for the government, according to the press lord whose family trust owned the newspaper.

'He said he had booked you in under a pen name, so I asked for Mr. Derek Westropp. Is that all right?'

'Oh. Yes, I suppose so.'

'I wanted to thank you for the other night, Michael.'

'It was only a fish and chip dinner.'

'Yes, but traditional. I loved the checkered tablecloth and the sharp white vinegar and the plastic ketchup container. Oh, and especially the mushy peas.'

'Are you having me on?'

'No, not at all,' she laughed. 'Look, the reason I'm calling is that by the funniest of coincidences I shall be in Geneva next week. Apparently this chap Alban made the difficult overland trek from England to Geneva sometime around 370 AD. He stayed at a monastery near Vevey for a few months, and according to Dr. Richards, the dean, the well-preserved remnants of a diary he kept about his journey across the channel and through France are to be made available for my perusal.'

'That's splendid,' said Vaux, impressed. 'You're really quite a scholar. Maybe Alban had something to do with the Holy Grail—you never know. You'll soon be a candidate for another doctorate by the sound of it.'

'The Holy Grail story develops somewhat later, Michael. But thanks for the compliment, anyway. Look, I'll call when I get there. You won't be too busy, will you?'

'No, not at all,' said Vaux. He put the receiver back, stretched out on the bed, and fell asleep.

* * *

That afternoon several key players in Operation Helvetia checked into the Hotel de la Paix. It was a relatively small hotel for Geneva's lakefront, and the lobby was crowded with new arrivals from the airport and the main railway station, which every few hours disgorged a few hundred passengers who had preferred to travel in the first-class luxury of the TGV from Paris.

When they finally got to the small reception desk, Chris Greene and Len Powell were asked if they wanted a twin room or one with two double beds. They said they had reserved a room on the third floor and asked to see the hotel's manager. He emerged from a small office, an aristocratic-looking gentleman with silver hair swept back in leonine fashion, a long, thin nose and immaculate black suit. They showed him some sort of document and he read its contents slowly. Then he looked up and told the receptionist to put them in room 301.

'I'm Otto Heinz, gentlemen, your host while you are in Geneva. Welcome. You will find the room very convenient. If you want anything, please let me know. I do hope you enjoy your stay.' He folded the document and put it in his inside pocket.

Chris Greene was about thirty, seconded to Operation Helvetia from the North American section of MI6. His job, he had been told by Sir Walter Mason at the Olympus on Jermyn Street, was to watch the key man in the operation, one Michael Vaux. It was not your usual gig, said Sir Walter (having learned the word from his eighteen-year-old niece the previous weekend); it was more a protective exercise than anything to do with watching out for suspicious activities. In other words, said Sir Walter, Greene's job was to look out for Vaux's safety and well-being, to try and make sure things went smoothly for him. Greene listened enthusiastically as he mopped up the remnants of his baby octopus in garlic sauce. He hadn't traveled on an active mission for some time and he was grateful for the opportunity to get out of Century House.

His roommate, Len Powell, had been trained as an electrical engineer, was old enough to have done national service in the Royal Corps of Electrical and Mechanical Engineers, and had put in ten years at GCHQ, the government's communications center in Cheltenham. He was an expert on radio technology and listening devices. Len was in his fifties, a down-to-earth technical man who didn't have much time for the young Turks who in his view had been handed everything—including their college education—on a platter. He didn't much care for sharing a room with Greene (an apt name, he told his wife on the phone that evening), but the job in question precluded any alternative.

When they got to Room 301, they realized why Otto Heinz, one of the firm's veteran Swiss helpers and facilitators, had selected this particular accommodation. There was a wide double door on one wall, clearly an entry into Room 302 for occupants who preferred a two-room suite. The only drawback was that their half of the suite was designed as a living room—with a big fold-out couch and a single day-bed. A wide armoire dominated the wall opposite the french windows.

Powell walked over to the connecting doors. They were locked, of course. He put his ear to the shiny white surface but heard nothing. It was an ideal location for his new probe microphone, which would listen to every movement and every conversation emanating from Vaux's room. All he had to do was to drill a small hole with a No.60-size bit and insert the mike. Whatever the ultra-sensitive microphone picked up would be transmitted to an already set up safe house located in the red light district, close to the Gare de Cornavin, the central railway station.

'This is very satisfactory,' he said to himself but loudly enough for Greene to pick up on.

'Except for the beds. I thought we ordered twins,' said Greene.

'Beggars can't be choosers, young man. That door is the key to the whole thing,' said Powell, opening up a small compact suitcase in which he stored the small drill and other tools of his trade. Greene thought he'd better respect seniority and asked Powell where he wanted to sleep.

'I'll take the bed; you can have the fold-down. It's bigger anyway.'

Greene had resigned himself to the inconvenience of having to go through the hassle of assembling the thing, but then he thought he could probably get the maid or housekeeping to do it. He mentioned the possibility to Powell.

'No way, young man. This room has to be secure. In fact, as far as I'm concerned, I'll be doing a lot of baby-sitting. You can go out and enjoy the fleshpots if you like—that's if our man lures you there.' This was the closest Powell got to joking on the job.

* * *

Just after Greene and Powell checked in, Monica Manning, feature writer and political reporter for the *Evening Standard,* arrived. She was tall, heavier than she wanted to be, with red hair and a pleasant if somewhat masculine face. She was carrying a brand new Apple 170 laptop computer and a handbag. Earlier, at the Gare de Lyon in Paris, she had boarded a TGV, hauled her heavy suitcase into the carriage, parked it in the luggage recess, and sat herself down with a pile of unread newspapers. She looked at her watch and saw that the train would be departing within three minutes. She thought it vaguely puzzling that she had the whole coach to herself except for a white-haired, elegant old lady with glittering earrings and necklace, clearly a denizen of Geneva. Manning had a habit of summing up people quickly and she guessed the old girl was probably a rich widow on her way home after a spring shopping spree in Paris. There was some harsh announcement on the intercom and she saw the woman stand up, grab her hatbox, and rush out of the carriage. Manning's French was somewhat rusty and she listened for another announcement. The old lady suddenly reappeared.

'*Madame! Ce train va pas a Geneve! Il faut debarquer. On a change la voiture.*' Manning got the gist. She stood up, retrieved her laptop from the overhead rack, grabbed some of the newspapers, and ran toward the door. She heard the hydraulic hiss as the automatic door began to close. There was no time to haul her heavy suitcase off the train, so she quickly squeezed through the rapidly shrinking exit space and jumped back on to the platform. The empty TGV, with her canvas suitcase packed with her favorite slacks, dresses, and pumps, then started to move slowly out of the station and into a siding. Then she just caught sight of the old Genovese hauling herself up into the train that stood on the other side of the platform. She scrambled into the same carriage and found the seat numbers coincided with those of the abandoned *voiture*.

She lost no time in finding the conductor, who promptly got on his two-way radio to tell the railway gendarmerie in Paris not to explode or destroy any suspicious suitcase that was found on the aborted 10:40 a.m. Geneva-bound TGV, Voiture No. 1, which had been shunted into the maintenance sheds for unexplained and unknown reasons. And he requested the lost item to be put on the next available TGV to Geneva in the secured luggage section. On the Swiss side, the stationmaster was informed of the expected delivery before midnight and agreed to dispatch the item at S.N.C.F's expense in a taxi. Manning's hitherto negative opinion about French railway staff was now appreciably modified. Even so, she was irritated and annoyed about the unneeded hassle and she wondered how the French could have muddled things so to direct her on to the wrong car. She arrived at the hotel in a bad temper, hot and in need of a shower and a double gin and tonic. She told

the reception staff at the hotel to expect late-night delivery
of a canvas suitcase. And could she please be shown her room
immediately. She had asked for one of the higher floors and was put
into Room 402, directly above Vaux. She knew him only as
Westropp, but she didn't know whether he had yet arrived.
She was anxious to meet this stranger who had been parachut-
ed in to cover some of the more arcane areas of the Mideast
Conference (or so she had been told by that idiot Nigel).

Vaux was semi-conscious after a short nap. He heard the
tinkle of the bedside phone, echoed, it seemed, in the bathroom, and lifted the receiver. He had no idea who it could
be, but he found himself hoping it was Veronica again. He was
disappointed.

'Mr. Westropp?'

Vaux said nothing. He'd been having a weird dream and
he tried to gather his thoughts. Of course, *he* was Westropp.
'Yes?' he said.

'I'm Monica Manning of the *Standard*. I understand we're
colleagues, at least temporary ones. I've just arrived and
thought we could have a drink downstairs or somewhere to
compare notes etcetera.'

Oh God, thought Vaux. *Hasn't she been told to lay off me?
Doesn't she know the story?* But of course she hadn't been told
anything and couldn't be allowed to know anything. It would
completely blow the whole gaff; the ensuing scandal and gossip would make a laughing stock of the operation. He simply
must make an effort to get on their wavelength—Mason's and
Craw's, that is. 'Yes, yes. Absolutely. When did you get in?'

'About an hour ago. Horrible experience. Came by the
bullet train. And would you believe they lost my luggage!
Should have flown, I suppose.'

Vaux felt like a scotch and thought a drink in the bar
downstairs with a female reporter from Fleet Street would
be more interesting than raiding the minibar in his room and

drinking in isolation. He looked in the minibar anyway, extracted two small bottles of J&B, and poured himself a drink. In the next room, Powell adjusted his headphones as he heard the bathroom tap turned on to dilute the scotch. He waited for the click of the door as Vaux left for the downstairs bar and moved toward the connecting doors. He took the hotel's skeleton key out of his pocket (supplied by Otto Heinz), made sure not to dislodge the microphone, and went into Vaux's room. Within ten minutes he had inserted another minute microphone into the phone's speaker and another probe mike on the top of the tall armoire. He stuck the last tiny mike behind the toilet in case Vaux made or received calls from the bathroom. Then he decided to check the armoire for the small safe hidden at the bottom of a series of shelves for shirts, underwear, and socks. He inserted the duplicate key Heinz had given him. The heavy metal door opened. He found one single object inside—the subminiature Minox C camera that had been among the accessories requisitioned for Vaux in London. Good man, he said under his breath.

* * *

'Where are you phoning from?' asked Craw, a tone of apprehension in his voice.

'A public phone in the railway station,' said Greene.

'Well and good. Now, we understand that Kadri has arrived with his team at the Beau Rivage. It's essential to get Vaux focused on the target. He's spent the last couple of days drinking with that woman from the *Standard* and generally behaving like a bloody tourist. He's got to get off his arse and get to work.'

'Yes sir. I'll see to it somehow that he's aware of Kadri's belated presence in Geneva. You do realize he was supposed to be here two days ago.'

'Yes, yes, yes,' said Craw impatiently. 'Your task, Greene, is not only to make sure Vaux knows Kadri's now in Geneva, but also to somehow engineer the critical meeting between Vaux and Kadri. The reunion of the two old college friends. Understood?'

'Yes sir,' said Greene, smiling to himself at what he considered the brilliant idea that had already surfaced in his fertile brain.

'So get moving. Anything else to report?'

'Only that the room and the phone are wired up. So far the recordings are innocuous—ordering room service, chatting with Monica Manning, rather heavy snoring—oh and the imminent arrival, apparently, of one Veronica Belmont. Any instructions with regard to her, sir?'

'None.'

* * *

If the essence of espionage is deception, then the ability to act will give the professional spy a big career advantage. Double lives or multiple roles require deceit and deception in the same way an actor can portray any character an author calls on him to play. And so in much the same way as Arthur Davis in his youth aspired to an acting career, so Chris Greene sometimes felt he had missed his true vocation. Acting was in Greene's DNA, his uncle having worked as a successful character actor all his life, culminating in a few memorable parts in some of David Lean's more opulent productions. The idea that had developed gradually over the past few days had now reached full maturity. He knew what he would do as soon as he put the phone down. Craw of course had been no help—no suggestions, no nothing. He had been left to his own devices; so be it. But he couldn't suppress an irritation at Craw's bland assumption—given his clear instructions to keep a discreet distance from Vaux—that he knew how to pull off the virtual miracle of bringing Vaux and Kadri together. A few suggested surreptitious ploys, a few lessons perhaps in classic tradecraft—all would have been welcome. In his youthful innocence, Greene, new to this clandestine side of the intelligence game, would have appreciated a more paternal handling by his immediate boss.

He walked into the lounge off the lobby and, as he expected, saw Monica Manning sitting on a high stool at the shiny zinc bar. She was drinking what looked like a bloody Mary with crystallized salt circling the rim of the glass and a piece of celery sticking up into her face. She was struggling with the *Herald Tribune*, unsuccessfully folding and shuffling the broadsheet's pages in order to present a more compact product to her bloodshot eyes. Gold-framed half-moon glasses were perched at the end of her nose and she looked over them at Greene as he sat down on the stool next to her.

'Morning,' said Greene cheerfully.

Manning looked him over as if he were an unidentified riverine object who had just crawled out of Lake Geneva. 'Morning,' she replied—clearly not wanting to be disturbed as she digested the morning's news.

He ordered a tomato juice from the white-coated, diminutive Italian barman. The order prompted Manning to look up from her newspaper again to reexamine the sort of timid subspecies that would order such a bland non-alcoholic beverage after eleven in the morning. Greene leapt at the opportunity.

He used the first two names that came into his head: 'I'm Malcolm Parry for the *Levenham Observer*. You, I believe, are the eminent Monica Manning of the *Evening Standard*?' He was sure she had never heard of his putative newspaper and equally certain that to be described as 'eminent' should surely smooth the way.

'The *Levenham* what-did-you-say?'

'You're forgiven. It's an East Anglian newspaper launched just last year. The proprietor thinks the east coast of England is woefully unrepresented among opinion formers, pundits, and the like. Anyway, we still aim for exclusives, and, boy, did I hear a juicy tidbit just now, from none other than my own news editor.'

Manning's ears pricked up. This guy was a loser, but sometimes even blind pigs find acorns. 'Oh? What's that then?' she asked in a tone that suggested extreme skepticism that anyone so junior in the profession could possibly come up with anything approaching a real scoop.

Greene sipped his drink. 'Well, it's to do with the Syrian delegation. Apparently they've sent a guy who'll be the next governor of the central bank along with the foreign affairs bigwigs. I understand the reason is that Syria's going to ask the U.S. for a big loan that could ensure Syria's support for any U.S. initiative in the Middle East peace process. In other words, Syria's finances are in shit straits and they're in dire need of a big loan to bail them out. With the Russians putting forward an alternative peace initiative, they're playing one off against the other. The key is they think they've got the U.S. over a barrel.'

Monica Manning took off her reading glasses and looked into the distance, beyond the bar and through the heavily curtained windows that looked on to the bustling Quai du Mont Blanc. This was moderately interesting. She wondered now whether this was the sort of offbeat news angle that Westropp was searching for. Should she keep it to herself or should she give him a morsel to chew on? After all, she had to admit she liked him. And she didn't feel professionally threatened thanks to her reputation, her undoubted abilities plus the incidental fact that she let Nigel Nutting fuck her on a regular basis.

Greene studied Manning's big, rather flushed face. The lipstick was plastered on, along with the mascara. Her eyebrows were uneven and the powder on her nose was smudged and caked. Here was a woman, thought Greene, who made token gestures to the cosmetic altar of feminine beautification, but who was much more interested in getting a real scoop than attracting the male of the species. In fact, he mistakenly thought, she may well prefer women.

Zeroing in on the bottom line, Manning asked Greene what the fellow's name was—this so-called Bank of Syria governor-in-waiting. Greene felt a surge of satisfaction, almost an orgasmic climax of a professional job well done.

He said slowly and with emphasis:'Ahmed Abdul Kadri—educated in Britain, fluent in French and English, and fiercely loyal to Assad.'

Sheer diligence in plowing through the newspaper archives at Century House had revealed several articles in the *Evening Standard* by Monica Manning as she toured the Arab capitals a few years back for a series of features and think-pieces whose stated aim was to create a better understanding of Arab policies, the Palestine question, and the role of Israel. She had interviewed Ahmed Kadri when he was deputy-governor of the central bank prior to his secondment to the Defense Ministry—of which she was unaware. Greene could have said the words for her.

'But I know that man—Kadri. Yes, Ahmed Kadri. I interviewed him three years ago when I did that series on Arabia. He gave me a backgrounder on the Syrian economy. My God, thank you. That's quite a tip. Are you doing a story on him?'

Manning was already wondering how she could scoop this undeserving and ingenuous young reporter when Vaux walked in.

She had to think fast. So did Greene. The less Vaux saw of him, the better.

'I have to file now,' he said, getting up and dodging him as Vaux headed for the bar and Monica Manning. She muttered something and was grateful she wouldn't have to make any introductions. Vaux sat on Greene's vacated stool and pushed away the dirty glass. He ordered a Stella Artois and asked Monica how she was.

'I'm fine, darling. Bit hung over, but what can you expect.'
She felt she had to report on the scoop that had landed in her
lap via a jejune reporter on an obscure provincial newspaper.

Vaux's eyes widened and he shook off some of the mid-
morning lethargy which came with the pre-conference phony
journalistic war that in the past he would have used to his
advantage: making notes, harvesting 'color,' perhaps landing
some key and exclusive interviews. But this was different.
He had been kicking his heels, suppressing an innate urge to
write something when he knew nobody wanted him to write
anything—let alone anything that would ever see the light
of day. Now at last he could spring into action. Manning said
something about whether he wanted to get an interview with
Kadri and if so she could help. Alternatively, she could get the
interview for herself if he wasn't really interested in this sudden offbeat angle.

Vaux wished he could be frank with Manning—she had
all the attributes of a good hard-nosed reporter, and it could
make the next few days easier if she knew he had no interest
at all in writing any articles or pursuing any fascinating stories
for her newspaper. But deception was now the game and he
had to play his hand.

'No, no. I'm pursuing other even more arcane angles,
Monica. I suggest you do it—after all you know him. The
strange thing is that I've a feeling he's the same man I knew in
my university days. That name Kadri definitely rings a bell. If
it's the man I think it is, I should certainly like to make contact
anyway.'

Manning wasn't interested in Vaux's musings about his
damned university days. She quit school at sixteen and went to
work as a copy 'boy' at the local weekly rag. It hadn't done her
any harm and she always harbored a suspicion about university
types in journalism. They often couldn't write simple prose
and found it difficult to shake off their liking for long words
that turned readers right off.

'I'll try and get through to him this aft,' she said. Sensing a sensational story—the Syrians literally extorting money from the Americans in return for their support of the U.S. peace plan—she felt warm and generous. 'Tell you what. I'll fix up an interview and you can come along as a colleague in search for background material. How's that sound?'

'Perfect,' said Vaux.

14

Ahmed Abdul Kadri sat on a high-backed Louis XV chair
in the reception room of a four-room suite whose view of
Lake Geneva was similar to the vista that Vaux had enjoyed
every morning while he ate the continental breakfast that was
brought up to him at 8 a.m. The hotel was a larger replica of
the Hotel de la Paix with a high atrium vaulting above a lobby
that boasted gilded marble columns and magnificent crystal
chandeliers. Kadri was dressed in a dark blue business suit,
white shirt, and what looked to Vaux like the old Bristol University tie. His short-cut salt and pepper hair was thin and
receding. He was still slim and Vaux thought he had shrunk a
little, though his well-tailored suit could have explained that.

There were two other men in the room. One, sitting on
an over-stuffed sofa, looked about the same age as Kadri, simi-
larly turned out in an elegant western suit. The other man was
about thirty, heavy and tall, with a swelling under his arm that
suggested an automatic weapon. He wore a gray, baggy suit
and his blue shirt was open at the neck. He had a neat black
beard, was darker skinned than Kadri, and wore several thick
gold rings on sausage-sized fingers.

Manning had finally organized the interview. It had taken
two days and at least ten phone calls to get through the staff
whose job apparently was to isolate Kadri from the real
world—at least that's how Manning saw it. Vaux placated her
and told her to persist and to make sure they understood that
she had met Kadri three years ago and had written positively
about the Assad regime. She couldn't recall whether she was

all that positive, but if Vaux thought it politic to say so, then
she would get that message across.

Now here they were. Vaux felt that just getting into the
same room as Kadri was in itself quite an achievement. Sir
Walter and Craw would at least now feel that their confidence
in him had not been totally misplaced. There was a lot of work
still to be done, and of course, Kadri didn't know him from
Adam. It was quite obvious when they walked into the suite
(and Kadri and Manning shook hands and then went through
the etiquette of introducing everyone to one another) that
Kadri failed to recognize him after nearly forty years. What
a surprise. He would never have known Kadri if they had
passed close to each other in Piccadilly Circus. On closer examination, though, the deep brown, hooded eyes and the thin,
straight nose would perhaps have sparked old memories of a
once-familiar face.

But mutual recognition would be no problem once Vaux
broached the subject. They had done so many things together
in those far-off days that no one could possibly fake the relationship. No, Vaux told himself, that wasn't the problem.
The problem, as he saw it, and which those brilliant spooks
had never thought through, was that he was being introduced
as a man called Westropp while at the auspicious moment he
would have to convince Kadri that his real name was Vaux.
And then Kadri and his cohorts would wonder why Vaux was
parading in Geneva under an assumed name. God knows how
that little problem could be resolved. He wondered if the B3
team had any bright ideas.

Manning got out her tape recorder and notebook. She was
not the sort of reporter who danced around the niceties. But
she thought she'd give Vaux an opportunity to remind Kadri
that they were old acquaintances from their student days. She
gave him a meaningful look, then a nod, and waited for him to
address Kadri. But in reply, Vaux shook his head slightly as if
to suggest he had been mistaken. Probably, she thought, Kadri
was as common a name in Arabia as Brown or Smith in Eng-

land. So she began the interview. 'Are you looking forward to
your new appointment as governor of the central bank—and
what will you do in your first few months that would mark
you out as distinctly different from your predecessor?'

Kadri tried to suppress a smile. He looked at Amin Hakki,
his colleague, who also looked amused. Manning waited for
the answer. Vaux sat far back in a corner chair next to a connecting door that led into one of the bedrooms.

'Well, Miss Manning, let's start with some facts. I don't
know where you heard that I was to be appointed the new
governor of the Bank of Syria, but it's just totally wrong. In the
first place, the present governor, my friend Gamal Gemayed,
is younger than I am and is doing a competent if not brilliant
job in the circumstances. Second, I left the bank two years ago
and I am now, well, shall we say, a roving ambassador. Is that
how you would put it, Amin?'

Amin nodded and cleared his throat. 'Yes, that's about
right, Ahmed. Mr. Kadri, Miss Manning, is one of President
al-Assad's close advisers. It's a bit like the White House, if you
like. Although there is an official cabinet, the president puts
more faith and trust in what they call the "kitchen cabinet."
And Mr. Kadri is a member of that small team of advisers.
When they travel they're called roving ambassadors or representatives, if you like, that's all.'

So they are not revealing the fact that Kadri, if not Hakki,
works for the Ministry of Defense, thought Vaux. But where
does that leave Manning? What can she interview him about if
he holds no official position in the government of Syria?

Manning was nonplussed. This, thought Vaux, didn't happen very often. She looked back at Vaux as if she thought he
could come to the rescue. But Kadri spoke first. 'Look, it's
very nice to see you again after all this time, Miss Manning.
But I'm afraid you came here under a false impression. As an
adviser to the government I can't really give you any substan-
tive news. Maybe it would be more interesting for Mr. Westropp, who you say is here for atmosphere and background

color. I don't know these journalistic terms, but I think I know
what you're getting at.'

'Well,' said Vaux, clearing his throat, 'perhaps you could
fill us in on Syria's attitude toward the U.S. peace initiative.
It would seem that some Arab states are still trying to decide
whether to back Russia's alternative proposals—'

Kadri looked again at his colleague, who looked at
his watch and tilted his head just perceptibly. 'Our time is
somewhat limited and you ask a big question, Mr. Westropp.
Perhaps we can get together—just you and me another
time.'

Vaux wondered if Kadri was just being evasive or whether
by some strange retroactive chemistry he had sensed he could
get on with Vaux and perhaps reach a sympathetic audience.

Manning was feeling like a second fiddle. 'What about the
story that's going the rounds that Syria is after a big loan from
the U.S. as a sort of *quid pro quo* for supporting the American
peace initiative?' She had hoped to leave this bombshell until
last. But she could sense that Kadri felt he had nothing much
to say to her.

Kadri again looked over at Amin Hakki whose expression
had turned glum. 'That's an absurd assertion, Miss Manning.
I don't know where you're getting these stories, but none of
them has any foundation in fact.'

Manning felt like strangling that ingenuous creep of a reporter she'd met in the bar. The atmosphere had turned un-
friendly. She tried one last gambit. 'Did you at least enjoy that
series on the Middle East I wrote? I seem to remember it was
fairly favorable toward Mr. Assad and Syria.'

'Well, I don't recall that it was all that favorable, Miss
Manning. At best it was neutral toward us and highly positive
toward Jordan with which, as you probably know, we have
some problems and which incidentally is an absolute monar-
chy. Anyway, we are thankful for small mercies. The western
press seldom sees or understands the Arab point of view when
it comes to the crisis with Israel, and we consider you did

your best to resist the inevitable pressures from your Zionist proprietor.'

With that, Kadri stood up and beckoned to the bulky bodyguard who had been standing at the main door of the suite. He opened the door and signaled to the two journalists that the meeting was over. Vaux had to do something to save the situation, so he walked over and again shook hands with Kadri. He fished in his top pocket for one of the business cards that B3 had printed for him, wrote on the back his hotel telephone number, and said he'd very much like to take Mr. Kadri up on his offer of a background talk covering the Middle East and Syria's role in any future peace negotiations. He was relieved when Kadri smiled and put the card in his jacket pocket.

'You're the journalist, Mr. Westropp. You call me. Ask for Marhaba, my secretary. She'll fast-track you through the phalanx of staff we are encumbered with.' Manning was walking out and Kadri raised his voice to wish her goodbye. He put his arm around Vaux's shoulder and said: 'Now don't forget, call me. I always enjoy explaining things to western journalists who have open minds. I sense that you do.'

Vaux and Manning walked back to their hotel in silence. When they got inside the lobby she suggested a pre-lunch drink in his room.

She was defiant. 'That bastard. That was a brush-off if ever I've seen one.'

Vaux was feeling pleased with himself but didn't want to show it. 'Look, you went in there like a bull in a china shop. You had these stories that you threw at him like hand grenades. You put his back up, that's all. And since he no longer works for the central bank he reckoned he couldn't help you with much.'

'You telling me how to conduct a bloody interview, Westropp?'

* * *

In the small, cramped room in the seedy pension on the Rue de Zurich, the technicians diligently taped the sounds emanating from Vaux's room. Suddenly both wore expressions of wonder and bafflement. They heard a door slam and a shuffle and then the tinkling of bottles and glasses. They then had to turn the volume down. Someone was very angry.

'That fucking bastard's just disappeared. There's no such paper as the *Lavenham* bloody *Observer* and there's no registered guest by the name of Malcolm Parry. It was a ruse to make me look silly. What the hell can I do about it, Westropp? Something has to be done!'

The two technicians exchanged glances. Len Powell stood behind them as he assessed the small speaker's sound quality while Chris Greene's grin betrayed his feeling of satisfaction with a job well done. Barbara Boyd, another B3 operative, lay on a shabby, silk-covered chaise longue on the other side of the room. She was paying her colleagues a social visit before resuming what Sir Walter had called her 'special assignment' within Operation Helvetia. Her expression was one of boredom rather than amusement.

In Room 302 at the Hotel de la Paix, the mood was somber and smoldering. In answer to her angry demand for some sort of action to be taken, Vaux said, 'There's nothing that can be done at this point, Monica. I can't think why anybody would mislead you like that. But let's face it, you did get an interview with a senior Syrian official, you did see Kadri again after a lengthy interval, and I certainly intend to follow up his invitation to get together later. I'm not trying to steal your thunder—I hope you understand that. But at least now you can concentrate on the main story of the conference or what comes out of it. Kadri would have only been a sidebar anyway,' said Vaux as he handed her a can of tonic for her gin.

'I'm going to keep my eyes skinned for that little bugger. Hopefully when I catch sight of the two-faced runt in one of the bars, I'll have a full glass of gin to throw at his weak face. He's obviously working for one of the *Standard's* competitors—probably the bloody *Mirror* or the *Sun*. I won't rest till I find the bastard. I'll rip his balls off!'

In the fug of the safe house communications center, Greene gave out a loud derisive hoot and instinctively placed his hands over his testicles. Powell warned gloomily he'd better watch himself. Barbara Boyd, flipping through *Le Monde,* gave a big yawn.

Meanwhile Vaux sipped on a beer and silently toasted Manning's latest enemy. Without the skillful planting of disinformation by the unknown young man, he would have found it very difficult to get his foot in Kadri's door.

After three more gins, Manning seemed to calm down. She had been sitting on the edge of the bed and now she kicked off her flat-heeled walking shoes and hauled her heavy legs up on the bed. She loosened her white blouse so that her cleavage became more obvious. 'Oh, Westropp, why can't you give me some comfort—a hug at least? I'm so bloody upset about this.'

'There's no time, my dear. I have a guest who right now is probably waiting in the lobby. She's an old friend, a professor of archeology—nothing to do with the conference or newspapers. I must go now, so drink up, there's a good girl.' It was a white lie. He had arranged to meet Veronica in an hour's time. Manning pulled a schoolgirlish face, quietly buttoned up her blouse, got off the bed, and left.

This last bit of disinformation roused Barbara Boyd from her boredom. Greene looked over his shoulder and gave her a cheeky wink.

'Curtain call for Miss Veronica Belmont!' cried Greene. But Barbara Boyd was in no mood for jokes. She gave Greene a forced smile and walked out of the room into the bright, narrow street. She passed a blonde, busty middle-aged hooker who was leaning against the entrance to a sex shop.

'Looking for something, *ma'moiselle?*'

Boyd looked the other way, her pace quickening as she made for the lakeside and her appointment.

* * *

The woman he knew as Veronica Belmont was waiting in the lobby. His plan was to have a few quiet drinks in the bar and then go across the bridge to the old part of town to a French restaurant that Manning had strongly recommended. Veronica looked more attractive that late afternoon than he remembered. Her dark looks and deep brown eyes contrasted with all the Swiss blondes Vaux had observed since he arrived. She also looked a little weary and travel-worn, and thus attractively vulnerable and in need of protection. Her hair had a gloss and a bounce that he wanted to run his hands through. The nipples of her small breasts pierced the fine cotton of her white blouse. She wore a black short skirt that provocatively showed off her slim thighs.

'I'm really tired, Michael. I caught the 6 a.m. train to Vevey this morning and I've only just got back. To make matters worse, I made very little progress. Abbot Jean, who was supposed to take me in hand, was off with the flu. So I got nowhere—a wasted day.'

'Oh dear,' said Vaux. 'Well, come and drown your sorrows with a good drink.' He led her into the crowded bar, now full of delegates to the peace conference. Many had already procured the security name tags that they attached to their jacket lapels, and Vaux was bemused to see Russians and Americans joking and socializing together—a sign perhaps that the Cold War was now really and truly a part of history.

He leant on the bar and asked her what she felt like drinking.

'Michael, do you mind awfully if we go to your room? We can drink there, can't we? I'm really not in the mood for crowds.'

Vaux was surprised but not unpleased. Were her defenses finally crumbling? If so he was just in the right kind of mood to take advantage—in a gentlemanly way, of course. 'Oh, sure, if that's what you want. Let's go.'

They got into the ancient lift that was too small to accommodate more than three persons. He felt a frisson of desire as he was forced to stand close to her, and seeming to sense this, she put her hand behind his head and kissed him gently. They said nothing.

Veronica kicked off her shoes and went into the bathroom. Vaux opened the minibar and took out a half bottle of Veuve Clicquot and found two flute glasses on the small writing desk next to the armoire. He had his back to her when she emerged from the bathroom, and when he turned, glasses in hand, he saw she had put on the terrycloth bathrobe that the hotel supplied. She had tied the belt tightly round her waist but he could guess she wore nothing underneath.

'Let's go to bed,' she said.

'A glass of champagne first?' Vaux knew he was stalling but didn't know quite why. Perhaps it was the brazenness, the totally unexpected invitation, the complete surprise that she was finally coming across.

'Michael, put the glasses down,' she commanded. She had got under the white Sea Island cotton sheet and now threw it aside for Vaux. Lying there naked, she reminded Vaux of a young dusky islander Gaugin would have wanted to paint. His heartbeat quickened, he threw his pants on a chair, pulled his socks off, and peeled the white shirt from his back. It landed on the plush multi-colored Aubusson carpet.

15

Sir Walter Mason stood at the grime-encrusted windows that overlooked the inside well of the 1930s office building on Gower Street. On the external window shelf lay a good three inches of gray pigeon droppings covered by a thin film of black soot. As on many other days, through the murky windows he watched and studied the hard-working competitors in the eternal rat race—the lawyers and accountants, the public relations people, the dealers in tea and coffee, and the stock brokers. What did these people care about Middle East arms deals, renegade dictators spending their nation's lifeblood on bigger and better guns, tanks, and guided missiles?

'You called, sir?' Craw had made a quiet entry.

Mason, roused from his meditations, turned round and went back to his worn leather swivel chair behind the mahogany desk. 'Yes, Craw. What's the progress on Operation Helvetia? Give me a run-down on what's happened. The D-G's coming down this weekend and he's bound to ask me about progress—if any.'

Craw drew up an empire chair of 1940 vintage. The seat was as polished as a mirror. 'Well, sir, we are indeed making good progress. First and foremost, I was able to employ a stratagem by which Vaux gained easy access to Kadri. Only a first step, mind, but he's met the man—'

'You mean they've had the hoped-for reunion?'

'No, sir. Kadri didn't recognize him, which in the circumstances is understandable. But the ice is broken and we understand from our monitors that another meeting is in the offing and it will be then presumably when Vaux and Kadri will wax all nostalgic.'

'What's this stratagem you talk about?'

'Well, sir, I conducted some useful research in the newspaper archives. Lo and behold I discovered that our Ms. Manning had met and interviewed Kadri some three years ago for some article she was writing on Syria and the Middle East. You know the *Standard* sometimes has pretty well-informed feature articles—'

'Yes, yes, go on.'

'So by foul means or fair I got the message through to her that Kadri was in town—and for other reasons than signing any deal with Russia. We gave her some false leads that she eagerly followed up. It's what I think journalists call a "bum steer."'

'All right Craw. Now what?'

'We are waiting for Vaux to make the move on Kadri. Meanwhile, as I say, we have lots of back-up. Powell is there to look after communications, Greene has so far done a good job, and the *piece de resistance* of course is our Barbara Boyd who, shall we say, will make doubly sure Vaux never wavers.'

'And that his overall security is not endangered.'

'Yes, of course, sir.'

It was a Friday afternoon and Sir Walter was anxious to leave for the Dorset countryside before the London hordes left for their homes in the suburbs. 'Fine, fine, Craw. You've done an excellent job. See you Tuesday morning,' said Sir Walter, thereby informing his assistant director that he would be taking a longish weekend.

But as Craw got to the door, Sir Walter had a sudden thought. 'Wait a minute, Craw. Vaux's *nom de guerre*, as it were, is Westropp, right?' Craw nodded. 'So when Vaux reintroduces himself to Kadri as Vaux how does he explain the fact that he's in Geneva under an assumed name?'

'Ah,' said Craw thoughtfully. 'I'll have to put my thinking cap on for that one, sir. We'll come up with something. Have an enjoyable weekend.'

'But why was it deemed necessary to give Vaux a false name in the first place?'

'Force of habit, no doubt, sir.'

Craw thought he heard a deep, forlorn sigh as he gently closed Mason's door. He lost no time in getting on to Chris Greene, the junior who had come up with the research that had discovered Manning's link with Kadri. The only mistake Greene had made was to think that by telling Craw of his coup, he'd be able to chalk up some brownie points at Century House. True to everything he'd learned in his public career, Craw had no hesitation in grabbing for himself the credit for such diligence.

'Greene, have you thought about Vaux's little problem of being introduced to Kadri as Derek Westropp? Won't this make things a little dicey when the time comes for Vaux to show his cards?'

'Well, sir, I hadn't actually given it much thought.'

'Well, bloody well do so, Greene. And let me know what you come up with. The problem is even if you do come up with some brilliant idea, how the hell do you convey it to Vaux with whom, of course, you must stay incommunicado.'

Greene was a young man who could think on his feet. 'I've got the answer to that one, sir. Our Miss Boyd has made what one might call a tactical breakthrough. She'll make an ideal conduit for guiding Vaux through the woods and thickets in the days to come.'

Craw hated the creative, flowery language of youthful enthusiasm. 'Oh well, that's some sort of progress, I suppose.'

* * *

Arthur Davis sat in his deep leather chair nursing a Glenmorangie 18, his favorite single malt. His side of the game had gone well: he had got Alec Abel, partner at Abel, Smith, Collins & Dalfen, solicitors and commissioners for oaths, to write a formal offer of £410,000 for No. 32 Willow Drive, topping Vaux's latest bid of £405,000. That should stimulate Vaux's enthusiasm and loyalty, which had, at times (in Davis's view), seemed to be waning. So far, the firm had pledged compensation of £100,000 for the job, but Davis had got authorization to pay Vaux a total of £200,000 out of the secret contingency fund—provided the final success of the operation was secured. It was some satisfaction to know that Sir Walter had left him to decide on the final sum Vaux could make within those parameters. Thus pressure on the man must be kept up. He was anxious to know just how Vaux was getting on, of course, but it would be highly unprofessional to call Sir Walter for a progress report. His duty was to do and die, not ask silly questions.

The doorbell rang. Ann Whitely had arrived. 'Darling, I can't stay. Just as I was leaving Brian called. He'll be back tomorrow morning and I'm going to pick him up at Heathrow.' Ann's husband, Dr. Brian Whitely, had just finished a nine-month tour in Ethiopia with *Médecins Sans Frontières*.

'But why come all this way—why didn't you phone?'

Ann, in a closely fitting cotton dress, stepped into the hallway and closed the front door. She stood on her toes to give Arthur a long, hard kiss. 'I have time for you-know-what but nothing else—no din-dins or drinkies. Just good old rumpy-pumpy, darling—a romp in the hay,' she laughed. She caught hold of his hand and they both went up the broad staircase in silence.

* * *

Davis was disappointed that Ann had to rush off like that. He sat alone at the kitchen table. Mrs. Fletcher's shepherd's pie was exceptionally good, succulent and strongly flavored because, according to what she had told him, she always got the butcher to grind up mutton rather than lamb. He had just put the plates and knives and forks into the dishwasher when the doorbell rang again. He hadn't a clue who it could be this late on a Friday night.

'Craw! How are you, old boy?' He couldn't stand the man, but professional courtesy came before personal feelings.

Alan Craw wore a navy blue blazer with brass buttons and an obscure insignia on the breast pocket. A silk paisley handkerchief poked out of his sleeve at the wrist. Fine worsted gray slacks and brown suede shoes completed the conservative weekend ensemble.

He sat down on the long sofa facing Davis. He refused a drink of any sort. He looked at his slim gold Piaget watch. His face betrayed a man who was seriously concerned and needed to talk. 'Problem?' Davis asked.

'Yes, Arthur—quite a serious one. I have been racking my brains all day trying to come up with a solution. Thought it might help to consult a veteran whom I truly respect.'

Like hell, thought Davis. 'If I can help at all I will.'

'I'll come to the point. As you know, Operation Helvetia is now underway. Progress has been made. But we're not there yet. A snag has arisen...'

Craw then informed B3's former agent-runner of the main details of the operation and the use of Vaux as the vital nexus in the bid to uncover the details of the Russian-Syrian arms deal. It was information that neither he nor Sir Walter had wanted to impart to the retired officer. But if the old warrior's experiences and seasoned judgment were now to be tapped, there was no way around giving the man the facts of the situation.

'So, Arthur, if it's not handled right the whole operation could be in jeopardy—'

'Bit dramatic, aren't we?' Davis couldn't think what had gone wrong to warrant such a dire prognosis.

'Here's the situation: Vaux has made contact with Kadri and has even been invited by Kadri for a press-type interview. He seems to have warmed to the man already. But the whole

point is that he doesn't know Vaux is Vaux. He failed to recognize him after thirty or forty years, which is not surprising.
In other words, he thinks he's a Fleet Street type named Westropp who writes for the *Evening Standard*. How the hell do we
get round that? When Vaux launches into the old undergrads
reunited business—former, long-lost friends and all that—
Kadri and his cohorts will immediately be suspicious. Why
has the man used an alias? Why a pseudonym? Very fishy—or
whatever the Arabic word for fishy or mysterious is.'

Davis went out of the room and poured himself a brandy.
He squirted some soda into the balloon glass and came back to
the living room. He looked through the windows behind Craw
at the clusters of people milling in front of the floodlit Pig &
Whistle. He thought he saw Goodchild's lad collecting bottles
and glasses from the stragglers. It was closing time.

'It could be a problem, but then again, if it is handled
imaginatively, it may prove no obstacle at all.'

'What do you mean, Arthur?' asked Craw, praying that
the old hand may have the germ of an idea—and incidentally
justifying his arduous trip from Knightsbridge through heavy
Friday night rush-hour traffic.

'Well, for one thing, as I understand it, pen names aren't
all that uncommon among writers—'

'I thought of that. But I bet you can count on one hand the
number of Fleet Street newspaper writers who don't use their
own names. Egotists to the last man, most of them, and too
bloody narcissistic not to try and impress all their friends and
old school chums that they've made the big time.'

'Maybe you're right. But maybe we could think of some
special circumstances where Vaux is concerned.'

'That's more or less why I'm here,' said Craw, a touch
sarcastically, thought Davis.

They sat in silence, the only noise coming from the crowd
of revelers who had closed the pub down. Craw looked disappointed that the veteran agent runner hadn't so far come
up with a watertight solution to his problem. If some idea

surfaced—at least a plausible pointer in which direction to go—then he'd be able to inform Sir Walter on Tuesday morning that all was under control.

Davis suddenly slammed his knee with a clenched fist. 'I think I've got it.' Craw looked like an eager child whose uncle had suddenly offered him the possibility of an ice-cream.

'Let's say Vaux had marriage problems—no lie, in fact. He's divorced. But let's say his ex has continued to harass him over the years, badgering him to increase the agreed-upon alimony and all that. Even going so far as to interfere with his love life—threatening his girl friend of the moment. All that sort of "hell hath no fury like a woman scorned" stuff.'

Davis paused for a moment to collect his thoughts. Craw said: 'Yes, go on, Arthur.'

'So our man decides to change his name by deed poll. Alimony payments are kept up, but the ex-wife can't tell where he's living or working. To make matters even more secure for our man with a changed name, he's decided to work in Europe or the U.K. and leave North America for good. The ex is hardly going to chase him to continents unknown. She was born American and she's reluctant to chase him around the world—her days of enjoying driving him up the wall are effectively over for good. Vaux tells this sad story to his old Arab friend from university days and they both have a good laugh at the wiles of women and how to defeat same.'

Craw adopted a serious, contemplative look. Finally he said, 'Arthur, you're a genius. That may well work. Now I'll have that drink—gin and bitters.'

Davis watched Craw get into the silver Aston Martin Virage that sat in the driveway. As he opened the car door, he turned round to face Davis. 'Is that the pub where Vaux stays?' he asked, nodding toward the Pig & Whistle. His expression was one of disdain and distaste.

'Yes, as a matter of fact,' said Davis. 'It's where I met him, so don't knock it.' Craw slammed the door, started the engine and reversed out of the driveway. Another one who married

money, thought Davis. Can't blame him, though. It would be
hypocritical.

* * *

The Pig & Whistle directly faced Sheridan Road, which
was at right angles to Watford Lane. The sash window of Vaux's
temporarily vacated small room looked straight up the road;
to the right stood the stately, baronial pile of The Cedars. It
took only about four minutes to walk down Sheridan Road, a
wide street lined by suburban houses of various designs from
detached dwellings with big gardens to small bungalows and a
few semi-detached houses with bay windows. The house that
would win the prize for the street's best design from the Royal
Institute of British Architects sat at the corner of Sheridan and
Willow Drive: it was the home, in fact, of an octogenarian
architect who designed it himself in the early '50s. A tradition-
alist, he built his dream home as an exact replica of an elegant,
finely proportioned red brick Queen Anne homestead. Turn
right at this elegant dwelling and you enter Willow Drive.

At No. 7, the Goodchild family—sans Mildred, the
mother—was crowded into the kitchen, all eyes fixed on a
new member of the family, a mutt that looked like a cross
between an Irish wolfhound and an Airedale terrier. He was
still a puppy and he had adopted his new family as if they were
all long-lost relatives. His saviour was Jason Goodchild, John's
twelve-year-old son, who had been told by a neighbor that
if he didn't take him (they were seen constantly playing together) he would have to go to a dogs' home where he could
pine away for months—or worse. His father was indifferent
toward domestic pets. They already had a black and white cat
named Whisky that they saw infrequently throughout the day
(he deigned to eat in the kitchen when he was hungry) and
never at night. But Jason caught his father in a rare mood of
magnanimity and he had said okay.

Now five-year-old Bobby chased Rex around and under the kitchen table and Rex, tail wagging furiously, sniffed umpteen legs of various sizes and shapes as he frenetically circled the clan. Then they all heard a bang as the front door was pushed shut. It was Patrick Goodchild, who hadn't been seen all day, not even for the one o'clock Sunday dinner.

Rex left the maelstrom for more interesting tasks and shot through the kitchen door toward Patrick, who was greeted as an adored brother. Rex jumped into his arms and, deftly gripped, gave Patrick's face a generous saliva wash with his tongue and cold snout.

When the excitement died down Rex was put in a big cardboard box with a folded blanket (his temporary bed). He slept deeply, contented that he had at last found a loving and interesting home with, he figured, fellow beings, some roughly his own age. John Goodchild then asked his son where the hell he'd been all day.

'Helping Betty move, Dad. Her old man's chucked her out, hasn't he?'

'Oh, he has, 'as he. So what does that mean? We've no room for more waifs and strays. Rex here's seen to that.'

'No, no, Dad. She's moved in with her friend Susan—you know, the estate agent with that firm on the High Street.'

'Who—Susan Appleby?' said John, wondering what the connection was between his son's girl friend and that fairly attractive older chick who drove around in a posh Jaguar.

'Yeah, that's her name. Anyway, she had nowhere else to go and this Susan's got one of those new flats overlooking The Heath. Big place it is and she's on the top floor. Lift and all that—plus a pool downstairs.'

'Sounds like paradise,' said John dryly.

'They get on well, anyway. Susan's a sort of aunt to her, you know. The main thing's she's got away from that bastard father of hers. Fancy throwing her out just because she's pregnant.'

'Some fathers are like that, mate.'

'You wouldn't be, would you, Dad?'

'Can't say, not having any daughters, can I?'

John then brought up the subject that had been on his mind since his son had confirmed that Betty was carrying his baby—and meant to keep it.

'What are you going to do, son? You're not ready to marry—you don't have a job and God knows I can't help you.'

'I'll think of something, Dad,' said Patrick.

16

Vaux felt queasy as he walked out of his hotel, turned left, and headed for the Beau Rivage. He hadn't eaten his usual continental breakfast because he had to admit a certain nervousness and lack of appetite. He supposed what made him feel less than his old confident self was something to do with the fact that he was now required to masquerade as a journalist and about to lie to and deceive an old and respected friend who had done nothing to deserve such abuse. He felt like a cheap con artist. It didn't go down well at all. He might have felt better if he hadn't worked as a journalist, if journalism and newspapers hadn't been his life's calling. He was betraying not only a friend but also his profession. He could hear Sir Walter, echoed by Davis, telling him that it was a patriotic duty, perhaps the only opportunity he would ever have of serving his country of birth in a noble endeavor. Somehow, he wasn't convinced.

Ahmed Kadri, looking suave in a dark blue silk suit and white striped shirt, sat alone in his Louis XV-style suite. This time the bodyguard disappeared as soon as Vaux and Kadri had shaken hands. They both sat down opposite each other, a round mahogany table between them.

'Would you like some coffee, perhaps tea, Mr. Westropp?' Vaux noticed that as he sat down, Kadri pulled at his shirt-sleeves to expose the cuffs. The gold cufflinks bore the miniature coat of arms of the University of Bristol. Vaux's heart beat a little faster now—for here was an opening for his rehearsed confession.

He had broached the subject with Veronica, who was all sympathy and understanding. The Arabs, he had said, had suspicious natures in any circumstances. He didn't want to start off on the wrong foot with his old friend. Kadri was potentially a great contact and a promising source for all sorts of stories that his editors would give their eyeteeth for. So Veronica looked pensive and thoughtful. Finally she quietly suggested that instead of resorting to the weak and perhaps implausible excuse of adopting a pen name—after all, there was no convincing reason why he should—she suggested another angle. Why not, she mused, simply say that your bitch of an ex-wife stalked you relentlessly all over the world and your lawyers had suggested a name-change to protect you from further harassment. Vaux thought the idea ingenious and wondered what other creative talents an academic researcher of medieval Britain could be concealing.

'I'd love some coffee, thank you,' said Vaux. Kadri got up and went to the door. The bodyguard had been standing outside. Vaux heard some verbal orders in Arabic and then heavy footsteps as the man walked on the parquet floor to a small kitchenette in the outer room. Vaux now took the plunge.

'You don't recognize me, do you, Mr. Kadri?'

Kadri looked surprised, took a closer look at Vaux, and smiled. 'Well, of course I do—you were the gentleman who accompanied Miss Manning the other morning. And you phoned me, did you not, for this interview just yesterday.'

'Yes, indeed. I didn't mean that.' Vaux shifted in his seat and tried to relax. The coffee arrived and the bodyguard placed the English bone china cups and saucers and a tall silver coffee pot on the table. Kadri asked the man for some tablemats. Vaux recalled that his friend had always been fastidious and careful about clothes and furniture.

'What I meant is that years ago, too many years ago, you and I crossed each other's paths. We both studied economics at Bristol—I see you're wearing the cufflinks. Ahmed—I'm your old friend Michael Vaux.'

He paused now to let the information sink in. At first Kadri's eyebrows rose, then his eyes opened wider, he smiled, got up, and put his arms in the air to invite a mutual hug. Vaux rose to his feet and they both clung to each other for what seemed like minutes. Then Kadri pushed him away.

'But why are you called Derek Westropp?'

'Before I explain that, I want you to tell me if you see any, *any* resemblance to the young man you knew as Vaux, what, more than thirty years ago? My eyes, for instance, or my nose. Because I can tell you that now I've had a closer look at you, I definitely recognize the eyes, the shape of the nose, even your mouth. You really haven't aged much, Ahmed. Your hair's a little thinner, but join the club. And I bet your weight is about the same.'

Kadri sat down carefully. He looked shocked but happy. 'To tell you the truth I see a glimmer of resemblance to my long-lost friend. Yes. I think the biggest change is in your weight. I remember a slim youth of about twenty—with an athletic figure, no? Now you have a little paunch, I think.' They both laughed and Vaux felt less tense even though he was now about to deliver the explanation that he hoped would sound convincing.

'Now the Derek Westropp bit. Ahmed, we have so much to talk about—our lives, our careers. But very briefly—I know the time available today is short—I had the misfortune to marry a real witch. Of course, she was wonderful in the early years, but you know how it is. We came to what I thought was an amicable settlement—all worked out with our respective lawyers. Anyway, she apparently decided to make the rest of my life hell. She harassed me and stalked me in every country I went to, on every job I had. She threatened every girl friend, especially the serious ones, some of whom were frightened away. So my lawyer advised me to change my name legally—and that I did, to Derek Westropp. The ploy worked. I haven't heard from her or of her since.' As he told this lie he wondered how sweet, dear Joan was getting on with her rich dentist husband in Los Angeles.

Kadri smiled, folded his arms. 'Well, my friend, this calls for more than a bloody interview. See, I haven't forgotten those swear words you taught me. We must get together for a proper reunion, a magnificent dinner, perhaps.' He got up and walked to the window. For some time he looked out to the lake. Without turning round to look at Vaux, he said, 'You are my brother, Michael, my long-lost brother, perhaps. For me, you will always be Michael Vaux, my best, and actually my only, friend from my college days. Can you understand that?'

Without waiting for an answer, he continued, 'I have some busy days ahead, Michael. I'm here on a special assignment, you know. Nothing to do with the Mideast Conference at all. We are using the international gathering as a convenient pretext for some very serious negotiations with another country— '

'You mean Monica Manning was right?' Vaux regretted the interruption immediately. It was the reporter in him.

'No, no, no, Michael. Not at all. We don't need any loans from the United States. In any case, our relations with the U.S. remain, shall we say, icy? No, it's something I can't go into. But suffice it to say that the time for socializing is limited. Somehow, we'll have to fix up something—or maybe you could come to Damascus— '

'And experience a Pauline conversion?'

'Why not?' asked Kadri.

Vaux was relieved that the explanation for his false name seemed to have been accepted without question or comment. But he couldn't be sure whether Kadri was simply exercising his seasoned diplomatic talents or if the joy of rediscovering an old friend swamped any concern about the double identity.

'Why not, indeed. But let's work on it. How many days do you have before you must leave? '

'It's open-ended, depending on the negotiations. So I shall tell Marhaba, my secretary, to get to work and arrange an evening together. Where are you staying?'

'Just down the road at the Hotel de la Paix.'

'Come, I will see you out.' He ushered Vaux past the bodyguard, through the outer room, and to the elevator. They stood together, waiting. When the ornate brass doors slid open, they hugged each other again and shook hands. Vaux said, 'See you soon, Ahmed.'

'*Insha'Allah*,' said Kadri as he raised his arm to say farewell.

* * *

The news traveled fast. The revelation that Vaux had won the confidence of the chief procurement officer of Syria's Ministry of Defense, cashing in on their earlier friendship and the intimate relationship that had built up in their early twenties, spread throughout Section B3 of MI6 like a brush fire.

Barbara Boyd first heard the good tidings during postcoital pillow talk. She had asked casually if Kadri had readily accepted Vaux's explanation of his false identity or whether he had shown any signs of suspicion or doubt.

'Oh no,' said Vaux, his hands behind his head, staring at the small chandelier that hung from the ceiling. 'Not at all. We didn't even discuss it after I explained about the bitch of an ex-wife. Kadri's been married thirty years or so and I'm sure he knows how fragile some marriages can be. I imagine he's pretty quick to understand about divorce battles and family feuds.'

He heard Veronica sigh with what seemed like relief. And for just a few seconds he wondered if she wasn't overly concerned about all this. Why should she care about his misgivings, about the fact that he didn't like misleading an old friend? But such suspicious thoughts evaporated as her hand again moved silkily down from his chest and over his stomach to what she called the nether reaches. She had ended a long dry spell, this exotic creature, and Vaux had no hesitation in making the most of it. He felt younger and more vital, yet he also sensed a feeling within himself that his sexual needs were not as urgent as once they were. He hoped this was another harbinger of a quiet and peaceful retirement.

Len Powell's miniature microphones picked up the bedtime talk (plus the sighs, moans, and groans of love-making) and Chris Greene telegraphed the good news to Craw in London via conventional public phone lines. 'The story is accepted by all concerned. The green lights are flashing,' said Greene, childishly but cryptically. Craw was delighted to report the positive developments to Sir Walter Mason, who in turn apprised the director-general. Craw made immediate plans to leave for Geneva. He told his secretary to reserve a room at the five-star Hotel des Bergues on the Quai des Bergues, equidistant from Vaux's hotel and the Beau Rivage.

* * *

'Look at this, Westropp,' said Monica Manning. She was having her eleven o'clock bloody Mary in the hotel bar. Vaux was playing a waiting game: he had called Marhaba (with a name like that, he told Veronica, she must be a beauty) and in perfect English she had said that she would get back to him within forty-eight hours. There was nothing for him to do except continue to perform the masquerade.

Manning showed him a headline in the *Herald Tribune*: the Group of Seven had negotiated a loan of $24 million to help Russia 'through its current transition from totalitarianism to democracy.'

'Funny coincidence, what? Why now, just as this bloody peace conference gets underway? There's an angle tailored just for you—an offbeat think-piece about the West's feeling it has to fund Yeltsin's Herculean efforts to put Mother Russia on the road to freedom and all that guff.'

'Twenty-four million won't go very far—it's probably earmarked for a few new independent news magazines and media outfits. But yes, you suggest a good angle, Monica. Are they trying to buy him off? Is the U.S., which virtually runs the Group of Seven, saying in effect, "Look, Boris, we'll help you financially and economically, but butt out of the Middle East game once and for all"?'

'Couldn't have said it better myself. There's a lot of news to go around, Westropp. Riots in Los Angeles, terrorism in Egypt—and look at this' (she slapped the front page with the back of a fleshy hand): 'Bush, it seems, has got round some sort of U.N. arms embargo by granting export permits for all sorts of weapons that Iraq will purchase thanks to a loan from the Banca Nazionale del Lavoro—some Italian outfit. There's a budding scandal if ever I've seen one.'

Vaux thought this latter piece of news got close to the bone. It tended to justify one of Sir Walter's favorite theories that an arms race was going on between various Arab dictators (read Iraq, Syria, and perhaps Egypt) so that the country with the strongest armed services and weaponry could call the tune in any future deal between Israel and Palestine. But he must keep his mind on the immediate matter in hand. How the hell was he going to get his hands on the key documents that would reveal and expose to the world the details of the secret Russian-Syrian armaments deal?

'Anyway, I'm off. It's registration day. Coming along?'

'No, I'll do it later.'

'Please yourself.'

'Did you ever locate that young journalist who gave you the bum steer?'

'Nah. Reckon it was some cub reporter sent over by the *Sun* or *Mirror* to make me look like a clown. Dirty tricks and all that sort of thing. They often resort to foul rather than fair means. The *Mirror's* people hate the fact that I've turned down three offers to join them. Could have doubled my salary and expense allowance, but I happen to like my rag. It's what I call a quality tabloid—none of the page three tits and arse crap the others serve up.'

* * *

Veronica had told Vaux she'd be spending a couple of days at the Benedictine monastery in Vevey; Abbot Jean had recovered from his bout with flu. It was a fine spring morning. A low-lying mist hovered above the still water of the lake and he decided to take a walk to digest his breakfast and then visit the bank to check on his newly opened account. Trust but verify, Reagan had said, and that's what he intended to do. The heavy hand of bureaucracy could easily have screwed things up and for all he knew he was working for nothing—except the expenses they had given him in Thomas Cook travelers' checks.

He crossed the low-lying bridge that led to the south bank, the old part of town where many of the big international banks had decided to open up their Swiss offices. Here was Barclay's Bank, Chase Manhattan, HSBC, Bank of America, Banco Milano, Banque National de Paris, the Saudi Banking Corp. Here also were the major Swiss banks; Credit Suisse, his destination, was located on the Place d'Italie.

As he walked over the bridge he could hear the churning turbulence of the water as Lake Leman (the French name for the lake) gushed into the Rhone. Swans and ducks nose-dived for fish and insects in small, protected enclaves built close to the river's banks from which they could swim out to the farther reaches of the lake.

Vaux found the city quite beautiful: the morning air had an Alpine quality despite the heavy traffic; the belle époque grandeur of the old hotels on the quays that faced the south bank's medieval rabbit warren gave the place a unique and charming character. It somehow made up for its reputation as a funk hole for the tax-shy super-rich and the seemingly consequential ultra-high cost of things—from $10 cups of coffee to small shots of whisky for $15. Such thoughts of mundane money matters prompted the question of whether he should withdraw some of his new cash or just leave it there to gain interest. He'd surely need it pretty soon.

He'd called Susan Appleby, who had told him of the latest bid for No.32. There seemed no end to the ever-upward spiral in the valuation of that jerry-built bungalow, but he could not waver: the southerly view of the lush, green fields and pastures, the hedgerows, and the magnificence of the willows, the beeches, and the Spanish chestnuts that seemed to have been there for centuries—this was a little tranquil corner of England that he had found and would not relinquish.

Suddenly he was standing in front of a disappointingly utilitarian five-story building of glass and steel that dominated the old cobblestoned Place d'Italie. He was ushered into a square, windowless waiting room. He had brought along the latest issue of the European edition of *Time* and read for at least fifteen minutes.

'Sorry to have kept you waiting, Mr. Westropp. But you didn't make an appointment and most of our representatives are in conference this morning. Will you come this way?' A middle-aged platinum blonde dressed in an elegant black knit suit addressed him. He felt duly reprimanded.

He spoke to her elegant back: 'Yes, I should have made an appointment. I'm used to just walking into my local bank and doing business quickly. In the little town where I live you can talk to the manager across the counter.' Vaux's attempt at light humor was ignored.

'Monsieur Blanc will be with you shortly,' said the lady, closing another door and leaving him again in a windowless room dominated by a big oval walnut table. He sat down and poured himself a cool glass of Evian from the bottle that had been placed in the center of the table. He heard the door handle turn, and in walked a tall, well-tailored man in his mid-thirties. He wore rimless glasses and his light brown hair was pasted back with gel.

'Ah, Mr. Westropp. Good morning. My name's Blanc. Sorry to have kept you waiting. May I first see your passport?'

Vaux took the new U.K. passport out of his inside pocket and placed it on the table. The man whipped through it, looked momentarily at the small photo and then up at Vaux, and handed it back. 'Would you care for a coffee, tea?'

'No thank you,' said Vaux, now feeling slightly claustrophobic. He wanted to get the business over and done with. M. Blanc opened a folder, looked at some printed papers and handed them to Vaux. 'As you see, a deposit of fifty-thousand pounds sterling has been made—two days ago, I think—the money having been transferred from Coutts & Co., London. Everything is in order, sir. Would you want to keep the money in sterling or change some to U.S. dollars perhaps?'

Vaux hadn't thought much about that. But then he thought of the house and he doubted the Kingston clan would want to be paid in greenbacks. 'Oh, no. I think I'll keep it in pounds. I take it there's no problem transferring it back to my bank in England.'

M. Blanc looked somewhat disappointed. 'No, of course not, Mr. Westropp. It's your money. But of course, if you repatriate the money, you'll be liable for U.K. taxes. Here there are no taxes to worry about.'

'That's a thought,' said Vaux as he saw the appealing sum of £50,000 sitting in the credit column of his new Swiss bank account.

'Perhaps you will want to place the money, or at any rate part of it, in a term deposit? We offer higher rates of interest on TDs, of course. At present, you only get 1.5 percent on the account. We could place the money in a three- or six-month TD and you'd get around 4.5 to 5 percent.'

'Annually, I presume,' said Vaux, half-facetiously, having read somewhere that a recent investment scam had relied on sky-high monthly interest rates to attract gullible punters. The financial writer had advised readers that the higher the interest rate offered the greater the risk.

M. Blanc was deaf to Vaux's quirky sense of humor—and he hadn't read the same magazine article. 'Yes, of course, annually,' he said, stunned that this naïve client could seriously believe otherwise—what, a Ponzi-like 5 percent a month from the venerable Credit Suisse?

'Frankly,' said Vaux, 'I'm not too sure when I'll be needing the money.'

'Well, in that case, let's leave it in the current account. Now do you want us to keep the mail and monthly statements or send them to you in the U.K.? Most clients prefer us to keep all mailings here—to protect secrecy and confidentiality.'

Vaux was feeling hungry now. He'd have a traditional Swiss lunch at that little restaurant with a terrace overlooking the Rhone he'd seen on the Rue Simplon.

'Yes, I think that's best. I'll leave everything here in safe-keeping.'

'Quite so, sir.'

17

'Look what happened in Madrid last October—nothing, nothing at all, a complete waste of time,' said Amin Hakki. He was expounding on the results of the Middle East peace conference called by President Bush in the wake of the Gulf War—the U.S.-led push to get the invading Iraqi forces out of Kuwait.

Marhaba, Kadri's secretary, had summoned Vaux only two hours earlier. In her best English, she said a 'window of opportunity' had opened and Mr. Kadri would like to see him at 11 a.m. for a general discussion and 'backgrounder.' Vaux had just got out of the shower. He dressed hurriedly. He opened the safe and put the tiny Minox camera into his jacket pocket, more out of respect for the Boy Scouts' motto on being prepared than in any hope of using it.

He was greeted at the elevator by the heavy Syrian bodyguard who failed to acknowledge him either with a smile or verbal greeting. He led Vaux into a large dining room where Kadri and Hakki both sat eating the remains of a continental breakfast. They didn't get up.

'Salaam!' cried Ahmed. 'Like some coffee? Something to eat perhaps?' he asked, gesturing to an array of breads, jams, some cheeses, and fresh fruit. 'There's some cold ham. They never learn in this hotel.' Vaux declined any food but poured himself a glass of mineral water. Kadri was apparently happy to let his colleague do most of the talking.

'You see, Mr. Westropp, Bush had to show he was a man of peace and not a warrior. It was a gesture, an attempt to persuade the public and the so-called Arab "street" that the U.S. cares about the Palestinian problem and wants to act as honest broker in any negotiations toward a peaceful solution. But in our view, it's all play-acting, propaganda. The Americans will always put Israel's interests before those of the Arabs. We know that—they constantly repeat that they have to stand by their great friend and ally. So why this charade, we ask?'

Vaux was still not used to being addressed as 'Westropp.' It seemed natural enough from Monica Manning. But from one of Ahmed's colleagues it sounded somehow artificial or forced. But it shouldn't, he told himself. It was, after all, his official name—and even Ahmed would in the presence of others presumably continue to call him by his alias. Perhaps he would revert to his real name when they were alone together, thus sealing a sort of bond between old friends, a pact or confidence that they could share. In any event, he was now thankful he had done his homework. Over the last few weeks he had bought a few books on the Middle East and the Arabs, read all the coverage of the Israeli-Arab dispute he could find in the newspapers and weekly magazines, and now felt qualified to ask some reasonably intelligent questions.

'But the Syrians attended Madrid. You must have felt then that something could have come out of it, that it wouldn't be a complete waste of time.'

'Mr. Westropp, please,' said Hakki, draining the last of his coffee from a small, delicate cup. He looked at Kadri whose eyes were fixed on Vaux. Kadri slightly tilted his head as a signal that Hakki should continue. 'We feel that for many, many years we have been ignored. While the Israeli occupation of the West Bank and Gaza are main stumbling blocks to peace, our own priority is quite simply that until the Golan Heights are returned to us—until Israel withdraws from Golan—there simply cannot be any comprehensive and lasting peace that Syria could sign on to.'

Kadri at last spoke. 'You see, Derek, to us, naturally, we want our land back. The Golan Heights is strategically vital to us. But the Americans have put this dispute on a back burner pending progress over the West Bank and Gaza. Our relations with the U.S. have remained cool in recent years, and they have made no gesture, despite our support for the U.S. position on the Iraqi invasion of Kuwait, toward any resolution of our main dispute with Israel.'

'So what you seem to be saying is that there are pre-conditions to a comprehensive peace: first Israel must get out of occupied lands including, of course, the Golan Heights—then we will talk about guaranteeing Israel its security,' said Vaux.

'Quite so,' agreed Hakki. 'The restoration of Palestinian rights is a prerequisite to our sitting down and hammering out an overall settlement.'

'And Israel's position is that progress can only be made when and if certain guarantees are made and a formal peace treaty is drawn up between them and the major Arab players. Then negotiations could get underway about the return of Arab lands. Is that right?' asked Vaux.

'Yes,' said Hakki. 'That sums it up pretty well. But don't forget that international law is on our side. An aggressor can't hold on to conquered territory forever. And key U.N. resolutions call for Israel to withdraw from those lands invaded in the '67 war.'

'And the purpose of your coming here to Geneva is that your government presumably thinks you may be able to break the logjam?'

Hakki said: 'This meeting has been called by the United Nations—that's the No. 1 point. The U.S. is not calling the shots, which they were in Madrid. Second point is that the new Russia is playing an increasingly important role. They have asked us to participate. And we feel that if they are offering their good offices toward an eventual settlement—as a sort of counterweight to the U.S.-Israeli alliance—then we should also make a gesture toward them. So we have agreed to attend this current meeting as observers and hope something will come of it. Do you want to add anything, Ahmed?'

Kadri smiled at Vaux and looked expansive. 'Have you studied our recent history, Derek? You know, back in '73, we really won that war. The Israelis called it the Yom Kippur war. Egypt attacked from the west, we attacked from the east. Kissinger's intervention, his old shuttle diplomacy, created conditions under which all the parties eventually agreed on a cease-fire. The world thinks Israel is invincible—but believe me, they came very close to being defeated. Perhaps when we get together again I'll have the opportunity to discuss these matters further. You would be doing your readers a favor by getting some of the real facts out rather than repeating the old U.S.-Israeli propaganda.' Kadri stood up. The meeting was over.

The breakfast session had lasted about an hour. When Kadri rose to accompany Vaux to the elevator, he said, 'Doesn't all this sound depressingly familiar, Michael? I mean we were discussing the injustices of the Palestinian-Israeli situation back in the late '50s—before the wars of '67 and '73 and the full-scale occupation of the West Bank and Gaza. The arguments don't change, do they? It bears out my old theory that you may or may not remember: the Israelis just dance around and play for time—and meanwhile build more settlements so that when final peace negotiations get underway, they will say the "facts on the ground" don't merit the sort of deal the Arabs want. Moving the Jews out of their scores of settlements is untenable and physically almost impossible, they will say. This is not acceptable to the Arab side and never has been.'

Vaux sighed at the seeming impossibility of the two sides ever coming to an agreement. 'One has to hope that one of these days somebody will come up with a formula acceptable to all sides, I suppose.'

'In the end, the only thing that will bring the Israelis to the bargaining table will be the same sort of thing that kept the world peace for forty-five years or so—the fear of mutually assured destruction between the U.S. and the U.S.S.R. Only when the Arab side is strong enough to pose a real military threat to their existence will the Israelis come to the table and negotiate seriously.' The elevator doors slammed closed as if to emphasize Kadri's point and before Vaux could say goodbye.

* * *

Alan Craw had installed himself in a three-room corner suite on the fifth floor of the luxurious Hotel des Bergues, just down the road from Vaux's hotel. The Bergues overlooked the confluence of the lake with the Rhone as the roiling mountain waters poured into the narrow causeway where the river began its long meander through southern France and eventually spilled into the Mediterranean. From his window, Craw could see the sweep of the busy street that hugged the lakeshore northwards, the Mont Blanc bridge over to the old town, and the historic buildings of the south bank.

'Dorothy, call Vaux and get him over here. Don't forget to ask for Mr. Westropp.' He had brought his secretary, just fresh out of Roedean, along with him. She was young and inexperienced but spoke well and, in his mind, looked as pretty as an English rose.

Vaux arrived. He'd had a heavy pasta-seafood lunch at an Italian restaurant next to his hotel. He was just contemplating a siesta when he was summoned. He had no idea Craw was going to appear in the war zone but accepted his arrival with equanimity. After all, he was making progress even though the ultimate mission was tantalizingly just out of reach.

'How are you, old boy?' asked Craw. He was dressed in a navy blue blazer, casual khakis, and highly polished Gucci loafers. No doubt, thought Vaux, his out-of-London attire. He remembered how he had looked like the quintessential City gent when they had first got together at that small hotel in Swiss Cottage. He even sported a bowler hat, still a part of English (and Ulster) sartorial pretensions but hardly seen elsewhere on the globe.

'I'm well. Probably eating and drinking too much, but Geneva's like that. An essentially boring city, but one that offers an abundance of good restaurants,' said Vaux.

'No time to be bored, Vaux. I'm in a debriefing mode. So spill the beans, please.'

Vaux sat down on a silk brocaded, high-backed chair. Craw stood at the heavily draped windows looking intently at the surging waters as they gushed into the narrows of the river.

'Well, of course, as you know, I have made contact. I've met Kadri three times—once with Manning. The last meeting was yesterday morning. Our second meeting was face-to-face and it was then I took the opportunity of pulling off my disguise. In other words I identified myself. He swallowed the story about a shrew of a wife and hence the name change. Incidentally, why *was* it so necessary to give me a phony name?'

Craw turned around and Vaux saw a face contorted by the horror of a bolshie question from an insubordinate staffer.

'My dear Vaux, that is how we operate. Precautions are vital in our business. Don't question our methods, dear boy. You haven't been around long enough. Were you wired for these get-togethers?'

'Wired?'

'Did you have a body mike to record your conversation?' said Craw impatiently.

'Er, no. Was I supposed to? Nobody gave me any equipment like that.'

'Ah,' said Craw thoughtfully. He would have to have a word with Len Powell. Clearly there had been a serious slip-up in the communications department.

'So we are relying on your reportage, Vaux. I trust it will be accurate. What did you discuss at the face-to-face meeting yesterday?'

Vaux told him about the Syrians' change of heart at the behest of the Russians. He also repeated Kadri's (and presumably the Syrian government's) belief that the only solution to the Israeli question was for the Arabs to arm themselves to the hilt and present a real challenge. It was as though the Syrians had decided that the Israelis would only negotiate in good faith once they were scared enough to realize armed conflict could destroy all they have built up over the years. He told Craw that at the one-on-one meeting, Kadri had implied that his business in Geneva had nothing to do with the peace conference. 'A special assignment he called it—which would confirm our suspicions of his real task in Geneva.'

Craw had decided to buff his fingernails as he listened to Vaux's report. The scratching sound of an expensive fountain pen could be heard as Dorothy, sitting at a mahogany writing desk, took what notes she could with her deficient shorthand.

'They're confirmed already, Vaux. Why else do you think he goes to the Russian consulate every morning?'

'I didn't know that,' said Vaux.

'We've been watching him since he got here. Now about future tactics. Any ideas?' asked Craw, who then decided to answer his own question. 'You must find out where he keeps his briefcase: the documents or procurement contracts are what we're after. As I told you, we know that he goes every morning to the Russian consulate, a big villa on the Rue de Lausanne perched on the lakeshore, fittingly close to where Lenin stayed when he was in exile, before he went back to Russia to lead the great and ultimately disastrous Russian revolution. He's always carrying a fat, lawyer-type briefcase. I have no doubt that's the target—that's where the details of the arms deal will be outlined. If and when you get your hands on the quarry, Vaux, you must just quickly photograph the pages. Don't bother reading them, it'll take up too much precious time. Understand?'

Vaux didn't reply. He felt a cloud of depression descending, a feeling of helplessness. Why would Kadri be so careless as to make his precious briefcase accessible? It didn't make sense. Surely Craw had some back-up plan.

Craw must have read his thoughts—and doubts. 'Look, Vaux, it's not that difficult. Why don't you waylay him on his return from the consulate and take him to a bar. He usually walks along the quayside in the afternoons—probably gets his daily constitutional that way. So you meet him, take him to a sleazy bar, maybe one of those strip joints near the railway station, get pissed for old time's sake. Pick up his bag by mistake. Take it to the *pissoir*, copy the pages, and come back to him apologizing.'

Craw looked over at Dorothy to see if he had impressed her with his worldly familiarity with low-life watering holes. But her eyes remained fixed on the shorthand notes.

'You make it sound so easy,' sighed Vaux.

'The alternative is breaking open the safe. Pound to a penny he keeps the secret papers in a safe while he's at the hotel. That safe will be in their suite. If necessary we can recruit one of our professional ex-cons to help you. It'll take twenty-four hours to get the best safe-breaker in the U.K. over here. He's out on probation from a ten-year stretch provided he behaves himself and works exclusively for us. Keep me posted.'

With that Vaux was dismissed. Dorothy accompanied him to the door. She smiled sweetly. 'Did you get all that down?' asked Vaux gently.

'I'll let you have the transcript. You can add to it and/or correct it. That's the usual procedure,' she said as someone who had more experience in such matters than Vaux might have thought.

* * *

Chris Greene entered the corner suite with the jauntiness of a young man on the way up. It was not the best way to present himself to a middle-aged MI6 officer who hoped to be in line for promotion to succeed Sir Walter Mason on his retirement. But Greene was not unaware of the laws of succession at Century House and knew that if Craw wanted to win the horse's race (there were the two other contending deputy directors) by a decisive head, he'd have to chalk up Operation Helvetia as an indisputable success. Greene knew that he was a key player in Craw's end-game—and he didn't doubt that Craw himself would, at least to himself, reluctantly acknowledge his decisive role.

'Sit down, Greene,' said Craw, gesturing to the long, curl-armed brocaded Louis Philippe sofa. Craw chose to remain standing, his arm propped up on the marble mantelshelf of a screened fireplace that had last seen a log or a piece of coal in the 1940s. 'Tell me what you have to report.'

'Well, sir, first of all the mikes in Vaux's room are working well—'

'That's Powell's department. I'm seeing him later. But while we are on the subject, do you have any idea why Vaux wasn't wired when he had those meetings with Kadri and Co.?'

Greene didn't know.

'Go on, man. Continue.'

'Well, I have scrupulously followed Kadri's movements since he arrived at the Beau Rivage. He goes with his associate Hakki to the Russian consulate on the Rue Lausanne by staff car. It's a Mercedes and one of a fleet of three from the Syrian embassy in Bern.'

'Bloody Arabs. Buy anything but British. They go around in Mercedes, Citroens, Cadillacs—but never, never a good British marque like a Bentley or a Rolls.'

'Hangover from imperialism?' suggested Greene.

'The Frogs were worse than us. No, I think the Mercedes thing has something to do with their latent love of things Germanic. Ever since the war when Hitler did a sort of Lawrence of Arabia thing—promising them self-rule and independence from the western powers if they helped him win—they've had a secret love affair with the Germans. Why do you think Assad's Baathist Party is basically national socialist?'

'You have a point, sir,' said Greene diplomatically.

'Well go on, Greene.'

'Around 3 p.m. every afternoon he leaves the Russian consulate and walks along the lakeshore back to the hotel. It must be at least a three-mile walk, but at this time of year of course it's quite beautiful. Hakki sometimes accompanies him, but more often goes back in the Mercedes. As I told you, Kadri always carries one of those heavy lawyer's briefcases. Even when he decides to walk. In other words he doesn't entrust it to Hakki or to the chauffeur to bring it back to the hotel.'

'Very, very interesting,' said Craw. 'It could almost be snatched from him, couldn't it?' Such a crude maneuver would eliminate Vaux and might well produce a totally successful result. Craw's heart was beating faster and he walked over to a large armchair and sat down. He immediately got up because the seat was so soft and deep that he was forced to look up to Greene. He began to pace the room.

'No sir,' said Greene.

Craw was deep in thought. 'What?'

'No sir. It couldn't be snatched. The briefcase is handcuffed to his wrist.'

'Oh,' said Craw, disappointed that he would have to rely on Vaux after all.

'The other point I haven't mentioned is that he is followed by the usual bodyguard, a big, heavy number who keeps about a hundred yards behind Kadri and sweats a lot. I shouldn't think he's used to all that walking. Oh, and by the way, he carries a weapon, probably a revolver.'

Craw now saw the total collapse of what he considered his highly original snatch-the-bag strategy.

Dorothy came into the room with a silver tray laden with cups and saucers and a white china coffee pot. She put the tray down on a side table next to the armchair. She smiled at Greene, who smiled back.

'That'll be all, Dorothy, thank you,' said Craw. She smiled again at Greene as she left. Craw had now lost his train of thought. He fussed over the coffee, added some milk and sugar without asking Greene about any preferences. Greene decided not to mention that at this time of day he liked his coffee black.

'Where were we?' asked Craw, handing the delicate Worcester china to Greene.

'Well, as you know, sir, Vaux has made good progress and the battle plan looks in place. It will require some luck, and if I can help Vaux in any way I'm available.'

'Of course, Greene. But you must still keep a low profile. Your job is to shadow him for his own protection. That's about it, then. Ask Powell to call me. I haven't time to see him now. Where is he?'

'Probably at the safe house, sir.'

Greene finished his coffee quickly and headed for the doors. As he grasped the shiny brass handle Craw suddenly asked him, apropos of nothing, what college he'd been to at Oxford.

Greene turned round. 'I didn't go to Oxford, sir.' He hoped he didn't sound apologetic. Craw looked dismayed. 'I was at SOAS in London.'

Craw's wide mouth broadened a little. 'Ah, I see. They teach Arabic there, don't they?'

'Yes sir. But I read politics and economics.'

'Oh, I see. Too bad, really. Damn few of us in B3 speak the bloody language of our antagonists. Oh well, good work, Greene. Close the door a minute.'

'Sir?'

'I forgot to ask you for some input on the Boyd saga.'

Greene had to think for a second. The Boyd saga? 'Ah, yes sir. Well they've hit it off, all right. We hear the bed talk when she stays over. And she was a great asset in passing on the solution to the false name business. He bought it and so apparently did Kadri.'

'Yes, yes—very satisfactory. And presumably Vaux hasn't cottoned on to the fact that she's one of us.'

'Oh lord, no sir,' said Greene.

'Any other gleanings from the phone taps, etcetera?'

'Not really, sir. He calls his estate agent in England every other day. He still keeps the act going with Monica Manning. She's actually impressed that he's so far failed to write anything for the *Standard*. She's bought his story that his task is the big definitive wrap-up, the think-piece, about the issue of war and peace in the Middle East and all that. Oh, and he went to the bank to check up on his money.'

'Yes, I'd imagine for him that was a priority.'

* * *

Craw heard the phone tinkle on the writing desk. Dorothy called from the other room. 'Mr. Powell on the line, sir.'

'Thank you, Dorothy. Put him on, please. And after I've finished with him would you call my wife?'

'Yes sir, of course. Here's Mr. Powell.'

'Powell, how are you. I presume this line's secure?'

'Otto Heinz and Swisscom, the phone company, have guaranteed it, sir.'

'Good. Now Powell, why didn't you think of wiring up Vaux for these face-to-face meetings with the Syrian party?'

'It wasn't on the requisition order, sir. Only the subminiature Minox and my eavesdropping equipment were required for this operation—or so I understood.'

'Damn the bloody requisition order, Powell. I thought you'd have used your own initiative. You knew the details of the operation.'

'Correction, sir. No one told me anything about what I now know as Operation Helvetia. I was never officially briefed, sir.'

'Well, that was an oversight. Greene should have told you all the details. Anyway, the result is we now have to rely on what Vaux says he said to the Syrian and what the Syrian said

back. Could be worse, I suppose—he was, after all, a reporter.
I just hope that the old saw that you can never believe what
you read in the newspapers doesn't hold true—in our case at
any rate. You're over on the Rue de Zurich, I presume.'

'Yes sir.'

'Put me on to Boyd if she's there.'

Powell didn't answer. Barbara Boyd's feminine voice
soothed Craw. He had been irritated at Powell's lack of imagination and incompetence. It was only his technical know-how
that saved him and his job.

'I want you to make yourself scarce, Barbara—for a while,
anyway. I don't want Vaux to be distracted. He's zeroing in on
the target and I want him to concentrate fully on his mission.
You do understand, don't you?'

'Yes, of course, sir.'

'Does he still believe you are in Vevey?'

'Yes sir. Only for a day or so, though.'

'Well, call him and say you're going to be staying there for
at least a week. Tell him you've uncovered some highly intriguing historical manuscripts or whatever.' Craw chuckled at the
shared conspiracy to deceive Vaux.

Boyd said, 'There's one snag. We've been monitoring his
phone calls, of course. And he spent the whole afternoon ring-
ing every hotel in Vevey trying to make contact with me. If I
call him he'll ask where he can get hold of me.'

'Well, tell him you're staying as a guest at the monastery,
or something. And there are no phones in the cells. That makes
sense, doesn't it? Monks are sworn to silence and all that.'

Boyd wondered, not for the first time, whether Craw was
deliberately playing dumb in order to extract a more sensible
solution from his interlocutor.

'Not the Benedictines, sir. However, I'll think of something. I'll tell him that poverty-stricken academics like me
can't afford posh Swiss hotels and that I'm staying at some
pension which boasts one public phone in the hallway.'

'That a girl,' said Craw. 'Good luck anyway.'

Boyd put the phone down and gave out a big sigh.

'Old man giving you a hassle?' asked Greene.

'I've been told to lie low, that's all.'

'Let's go for a drink,' suggested Greene eagerly. Powell and the two technicians were fine-tuning the transmission receiving equipment which had been activated by Vaux's picking up his phone.

'Not another marathon session, I hope,' said Powell.

'There's only so many hotels in a small place like Vevey,' said the technician.

'Now he's dialing the bloody Montreaux Palace—a five-star super-luxury place,' said Powell.

'He must be keen to see you again,' said Greene.

'Let's go for that drink,' said Boyd.

18

Vaux decided nothing could be lost by taking the initiative. He wanted to get the whole sordid business over and done with and then go back to England. He was anxious to clinch the house purchase—especially now that his latest bid of £420,000 had not, according to Susan Appleby, been immediately topped by the rival would-be buyers. He wanted to get on with the sort of life he had all along planned for. The earnings from the Geneva caper (as he termed it when muttering to himself) would go up in smoke—but it would at least mean he would get the house he wanted in the location he wanted. Then he would get down to the drawing board—literally. Plans would have to be drawn up to remodel the bungalow to his tastes and at that point he would probably have to call in an architect or reputable builder.

'Yes, Michael, what can I do for you?' Ahmed Kadri had picked up the phone in his bedroom. He had been lying down after walking back from the consulate and he felt tired. It had been a long day of haggling and bargaining with an arrogant, pushy Russian negotiator who had adopted the attitude that the arms and military equipment Syria had on its shopping list were his own personal assets. Now he wasn't at all displeased to talk to a civilized Englishman.

Vaux invited him for a drink at his hotel and then dinner perhaps at the elegant Pavillon, the hotel's popular French restaurant.

'Would you forgive me if I decline? I've had a rough day and I think I'd like an early night. Perhaps tomorrow. Why don't you call me at about the same time?'

Vaux put the phone down and swore just audibly. He decided to go down to the bar and treat Monica Manning to a few drinks. She was working her rather fat ass off writing news stories every day and he felt peculiarly guilty at not having done anything at all even though he wasn't required to do anything. Withdrawal symptoms from a life of reporting and writing, he told himself.

She sat on her usual stool at the end of the bar, a gin and tonic within easy grasp as she perused her written copy of the day's proceedings. She looked up at Vaux over her half-moon reading glasses and greeted him with the usual enthusiasm.

'Westropp, old chum. How the hell are you? Still working on that definitive wrap-up piece the world's been waiting for with bated breath?'

'Sometimes you can be quite cruel, Monica.'

She laughed raucously. Heads turned. She stubbed out a half-smoked Gold Leaf. 'Oh, I'm bloody fed up with this town. It's been all work and no play. Why don't you take me out to dinner tonight, Westropp? On your *Standard* expense account, of course.'

'That goes without saying,' said Vaux.

'Jolly good. It'll be good to forget the bloody conference for a few hours. I've just got to fax this stuff over. Want to read it?'

Vaux said he'd read it tomorrow when they flew in the London papers. But he suggested she could give him a verbal summing up of the talks to date.

'Listen, it's a complete fiasco. The Arabs talk over the heads of the Israelis and vice versa. The Americans back the Israelis about the need to end terrorism and the Russkies are sympathetic to the Arab point of view that terrorism will only end when their land is given back. So it's a Mexican standoff, if you'll forgive the mixed metaphors. A stalemate, if you like.'

The diminutive Italian barman loomed over them. 'Mr. Westropp? Phone for you, sir.' Vaux thought it had to be

Veronica—finally. Thank God for that. The white phone was placed in front of him together with a tumbler of Cutty Sark.

'Excuse me, Monica. Hello?'

'Michael—it's Ahmed. Look, I'm sorry I declined your invitation. But is it too late to change my answer? I feel a lot better now I've had a shower and a pick-me-up. But let's start off here. Come to my private quarters at 7:30. We can have a few refreshments and a chat and then maybe something to eat.'

Vaux was elated. He looked at his watch. He had about an hour. He bought Manning another drink, drank his, and ordered another. He told Manning he'd landed a key interview with a top Syrian official.

'The foreign secretary—old Farouk Al-Zubaidi or whatever his damned name is?'

'No, his right-hand man. See you later.'

* * *

Kadri's private rooms were on the same floor as the rest of the delegation, but he had his own entrance at the end of a long, thick-carpeted passageway. Vaux rang a bell outside the double doors. He heard some shuffling about, then a short cough, and the door opened. It was Ahmed, in a polka-dot silk dressing gown with a cigarette in his mouth and a glass in his hand.

There were no servants or bodyguards this time and Kadri suggested Vaux get his own drink.

Vaux saw an array of wines, spirits, beer, and a big silver-plated ice bucket. 'I take it the Syrians aren't averse to alcohol like their Saudi brothers,' said Vaux, remembering a long-ago assignment in dry, abstemious Riyadh.

'You don't remember our drunken orgies at Bristol?' Ahmed laughed as he pointed to where Vaux should sit. 'Well,

well. It's nice to meet informally for a change. How are you getting on with the conference?'

Vaux thought he'd take a plunge. 'How come I never see you there with the Syrian team?' he asked, guessing that Kadri's time was totally taken up with the arms negotiations with the Russians. Perhaps the question would prompt his friend to embark on a long discourse about the Syrian-Russian talks.

But Kadri seemed reluctant to broach that sensitive subject. 'I'm a behind-the-scenes man, Michael. I report to the president and his close advisers, as Hakki told you. I'm not even in the Foreign Ministry. But you answered my question with your own question: I repeat, how's it going over there? What's your assessment—what are you telling your readers?'

Vaux hedged. 'Manning's doing the day-to-day reporting. I'm supposed to be writing a series of articles that will sum up the results of the conference—whether it's achieved any modicum of success, that sort of thing.'

'Ah, I see,' said Kadri. 'Well, you know, we never feel that you in the West really understand our viewpoint. Did you know, for example, that in '73 the Israelis were so panicked that Golda Meir actually told the U.S. that she might well have to use her country's nuclear arsenal to "ensure national survival" as she put it?'

'I had no idea,' said Vaux.

'Did you even know that the Israelis had nuclear weapons back in the '70s?'

'I've heard talk that they now have the bomb, but I had no idea they had usable nukes twenty years ago.'

'Well, they did—and they do.'

Vaux sensed that Kadri was about to tell him of Syria's ambitions in the nuclear field—or at least of the necessity of equipping the armed forces with the best possible weaponry. He looked around for the famous briefcase but saw nothing. Of course, there could be a safe concealed at the bottom of the tall walnut armoire that stood in the corner of the room.

'So, Michael, just for your own background, I'm going to tell you something that I think will be useful when you come to assess the "big picture," so to speak. But it's in complete confidence. You must promise me that you will never attribute this information to me. You are my dear brother and I think I can trust you. Well?'

Vaux hated what he was hearing but at the same time sensed it was the Holy Grail. 'Yes, of course, Ahmed. For my ears only—to be used strictly to help me form the right conclusions on this very complex question.' He hoped he didn't sound as hypocritical as he felt.

'My job here has been to confer with the Russians. We are talking to them because, as Hakki told you, they are trying to supplant the U.S. role as honest broker—or at least become a partner in the brokerage business! Now Russia under Yeltsin believes, as we do, that the only concessions we're ever going to wrench from the Israelis is through strength, the strength of arms. Our military, to put it mildly, is run down. We need all sorts of weaponry and armaments and replacement components. Israel could walk over us today. They have complete air superiority, hundreds more tanks and armored vehicles. That's what I am talking to the Russians about.'

Vaux realized that what Kadri had told him didn't get him any further. He couldn't tell him the Brits already knew all this. Even so, he was at last opening up—and he should show gratitude for Kadri's clear willingness to give him the inside scoop on Syria's current political strategies.

'Fascinating stuff, Ahmed. I trust the talks with the Russians are going well.'

Kadri got up to pour himself another glass of white wine. 'Yes, they are, as a matter of fact. Wait a minute: something just occurred to me that I must check now before I forget.' He left the room. When he returned he was carrying a fat briefcase, which, Vaux reckoned, had to be *the* case in question. He started to delve through sheaves of papers, took out and read a few, his eyes going up and down the typewritten columns. He

took a Mont Blanc fountain pen out of the briefcase and started
to mark certain items, crossing and ticking, underlining.

'Excuse me, Michael. My bladder's working overtime,'
said Kadri suddenly. He left the room again—with the briefcase still sitting on the floor, wide open.

Vaux snatched the Minox out of his side pocket, knelt
down beside the case, and began to click away at every document he could pull out. The beauty of the subminiature Minox,
he had been told, was that you didn't have to focus it—just
hold it in the palm of your hand a few inches from the object
and press the shutter release with your thumb. He listened
intently for any movements and knew he had to act fast. Was
Kadri taking a piss or would it take longer? He didn't know.

After about twenty takes he heard a slight shuffle at the
door. He quickly shoveled the documents back in the case and
sat back up in his chair. He slipped the Minox into his inside
jacket pocket. Then he looked up and saw Kadri standing at
the door. Veronica was at his side.

'Veronica! What are you doing here?'

'First, let's have the camera,' she said coldly.

'What on earth are you talking about?' said Vaux knowing he sounded as guilty as a kid caught scrumping apples in a
private orchard.

'Michael. Don't play games. They're over with,' said Veronica.

He looked at Kadri, expecting (stupidly) some support.
'What does all this mean?' he asked.

'Michael, my friend. That was very careless of you. And
by the way, this is Barbara Boyd, not Veronica Belmont. And
she's not a medieval archivist.'

'Then what the hell are you?' asked Vaux angrily.

She stretched her hand out and told him to give her the
camera. He knew there was nothing more to say so he did so.
But the biggest shock was the heavy Mauser revolver she now
aimed at his chest.

* * *

He was struggling hard to gain consciousness. It was as though an impenetrable ceiling prevented his mind from surfacing beyond the dark, gloomy world of deep sleep and into sentient reality. With a conscious effort, he at last opened his eyes and was now looking up at a real, yellowed ceiling with curlicue cornices and arabesque friezes. In the center hung a small crystal chandelier whose short electric candles gave out a dull glow. His eyes moved to the high dormer windows through which he could see bars and a bright blue sky. It looked like the afternoon. He looked at his wrist, which was usually adorned with his old Accurist watch, but it wasn't there. He tried to sit up, but his head started to pound. He closed his eyes and forced himself to think.

He remembered now. He had been confronted by Kadri after he'd successfully stowed the Minox back in his jacket pocket. It must have been a set-up. What a fool not to have seen it coming. But then he felt a deep emptiness from the pit of his stomach: he had remembered Veronica appearing out of the blue—and worse, her taking the camera from him. The last thing he could recall with any precision was the gun she pointed at him. Did he pass out? No, he couldn't have.

He now recalled the familiar muscular bodyguard rushing into the room, cuffing his hands behind his back and pushing him into an adjoining bedroom. There the handcuffs were taken off and he was told to relax and lie down. A bottle of Cutty Sark had been standing on the bedside table with a glass. He lay there thinking for a while and then got up. He tried the door and of course it was locked. The windows. They were old french windows, which were jammed either deliberately or because they were sealed to enhance the hotel's air conditioning system. He was on the fifth floor and the drop to the street—even if he broke one of the glass panels—would be fatal. So he poured himself a generous glass of scotch, stretched out on the bed, and waited.

The next thing he knew he was waking up, fully clothed, in this big garret of a room. England's green and pleasant land seemed a long way away.

* * *

The alarm had sounded loud and clear. The boys from B3 on location in Geneva, headed by Sir Walter Mason's aspiring successor, Alan Craw, were told of Vaux's disappearance as early as 4 a.m. The duty technician monitoring Room 302 reported to Powell that the protected target had not returned from a night out on the town. Powell had been sleeping in Room 301 when his phone rang. He looked over at the pull-out couch and saw Greene lying on his back with his mouth wide open snoring lightly. He wasn't wearing pajamas and his hairless tanned chest moved up and down with the regular inflation of his lungs. Powell wondered for a moment where Greene had gone on holiday to get a tan this early in the year. Then he heard the report from the Rue de Zurich.

'Greene! Get up, you lazy bastard.' The pleasure of waking up a young man who enjoyed his sleep recalled his national service days as a staff sergeant in the REME.

Greene stirred, opened reluctant eyes, and looked at the windows. He saw a black, velvety sky glittering with stars. 'What's going on?' he grumbled.

'Emergency, old chap. Vaux's disappeared.' Powell threw the bunch of duplicate keys at Greene. He kept them in the small drawer of his bedside table. 'Go into his room and take a look. I'd better notify Craw—or do you think we'd better wait? It's only 4 o'clock. Vaux could be in a brothel or spending a night with Babs Boyd.'

'Unlikely' said Greene, whose dulled brain was now gearing up for what promised to be a hard and long day. 'Vaux is no alley cat and he thinks Boyd's in Vevey with the monks.'

'Where is she, anyway?' asked Powell, who never thought it particularly important to know where every one of his colleagues chose to stay.

'She's staying at the Warwick, opposite the railway station. Big modern monstrosity but comfortable.'

Greene opened the double doors into Vaux's room. Everything seemed to be in order. His bed was still made. An empty glass stood on the minibar next to a miniature bottle of Dewar's. The ice tray looked forlornly empty with dregs of water resting at the bottom of the little cube molds. He opened the doors of the armoire and kneeled on the floor to open the small safe. It contained Vaux's U.K. passport and a wad of Thomas Cooke travelers' checks. But no Minox.

Powell was dialing the Warwick Hotel. He asked for Miss Boyd.

'Hello?' A sleepy, muffled voice.

Powell didn't know how to put this but it had to be done. 'Barbara?'

'Yes, who's this?'

'Len Powell. Sorry to wake you up. But I have to ask you a question. It's an emergency.'

'What on earth are you talking about, Len?'

'Look, is Vaux with you by any chance?'

There was a pause. Powell hoped that maybe he was and that all this fuss was unnecessary and unjustified.

'No, no. He's certainly not. I'm alone and trying to get some sleep.'

'Did you see him last night?'

'No, of course not. He thinks I'm in Vevey. Everyone on the team knows that—have you forgotten?'

'Well, he could have bumped into you or something,' said Powell apologetically.

'He didn't. I make myself scarce if I think he's roaming the streets.'

'What do we do now?' asked Powell, who recognized Boyd's superior field experience.

'What exactly is the problem?'

'He's disappeared. Never slept in his room. And it's nearly dawn.'

'Call Craw. I'm going back to sleep.'

* * *

But Powell did not call Craw. Indecision and procrastination set in while Powell discussed with Greene the best plan of attack.

'Look, I don't want to bother Craw just yet. I'm still pretty sure that Vaux went out on the town last night and got mixed up in some low-life situation. If he suddenly shows up at 6 a.m we'll be thankful we never informed Craw and the whole thing will blow over.'

'Except that I'll be blamed for losing him. I'm supposed to be watching Vaux and here I was assuming he'd have his usual quiet night and go to bed early,' said Greene, who was now wondering what long-term career repercussions could arise by this lapse of devotion to duty. Since he'd been in Geneva he'd been told that together with Barbara Boyd, he would play the watching game in reverse: his job, Craw had told him, was not to follow a suspected traitor but to shadow Vaux for Vaux's own safety and security. That was what was asked of him and he had failed in that task.

'That bitch Boyd deserves some of the responsibility,' said Powell. 'Her remit, if anything, was clearer than yours—and she got a lot more fun out of it from what I've gathered.'

'She knows when to employ her feminine wiles,' agreed Greene.

'Her job was easier. She could show herself—you had to keep your head down and your trench coat collar up.'

They decided to wait until 7:00. But there was still no sign of Vaux. At this slightly more civilized hour they thought it probable that Craw would at least be thinking about getting up for one more day in the waiting game.

* * *

In fact, Craw, who wasn't used to sleeping alone in a big king- sized bed, had been tossing and turning all night; as dawn broke he had managed at last to get off to a deep, dreamless sleep. His phone in any case was disconnected so that Dorothy, in another bedroom, could take all in-coming calls.

She pouted her lips in front of the big bathroom mirror, looking closely for skin blemishes (she suffered from acne) and examined her perfect white teeth when the wall phone over the W.C. softly purred.

'Hello.'

'Oh, is Mr. Craw there. This is Powell, Miss er—'

'Booker. I believe he's still asleep. Is this urgent?'

Powell couldn't pretend it wasn't. 'Yes, Miss Booker. Very urgent indeed,' he said.

'Please hold on.' She thought she recognized the slight Yorkshire accent that their Mr. Powell sometimes affected. 'You're Mr. Powell of the firm, I take it...'

Powell hated that sort of loose talk. And protective young secretaries pissed him off even more. He confirmed her supposition.

After precisely five minutes—Powell kept his eyes on his Seiko Chronograph—he heard shuffling and the loud sniffing and snorting of a man troubled by a flood of early morning mucus. Then: 'Yes, Powell. What is it?'

'Well, sir, some rather troubling news, I'm afraid. Mr.
Vaux seems to have disappeared. His room hasn't been occupied since last evening...'
    Craw said nothing as his mind sped to all sorts of grim in-
terpretations. But he must not show panic. 'Well, he probably
met some woman and slept over. Don't let's imagine all sorts
of grizzly scenarios at this early stage, Powell.'
    'I had to report it, sir. We've been up since 4 a.m. when
the boys on Zurich Street notified me and Greene.'
    'And no clues, no information at all?'
    'No sir.'
    'Where's Greene? It was his job to shadow Vaux.'
    'I'll let you speak to him, sir.'
    Powell passed the phone to Greene.
    'Hello, sir.'
    'Where the hell were you when all this happened?'
    'I last saw him at the hotel bar, sir. He was talking with
Monica Manning and it looked like they were set for the evening.'
    'You should assume nothing in this business, Greene.
Look, you'd better come over here now. Bring Powell with
you.'

* * *

    Vaux heard a clanking noise and a strange whirring sound.
It seemed to come from a corner in the room that he hadn't
yet examined. He saw what looked like an in-built wooden
cabinet with a sash-like lower panel. Attached to it was a bright
brass bracket that could be gripped to slide the panel upward.
It was an old-fashioned silent waiter. He pulled up the panel
and saw ropes and pulleys moving slowly in up-and-down mo-
tions—presumably a prelude to the arrival of something to
eat. He was grateful because he was ravenous.

A tray emerged on which was placed a large bowl of goulash on a pile of pasta. A side plate offered diced zucchini. Plastic knives and forks and spoons were supplied along with a paper serviette. A baguette and a bottle of Evian completed the meal. At least they weren't trying to starve him into submission. But he heard no human sounds at all. He was as isolated as if he'd been locked up in a monk's cell at that Vevey monastery where Veronica had claimed she was doing valuable historic research. He took the solitary upright chair in the room to stand on and, with a stretch, looked out of the windows. The view was similar to his hotel's. The villa, for that's what it seemed to be, looked over manicured lawns and large plane trees onto the shimmering lake where small craft and pleasure steamers constantly plied up and down. But he could hardly see the far shore, so presumably he was north of the town where the lake got much wider.

Suddenly he heard footsteps. Then the sound of several locks turning. He now knew what it felt like to be a prisoner and grateful for any sign of life outside the cell. At the door stood a tall, heavy, totally bald man whom he didn't recognize. He wasn't wearing a jacket and Vaux saw the ominous holster under his arm.

'Please come with me,' said the man as he held the door open. The accent was Eastern European. But at that moment Vaux was more concerned with basic cleanliness. He hadn't had a shower for over twenty-four hours and his bowels were also objecting to the break in routine. 'May I go to a bathroom first?' he asked, hoping he sounded adequately deferential. The man grunted and gestured to a nearby door marked MESSIEURS.

After fifteen minutes Vaux emerged, relieved but still unshowered. He decided to say nothing and trusted that fate would soon release him from this hellhole. Perhaps it had all been a mistake. But then he remembered the farce of his first

attempt at espionage and the deep hurt he had felt at Veronica's
elaborately planned betrayal. But then again, he wondered if,
perhaps even hoped that, Veronica was playing a triple game—
and that she would suddenly reappear and take him back to the
real world.

The burly guard beckoned him to walk ahead down a long
stone-floor corridor, then down a spiral staircase to another
floor. They came to a pair of doors that were flung open. At
a large desk in front of tall french windows sat Ahmed Kadri.
Opposite him, turning his head as Vaux came into the room,
was Amin Hakki. Both men looked, as always, neatly dressed,
freshly groomed and shaved, and had obviously had a good
night's sleep.

'Ah, Michael, sit down please—over there.' Kadri nodded toward a hard wooden armchair, about three feet away
from the desk.

Vaux's first thought was that he was damned if he'd play
docile. Guilty he might be, but he would not take the subsequent uncivilized behavior of a friend—two friends, in fact—
lightly. 'Look here, Ahmed, what the hell do you mean by first
of all bringing me to this place after I was presumably drugged
and secondly—'

Kadri raised his hand for silence. 'Please, my brother—
don't go on so. What the hell do you expect? You betrayed my
trust in the worst possible way. I'm supposed to embrace you
and open a bottle of champagne?'

At least his friend hadn't lost his sardonic wit. But what
had been lost? Was it ever retrievable? Vaux decided to stay
quiet. He had little choice.

Kadri shuffled some papers on his desk, looked at Hakki,
and gave a slight nod. Hakki turned toward Vaux with a faint
smile.

'I've been assigned the job, Mr. Vaux, of trying to discover
what sort of man you really are. Where perhaps your political
sympathies really lie. What sort of decision you may come to
about certain matters if you are given accurate and unbiased

evidence that would support a definite outcome. Am I clear
so far?'

'If we are in for a long discussion, can I first ask for a
shower? I feel dirty and uncivilized. I'm sure you understand,
Ahmed.'

'Detainees aren't in any position to dictate the terms of
any discussion—'

'Let him,' said Kadri. He pressed a button on his desk to
summon the guard. Kadri, to Vaux's astonishment, spoke Russian to the man.

'Follow him. And be back in fifteen minutes, please,' said
Kadri.

Vaux was grateful and leaped up to follow the Russian.

* * *

At the Hotel des Bergues, the inquest was in full swing.
Craw had summoned Barbara Boyd to join Greene and Powell. Dorothy had been asked to go shopping, specifically to buy
a diamond-studded gold Piaget watch for Jessica, Craw's wife,
as an anniversary present. They had been married twenty years
and Craw couldn't resist the opportunity of buying what she
had asked for—as a visitor to Geneva, it would be duty free
and tax-free. Dorothy had been given a wad of high-denomi-
nation pounds sterling, which she would have to change into
Swiss francs. Craw had recommended the foreign exchange
boutique at the railway station where he had discovered, after
shopping at American Express and some of the major banks,
they gave the best rate for the pound.

'Now then, Barbara, where were you when you were
needed?' said Craw dryly.

'First off, I was in my room all evening and all night. As
you are fully aware, Vaux was under the impression I was in
Vevey for five days or so, so I could hardly run the risk of being seen on the streets or in some restaurant in town, could I?

I left the Rue de Zurich premises about 5 p.m., took a taxi to the Warwick, made my way to the room, and ordered some food to be brought up. You can check it out if you like.' She wanted to sound annoyed that anyone should question her movements and she succeeded.

'That won't be necessary,' said Craw in retreat. He turned to Greene. 'Dereliction of duty, Greene, or just one of those silly but fateful oversights?'

Greene blushed. He didn't know if Craw was giving him the benefit of the doubt or whether he was being bloody sarcastic.

'Well, sir, with all due respect, you will recall that my assignment in the late afternoons is to follow Kadri from the Russian consulate and basically to watch his movements until he makes it back to his hotel. He usually gets in around 6 p.m. and then I take a seat in the lobby and hide behind a newspaper. Otto Heinz keeps me posted on Vaux's movements, and when I get back to the Paix I double-check Vaux's whereabouts—he's usually in the bar or in his room for an early night. Some evenings, it's true, I have followed Vaux into town to the odd bar and have watched him go into a restaurant. He's always been by himself.

'But last night I saw him go into the lobby bar, greet Manning, and settle down for an old chinwag. He bought a few drinks and he took a phone call. Now I checked with the technicians and he had made a call to Kadri earlier from his room. He invited him over to the Paix for a drink and then to dinner at the Pavillon. It was all in the line of work—what he was supposed to do. But Kadri declined, pleading fatigue.

'In the bar I did see him take the phone for an incoming call. We checked with Otto who checked with Swiss Telecom. It appears the call was made from a public phone, so we can't say who made it.'

'And then?' asked Craw, sensing he was getting to the crux.

'Well, sir, then I went up to my room to put my feet up. I fell asleep and the next thing I knew Powell was waking me up. It was 4 a.m.'

'You didn't think of staying with Vaux to see what transpired?'

'I honestly thought he was in for the night—probably a dinner with Manning, drinks, and then to bed. That's what he's done on numerous other nights.'

'Yes! But not last night, Greene.' Craw was pacing the room now, hands gripped behind his back, in two minds whether to inform Sir Walter. Should he burden him with the disastrous news or wait until the full dimension of the debacle—for debacle it appeared to be—were fully apparent? What really bothered him was the disappearance of the Minox spy camera. Did Vaux always carry it with him or did he take it because he was getting together with Kadri and thought he had a good chance of finally getting a look at the Syria-Russian arms deal?

19

Vaux felt almost normal. A clean shirt would have completed the feeling of well-being, but beggars can't be choosers. He waited for Hakki to resume his speech. Kadri made notes and avoided eye contact. It was the opening game in several sets and finally a match.

The sessions lasted for four hours; there was a break of half an hour, and then another session. There were three four-hour meetings per day and then Vaux was led to his garret. He ate some meals in a small room next to Kadri's office, which he guessed was temporarily loaned him by the Russians. Apart from his near certainty that the villa was the Russian consulate, he never saw any of the personnel except for his guard, who chaperoned him around the corridors when he signaled he needed to take a leak or have a shower.

Hakki did most of the talking, but Kadri sometimes intervened to make a point clearer. The object of the marathon sessions, Vaux quickly realized, was to educate him in the ancient, modern, and more immediate history of the crisis-torn Middle East region. Facts were piled on facts, anti-Arab arguments put up then knocked down by logic and truth. Received opinions—many that he discovered he had held himself, almost unquestioningly—were crushed by the litany of historic data, buttressed by objective arguments and examinations. The labyrinthine twists and turns of the Arab *souk* were reflected in the circular but seemingly unassailable arguments of his interlocutors. He experienced a sort of conversion, a new way of seeing and interpreting the tragic story of the

Arabs—liberated finally from western imperialism only to then be dominated by an imposed pro-western, alien power populated by Semitic cousins who seemed to view the Arabs as mere subjects or, at best, second-class citizens. And then it was Barbara Boyd's turn. He was resting on his spartan cot after another round of 'instruction' when he heard a knock at the door followed by the jangling of keys. The door was pushed open by the guard and in walked the woman he used to know as Veronica Belmont. Despite all that had happened, he was glad to see her. She wore a short khaki skirt, an open green shirt, and flat-heeled shoes. They looked at each other for some time, each wanting the other to say something first. Finally Vaux spoke: 'Well this is a fine how-do-you-do, isn't it?' He surprised himself with the banality of the observation.

At least it produced a titter of a laugh. Her eyes darted around the room as if she were looking for something. Then she focused again on Vaux. 'How have you been bearing up, Michael? The sessions haven't been too grueling, I hope.'

'It used to be called brain-washing, didn't it? But since you're on their side, I'd better keep my opinions to myself.'

He was standing in front of the bed and she walked toward him. 'Don't be bitter. You may think I'm a liar, but I think you should know that, despite everything, I am very fond of you and I wish no harm to come to you.'

They stood close to each other and Vaux fought off the impulse to hold her in his arms. 'I don't know what to say, Veronica. That will always be your name as far as I'm concerned. But if you—well, if you have some feelings for me, perhaps you could do me the favor of telling me what's going to happen. What are their plans for me?'

She sat down on the bed and looked up at him. 'We want you to see our point of view. To realize that our cause is just and honorable. If by now you can see things from our perspective then that's progress. But we want more from you. We want you to—you know that English expression. We want you to "bat for us." But we also want you to stay where you now are—in the British Secret Service. You could, if you so choose, help millions of poor, downtrodden Arabs improve their lives, reconquer their lands peacefully through changing public opinion in the West—'

'How on earth could I do that?' demanded Vaux. 'You forget I'm not writing for newspapers any more.' He was half amused, half dumbstruck.

'Tomorrow morning it will all become clear. I think you will want to work with me, Michael. It's not an evil thing we do. It's the only thing that can be done to help the Arab cause,' said Boyd.

'Basically, Veronica, you are a spy for the other side. Is that not right? And you expect me to follow you into treachery, for God's sake.'

'You're being over-dramatic.'

'Let me ask you this, then: why? What brought you to this—a sort of living deceit? I don't know how you can put up that act of pretense and deception all day and every day.'

'I will tell you why, Michael. My mother was English. She was a nurse when she met my father, who was training to be a doctor at University College Hospital in London. He was a Palestinian refugee whose parents were slaughtered in the massacres that followed the Israeli so-called War of Independence. That of course, as Hakki has probably told you, was the first of several Arab-Israeli wars—not just the '67 and '73 armed conflicts that most people are familiar with.

'They married in '58. I came along in '60 and my brother, Neguib, was born in '62. When he was twenty he had a gap year at university. He chose to go to the West Bank to see for himself what sort of conditions our people live in—the squalor of the refugee camps, the aimlessness and despair of ordinary life. While he was in Ramallah, some sort of demonstration took place. Israeli soldiers had roughed up a group of kids they thought were probably carrying weapons. The situation got ugly. Neguib was caught up in the melee and he was shot dead. He was twenty, Michael. In his homeland, doing no mischief, just learning about his heritage and the country of his father's birth. He had dreams of becoming a lawyer.'

Vaux put his head in his hands as he sat down beside her. 'I'm so sorry.'

* * *

'How long has he been gone?' asked Sir Walter Mason. Alan Craw, his deputy, had just informed him that Michael Vaux was missing in action. 'And I regret that turn of phrase, Craw. Most inappropriate.'

'Yes sir. Sorry. He disappeared three nights ago, so he's been gone seventy-two hours, give or take.'

'And you have waited three days to inform me, Craw. That's inexcusable. The whole operation could be doomed. And it seems we've made asses of ourselves.'

'No, no, sir. I don't look at it that way. My sense is that it's too early to say that the operation is in jeopardy. I nurse this strong suspicion that the man's had a bit of a nervous breakdown and that he went on a bender, got mixed up with some woman and is enjoying the break away from all the tension and stress. Don't forget he was never trained for this type of job, sir. And I don't think deception and double-dealing come naturally to him. So he got stressed out and, true to the reputation of all the newspapermen I have ever encountered, got plastered to ease the pain.'

'Well, you may be right,' sighed Sir Walter as he beckoned Major Eric Short, hovering at the open door of his office, to come in and sit down. Major Short, just out of the Royal Horse Guards, was a newly appointed deputy director of B3, filling a vacancy in the designated Establishment. A man Sir Walter instinctively felt comfortable with, despite the ginger hair and freckled face. He switched on the speaker phone so that the major could listen in.

But now the conversation between Mason and Craw dried up. Craw was wondering if the old man had some bright ideas on where to go from here. But Mason wanted more facts and theories about the probable whereabouts of Operation Helvetia's chief operative.

Then he had a thought. 'Looking at this thing coolly and objectively, I'd have to say that you're probably right. However, I want to know what your investigations so far have come up with. I presume you have conducted a thorough inquiry into this potential fiasco?' His eyes fixed on Major Short then rose to the ceiling in a gesture of infinite patience.

'Yes sir, of course. I've put the whole matter in Barbara Boyd's hands. She was close to him, extremely close to him, and if anyone has an incentive to find him and resurrect him, she certainly has. So far, however, she has come up with nothing except a vague suspicion that he may have taken the train to Vevey on a sudden crazy whim to find her. Many men seek solace in feminine company, and perhaps he'd had it up to here, so to speak, and determined to find her. She had said she would be in Vevey at the monastery for at least a week.'

'Why did she do that? I thought she was a key watcher.'

Craw hesitated. He remembered ordering her to make herself scarce so that Vaux could better concentrate on the job at hand. 'I forget the exact reason, but I think we all agreed that she was proving too much of a distraction for him. Better that he get on with the job and get the operation completed.'

'Well, that's hardly happened, has it?'

Major Short stretched for a pen on Mason's desk and scribbled on a piece of paper. He pushed it within Mason's view. Mason's eyebrows rose in interest and perhaps a recognition that the selection of Major Short as a new deputy had not only been a good choice but, in view of Craw's apparent bungling, a timely one.

'Look here, Craw. Let's assume your first theory is rubbish. If we eliminate the possibility that Vaux resorts to booze when stressed out, then we are left with a second possibility.'

Here he referred to Major Short's one-word notation. 'We
could have a mole within our midst.'

The statement stunned Craw. He closed his eyes tightly
and pursed his lips. The last word he ever wanted to hear had
been uttered. And the implication was that he, as the No. 1 in
charge of Helvetia, had been negligent and incompetent not to
detect such a heinous breach of trust.

'There's simply no evidence of that, sir.'

'You've only a small team there—it should be easy
enough to zero in on the culprit, assuming there is a mole.
The third theory I want you to consider is that in fact Vaux was
kidnapped—caught perhaps *in flagrante delicto*. In other words,
they are holding him until they feel inclined to contact us and
make us look like chumps and probably extract a king-sized
ransom for his bloody return. Not to mention the public relations bonanza they'll have in saying the Brits are once again
showing their colonialist arrogance by attempting such a bla-
tant act of espionage.'

'I have in fact thought of that, sir,' said Craw. 'So, with
all due respect, I am acting on two theories that (a) he's on a
bender and/or decamped for Vevey; and (b) that he is being
held by our adversaries.'

'That's three theories, but never mind. All right, get on
with it, Craw. England expects and all that. And please call
me if there are any developments. The last thing we want is
a total bloody fiasco and yet another bullfrogs' chorus. Call
me tomorrow at this time whether there's anything to report
or no.'

'Yes sir,' said Craw, thankful that the carpeting was over.

Mason was shaking his head. 'You know something,
Short?'

'What's that, sir?'

'I never did have much faith in this university contingent we started to recruit in the '60s. Never had the military
background, never knew what discipline meant. Craw's just
confirmed my worst fears. They should never have left Vaux

out of their sight. They should have followed his every move, watched every building he entered, had back-up for the worst possible scenarios. So that if, for instance, he went on some bender, they could have arranged a polite Swiss police escort to get him home—all that sort of thing. By the way, how did you like my reference to a bullfrogs' chorus?'

'I wasn't quite sure what you meant, to be honest, sir.'

'When one bullfrog starts to croak, all the others follow. If one enterprising reporter gets hold of this mess, they'll all chase it like the biggest story since Blunt.'

'Ah, I see what you mean, sir,' said Short. Then he produced a packet of Sobranie from his pocket. Sir Walter accepted the proffered cigarette. Short bent over the desk to light it for him with a quick click of his gold Dunhill.

* * *

Amin Hakki sat behind the desk usually occupied by Kadri. It was still dark outside and Vaux steeled himself for another long day of indoctrination. The marathon sessions with Hakki had revealed a good deal, and the arguments in favor of the 'greater Arab cause' seemed at times unassailable. He had been told that his mind was preconditioned by forty years of propaganda inspired by the Zionists and their U.S. allies. The West (Britain, France) had simply taken the line of least resistance and gone along with the injustice of first recognizing the Israeli upstart state and then agreeing that its existence had to be guaranteed against Arab regimes that had sworn to destroy it.

The problem, as Vaux saw it, was that, despite the Arab's arguments, the fact remained that after World War II surely it was better to set up a home for the Jews than risk another holocaust. The truth was that Vaux had never taken much interest in Middle East politics and what interest he had been able to muster was often stirred by outright horror at the sort

of terrorism that killed innocent women and children to make
a political point.

'Your friend Kadri has just phoned,' said Hakki. 'He wants
to know if it is time, as he puts it, to "talk turkey." In other
words, Mr. Vaux, do you think there's any purpose in going
on with our tutorials or do you believe that we have reached
the point where, shall we say, you have at least seen our point
of view?'

Vaux thanked an invisible but merciful God. Suddenly he
could see his confinement coming to an end. He felt some
positive comment was in order.

'Amin, obviously I now have a more balanced view thanks
to your efforts. You could use some of your talent in the West.
I've always thought that your side lacks good P.R. Israel, as you
know, hires the best lobbyists in Washington, not to mention
the lavish junkets they give to visiting western politicians.'

'Maybe that's where you can help, too. Meanwhile, you
are very lucky to have such a good friend in Ahmed. There
were, you know, other recourses open to us—I'm sure you
understand.'

'You mean, I presume, a trial and conviction as an enemy
spy.'

'Or worse,' said Hakki ominously. Then he got up and left
the room.

The first pink and orange smudges of sunrise were beginning to lighten the sky as Vaux looked out from the big,
ornate, gilt-paneled room. The villa's long lawn swept down
to the banks of the lake. Sparrows and blue tits rummaged for
insects in the recently cut grass. The lake was like a sheet of
glass. Some white-collared mallards glided past in a v-shaped
convoy. Lake gulls swooped just above the placid surface. The
day promised to be bright and warm. It didn't take long for
Vaux to decide on his basic strategy.

Kadri entered, walked over to his usual seat behind the
big mahogany desk, and sat down. Vaux stood up and leant

over, arm stretched out to shake hands. Ahmed gripped his
hand warmly and tightly.

'Let's cut this short, Michael. Do you think we can rely
on you for some real help in the future—the very near future?
Particularly in our efforts to thwart the attempt by the Brits'
intelligence services to basically steal and expose our plans to
re-arm and boost our defenses?'

'I'm going to have to take it one day at a time, Ahmed. But
you can rely on me to do my best.'

'Ah *hamdoul'lah!* Thanks to God! So here's the gameplan,
my brother. You will wander back to your hotel—somewhat
disheveled, somewhat disoriented. Your cover story is that you
had decamped to Vevey to find Barbara—sorry, I should say
Veronica. You had got bored and depressed with all the waiting
games and the on-again, off-again meetings with me and what
you had decided was the hopelessness of your mission.

'You apologize. And you say you will try again. If I know
the Brits, they will forgive you and take the line of least resistance—that's to use you so long as you are willing to complete
the job. Then, my friend, it will get interesting. I will contrive
a way to let you photocopy my armaments procurement deal
with the Russians. Of course, it won't be the real deal, but it
will give them something to think about.'

'You mean I'm to provide disinformation,' said Vaux as
he realized the stark truth and consequences of what he had
promised Ahmed to do.

'Yes, it's what I think your agents call "chickenfeed," Michael.'

'Do I say that I found Veronica?'

'No, of course not. She's been in Geneva all the time.
They know that. You discovered you'd been on a wild goose
chase, so you got drunk, and the next thing you knew, three
days had passed. You came back on the train as soon as you so-
bered up—didn't even take a shower, let alone have a change
of clothes.'

Vaux was silently overjoyed. He was getting out of this hornets' nest; he could smell freedom once again. He thought of the rolling hills of his Hertfordshire, of the green meadows and leafy woods within his purview—once he'd acquired No. 32. Then he thought it appropriate to show some earnestness. 'Tell me something, Ahmed. Why are you dealing with the Russians? Why not try and buy arms, say, from China or even the French, your old protectors?'

'Protectors! Oh, Michael, I don't know whether we've done as good a job on you as Hakki claims. France is the colonial power that ruled us between the First World War and the Second. What did they protect us from? Our own self-determination?' He took a packet of Camels out of his side pocket, offered one to Vaux, and pushed a large black ceramic ashtray to the middle of the desk.

'We have a long history of arms deals with the Russians—from the time, of course, when they were the Soviets. Goes back to the mid-'50s and grew tremendously after the '67 and '73 wars. They built SAM missile sites for us and taught us how to operate them. In the '80s, they installed SAM 5s and SAM 9s and then the sophisticated SS-21 missile systems, which covered the major part of our region, including, of course, Israel. They helped us equip our air force with vital strategic aircraft—MIG fighters and SU bombers. Without the Russians, we'd have nothing—no mechanized divisions, no artillery, no effective air defense. And by the way, you asked about China: in fact we are working now to buy some of their state-of-the-art missile systems.'

Vaux was now impatient to get back to the normalities and comforts of his hotel. 'So what's my schedule?'

'Mikhail, the man who has been looking after you, will take you down to the Quai Mont Blanc where you can start your walk back to the hotel. You will report to Boyd if anything untoward occurs. She's staying openly at the Warwick Hotel and you can work out your own codes. The beauty is that your relationship is known and tolerated, so communications should be easy. I shall let you know when I'm available for another interview and then we'll let you have a free ride over various documents. They are being prepared now.'

Vaux got up, relieved but perplexed. Who was it that said that once you start playing the betrayal game, you are lost? 'One last thing, Ahmed. I presume the Russians aren't interested in me. For my own piece of mind, I wouldn't want them to dream up some reason for seeing me as an enemy.'

'No, they know it's our show, this. We have convinced them we are quite capable of handling the affair ourselves. But if it had gone the other way, there were contingency plans. They had a tramp freighter docked in Marseilles should you have decided not to cooperate. However, I always knew you were a good man. I'm happy our friendship has meant something to you over all these years. Without our mutual respect for each other and indeed my real fondness for you, Michael, I'm doubtful that such a happy outcome for us all could have been achieved.'

Vaux was taken aback by the reference to Marseilles. 'Sorry, Ahmed, you've lost me. What's this about a freighter docked in Marseilles?'

'My dear Michael. If you had not seen the light, as it were, we were quite prepared to spirit you out of Geneva in a car to Marseilles, then deposit you on board the Russian freighter. Its next port of call was to be Latakia, one of our ports on the Med.'

'And then?'

'Then a show trial with all the propaganda benefits flowing to our side.'

'And then the ultimate punishment, I suppose.'

'Good God, no. We're much too civilized for that. A long-term prison sentence, probably shortened by some eventual deal with the Brits brokered perhaps by the Russians. They still have some spies languishing in British jails.'

'How could you smuggle me out of Switzerland? If memory serves, they still have guards and custom agents at the borders.'

'They never search a limo with diplomatic plates, Michael.'

20

Vaux slumped back in the comfortable leather seat in the black limo, occasionally glancing in the rear-view mirror at Mikhail whose face only betrayed boredom. Opposite the manicured lakeside Parc Mon Repos, the car merged into the Avenue de France, which becomes the Quai Wilson as the road winds south along the lake. At the junction with Rue du Leman the car stopped and Vaux heard the snap of the released locks. Mikhail said nothing, but it was clear that this was the point of exit. Vaux had no baggage, so he opened the door and stepped out of the car. He acknowledged Mikhail with a polite wave that was ignored. The Mercedes slowly weaved into the heavy early-morning traffic.

The sense of relief was almost overwhelming and he sat on a bench opposite the *bains*, a public swimming area marked by buoys and floating barriers. A few youths were diving off a nearby jetty into the lake itself, defying official posted advice to stay within the barriers. The beauty of the lake and the sudden skyward propulsion of water as the distant *jet d'eau* sprung to life for another day—a reminder, Vaux mused, that normal everyday existence continues despite man's treacheries and betrayals. He put his head in his hands and for the first time in many years thanked God for his deliverance.

After about fifteen minutes, Vaux stood up and walked slowly toward his hotel. He stopped at a kiosk that sold fresh fruits and juices and bought an apple with some of the loose change he must have had on him when he went to visit Kadri

that evening five nights ago—a time gap that seemed more
like four months.
   Otto Heinz was in the small office behind the reception desk when Vaux walked into the hotel. He picked up the
phone and dialed Room 301. There was no answer so he called
the technicians at the small hotel on Rue de Zurich. Powell
answered. He immediately called Craw at the Bergues. Dorothy told him that Mr. Craw was probably in L'Amphitryon,
the grand restaurant where the hotel provided a sumptuous
buffet breakfast.
   Vaux by now was in his room. He looked for the DO NOT
DISTURB sign on his small writing desk, found it, and placed
it on the outside handle of his door. He showered and went
to bed. Meanwhile, Greene had been dispatched at Powell's
suggestion back to the hotel. He saw the sign outside Vaux's
door as he let himself into Room 301. It was his assigned task
to speak to Craw a.s.a.p.

                          * * *

   Vaux lay in a state of semi-consciousness: he was awake,
but his thoughts were indistinguishable from fanciful but benign dreams. He was struggling to surface and couldn't grasp
where he was. But the comfort of the bed, the crisp and fragrant sheets, produced a sudden realization that he was no
longer on a hard cot in a virtual prison. Then he heard the tapping on the door. He got up and put on the hotel's terrycloth
bathrobe.
   Monica Manning stood in front of him. She was wearing a
business-like dark blue pantsuit and it looked as if her reddish
hair had just undergone the skills of a stylist.
   'Westropp, old-timer! How the hell are you? I was getting worried. Nobody knew where you were—not even Nigel
fucking Nutting, who, by the way, didn't seem at all put-out.
Said you had a habit of disappearing.'

Vaux beckoned her into the room. The tapes at Rue de
Zurich were triggered and Powell wondered where Greene
had got to.

'I took a couple of days off, that's all,' said Vaux. 'Went to
Vevey and took the waters.'

'That's Evian, isn't it?'

'Well, anyway. It's a beautiful place on the lake. Small and
ideal to relax and wind down.' Vaux had read the description
in a travel brochure.

'Good for you, kiddo. Did you ever get down to finishing
that definitive wrap-up?'

'Haven't even started it,' said Vaux, now feeling defen-
sive.

'I heard you were back, anyway, so I thought I'd just look
in. Got to be off to the Palais now. The Russians are making
some formal peace settlement proposal this morning. Dead on
arrival, according to my contact with the U.S. delegation.'

Vaux was beginning to wish he'd never heard of the bloody
Middle East peace process. 'What else is new,' he said wearily.
He opened the minibar and took out a small bottle of orange
juice. 'Like something?'

'No thanks. I'll be off. Let's meet this aft'—around
5:30.'

'Downstairs?'

'Where else?'

She was off, her briefcase bulging with files and press re-
leases, looking forward to reporting on another tedious day
at the international peace talks. Enthusiasm was never Manning's problem. She felt a rush of excitement and elation every
time she saw her byline—especially if it was on the front page.
Vaux instinctively knew this and remembered the halcyon days
when he enjoyed the same professional kicks.

In the adjoining room, Greene removed his headphones,
opened his door, and watched the receding bulk of Manning as
she walked with her habitual slight limp toward the elevator.
He went back into his room and picked up the phone.

'Greene here, sir. Vaux confirms through his conversation with Manning that he did indeed go to Vevey—'

'Ha! My theory was bang on, then. That's all that happened. Nothing serious,' said Craw. The self-congratulatory tone was almost palpable.

'Basically he said he wanted to get away for a few days for some fresh air and quiet, sir,' said Greene.

'Yes, yes. All right. Leave it to me. But please will you now realize that he should be watched twenty-four hours a day? It's your job, and don't let us all down, Greene.'

'No sir. Will do.'

Craw was jubilant. It was a victory of sorts. Mole theories be damned. He'd put Sir Walter's mind at rest. And he'd make it plain that he didn't want any more interference from this new deputy—Major Bloody Whatsis Name. He was pretty certain it was this new man who'd planted the seed in Sir Walter's mind about the possibility of his little tightly knit team harboring a bloody traitor. He'd call Sir Walter after debriefing Vaux.

* * *

Ahmed Kadri had asked Barbara Boyd for a meeting on strategy. She suggested a restaurant in a seedy hotel behind the Gare de Cornavin, which was usually quiet despite its central location. She sat at the bar and sipped a Coke. Kadri walked in and sat at a table. He looked at her as if he didn't know her. He ordered an espresso from a waiter, and five minutes later Boyd joined him. The few people in the restaurant registered no surprise at this encounter—it was that kind of place.

Kadri liked to use her Palestinian name. 'Alena, my dear, how are our friends reacting?'

'We'd better be brief. Now the prodigal son has returned, there's a new conscientiousness among the workers. They never want it to happen again. They've come out of shock with a

renewed sense of duty. I have to report back to the Rue de Zurich within twenty minutes,' she said.

'Let Vaux know that he can come and visit me at the Beau
Rivage. It will be déjà vu, I'm afraid. He'll use his little Minox to
copy the documents we've prepared, and then he'll take them
back and the Brits will think they've discovered the Holy Grail—
everything they'd always wanted to know about our arms deal
with the Russians. No doubt their Foreign Office will protest—
in private, of course—as a matter of principle and they'll go like
a lap dog to the Americans who in turn will inform the Mossad.
All well and good. Our mission is accomplished.

'The next phase involves you staying in place and keeping
a close eye on Vaux. We can't be sure whether he'll stay with
us or, frankly, betray us—and you into the bargain. Do you
have any ideas, apart from the obvious, how we can forestall
any weakness on his part?'

'A mixture of gentle and tough love, I'd imagine. I'll continue to accommodate his sexual appetites, such as they are,
and at the same time drop the odd hint about what could happen to him if he ever contemplated triple-dealing,' said Boyd
in a low, seductive voice, looking into Kadri's hooded eyes as
if she was contemplating a sexual assignation.

'Try and get him over at the hotel tonight. I want to get
this business finished. We're signing the deal tomorrow morning.' He looked up at her and put his hand on hers. She couldn't
know, thought Kadri, that it wasn't a theatrical gesture. It was
in fact an impulse to touch her warm, silky skin. Kadri never
mixed business with sexual pleasure, but he did find Boyd attractive—admirable, too, in her steadfast loyalty to the Arab
cause. He knew her personal history and felt a surge of sympathy as she sat there defying the vulnerability of her sex.

She said: 'Did you ever mention the financial incentives
on offer?'

'Yes. I said he was only to ask you. He could expect expenses and a lump sum at the end of the day. He didn't even
ask how much. But I'll see to it that at least, say, $40,000 to

$50,000 is put aside for him. You have to ask him where he wants it deposited.'

'And as he rides into the sunset, what then?'

'It depends. They may want to use him for another assignment. All well and good. If they drop him completely, then it will depend on what we feel about him. In other words, whether we can trust him to stay quiet or whether he could be vulnerable to certain pressures—such as appeals to patriotism or his own conscience acting up. Who knows at this stage?'

Boyd could interpret the coded language. 'But you're his old college friend, Ahmed. You wouldn't want anything to happen to him, surely.'

'I love the man. That may be hard for you to understand. But it's a love that stems from a very close, youthful friendship; sadly, of course, it's ancient history, isn't it? And this is a crucial time for the collective Arab nation, Alena. So if after all the talk, after all the debates, all the arguments, and the overwhelming evidence that he has acknowledged supports our cause—then if he decides to betray us, the consequences to him would be simply unavoidable. There's nothing I could do to stop the process of elimination.'

They stood up together. Kadri paid both bills and then they left. Once they passed through the rear entrance of the railway station, Boyd walked into a magazine outlet. Kadri walked on through the station's underpass and toward the taxi rank.

* * *

Ahmed Kadri showed his friend and associate Amin Hakki the highlights of the pending Syrian-Russian arms deal. Russia was to supply within a nine-month period the following:

Mig- 27 fighters   *50 — equipped with air-air*
SU-27K bombers   *20 — missile systems*

T-72 tanks   150
Armored personnel
carriers BTR 60/70s 100
Armored recon
vehicles BRDM-2s   100
Self-propelled
artillery 122mm   50
Multiple rocket
launchers 122mm   25

MISSILE COMMAND-ALEPPO

FROG 7s SSMs
SCARAB SRBMS   5
SS-21s
SCUD B miss.   8
SS-1s
SCUD-D   20
Longer range   75

NAVAL BASES: LATAKIA, TARTUS

SSC-3 STYX
Missile systems   5
SSC-1B SEPAL
Missile systems   5
Zsu-23-4 self-
propelled guns   25
SA- 9 & SA- 13
Mobile surface-
air missiles   100

ESTIMATED COST: $4.5 billion.
Delivery by airlift and sealift (Latakia)
Payments to be staggered.
ANNUAL SUBSIDY FROM RUSSIA ['92-'96]: $850 million

Hakki leaned back in his chair and wiped his brow. 'Assad will award you the Order of Omayyad, our highest honor, Ahmed. You have brought off a miracle. These are not the old Soviets. We didn't quite know where we stood with Yeltsin and his gang, but thanks to Allah, they are still our friends.'

Kadri smiled at his colleague. 'You deserve some credit, too, my brother.'

'Come, come. You were the chief negotiator. You left me the footnotes and sidebars—oh, and the financing details to work out.'

'We shall be stronger than ever, Amin. Our aim to hit Israel with an early knockout blow in the event of a conflict should be assured. Meanwhile, if Israel launches a surprise attack, our defenses will present a formidable challenge to them. All-out victory for the Israelis is far from certain now.'

The two men looked at their respective copies of the agreement, a deal that took just three weeks to hammer out. Kadri got up and stretched his arms.

'Now for the other version. The deal the Brits will think we've made. It shouldn't take long to draw up. A few rifles, perhaps, maybe five tanks and personnel carriers, the odd reconditioned Jeep. They'll wonder why they went to all this elaborate play-acting and deception—why they got so excited about our parlay with our old allies.'

'You don't think they'll be somewhat suspicious? They will have found a two-man pill box where they had expected to discover an elaborate and heavily armed fortification.'

'They trust this man Vaux, my old college friend. He's the last man in the world they would expect to turn on them. In selecting him for the assignment they thought he would find it easy to get along with me, to sort of seduce me, if you like, into being lax and open about our plans. After all, they sent him under the cover of a newspaperman—why would I think he was working for MI6? We were both left-wingers in our university days and they played on the fact that we had so

much else in common. Without Alena, of course, I may have
fallen for the ruse—in the sense that I probably would have
been tempted to give him some exclusive information to help
him with his editors and enhance his reputation.'

'Boyd was a lucky find,' said Hakki.

'She's the GSD's major asset in London. She came to *us*,
you know. Walked into the PLO offices in Knightsbridge and
asked if she could help. They steered her to us. What poetic
justice! The country perhaps most responsible for the Palestinian diaspora should end up being betrayed by one of its victims. But how typical. Did they not vet her background? Did
they not discover that her young brother had fallen victim to
Israeli bullets?'

'The British Secret Service surely lives up to its reputation—sloppy background checks of their top personnel.
Quite unbelievable,' sighed Hakki.

Kadri said: 'I think the Brits were banking on a big intelligence coup here to impress the CIA. I'm afraid their hopes
will go up in flames. It's quite conceivable, however, that the
hard heads at the CIA will recognize chickenfeed when they
see it. But that'll only make the Brits look silly once again.'

As Hakki got up to leave, he pushed various documents
into his briefcase and shook on his jacket. 'I'll get the car back.
Are you going to walk, Ahmed?'

'Yes, I think so. I need some exercise. By the way, how are
we going to find that $4.5 billion? Any idea?'

'The Russians have been very good. They say it's a sort of
lend-lease deal. We pay them back the subsidies as and when
we can—on a long-term basis. But the Saudis have committed
to helping us, too.'

'*Tamam al-hamdoulilah,* thanks to God,' said Kadri.

Hakki bowed and left the room.

* * *

Craw pored over the developed exposures with the help
of a large Schweizer magnifying glass. His heart began to sink
in disappointment. The copied documents revealed the following procurement requirements of the Syrian government:

AK-47 assault rifles	*100,000*
T-72 tanks	*50*
RPG-7 rocket-	
propelled grenade	
launchers	*100*
Dzik-3 armored	
personnel carriers	*100*
M113 personnel	
Carriers	*50*
Used Jeeps	*50*

ESTIMATED COST: $250 million

Craw threw the enlargements on the desk. He was alone
but heard Dorothy on the phone in the other room. This was
the sort of deal the Syrians could have arranged by bloody telephone! Why come to Geneva? Why go to the fuss and bother
of having the talks camouflaged by the concurrent peace conference that the representatives of both countries would attend? This was a picayune, trivial piece of trade between two
friendly countries—an arms deal that could only meet the
small needs of the domestic police force and a ragtag army!

Dorothy entered the room. She was wearing a gray and
white checked full-length Burberry topcoat.

Craw was mystified. 'Is it cold out?' he asked.

'The wind off the lake is fresh, sir. And I have to finish up
some shopping for your wife.'

'What does she want to buy now?' asked Craw wearily.
He was now feeling the first stirrings of a strong desire to
leave Switzerland and go home. Jessica's shopping bills had
been astronomical. It was as if the anniversary Piaget watch

had been a mere appetizer. He had explained to her that just because everything was duty free and tax-free didn't mean that all articles were bargains. The place was brimming with Arabs—super-rich Gulf Arabs and Saudis—and the Swiss, traditionally savvy in the ways of commerce, simply marked up the prices of their wares and products to test what the market could bear.

But it was to no avail. Her shopping lists came in every morning by phone and Dorothy copied down the instructions. She was handed big wads of sterling and by now she was an expert on the daily fluctuations in the foreign exchange markets. The pound seemed to get weaker against the Swiss franc every morning—nothing, she hoped, to do with her own dealings on behalf of her boss's wife.

Craw read the note. A Gucci watch for their daughter; a pair of Yves Saint Laurent velvet moccasins (size 6); and a Roberto Cavalli patent leather skirt. His heart sank for the second time that morning. 'And how much do you estimate you'll need for this little lot?'

Dorothy was happy to allay some of his worst fears. 'The Gucci watch will be quite cheap, really. It's just the name. Probably under £500. The shoes and skirt may come to a total of £1,000—to be on the safe side, sir. I'll bring the change back, if any.'

'I suppose I should be thankful for small mercies, Dorothy.' He found another £2,000 in the safe and waved her goodbye.

21

Vaux had no idea what to expect. Would the phony documents raise a warning signal, a doubt about their authenticity that would inevitably reflect on his own integrity? Or would Craw and Co. believe that he, Vaux, had been hoodwinked into thinking he'd taken copies of the real deal? Would they think him a naïve clown or would they give him full marks for trying. On the other hand, perhaps they would settle for what he had finally delivered: they would take the evidence as genuine, decide they had built the deal up in their own vivid imaginations, had over-reached in their ambitions—driven perhaps by the fervent, pervasive goal of showing the skeptical American cousins how clever they were.

His self-agonizing would soon be over. Craw had called him, congratulated him, and told him to come over to the Hotel des Bergues around 3 p.m. Meanwhile he lay on the bed, wrapped in the terrycloth bathrobe, patiently waiting for Barbara Boyd to finish in the bathroom.

She had come over—in blue jeans and white t-shirt, very European—at 11a.m. She gave him a wan smile, stripped off her clothes, and silently went about her debugging plan: she reached up to the top of the armoire, grabbed the tiny button microphone, and put it in the safe. She shut the safe door and turned the lock. Then she grabbed two thick blankets from the bottom drawer of a chest by the side of the bathroom door. She produced some masking tape and attached the blankets to the connecting door between Vaux's room and No. 301. She quickly went into the bathroom and turned on all the taps plus the shower. She left the bathroom door open. She went over to the phone. She picked up the receiver, unwound the mouthpiece, and plucked out the tiny mike. Then she jumped triumphantly into the still unmade bed, her jeans and t-shirt in an untidy pile on the floor. Vaux had watched the debugging process without saying a word. He wondered why his own side should have wanted to listen into his life but supposed it had all been for his protection.

He opened a small bottle of Veuve Clicquot and sat on the side of the bed while they both drank from the fluted glasses. She had pulled the sheets down, exposing her small, perky olive breasts.

'I don't know that I'm really in the mood, Veronica.' He had promised himself he would always call her by the name of the woman he had met 'by chance' a lifetime ago in the Pig & Whistle.

She smiled and put out her hand to grip Vaux's arm. '*I* am. The last time was, well, the last time we did it.'

'I should hope so. Unless you're also getting it off with Ahmed—or perhaps Hakki,' he said, hoping she would take the remark as the joke it was meant to be.

She decided to take it seriously. 'No, darling. I'm a one-man kind of female. By which I mean that so long as I have something going, then I stay loyal and faithful until it doesn't work out. And that means for both of us. If you are tired of me, Michael, then tell me. This isn't part of the deal—I hope you don't think so, anyway.'

'No, of course not,' said Vaux, knowing that he wanted to avoid any serious discussions about what they had got him to do or whether there was any connection between her professed feelings for him and his surrender to treachery. To forestall the self-examination he knew he owed himself, he decided to play along. He got into bed.

She put her arms around his neck and pulled him down to kiss him. He didn't respond because there was one question that had been obsessing him. 'Tell me something, who decided to plant you in the Pig & Whistle that night, so that we could meet up—the Syrians or my own people?'

'Michael! What does it matter? Actually it was MI6, or to be more precise, Sir Walter and his gang. Of course my Syrian controller waxed all enthusiastic. It fitted in perfectly with our own designs.'

'But why would B3 think it advantageous for me to get together with you—have an affair, if you like?'

'It's their convoluted thinking. They go by the book. I was to watch you, keep tabs on you, detect any wavering on your part to come in from the cold and work for us.'

'I see,' said Vaux wearily.

She was like a gamine, feverish and hot, impatient, hungry to extract what she could from him. It was as if he were there as an extra—the object of her desires and little fetishes.

* * *

'You look worried' she said, pulling on her jeans.

'Well, I am, really. I don't know what the reaction's going to be, do I? Whether they're going to swallow our little fraud or whether they'll give me the third degree to find out if I've betrayed them.'

She snorted at such a silly idea. 'Oh really, Michael. There's nothing whatsoever they can be suspicious about. You both got into the sauce while doing your "down memory lane" bit. Ahmed had got paralytic, and you had to put him to bed. He was stupid enough to leave his briefcase invitingly open, and you quickly copied the documents while he snored away in his bedroom. What could be more likely between two old friends?'

'I suppose so,' he sighed. 'It sounds plausible enough.'

'Well then. And don't forget our work isn't finished.'

'What do you mean?'

'I'm still there—with B3, a prized operative, fluent in Arabic. And I've no doubt they'll try and use you again. Keep up the journalist cover and all that. I'll be your appointed chaperone, darling. And all the time we'll be working for the people we love and trust, the people you yourself now agree have been betrayed all these years and have lived in poverty and without a homeland because we have lost a series of battles. Now we can help them win the final war.'

Vaux looked at her and saw a woman who could instantly change from a sex-hungry animal to a decidedly unromantic political idealist—even a fanatic.

'That was quite a speech.'

'I know you can't feel about it the way I do,' she said. 'But don't waver now, Michael. It could be dangerous for you. I am too fond of you to want anything to happen to you.'

'What do you mean, "waver"?'

'Sometimes your flippancy betrays a certain lack of enthusiasm. Ahmed has noticed that.'

'So has Craw, for that matter.'

He watched her pull on her t-shirt, then shift into her brown loafers. Somehow she seemed a stranger now. A beautiful girl who had so easily led him by the hand into a moral quagmire. He had postponed the inevitable debate with himself, but he knew it would be a solitary conversation between him and his alter ego—perhaps, in his case, Derek Westropp. The idea made him smile.

'Ah! Not so serious now. Thank God for that,' said Boyd, who had observed the upward curl of his lips. She was now putting the room to rights and was about to open the safe. Vaux raised his hand to stall her. He still had something to ask her that he didn't want the technicians to pick up.

'Who do you work for, anyway—Ahmed?'

'I'm a lieutenant in the General Security Directorate, darling. We all have military ranks, but it's our equivalent of the CIA or MI6.'

'Well, well. And don't you ever worry about this double life you're leading? Or getting found out?'

'Such talk. Try and smile again and stop worrying.' She swiftly opened the safe, replaced the microphone on the top of the armoire, tore down the blankets from the connecting doors, and turned off the shower, the bidet, and the gushing wash basin faucets.

'That was a bloody long shower,' muttered Powell to one of the technicians at the safe house on the Rue de Zurich.

* * *

'Come!' shouted Craw as Vaux lightly tapped on the door of his hotel suite.

'Ah Vaux, old chap. Do come in. Sit down. Can I get you anything?'

'No thanks. I've just had lunch.' Vaux sat on the gold-green brocaded Louis Philippe chaise longue. Craw remained standing. He was looking out of the window to the lake.

'Well, I suppose I have to say "mission accomplished."'

'Yes sir,' said Vaux, who had, for now, decided to be deferential.

Craw stiffened, his head held high, hands clasped behind his back, his eyes now focused on the far shore of the lake. 'But I have to say that the whole operation was badly conceived, poorly planned, and shambolically executed.' He paused, turned round, and faced Vaux, who had decided at this moment to polish his recently purchased Bulgari shades. He put a crumpled Kleenex back in the top pocket of his blazer and lifted his head. Craw was looking at him with narrowed eyes.

'However, I do not blame you entirely.'

He is going to let me off lightly, thought Vaux. But he had foreseen the disappointment and sense of failure that the final outcome of the mission would have generated. He had prepared a little speech.

'Look, Alan, I did my best. I can hardly be blamed for the fact that the arms deal that was supposed to rock the Middle East turned out to be a non-event. I did my part, and frankly, I fail to see how you could suggest I was even partly to blame.'

Craw's cheeks displayed a slight flush. 'Well, perhaps I'm being a little harsh. My main beef is with the top brass. The director-general and, of course, Sir Walter, were adamant. As they saw it, this new arms deal would upset the balance of power in the Mideast and set back any real chance of peace for years. And they were frankly astonished and shocked that the new Russia would resort to the same old game as the So-viets—selling arms to the Syrians, giving them financial as-sistance and training their personnel to fly their aircraft and operate the missile batteries. That's the way they saw it. But as it turned out, it was way off the mark.

'Then there's the fact that we've been sloppy in execu-tion. For example, we should never have lost you for three days. And perhaps we could have used more in the way of old-fashioned tradecraft to get hold of what we wanted.'

'But with all due respect, Alan, what you wanted wasn't there. Or so it turned out,' said Vaux, now feeling the harrow-ing emptiness of guilt and betrayal—and wondering whether he shouldn't make a clean breast of it here and now. But he remained silent.

'Your job is done, Vaux. You can return to England tomor-row. Stay there until you are called for an official debriefing in London. I suggest you contact old Arthur Davis since you still have no fixed address in the U.K.'

Craw's ironic tone seemed to imply that he had joined the ranks of common criminals and wanted fugitives in having no permanent abode. He got up to go. As he opened the door, Craw said, 'Vaux—just a minute. Shut the door, please.' Vaux stood, his hand still on the brass handle of the door.

'Did you ever think that those documents you photo-graphed were switched? In other words, could it have been possible that the final deal that we saw was not the real deal at all? That the docs were a sham or what the military would call a feint?'

'You mean a deliberate hoax. They knew I was after the real documents, so they made it easy for me to copy the phony deal?'

'Yes.'

Vaux felt blood rush to his face like a schoolboy whose teacher had seen through his lies. 'I was there because I was a long-lost friend of Ahmed Kadri. Nobody else could have gained entry into his quarters. Nobody else would have been a drinking companion, an intimate from a long-ago relationship. I played the role you had planned for me, and I was perfect at it, if I say so myself. And now that I've produced a mouse rather than an elephant, you suggest they knew what I was playing at all the time. They saw me coming, in other words.'

'It's a plausible theory, what?'

'The big flaw is that they couldn't have known my real purpose. I simply can't believe that Ahmed was in any way suspicious. Yes, I represented a country most Arabs have learned to despise, but he is far too intelligent to cast me as an envoy of "perfidious Albion." I never asked Kadri any searching or penetrating questions that could have made him suspicious. He saw me first and foremost as a working newspaperman, still practising my old profession, if you like. He never betrayed the slightest hint that he knew what my true mission was about. And, actually, he did most of the talking. A lot of it was about the plight of the Palestinians—'

'Oh that,' sighed Craw.

'Yes, that. It's a long-festering sore. They feel very strongly about the occupation of the West Bank and Gaza, and they certainly want their Golan Heights back.'

'All good stuff, Vaux. Remember to include everything they said to you in your debriefing statement. It's vital that we at Section B3 know the way the Arabs are thinking and feeling. Excellent. Have a good trip home.'

* * *

Vaux went to the front desk, traveler's checks in hand. Otto Heinz, looking dapper in black jacket and striped gray pants, looked up from the computer to attend to a departing guest.

'Ah, Mr. Westropp, you are leaving us. I hope you had an enjoyable stay?'

Vaux realized, when asked the question, that he hadn't had an enjoyable stay. In fact, the whole episode, except for Veronica's finally coming across, was one he would like to forget. Geneva had its attractions, but the circumstances were all wrong and he was leaving with his head down and a sense of shame about the whole episode. He now felt a real affection for a woman he may never see again and whom he could put behind bars. He had betrayed the country he had returned to in the hope of spending perhaps ten to twenty years in untroubled retirement. He had found a place to live that he loved and could now, thanks to his putative services to the government, probably afford to buy. Yet he was happy to have found Ahmed again, and despite everything, he treasured their renewed friendship.

But there was this sense of emptiness. In his career he had drawn deep satisfaction from completing an assignment. Once the reporting was done, the articles written and dispatched, he used to sit back and bask in a professional pride that could have been confused with self-satisfaction. But it wasn't that. It was the firm knowledge that he had done the job as well as anyone could—and that came with the inner conviction that, unlike so many world-weary toilers, he had chosen the right and perhaps only occupation in which he could excel. Now he felt the sensation that he supposed a plagiarist might feel—a sense of guilt at taking credit for a fraud.

'Well, yes, thank you,' he lied. 'What do I owe you?'

'Nothing, sir. Everything's been taken care of,' said Heinz. 'Shall we call a taxi?'

Vaux felt a heavy hand on his shoulder. He turned around and was relieved to see Monica Manning—even though her expression was one of stern disapproval. 'Where the hell are you going now, Westropp? Running out on us again, are we?' 'Monica! No, I've been told to get my ass back to London, that's all. The conference ends in two days and I've done my piece. No point in hanging around for the cocktail parties.' 'Why not? That's the best part of the bloody conference. You really are a party-pooper, aren't you, Westropp. Anyway, guess who I'm off to see?'

'Haven't a clue.'

'Our very aristocratic Foreign Secretary, Douglas Hurd.'

'An exclusive interview?'

'Of course, my dear. And I've got some tough questions for the old bugger. Our Foreign Office team have been like a bunch of lapdogs, echoing Washington's line on every bloody issue. Major's a fucking disaster. I never thought I'd yearn for the return of that old harridan Maggie Thatcher.'

'Would she have been any different? There wasn't much daylight between her and Reagan, was there?'

'Oh, Westropp, you're so perceptive. Anyway, don't you think I should read your piece, the wrap-up or whatever it is—to be in the loop, as it were?'

'I'll fax it over when I get to London. And don't forget to ask for a signed copy of Hurd's last novel—that'll butter him up nicely.'

Manning looked skeptical. Westropp was probably having her on. 'Hurd writes novels? What sort of novels?'

'Political novels.'

'Well, I'm buggered. Thanks for telling me, love.' With which she swept out of the lobby, pushed through the fast-spinning revolving doors, and marched toward the Palais des Nations.

PART THREE

22

Ten days after returning to England, Michael Vaux successfully purchased No. 32 Willow Drive. Three weeks later he was sitting on what had passed for a patio (chopped up paving stones in various shapes and sizes) in the bungalow's first sixty years of existence. Beneath his feet a variety of weeds pushed up between the cracks and crevices. He had upturned one of the stones and was mesmerized by the hyper-activity of the suddenly disturbed insect world: red ants, beetles, woodlice, earwigs, and what looked like tiny scorpions—all rudely awakened from their benighted slumbers as they struggled to understand the nature of the earthquake that had exposed their habitat.

Mrs. Parker, who had hired herself as a sort of general help, housekeeper, and cook—with up to now no discussion about compensation—came through the open french windows with a tall glass of lemonade. The late May days had become warm and humid, and during her inventory-taking on arrival she had noticed a case of lemonade in the pantry.

''Ere, sir, have a nice refreshing drink. I've put a few ice cubes in an' all.'

Vaux looked up and smiled. 'You think of everything, Mrs. P.' (She had told him that everyone called her "Mrs. P.")

She saw the swirling mass of crazy insects. 'Ugh—that's horrible. What did you do that for, Mr. Vaux?'

'No reason. Just curious, that's all. They're only bewildered—like we all would be if our roofs were suddenly torn away.'

'Sooner you get that Mr. Grainger to come and fix this place up the better. You should start right here and make a proper terrace like.'

'That's what I plan to do, Mrs. P. He should be here to-morrow.'

Bill Grainger was a portly, red-faced builder, general contractor, and odd-job man who had told Vaux not to waste his money on any 'useless architect'—he could do as good a job and cheaper. All Vaux had to do was to tell him—with the aid of the odd drawing—what he wanted done. Vaux had agreed but warned the contractor that there was an awful lot to be done—from a brand new kitchen to a refitted bathroom and a few internal walls pulled down plus a wide and deep terrace.

Grainger had given him some cost estimates that seemed on the high side. But he'd come with the recommendation of Susan Appleby who, unbeknownst to Vaux, helped herself to an undisclosed 10 percent of the bottom line estimate on all the jobs she procured for her old friend.

'I've left you a lamb casserole. All you have to do is put it in the oven for an hour—low heat.'

'That's very good of you, Mrs. P. How much do I owe you?'

'I don't want to discuss that right now, sir. I'll put the receipts for the shopping in a biscuit box I saw on the kitchen dresser and we can have a good old session when you're ready—and not before.'

'But I'm ready now, Mrs. P. Let's get the thing over with so we know where we stand.'

'I've got to be off now. I'm cooking some scones and cakes for the church fete, you see. There's plenty of time to talk about money later, Mr. Vaux.'

* * *

Within a few weeks, the front garden at No. 32 was transformed into a builder's yard. Sacks of plaster, piles of sand,
copper piping, and stacks of two-by-fours littered the lawn.
A miniature pyramid of gravel rose up before the front porch.
The thunder of falling bricks and plaster, the shrill scream of
drills, and the persistent knock of hammers formed the combined cacophony of the plasterers, the plumbers, the masons,
the tile-layers, and the 'contractors.' Most of the initial work
involved the noisy demolition of walls and old doorways.

Amid this world of hyperactive entrepreneurship, Vaux
tried to lead a normal sort of existence. He slept on a bed
recently purchased from a department store in Watford along
with blankets and sheets. He had very little other furniture
except for a few deck chairs and a marble-topped bistro table
on which, weather permitting, he ate his al fresco meals. He
would usually walk to the Pig & Whistle around noon, the
hour he had realized his work force decided it was time for
lunch.

Most of the craftsmen were self-employed. But a century of trade unionism had inculcated an instinctive aware-
ness of the rights of the British working man. Work started
at 8 a.m., there was a mid-morning fifteen-minute tea break
at 10:30 and then lunch at noon. When Vaux returned from
his own liquid lunch at 2:30, the men were all working furiously in anticipation of the afternoon tea break at 3:30. They'd
resume work at 3:50 and pack it in by 5 p.m. Some of the
more zealous artisans would work until 6 p.m. Vaux thought
it good politics to offer this last contingent free beer. At that
time of an early evening, he'd often play some jazz tapes (John
Coltrane, Miles Davis) that he'd recently bought along with a
small portable radio and cassette player. He was resigned to
a long, inconvenient reconstruction and remodeling job and
viewed Grainger's optimistic estimate of completion ('We'll
all be done by September 1, Mr. Vaux, don't you worry.') with
the heavy dose of skepticism it probably deserved.

Vaux enjoyed his midday escape to the Pig & Whistle. He would usually exchange small talk with Pete or Harry who both insisted (in vain) he should come back to his old room while No. 32 was undergoing its renovations. His first pint of Watney's was often on the house. He'd take it to the back of the bar and sometimes sit in the small flagged garden. After checking the *Daily Telegraph,* he'd lapse into his daily session of self-agonizing. Should he continue his life as if nothing very significant had occurred or should he make a clean breast of the whole miserable situation? If he did so, would he be morally obliged to return the money he had earned from services rendered to HM government and, if so, could he now afford it? He had paid £430,000 for No. 32, and the reconstruction and refitting work would probably cost another £30,000 to £40,000. But then again, he told himself, this isn't a matter of money, it's a matter of honor. It had to be as simple as that. Could he live with his continuing silence, his own private conspiracy that had protected himself, Veronica, and the clandestine Syrian arms deal?

At this point of his self-examination, he would recycle the arguments in support of what he did: Ahmed Kadri was still a good friend and a treasured soul mate. Ahmed had no choice but to do what he did because he was fiercely loyal to the greater Arab cause and probably also to the regime that had given him a good and rewarding career. He and his colleagues were confronted with the report—delivered by Barbara Boyd, their faithful agent—that he, Vaux, was in fact a Trojan horse, sent by British Intelligence to exploit their mutual friendship and use him to glean information about the pending Russian-Syrian arms deal. They saw him as an instrument of the British government and, by extension, probably the CIA and the Israelis.

Vaux would drain the last dregs from his pint glass and walk back to the bar for a refill. Pete and Harry would both look at him, look at each other, and once again mutually confirm that somehow these days Vaux was in another world, miles

away—perhaps homesick for America or Canada or wherever
he came from. Or was it worry about the new house, the cost
of the virtual gutting of the old bungalow? Who knows what
they may have found—mold in the walls, dry rot in the floor-
boards, shaky, sinking foundations? Then again, perhaps he was
pining for a lover he had met while he was away on that Swiss
vacation he had said very little about.

Vaux would go back to his table, nodding greetings to the
odd solitary customer who would return a smile if not totally
absorbed in the pages of the *Mail,* the morning paper of choice
in this particular neighborhood. Where was he? Ah, yes. Well,
of course he'd do anything for Ahmed and he knew that Ahmed
would reciprocate if and when it ever became necessary.

He felt nothing but affection for Veronica—and sympathy for the cruel loss of her young brother. It wasn't hard to
understand why she had become what she was. She wanted
to serve in her own way, avenge her brother's wasted life and
pointless death. But then again, he had an innate loyalty to
England. Being born here, growing up in an English family,
attending a local school and then university—all these things
had a subtle effect on one's sense of belonging.

And after the soul-searching came the flashbacks. How
many times had he sat alone in this bar remembering the days
when he was left outside, perched on a narrow wooden bench
while Uncle Aubrey bought him a Tizer and a bag of salty potato crisps to keep him happy for an hour or two? Often, little
John Goodchild would be with him—they'd both be wearing
their yellow school caps, gray short trousers, and, in John's
case, his usual black ankle boots.

It was some years after the war, but Uncle Aubrey was still
in his naval uniform with three gold braid stripes on the jacket
sleeves and the R.N. gilt crown and wreathed silver anchor
insignia on his cap. With his wife, Iris, his mother's sister, they
had often stayed at Willow Drive in the war and the immediate post-war years. They were a happy armed-services couple;
hard smoking, hard drinking, but always in control. Uncle

Aubrey was Vaux's own personal war hero. He had commanded a destroyer in the perilous navy convoys across the Atlantic,
took part in the famous PQ 1 convoy to transport vital military supplies to a beleaguered Russia, and helped break the
Nazi siege of Malta. And he had survived until his retirement
at the age of fifty in 1950.

Vaux had never minded being abandoned while his uncle
had a few scotches (his usual drink) and socialized with the
locals and Florrie, the flashy, brash landlady who ran the Pig &
Whistle at the time. (Florrie was a man's woman, disliked by
his mother and Auntie Iris and most other local females probably because—to a man—the pub's male customers adored
and loved her.)

Rather than sell out his country, Uncle Aubrey would have
chosen death—probably by drowning, along with so many of
his comrades, in the frozen, roiling seas of the Atlantic. Vaux
knew he lived in another world, that his long-dead uncle's antagonists were painted black and white—first, what he would
have called the Krauts and Japs, then the Cold War Reds. What
would Uncle Aubrey have said about the Middle East mess,
about Britain's economic decline (symbolically, the pound was
beginning another sharp descent against other major curren-
cies), about the Royal Family's sad ongoing soap opera? Vaux
concluded that he would have told him that no matter what
his personal views might be, his duty was to the country of his
birth, a country that despite all its faults and mistakes stood in
the end for honor and dignity. The Empire may have implod-
ed, he would have said, but British history and traditions in
themselves were worth the loyalty demanded of its subjects.

Yes, Uncle Aubrey would have said just that—probably
with more pithy and earthy language so that there could be
no doubt in his mind about how his once tiny and beloved
nephew should act. Vaux was overcome with guilt now, but he
knew the antidote. He owed Ahmed Kadri the steadfastness of
a friend. It also seemed to him that Ahmed's argument—that
the Middle East nations should be free from western meddling

and challenges to their sovereignty—was as legitimate as the struggle of Britain's former colonies for the same thing.

He had heard nothing from Alan Craw or Sir Walter Mason since his return. The promised money had been deposited and they had therefore kept their side of the deal. But so far there had been an absolute silence from Century House and Gower Street. Was the silent treatment deliberate—a ploy to shake his confidence, stir his conscience? And where the hell was Veronica? He had been told to make no effort to get in touch with any of the people he had met at Section B3. Well, they knew where to find him if they wanted to go through the promised debriefing. It would be an ordeal and, if he had come to a decision by then, the right moment to confess. At this point of the familiar internal dance, Vaux could feel his stomach rumbling for more solid sustenance. He got up and ordered bangers and mash.

* * *

On this particular afternoon, John Goodchild decided to have a beer while checking out the schedule for that day's races at Aintree and Cheltenham. Vaux was at the counter ordering his food.

'Well blow me down—you're back then. Where the 'ell have you been, Mike?'

Vaux had studiously avoided making a call at Goodchild's house, figuring that he would soon enough notice the frenetic activity at No. 32 and satisfy his curiosity by seeking him out on site.

'I've been back a few weeks, John.'

'Did you go back then?'

'Back where?'

'Well, wherever you came from originally.'

'No, no. I had a short vacation on the Continent, that's all.'

'Ah, the Continent. Haven't been there since I was a young man. Changed a lot, I should imagine. All this ecu and euro nonsense. Glad we're staying out of it. The Tories are right about that, I'll give 'em that much.'

'Probably,' said Vaux. 'Come on back and talk.'

'Sure, mate. Only one problem. Just discovered I've come out without any cash. Could you…'

'Put it on my tab,' Vaux told Pete as he retreated to the garden.

'What's all this about Mrs. Parker working for you then?' asked Goodchild as he sat down and watched Vaux scrape some baked beans onto a side plate.

'I always tell them to hold the baked beans but they always forget,' said Vaux.

'That's because it doesn't mean anything.'

'What doesn't?'

'We don't say "hold" anything. We talk English here, not American. We say, "Please could I have the sausages and mash without the beans,"' said Goodchild in a phony refined accent.

'I'll remember next time,' said Vaux.

'So what about Mrs. P? She's a real old gossip, you know. She'll know everything about you in no time and it'll be all round the neighborhood.'

'She saw me moving in—well, she saw me arrive. I was cooking bacon and eggs on my first evening and making a mess of things and she seemed like a godsend. She'll be handy, that's all. And I don't give a fig about whether she's nosy or not. I've got nothing to hide.'

Vaux looked up and into Goodchild's eyes. The whites showed a yellowish patina and the lids looked puffy. He looked straight back at him and Vaux wondered if he had observed a momentary glint of skepticism in the exchange.

* * *

He had parked his new black Vauxhall Calibra where he used to park the rental car—just round the corner on a side street. Goodchild made himself comfortable and suggested a quick visit to the variety store where Vaux could buy the whisky he knew he liked. As for him, he'd settle for some beer.

'Don't you want a lift home first to get your cash—you may want to buy something yourself,' said Vaux, privately amused at the suggestion he knew Goodchild would reject.

'Oh blimey, Mike, the missus ran off with my wallet to do her shopping—a habit she never seems to be able to cure. Sorry about that.'

Vaux hadn't underestimated Goodchild's ability to come up quickly with an original excuse for not spending his own cash.

Back at No. 32, Goodchild made the rounds. He shook hands with most of the men, who showed scant patience with the interruption but also a nodding confirmation that they had seen him around the neighborhood.

'What's your son been up to then?' asked Bill Bromley, the master plumber who had tried to apprentice rebellious Patrick. He was belly-flopped on the bathroom floor, trying to get his hand round the main cock of the cold water pipe. The water supply had to be turned off so he could replace the old corroded lead pipes with narrow-gauge copper tubes.

Goodchild addressed the back of Bromley's head. 'Don't ask, mate. Nothing but trouble and part-time jobs since he left you.'

'Yeah, not surprised. Still girl mad, I shouldn't wonder. Like a bloody tom cat.'

'It gets worse. He's going to be a father. Maybe the best thing for him—getting married and all that.'

'Some kids grow up. My lad's doin' all right. Off to uni next year. Don't know where he gets his brains from.'

'Your missus probably.' Bromley gave out a big skeptical guffaw that coincided with a weird, vibrating moan as the rusty main faucet was firmly twisted off.

* * *

Vaux and Goodchild sat down at the recently purchased bistro table on the now half-finished terrace. Two bottles of Heineken had been opened, still chilled from the variety shop's freezer.

'You're really going to town on this old house, aren't you, mate?' said Goodchild, lighting up another Rothman and looking around for a makeshift ashtray. He saw a broken roof tile on the grass beyond the terrace, retrieved it, and wiped it off with the leather-rimmed cuff of his shabby tweed jacket.

'It's where I'm going to spend the rest of my life, so I might as well make it the way I want it now rather than later. Besides the place was a mess—'

'No more so than most of the other bungalows on this street. Look at my place—unchanged since my old dad moved in before the bloody war.'

'If the price I wound up having to pay has any relation to reality, you've got a small fortune tied up in that house, John. Stop whining.'

'I'm not complaining. 'Course you've got this view. All we look out on is that copse that separates us from the field along Watford Lane.'

'There you go again. Most people would give their right arm for a bosky view of an overgrown English spinney. And the only building you see from your place is old Davis's, and that's far from an eyesore.'

'Bloody old phony Tudor—like 'im, if you ask me.'

Out of the mouths of babes—or at least the uninitiated, thought Vaux.

A comfortable silence descended on the two old friends, broken only by constant hammering and sawing and the distant whirring grind of the small cement mixer in the front of the house as the foundation for the macadam driveway (to replace the rutted, coal-cinder path built painstakingly over the

years by the late Mrs. Kingston) was put down. The hubbub
of construction activity was punctuated by loud shouts and
belly laughs as the craftsmen discussed the work at hand, the
latest row with their old ladies, or, among the younger men,
pithy anecdotes of recent sexual conquests of unnamed cool
local chicks.

Vaux looked beyond the garden to the glorious view. It
was a mild spring day and the worries and the self-examination that had obsessed him at the Pig & Whistle seemed to
float away to the distant horizon, along with a few cotton-
wool clouds that drifted across the sky toward London. He felt
the strong afternoon sun on his face and realized that before
long he would have to add a canvas awning to his shopping list:
he visualized long, languid summer afternoons on the shaded
flagged terrace, a tall jug of pink lemonade or golden Pimms
by his side and a good book in his lap.

They talked desultorily for an hour or so. Goodchild
spoke of his boys. Vaux realized that he surely loved his three
sons and was proud of them all. His loyalty to his peripatetic
wife seemed unshakable. So to have written him off as a lost
soul was probably unfair. For one thing, here he was in late
middle-age enjoying what Vaux sensed was a world he would
never know—the joy of seeing his own kids grow up, the sta-
bility of an apparently sturdy marriage, the earthy satisfaction
of winning the struggle to keep one step ahead of the bailiffs
or the banks.

Suddenly Goodchild got up. 'Got to skedaddle, old chum.
Mrs. Goodchild will be back and wondering where the 'ell
I've got to.'

'You won't have one for the road?' asked Vaux.

'Had one too many already. See you.' Goodchild went
round the back of the house rather than through the skeletal
construction that remained. Vaux wondered if the sight of so
many men working their butts off made Goodchild feel uncomfortable.

23

Alexander Vidal Simonds checked into a small inn near Padstow, a picturesque fishing village on the Cornish coast. It was the sort of quaint place he liked partly because it reminded him of what he thought a cozy English country hotel should look and feel like, but more importantly, because it was tucked away in a quiet hamlet, hardly visible on a map yet only about an hour from Bodmin, the railway junction that served Padstow since British Rail closed the town's own hundred-year-old rustic and uneconomic terminus.

A young man in blue jeans and incongruous roll-neck Argyle sweater carried his suitcase up the narrow stairs, unlocked a glossy black door, and informed him that dinner was from 7 p.m. to 9 p.m. and breakfast started at 6:30 a.m. Breakfast could also be brought up to his room provided he left the order on the door before retiring.

'Thanks a lot, guy,' said Simonds. The accent confirmed to the young man that the new guest was American. Yanks weren't all that unusual, he thought, but what did seem out of the way was the man's arrival by taxi rather than a private car.

'Enjoy your stay,' said the young man.

'Thanks, I'm sure I will,' said Simonds. He burrowed in his pocket for a couple of one-pound notes, gave them to an outstretched hand, and looked around the room. The ceiling was low and he had to stoop slightly in some areas to avoid the dark oak beams that traversed it. He went into the small bathroom, again having to duck his head, and did a cursory inspection. He sat on the high double bed and tested the springs. He would sleep well here, he thought. Then he got up and looked through the sash windows. He could see the white-specked blue Atlantic in the distance and the big rollers sweeping into the bay and crashing onto a beach about a mile away. A few surfers in wetsuits were braving what he thought must be the still chilly waters. He looked at his watch and went over to the phone.

'Has a Mr. Lawrence checked in by any chance?' he asked the girl at the reception desk. He was asked to hold.

'Yes, sir. He's in Room 5. Shall I connect you?'

'Yes, please.'

'Yes.'

'Simonds here.'

'Room number?'

'10—right at the top of the stairs.'

'I'm leaving in about an hour. We shall just have time.'

'Great.'

Simonds, a tall, gangly man in his mid-forties, was to most cynics a living contradiction of the orthodox belief that America's society is classless. From a wealthy New England family with a vast estate in Connecticut, a four-story brownstone in Manhattan, and another big spread in Palm Beach, Florida, he owed his Yale education to his father's gifts and pledges to that great university and, perhaps more important, to the affirmative action program that benefited the offspring of its alumni. The loyalty and devotion of such scions of the American establishment could never be doubted. And so, on graduation, he was recruited by the Central Intelligence Agency. He became an intelligence analyst at Langley, and a few months later married the daughter of a wealthy media mogul whom he met at a debutantes' ball at the Waldorf-Astoria in New York. He fathered three sons. His career as a desk-bound analyst did not impress some of his more discerning superiors and so, at the age of thirty-five, he became a field operative under the guise of a commercial attaché. Postings in Beirut,

Rome, and Helsinki followed and he had now been in London just twelve months.

There was a soft knock at the door. Simonds, head bowed to avoid self-injury, strode to the door. He had to tug it open, either, he figured, because the door had recently been painted or because Cornwall's damp sea air had warped the door-jamb.

Before him stood a man of medium height, dark, tanned complexion, short, black hair severely brushed back from his forehead, and a neatly trimmed beard. He was wearing an elegant dark blue Savile Row suit, a white shirt, and striped maroon and yellow club tie.

He was the man Michael Vaux had known in Geneva as Amin Hakki.

He put his hand out to Simonds. 'Lawrence.' It was a throaty, slightly guttural pronunciation and reminded Simonds of the way the Arabs spoke to their hero in *Lawrence of Arabia*. In one of his spasmodic half-hearted attempts to understand the Arabs, he had rented the video just recently.

'Simonds. Come in.'

Lawrence opened a briefcase he had placed on the bed and drew out a manila envelope. 'It's all there. The full details of the Russian-Syrian arms deal. Two foolscap pages—doesn't seem much, but it'll cost them a monumental $4.5 billion.'

'That's just great,' said Simonds, relieved that the business part of his visit would be over in less than five minutes. He went over to the suitcase the bellhop had placed on a canvas luggage stool. He retrieved a nylon Samsonite money belt whose bulging zippered pockets suggested a handsome stash.

'Walking around money. About twenty grand. You can keep the belt. The balance will be deposited in the U.S. account we've set up for you in Washington.' From his blazer's inside pocket Simonds then produced a new U.S. passport.

'As promised,' he said.'

'Thank you. One thing: did you pass on the information I gave your people ten days ago to your colleagues at MI6?'

'About the mole?'

Lawrence nodded.

'Yep. That's all taken care of.'

After a pause, Lawrence asked: 'May I ask why you chose to be so careless as to call my room?'

Simonds sighed. He sat down on the only upright chair that stood by the bathroom door. 'We're out in the boondocks here. I mean heavy-duty boondocks, man. Discovered the place last summer with the family. Miles from nowhere, for chrissakes. Why, it beats an official safe house.'

'Unless there's a tail,' said Lawrence, putting the passport in his jacket pocket and the money belt in his briefcase.

'No chance. Never be paranoid—that's one of the first rules of the big game, or so our instructors told us at Langley.'

Lawrence, a.k.a Hakki, smiled. He had never failed to antagonize his American friends. The pomposity and arrogance were always near the surface. This was a true blond specimen of what they called the WASP species. He would now have to get used to them. 'I hope you enjoy the rest of your stay here.'

'Thank you. Did you come by car?'

'Yes—the embassy's. The chauffeur's an old Cockney and thinks I just wanted a forty-eight-hour break. He enjoyed himself in the Padstow pubs. He can be trusted—especially with the substantial tip I shall give him.'

'Oh great. Have a good trip back to the States.'

'Yes. God willing.'

'Sure,' said Simonds, a little bewildered.

* * *

As soon as Hakki shut the door behind him, Simonds delved into the suitcase to retrieve a little diary. He looked up a London telephone number, grabbed the receiver on the bedside table, and dialed.

'Hello, this is Stateside.'

'Yes?' asked a rather high-pitched voice.

'What books are you recommending for the classics club to read this week?'

'*Nicholas Nickleby.* And the paperback is *The Old Man and the Sea.*'

'Very well. Any pages of note?'

'Yes. Page 429 in Dickens.'

'Thanks.'

Simonds put the receiver down. He got up and fished in the suitcase again. Among four hardback novels and six paperbacks he selected the Oxford University Press edition of the Dickens novel and a paperback of Hemingway's slim classic. He turned to page 429 in Dickens and the first full paragraph on the page. The first line read: *It was four in the afternoon—that is the vulgar afternoon of the sun and the clock—and Mrs.Wititterly reclined, according to custom, on the drawing-room sofa...*

The day's book code was easy enough to understand, but why anyone would want to read such old-fashioned garbage Simonds failed to comprehend. He began to put the consecutive letters of the alphabet above the letters in the appropriate passage until he came to *a,* the twenty-sixth letter in the text, which would represent the real *z.* Then he turned to the paperback. He flipped the pages: the final page in his edition was numbered 127. So the code would place 0 at 128, 1 at 127, 2 at 126, and so on. Double-digit numbers were simple double-ups: thus 11 would be represented by 127-127. The dodgy parts—he was never much good at numbers—came when he had to transcribe a complex number like 3,300, which would be represented as 125-125-128-128.

He began transcribing the details of the Russian-Syrian arms deal.

* * *

The taxi had taken her from the Newquay Cornwall Airport to the Arundel Hotel, a large gothic pile perched on the cliffs overlooking the bay and offering a dramatic view of the rugged coastline. She checked in as Veronica Belmont with a home address in Maida Vale, London. The reception clerk wondered why she was smiling to herself—perhaps the sheer relief at the prospect of a few days in a luxury seaside hotel. When she got to the room, she kicked off her black suede pumps, took off her navy blue jacket, and sat down on the bed. She picked up a Yellow Pages directory and looked for a name among the hotels and b&bs in Padstow, about, she guessed, ten miles away. Tomorrow morning she'd rent a car from the hotel and drive to Padstow on the B3276, the scenic highway that hugged the coast northward through tiny villages like Trenance and Porthcothan. Then there would be the romantic reunion with that wife-cheating, middle-aged, sadistic creep.

Her phone jangled.

'Belmont,' she said coldly.

'Joe says he's returning with Hakki this afternoon. So you must act by noon tomorrow.'

'Will do. Is it confirmed that he met the American?'

'Yes. They met for about five minutes. That would be all it would take. Good luck,' said her controller.

* * *

She had met him the previous summer. Simonds was known to them as one of the CIA's senior operatives on the North Africa-Middle East desk. Her detail was to watch him, make contact, flirt with him and, if at all possible, consummate a new affair. In short, play the classic 'honeytrap' role. Boyd had no hesitation in obeying the instructions to the letter. For one thing, he was quite attractive in that clean-cut, healthy American way. But naturally she harbored a particular dislike for any citizen of that benighted country. In her mind, the Americans were the chief protectors of Israel, bestowed billions of dollars of no-strings-attached financial and military aid, and were willfully blind to the injustices suffered by the Palestinian people. Thus she embarked on the latest mission with a cold heart and steely determination.

Her GSD controller had confirmed that Hakki, on a tour of Syrian embassies to acquaint ambassadors and top military aides on the details of the deal with Russia, had contacted the CIA while on his way to London. Only three days ago, informants had told them that Simonds had arranged to meet the Syrian traitor in a remote area of southwest England. Atlases were consulted. Flights booked. And Joe Baker, the senior chauffeur at the Syrian embassy, was told to report on Hakki's every movement.

* * *

Major Eric Short's first important assignment at B3 was, in Sir Walter Mason's words, to look after the 'B.B. affair.' That was schoolboy code for the suspected defection of Barbara Boyd as reported to an astonished Sir Walter by Russell Cameron, the CIA's liaison officer attached to MI6. They only ever saw each other in times of possible or pending crisis—such as the imminent defection of a British agent. Which was why old Russell was affectionately referred to as the 'cock-up boy.' And this, Sir Walter had to admit, was a monumental cock-up. B.B. had been in on Operation Helvetia from the start; she had helped to suborn Vaux, and she had clearly forewarned Kadri and the Syrians of their elaborate scheme.

Sir Walter had considered Craw as chief handler of the B.B. affair but ruled him out as too close to her and perhaps dazzled by her beauty. After all, she had successfully carried out her evil deception right under Craw's unseeing eyes.

Short was therefore put in charge and left to his own devices.

The only positive and unchangeable instruction he had received from Sir Walter was that the matter be resolved without any recourse to a time-wasting official inquiry, let alone some plodding police procedures. The law courts would be kept out of it, as would the press—which should and would never know a thing. There must be no adverse publicity. The public should not and would not hear of this latest betrayal by a hitherto trusted colleague of all who worked at Section B3. Thus, hinted Sir Walter, the way ahead was clear.

The first people to contact would be the Special Investigations Branch (SIB) who distinguished themselves as a ruthless and efficient service, vastly superior to their counterparts in the regular police forces. They were decisive and effective and would ask no questions once the highest authority, usually the PM's office, had given the go-ahead for whatever ultimate action was deemed necessary.

And so it was that on a bright and warm mid-May morning, Major Short had given certain instructions to Chief Inspector Armitage and his small team of seasoned Special Branch officers from the anti-terrorist SO13 group of the SIB. They arrived in Newquay by road from their Aldershot headquarters the day before Barbara Boyd checked into the Arundel Hotel as Veronica Belmont.

* * *

When Boyd drove out of the hotel's car park, the three-man SIB team, in an olive green Range Rover, slowly followed. They picked up speed as her rented Honda Civic headed for the narrow two-lane coastal road toward Padstow. They were not sure of her final destination but were surprised when, after about eight miles, she swung off the B road into a narrow country lane that, according to the signposts, led to a place called Trevone and farther on to Trevose Head, a craggy promontory on which stood an old lighthouse.

They kept their distance and the Range Rover braked suddenly when the driver noticed the Honda pull into a small lay-by about a hundred yards from what looked like an old stone farmhouse. There was nowhere for him to go except straight ahead, so he picked up speed. As they passed the house, they saw a sign hanging precariously from a tall gatepost. It read 'Highcliff House—B&B'. At the entrance to a field, behind a high slate wall, the driver pulled up.

'This must be it,' he said. 'Now let's hope we don't have to wait too long. Bob, you go and sniff around. Say you are thinking of coming back for a room tonight. Reg, get in touch with the truck team now, will you?'

Sergeant Bob Jamieson got out and walked toward the b&b. Then the driver drove for about five minutes until he found a widening in the road that facilitated a 180-degree turn. Constable Reginald Coleman was so busy chatting on the two-way radio he hadn't noticed until he looked up that the Range Rover was now facing the opposite direction.

* * *

She was dressed in tight black leather pants, black pumps with stiletto heels. A blue jean jacket covered an open-necked white shirt. And she carried a Prada faux crocodile-skin handbag.

'You look marvelous,' said Simonds. 'Come in, sweetheart.'

She gave him a long, affectionate hug. He smoothed the back of her straight black hair and pushed her away to look more closely.

'God, you're beautiful,' he said. 'I thought this place would be nice for our little tryst, but we can always book into something more luxurious if you like, honey.'

'This will do fine,' she said. There was something Simonds found a little cold or distant about her this morning. She didn't seem like her usual self.

'Is anything the matter?' he asked.

'No, just a little tired, that's all.' She took off her jacket and then her shoes.

'There's nowhere to sit, so let's go to bed,' she said.

'That's what I like about you. No foreplay. Just let's do it,' said Simonds with a laugh. 'I enjoyed doing it in the dunes last summer.'

'Too early in the year for a repeat performance, don't you think?'

He quickly undressed and got into the unmade bed. Then he opened a drawer and took out a ten-inch single blade knife. She had wondered where he had stowed his usual sex aid. He was the only man she'd ever known who had this particular perversion. To get a long-lasting, hard erection he had to hold the knife to her throat. He called it a bowie knife, apparently an old Wild West weapon. He never as much as scratched her—the thrill of threatening her with disfigurement or death was all he needed. Or perhaps it was the atmosphere of coercion that powered his libido.

'Let me wash that first,' she said. 'Just in case you nick me accidentally, darling.' She had rehearsed that line for some days and hoped to hell it sounded normal and convincing.

Simonds' eyes widened in surprise. He kissed her small breasts and resigned himself to another female whim. She got up and went into the small bathroom. She turned on the tap. He hadn't noticed her grab her handbag but wouldn't have thought it odd anyway, she guessed. She opened the bag and took out a small vial. She removed the rubber cap. Then she put the sharp point of the dagger into the vial's powdery contents. She held the knife firmly as she came out of the bathroom. He thought she would put it on the bedside table but she still held on to it.

'Give it to me, honey,' he said. The sight of the knife thrilled him. His erection was building, his eyes focused on the smooth olive skin of her throat. He put his hand out to receive the knife from her, but as he did so she jabbed the knifepoint into his forearm.

'Sorry! Sorry!' she murmured. 'Did I hurt you?'

'No, it's all right.' He grabbed a Kleenex from the side table, dabbed the small cut, and looked for blood. A small red blob appeared on the white tissue. She got up and went again to the bathroom. He sighed, more out of impatience than frustration.

She waited, looking at the rotating second hand of the small Longines watch Vaux had bought her in Geneva. Then she heard a groan. She opened the door. He was lying on his back, mouth and eyes wide open, as if taken by complete surprise. It was over.

She riffled through his leather suitcase. The documents were in the opened manila envelope. She took a quick look and knew she had found what she wanted. Why he had come with all those books she had no idea. In the eight months or so she had known him he had never discussed book reading, let alone classics. She flipped through a few pages and shook the books for any enclosed messages but found nothing. In a side pocket she fished out a photograph. It was of Simonds, his smiling, happy wife, and three healthy-looking, blond boys whose ages, she remembered, were eight, eleven, and fifteen. She stuffed the document envelope in her handbag. She quickly washed the knife and placed it on his hairless chest. The local constabulary would no doubt come to the quick conclusion that it was rough sex gone horribly wrong.

* * *

The Range Rover had parked in a narrow farmer's entrance to a field where cattle grazed contentedly. The few trees around had branches permanently bent by the prevailing westerly winds and the ground was wet and soggy after a rainy late spring. Chief Inspector Peter Armitage looked intently in the rear-view mirror. He could just see the front porch of High-cliff House supported by two white stucco columns. Now he had a better view of the parked Honda. They sat and waited. The windows were wound down so that gray-blue wisps of the smoke generated by three impatient smokers dissipated into the warm, salty air.

Sergeant Bob Jamieson had reported that the hotel was quiet. A young man at the desk was the only staff he'd seen. He told him there were plenty of rooms if he wanted one later. The only noise he heard was a television—probably from the guests' sitting room. The stink of the previous evening's dinner lingered in the small reception area and had reminded him of the boiled cabbage in the school meals he'd had as a kid.

'Here she is,' murmured Armitage. He started his engine and drove down the narrow lane to its junction with the B3276. He turned right toward Newquay, keeping the Honda a safe four hundred yards or so behind him. Several cars overtook the Honda and then the Range Rover. As they approached Porthcothan, the small coastal fishing village about seven miles north of Newquay, he told the wireless operator to give the truck team the signal. Then he slowed down to twenty mph. The Honda loomed up behind him, a young woman in dark shades shaking her head out of impatience. Then he saw the concerned face of a driver who wants to overtake quickly and safely. He sat the Range Rover deliberately over the solid, white 'No Passing' line, making it more difficult for the lady to pass. She tooted the Honda's thin, apologetic horn continuously.

Just past Porthcothan there was a sharp hairpin bend. Armitage pulled the car over a little as if to invite the Honda to pass. The solid white line still warned her that it was a no passing zone. But, as he expected, she took her chance—judging that the Range Rover's speed would stay irritatingly slow. She pressed down the accelerator, felt the Honda give a powerful surge, and guessed she would make it before anything came around the blind bend.

But then the Range Rover picked up speed. She saw a huge twenty-ton Mercedes Piefer haulage truck bearing down on her and she gestured helplessly to the Range Rover's driver to let her into his westward lane. But he ignored her as he picked up speed and paced the Honda along the two-lane highway. It was too late to brake and get behind the Range Rover. She heard the loud wail of the truck's powerful horn and closed her eyes to the inevitable. She never saw the impact, nor did she ever hear the shattering of metal and glass as the giant truck crushed the Honda to a flat sheet of metal with embedded fragments of human body parts and clothing.

* * *

Amin Hakki knew he must not relax or nod off as the comfortable Daimler limo purred along the M4 toward London and, according to Joe's instructions, on to his hotel on Park Lane. He had read the *Economist* from front to back then flipped through the *Playboy* he had retrieved from the paper rack at the back of the chauffeur's seat.

As the car neared the M25 interchange close to Heathrow Airport he stirred himself. He took out a small revolver he prayed he would not have to use. Joe's eyes were on the thickening Heathrow-bound traffic. He swung into a far side lane that would take the limo into the center of London. It was time to act.

'Stay in the lane for Heathrow, Joe,' ordered Hakki.

'I was told to bring you back to the Four Seasons, sir.'

'I'm giving the orders now, Joe. Do as I ask.'

Still Joe Baker stayed in the Central London lane. Hakki leant forward, showed his Colt Python, and said firmly. 'I'm asking you to go to Heathrow. You can say I threatened you. It wouldn't be a lie.'

Joe's eyes widened in surprise and horror. Oh Christ, and only six months away from a comfortable retirement as promised by the Syrian embassy after forty years of devoted service.

'Keep your 'air on, guv. Heathrow it is. What terminal?'

'American Airways, wherever they are.'

'It'll be sign-posted.'

* * *

Joe had been told to deposit Amin Hakki in front of the main doors of the Four Seasons on Park Lane. Three men sat in the deep leather chairs that looked out from the lobby to the sweep of the hotel's driveway. A doorman in gold and blue livery, top hat and white gloves, opened doors for new arrivals—some in taxis, others in private cars. Busboys rushed in and out with suitcases, trunks, hatboxes, and heavy fur coats.

One of the men responded to a beep on his pager by walking over to a battery of public phones close to the elevators. He dialed a number and listened for a few seconds. Then he ran toward his two companions.

'The bastard's given us the slip. Walid, get the car round. We've got to get to Heathrow!' Walid Husain ran down the lobby's fire exit to get to the Jaguar XJ, parked in the hotel's basement.

Apart from the location, their orders hadn't changed: shoot to kill on sight. They had planned to surround Hakki before he entered the hotel. Two shots to the chest from two silencer handguns would have completed the mission. Then they were to run through heavy afternoon traffic, dispersing in various directions from Shepherds Market, a warren of small streets and narrow alleyways behind the hotel. Walid Husain, a twenty-three-year-old GSD trainee, was to have casually picked up the Jaguar the next morning.

The three men rushed into Terminal 3, hands tucked into their jackets where they stowed their heavy handguns. They looked up at the big screen that showed DEPARTURES.

An AA Flight 301 to Washington was now boarding. Their chances of rushing Hakki as he got on the Boeing 737 were nil. They had no boarding passes and they'd never get past security. The game was up.

They sauntered back to the Jaguar. Insult was added to injury when an attractive blonde traffic warden handed them a ticket for illegal parking. 'Saves sticking it on the windscreen,' she said cheerfully as Husain put out his hand.

'Thank you, ma'am,' he said politely.

24

London's secret intelligence grapevine hummed with false reports, rumors, and the odd factual truth. There were whispers at MI6 that a top Syrian bureaucrat had defected to the U.S. after giving information to the CIA about President Al-Assad's long-term plans to develop weapons of mass destruction, including a nuclear bomb and nuclear tactical weapons for the battlefield.

In its turn, MI6 had put it out to the cognoscenti that a respected, top operative had been killed by a freak road accident while taking a short but well-deserved vacation in Cornwall.

The CIA, with the cooperation of MI5 and the local Cornwall constabulary, had confirmed to his wife and family and staff at the United States embassy in London that Alexander Vidal Simonds, one of their own, a loyal and patriotic toiler for the U.S. of A., had succumbed to a heart attack while taking a few days off in an idyllic location he had discovered while on holiday last summer. His wife was bewildered. He had told her he was on a top-secret mission and only those colleagues who needed to know would be informed of his destination. But he had expected to be back in London within five days. Mrs. Pearl Simonds, distraught and upset, knew better than to ask any further questions.

Only one man now knew all the facts. But Sir Walter Mason, veteran spymaster and chief of MI6's Section B3, still struggled to make sense of it all. *I have to connect the dots*, he told himself. And in the wake of the long chat he had just had with an infrequent visitor to Gower Street, Colonel John Freeman

(Ret.) of the U.S. Marine Corps and currently head of CIA's operations in London, he knew he faced a formidable task.

* * *

It was a dark morning for late May: heavy, ominous clouds blanketed the city and a constant drizzle added to the gloom. Lights were on in the offices opposite Sir Walter's, and he could see various new arrivals shaking their umbrellas and taking off soaked raincoats.

Ms. Dimbleby, who always thought the tall and handsome Freeman resembled Walter Pidgeon, took his trenchcoat and hung it on the ancient coat tree beside Sir Walter's door. Greetings were then exchanged between Sir Walter and the CIA chief while Ms. Dimblebey brought in a tray laden with digestive biscuits and and two mugs of coffee.

'You asked to see me, John, so I'll let you do the talking.'

'It won't take long, Walter. It's not exactly good news, but the sooner you know the facts of the situation, the better. Then I think you'll agree that you'll have to take immediate remedial action.'

Sir Walter thought he knew what the colonel was going to talk about. So he preempted him. 'If you're referring to our action against one Barbara Boyd, you need go no further. What was done was fully justified. We know we owe you one for discovering that she was working for the Syrians. We didn't want to go the inquiry route, then an arrest and the usual press sensationalism. We had to avoid another scandal. So it was the best way to deal with a lamentable situation.'

'We understand perfectly. However, this is not the reason why I requested the meeting.'

'Oh?' Sir Walter sipped his coffee and looked through the grimy sash windows and the misty, drizzly inner well of the building to a particularly young and pretty secretary he'd noticed had recently joined the firm of accountants on his floor.

'Our man Simonds was killed by a ricin-tipped knife, or dagger, if you like. It was found, washed, of course, on his body. But the autopsy discovered that that's how he died.'

'Good God. Well, I'd heard that you'd lost one of your best men, but I assumed it was one of those sudden cardiac arrests we are always reading about.'

'It was a cardiac arrest, all right—induced by the ricin, the same powerful poison used by the Bulgarians back in '78 against Georgi Markov, if you remember.'

'Markov,' said Sir Walter dubiously.

'The Bulgarian dissident. Killed by the Bulgarian secret service on a London street with a ricin-tipped umbrella.'

'Ah yes. It rings a bell. Go on.'

'Before Simonds was killed he had an assignation with Amin Hakki—'

'The man who tipped you off about B.B.?'

'Boyd, yes.'

'The same man who was with Kadri in Geneva when we were conducting Operation Helvetia,' said Sir Walter, as if that fiasco had been chalked up as quite an achievement.

'The same. The point is this: Hakki has proved enormously helpful to us. He not only tipped us off about Boyd, which we informed you about immediately—'

'Yes, yes.'

'But he also gave us all the details about the Russian-Syrian arms deal—the paramount object of your Helvetia escapade.'

Sir Walter did not much like the word 'escapade' to describe the heroic efforts of his B3 team to penetrate the dark secrets of the Russia-Syria accord. It had been a good try, and the use and exploitation of Michael Vaux had been a stroke of pure genius. In his book, nobody could diminish that achievement. However, the colonel appeared to be pregnant with new information.

'Do go on, old chap.'

'Poor Simonds had the foresight and, of course, the excellent training to encrypt the documents and then fax them to us from the small hotel where he was staying within half an hour of Hakki's visit. He would have hand-shredded the encrypted documents and thrown them down the toilet, of course. The original documents themselves were taken by whoever killed him. But I'm proud to say that Simonds' last service to his country will be remembered and honored if I have anything to do with it.

'We now have the Syrians over a barrel. A propaganda coup of mammoth proportions. Their hoped-for arms build-up—clearly directed against Israel—will soon be in the public domain. And they will be seen as the deceitful, secretive thugs they undoubtedly are.'

With that declaration, Sir Walter observed his American comrade-in-arms fish an envelope out of his briefcase. He handed it to Sir Walter, who quickly scanned the contents. He saw the bottom line.

'Um—much bigger than we thought. If the deal were to be completed, it would, as we originally suspected, indeed change the balance of power in the Middle East. Clearly, in the event, we were totally deceived into thinking the arms accord was a mere shopping list for a somewhat depleted military.'

'Somebody pulled the wool over your eyes, that's for sure,' said Colonel Freeman.

Silence descended as Sir Walter waited for the next shoe to drop.

'And we now believe that Simonds' killer was none other than your Ms. Boyd.'

'She's not one of us any more. But besides that, what evidence do you have for such an assertion?'

'Circumstantial, it's true. She was killed just a mile or so away from the bed & breakfast where Simonds met up with Hakki. He sent the fax to us about one hour before she was killed by that truck. The local police confirm that a Veronica Belmont, the alias she often used, had checked into the Arundel Hotel in Newquay, had rented the car, and had never returned to the hotel. We reckon she killed him to get her hands on the Syrian-Russian procurement details so that our side would still be in the dark about the real deal. She hadn't figured out he might have faxed the documents in code—and even if she had, it was too late to do anything about it.'

'Did the local police find any documents on her or in the car?'

'Walt. The gas tank exploded on impact. She was incinerated along with anything she possessed in the way of records or documents.'

'A horrible business,' sighed Sir Walter. 'What about the people who run the b&b? Did they see a female visitor or any other visitor?'

'The local police say no. But I think that's because they don't want to get involved. Bad for the tourist business.'

'You don't think Hakki could have done it?'

'It doesn't make sense. He met Simonds to give him the documents and to receive some cash—and to be provided with the U.S. passport he needed to get out of the country.'

'But he could have double-crossed him. Taken the money and the passport and then knocked him off,' protested Sir Walter, who for some reason he didn't understand himself was trying to find excuses to exonerate B.B.

Freeman rejected Sir Walter's flimsy theory. 'But we received Simonds' encrypted version! And don't forget that Simonds was found dead in his bed stark naked.'

'Yes. I forgot that small point. Well, then. She got her comeuppance a bloody sight sooner than she could have expected. All's well that ends well.'

'Except that it leaves an untidy end to the matter, some leads, shall we say, that have to be followed up,' said Freeman.

Sir Walter looked pensive. 'How do you mean?'

'To put it quite bluntly—'

'Yes, yes, I always appreciate that in your countrymen.'

'Was your Michael Vaux duped—or was he in on the deception? If he was a co-conspirator who funneled you false information via fraudulent documents, why then some pretty serious action must be taken.'

Sir Walter Mason looked longingly through the sooty windows at the young secretary he'd like to hire if only Miss Dimbleby would act on her oft-repeated threat (or promise) to retire. Colonel Freeman waited for some reassurance that his sister agency would act with haste and little mercy.

Mason said, 'Yes, of course, Colonel.'

'Did you debrief Vaux after the Geneva mess?'

'What mess?' Sir Walter was still in denial.

'Well, I thought we'd agreed that the whole exercise produced a mouse when we were expecting an elephant. Now we've discovered the real elephant lurking in the bushes, and obviously the mouse was put there to run rings around all of us. The big question, therefore, Sir Walter, is by whom. Who put the goddamned mouse under our twitching noses?'

Sir Walter preferred straight talk to mixed metaphors that he didn't understand and he was beginning to feel uncomfortable. 'My deputy, Major Short, is to go down to Hertfordshire very shortly. Debriefing Vaux had been postponed to make time available for other very serious matters concerning Section B3. The B.B. bombshell didn't exactly lift the staff's morale, you know.' He said this in a tone of quirky reproof, as though Barbara Boyd would never have betrayed the British Secret Intelligence Service if the Americans hadn't found out via Hakki.

'I can understand. I shall be in touch. I look forward to learning the results of the debriefing and the vital post-Operation Helvetia inquiry—in the light of what I have told you today.'

Sir Walter, who had known some very pompous Englishmen in his professional and private life, now thought that the American cousins were probably his countrymen's equals in sheer unadulterated arrogance.

'Inquiry—yes. It will be behind closed doors, of course. But rest assured I shall keep you "in the loop," as they say in Washington, I believe.'

'Sure thing, Walt.'

25

A big, unanswered question, more perhaps a conundrum, had hovered like an impenetrable dark cloud above Sir Walter's head since his meeting with Colonel John Freeman. He couldn't quite grasp it. It was like trying to remember the name of an old film star—tantalizingly on the tip of the tongue, but beyond final recognition until hours later or perhaps days, when the brain, like a computer, sorted through all the irrelevant information and permutations and came up with the right answer.

Sir Walter recognized a total defection when he saw one—like Burgess and Maclean. And then there was Philby some years later, a particularly heinous defection, in Sir Walter's view, since he had been instrumental in getting Philby a staff job at his beloved *Economist*. So Hakki had clearly done the classic moonlight flit, in his case to a comfortable life in the United States.

Over the years, Sir Walter had often thought about the fates of Burgess and his cohorts—living their lives out in genteel poverty in dreary Moscow apartments; Burgess with his male Russian lover, Maclean and Philby with their deracinated, disillusioned English wives. But unlike these English traitors, defectors to the rich and now only superpower had it made— new identities, lump-sum payments, and generous pensions for the rest of their clandestine lives.

It wasn't until Sir Walter was reading the *Times* over breakfast at his Westminster mansion flat the next morning that it suddenly hit him. Hakki had fingered the traitor B.B.

to the CIA rather than to the Brits, obviously to curry favor. He wanted to get away from the Middle East, geographically as far as possible—hence the U.S. was his logical savior. Then he had promised them more goodies: the real truth about the Russian-Syrian *entente-cordiale* and the genuine details of the new arms deal.

But why, wondered Sir Walter, if Freeman's suspicions were on target, had Hakki not exposed Michael Vaux as a double-dealer who had gone along with Kadri and the Syrians in a scheme to deceive and mislead British intelligence? Craw had told him that Vaux met both Kadri and this man Hakki who, according to Vaux, was a colleague or perhaps a watcher who sat in on their meetings at the Beau Rivage.

In other words, if the colonel suspected that Vaux was a traitor (and demanded a thorough internal inquiry to find out), why hadn't the over-confident American found it curious that Hakki had never mentioned anything incriminating against Vaux? Sir Walter, decapitating his boiled egg in one fell blow, suddenly felt better.

In his mind, the fact that Hakki had not fingered Vaux along with B.B. clearly exonerated the poor bugger. As far as Sir Walter was concerned, Vaux was clearly duped by his old friend Kadri. He found it impossible to believe that Vaux had conspired with Kadri to deceive his team at MI6. Yes, he appeared to have hit it off with Kadri, and yes, they had been close friends in their college days—but it was now pretty clear that Vaux, after all, could never have deliberately entered into a deceitful stratagem with the Syrians to produce a totally misleading and fraudulent document. Sir Walter had always considered himself a good judge of men, and now he felt reassured that his initial trust in Vaux had not been misplaced.

He shouted goodbye to Lady Sybil, his wife, who as usual had gone back to bed after making him a pot of tea, some toast, and boiling an egg. He had called Major Short and told him to be at the Gower Street offices at 10 a.m. sharp.

* * *

That evening, Sir Walter Mason called his old friend and colleague Arthur Davis. Mason respected the former talent spotter, who had been instrumental in discovering Vaux as a likely recruit when he conveniently arrived back in England for a cozy retirement after a life that seemed to be that of a wandering newspaperman. Good old Davis had seen the man was at a loose end and had successfully engineered the financial crunch that had finally pressured the reluctant hero to work for queen and country. Something about a house purchase, recalled Sir Walter. Anyway, it worked, and Vaux proved an intelligent, conscientious operator who brought home the goods—even if the final outcome of Operation Helvetia didn't live up to its advanced billing.

He told Davis of Hakki's defection and of the CIA's interest in the whole Helvetia affair. He chose not to tell him everything: the sad case of B.B.'s treachery would remain under wraps for the time being even if they were talking on a secure phone. Then he suggested to Davis the desirability of inviting Vaux for dinner some evening this week. The object would be to introduce Vaux to Major Eric Short, the new member of his triumvirate of deputies, prior to the official Vaux debriefing that would have to be done on a one-on-one basis probably in London.

'What happened to Craw?' asked Davis, always eager to learn who was the new golden boy, who was in or out of favor.

'He hasn't been fired, if that's what you mean. He's still one of my deputies, but I've taken him off the Vaux case. He was too close to the shambles in Geneva. He's on an Arabic language course at the School of Oriental Studies or some such. Anyway, it's Short I want you to meet. Thoroughly trustworthy military type. Ex-Guards, of course.'

Sir Walter couldn't know that Davis detested those of Short's ilk even more than the university types whom he still blamed for his lack of progress on the promotion ladder.

Sir Walter continued: 'Now, Arthur, I want to pick your brains.' He told him of Hakki's revelations about the Russian-Syrian arms deal and of the CIA's suspicions that Vaux might have been seduced into a conspiracy to plant the false intelligence that led MI6 finally to dismiss Syria's modest military shopping list as insignificant.

There was a pause on the other end of the line. Sir Walter sighed as he heard the tinkling of ice cubes and the familiar sound of someone taking a long pull at a good drink. He thought he'd let Davis know of his sensitive powers of detection. 'Bit early for that, isn't it?'

'This is a Coke, believe it or not,' said Davis, cursing the old man's perceptiveness. In any case, even if the sun wasn't over the yardarm, it was 5:30 p.m., for God's sake. He put the whisky down gently on the sidetable. Mrs. Fletcher, who at the time happened to be whisking a feather duster over various pieces of furniture, gave a look of disapproval and quickly placed a silver coaster under the old-fashioned.

'Well, Arthur. Any thoughts?'

'I can understand their suspicions. They're like that, aren't they? Paranoia reigns supreme in the U.S. intelligence agencies—in the whole bloody country for that matter. Now they've beaten the Soviets, they're looking for other fish to fry—new enemies under every bed. So they latch on to this chap Hakki, think the sun shines out of his arse and believe everything he chooses to tell them—'

'Yes, but Arthur, my point is just the opposite. Hakki has not suggested that Vaux cheated on us. It's Colonel Freeman who has raised suspicions. Don't you think that if Hakki in fact had uncovered Vaux, Freeman wouldn't have gloated even more? They just relish telling us that we're a bunch of incompetents, you know that. They'll never forgive us for the series of fiascos that started with Maclean and Burgess and went on through Philby and Blake.'

His mention of Blake prompted bitter memories. Blake's particular treason had produced a horrific and singularly disastrous episode in the annals of bungled joint MI6/CIA operations.

'That bloody tunnel dig under Berlin was supposed to be the greatest post-war intelligence coup by any major intelligence organization. 1956 I think it was, and here we were, full and equal partners with the CIA, tapping into the Soviet's telephone communications—orders from the Kremlin to the Soviet Army command in East Berlin and reports from spies to their controls all over Europe. What a bloody total disaster. Aptly called Operation Gold. Fool's gold, more like. From day one, our own Mr. George Blake, the secretary to the planning committee, told the Russians every damn thing there was to know. They laughed their heads off as we toiled away in a joint exercise, working to regain the Americans' confidence after the debacles of the '50s. They fed us false leads, encrypted key messages in new codes, gave us a load of chickenfeed—until one bright spring morning they entered the tunnels in the eastern zone and we all had to scarper like scared rats in a sewer. It smelled like a bloody sewer, too, if you remember.'

'No, I never visited—stuck behind my desk as usual,' said Davis, who fully understood Sir Walter's lament.

'Where the hell was I?' murmured Sir Walter. 'Ah yes. I suppose what I'm trying to say is this: if this Arab, Hakki, gave the genuine article about the arms deal to our American friends—essentially the price for taking him under their wing—why, if Vaux had been a party to the deception perpetrated on us in Geneva, did Hakki choose not to reveal this small fact along with the mother lode? Doesn't it suggest that Freeman's suspicions are groundless?'

'I see what you mean. I think you're probably right. But there could be other motives involved. I've dealt with defectors over the years—East Europeans who came over to our side to become double agents. They're a devious lot, Sir Walter. This man Hakki could simply be keeping other information that he knows would be useful to us under his bloody hat.

More arrows in the quiver, so to speak. Why should he spill all the beans in one go? He could simply be playing it canny to protect himself. The more information he dribbles out slowly, the more assured he'll be that they'll feel they need him.'

'Maybe, Arthur. You're right, by God, traitors are a deceitful lot of two-timing bastards.'

* * *

As Davis put down the receiver and replaced it in the drawer, Michael Vaux was making his way over Watford Lane after one of his long late-afternoon liquid lunches at the Pig & Whistle. Davis caught sight of him through his leaded windows, put his drink down, and rushed out of the house. Vaux was just disappearing round the corner when he shouted his name.

'Oh, hi, Arthur. Long time no see.'

'Yes. Hear your house is going well. Old Goodchild keeps me posted.'

'Well, these things never go fast enough, but we're making progress. The bills mount by the day. A veritable money pit.'

'I can imagine. Look here, Vaux, I'm having a small dinner party on Wednesday. I'd love you to come. Perhaps when the guests have left we can chat about your experiences. I'm a bit surprised that you never contacted me when you got back from that assignment.'

Vaux felt a pang of guilt. He hadn't got in touch with Davis because he didn't want to have to spin another phony version of what really happened in Geneva. He had a natural aversion to repeating falsehoods and so he had avoided anyone who might be curious about the ultimate outcome of Operation Helvetia. As far as he was concerned, he'd been paid by both sides, could now afford his renovated dream house, and, although he knew it was probably a forlorn hope, did indeed

pray that the whole episode would evaporate under 'the sheltering sky.' (He had been reading Paul Bowles' *The Sheltering
Sky*, a novel about three young Americans in Morocco, recommended by Ahmed during one of those long late-night discussions at the Russian delegation's villa in Geneva.) But he now
realized that shunning a man like Davis would only help stir
any suspicions that might be lurking in the corridors of Century House—or in Davis's own shrewd mind.

'I'm sorry about that, Arthur. I've been so damn busy
with the house these past few weeks. I'll make it up to you by
accepting the invitation.'

'Very well, old chap, around 7 p.m., Wednesday.' Davis
walked back over the gravel pathway to his house. But he felt
uneasy. Vaux had clearly been avoiding him—yet Vaux was intelligent enough to know that an old hand like himself would
recognize such obvious evasive tactics. If he really had something to hide, he would have acted in just this way. He would
have wanted to avoid anyone who was curious about the final
outcome of his engagement with the firm. And Davis had been
his recruiter. Sir Walter had told him that Vaux hadn't yet been
fully debriefed—which he found curious in itself. Perhaps
Major Eric Short will fill in a few blanks.

* * *

When he got back to No. 32, Mrs. Parker, busy rubbing
down the new Aga range, pulled out a postcard from the pocket of her flowered blue and white apron. 'Right name, wrong
address, sir. It's been sitting at No. 23, opposite, these past few
days. They apologize. Give it to me this mornin'.'

The postcard came from Newquay. It showed a wide
crescent of golden sand with children playing catch-ball
and building big sand castles with towers, battlements, and
moats. It wasn't signed. The handwriting was neat and elegant.
It read:

I hate the idea of causes, and if I had to choose
between betraying my country and betraying
my friend, I hope I should have the guts to
betray my country. —E.M.Forster

Mrs. Parker went on wiping down the dusty surface of the
new stove. He was vaguely familiar with the quotation and had
read Forster's *Where Angels Fear to Tread* ages ago—probably, he
guessed, as part of his 'A' levels.

He looked over at Mrs. Parker to see if she was betraying a
natural curiosity. But she had clearly decided to mind her own
business. Her head was thrust into the depths of the big oven
as she searched for any unpleasant grime accumulated while
the appliance sat in the showroom. Vaux recalled John Goodchild's friendly warning about Mrs. P.'s news-gathering and
broadcasting talents. He put the card in his blazer pocket.

Then, amid the sudden clatter of falling bricks as one more
wall was demolished, he went to find Grainger, the building
foreman. Another list of 'Things to be purchased' if the job
was to be done to Mr. Grainger's satisfaction would help to
keep his mind off the anonymous and mysterious postcard.

26

The contractors had been given the afternoon off. Vaux had suggested to Major Short that they meet at 3 p.m. They would sit on the newly built terrace. The day before, the yellow and white striped awning had been erected. Vaux was already enjoying the shade it provided. The sun was strong this mid-June afternoon and the day had promised to be one of those close, windless, humid days when the English begin to think about air conditioning but put the thought out of their minds when the weather turns more typically temperate a few days later.

Vaux had acquired a square, glass-topped table with white cast-iron legs to replace the second-hand, stained bistro table he had used while the new flagstones were being laid. The table sat low to the ground, surrounded by white-painted, cushioned rattan chairs. The french doors to the now enlarged sitting room were open and new double sliding doors from what was originally the back bedroom also gave access to the wide patio.

Mrs. Parker, who today wore a white kerchief around her grizzled locks, ushered Short into the living room and out to the terrace. He was wearing a blue blazer, an open white shirt, and khaki cavalry twills. Vaux had been reading the final depressing chapters of *The Sheltering Sky*. He put the book down and the two men shook hands.

'That was quite a dinner old Davis put on. The people round here seem very nice. Good choice of place to retire to, I should think,' said Short, assuming, thought Vaux, such pleasing remarks would break the ice.

Davis had invited some familiar faces. Susan Appleby, the estate agent, was there along with Ann Whitely, accompanied by her husband, Brian, the young doctor who worked for *Médecins Sans Frontières*. Vaux had detected for the first time a sort of intimacy between old Davis and the house agent, while Ann's attitude toward Susan was icy. Peggy Brown from the local supermarket was her usual cheery self, oblivious to both the hostile and the friendly crosscurrents that Vaux's attuned antennae had picked up.

But on the whole, it was an enjoyable evening, jarred for Vaux by Susan Appleby's blithe remark that the developer who had been his second antagonist in the price war for No. 32 had failed to get the local council's planning permission to tear down the bungalow and build a large two-story house. So he had eventually withdrawn from the battle.

'So why on earth did I have to pay what I did if I was competing against no other bidder?' he had asked in a low voice.

'He withdrew his offer just days after the Kingston boys accepted your own bid. So you won the war, but the enemy was in retreat already. It was too late legally to go back to square one, as it were. Isn't that right, Arthur?'

Davis had been listening to Short praising the merits of his new Volvo while also monitoring the conversation between Vaux and Susan. The exchange had gone far enough. Susan was treading on thin ice, and with three large gins down her already, he had to shut her up. He turned his head. 'None of it had anything to do with me. But that's what I heard from my solicitor friend who acted for the developer. Now children, no more shop talk tonight. Susan, a refill?'

Major Short, red-haired and freckled, looked young and vigorous, and portly Peggy took to him immediately. Vaux, knowing Short's true mission, felt for the man but was grateful that the social setting obviated any possibility of his bringing anything up to do with the firm.

In any case, Davis's sense of security was in full throttle, at no time hinting that the two men might need some privacy to talk or discuss things. They had nothing in common—this ex-professional soldier and the former newspaperman—except that they both were his friends. So there was no way that his guests would be able to report that the two men, later in the evening, had huddled together in the library for a quiet secretive chat. Vaux had also avoided the post-prandial talk Davis had said they might have (in the hope of hearing Vaux's version of the Operation Helvetia balls-up) by taking up Peggy's offer of a lift back to No. 32.

Vaux agreed that it had been a pleasant evening. 'Can we get you something?'

Mrs. Parker waited for the order. 'Just a mineral water, if you have it.'

'You, sir?'

'I'll have the same, Mrs. Parker. Thank you.'

'No one else here, I presume,' said Short, looking around him and back into the sitting room.

'No, the workmen have got the afternoon off. We're completely alone. Mrs. P will be busy in the kitchen. She likes experimenting with the new Aga. One-pot meals, she calls them. I just heat them up when I want them.'

'Of course, you could get a wife.' Vaux looked at him sharply. A busybody remark that didn't augur well for the interrogation ahead.

'Anyway, old chap, I think you ought to know that Sir Walter would like to see you very soon in London for an official debriefing. Today's little chat will be just a preliminary fact-finding question-and-answer session.'

'Under oath?' Vaux thought it was his turn to make a smart-ass remark. But Short took what he said seriously.

'No, that won't be necessary.'

Mrs. P came in with a large bottle of chilled Strathmore mineral water and two long-stemmed wine glasses. A small white plastic bucket contained irregular pieces of ice spewed

out by the new icemaker. She exited through the newly installed sliding doors, making sure the fly screens were closed
after her. Vaux was amused by the window-fitter's insistence
on the American-style metal meshes, particularly since the
original french windows were left wide open for the moths,
butterflies, houseflies, and even the odd dragonfly to enter
and peruse the décor and otherwise enjoy the coolness of the
rooms and passageways of the bungalow.

'The questions that have arisen and which need some
sort of resolution are fairly obvious in the light of subsequent
events.'

'What subsequent events are you referring to?'

'Let's start from the beginning.' Short grabbed some ice
from the bucket. Mrs. P had forgotten the new plastic tongs
Vaux had bought to match the ice bucket. Short looked toward the garden and on to the green meadows that stretched
for miles. The day's heat was beginning to generate a shimmering veil over the countryside.

'God, you have a wonderful view, Vaux. I can understand
why you fell in love with the place as you were saying last
night.'

Vaux did not reply. He waited for Short to get on
with it.

'A few weeks ago, the Americans came to us with some
intriguing and disturbing information. The intriguing bit was
the news that a man called Amin Hakki, a Syrian diplomat, had
come over to our side.'

'Good God,' said Vaux. He immediately felt concerned
for Ahmed. What could it mean for him? Kadri and Hakki
were colleagues and friends. And then it dawned on him:
Hakki could have told them everything. The luxury of debating with himself over lunch at the Pig & Whistle had suddenly
been taken away. His decision whether to confess all and rid
his conscience of the burden—for burden it was becoming—
could now be out of his hands.

Short related the story of Hakki's defection. How he had revealed the full dimensions of the Russian-Syrian arms deal and, by implication, how misleading and false were B3's assessments based on the information Vaux had supplied.

Vaux listened carefully. At no time was any hint given that they knew, through Hakki's debriefings, what game he and Kadri had played.

'So it looks to us that the Syrians saw you coming, doctored the documents, and gave them to you on a platter.'

Vaux shook his head in feigned disbelief. 'Son of a bitch,' he muttered.

'Did you ever suspect that this might be the case? I mean at the time you were able to gain access to the details of the arms deal, did it occur to you that it was all too easy?'

Echoes of Alan Craw's quickie debriefing in the immediate aftermath of Operation Helvetia, mused Vaux. 'Not really, no. Kadri got blind drunk that night. He was paralytic. I had to put him to bed and the documents were just sitting there in the other room. He had a large suite. I shut the bedroom door after stripping off his pants and socks and putting him under the sheets. He hadn't a clue about my mission, I'm convinced of that. He was an old friend and we hit it off so well that I actually felt bad about betraying his trust.'

Short nodded, sipped some water. 'You like the Arabs, don't you?'

Vaux pondered the question and tried to compose an answer that would block the direction Short seemed intent on going. 'I knew Ahmed Kadri at university. We were in the same department, went to the same lectures. He helped me in my weak subjects—statistics, for one. I helped him get over the disadvantage of English being his second or perhaps, after French, I should say third language. We were both young and we both discovered that despite vastly different upbringings and backgrounds, we had a lot in common. We traveled together in the summer vacations, we partied together. What

more can I say? If you mean to ask whether I hold any preju-
dices against the Arabs in general I'd have to say no, of course
not. Anymore than I dislike Pakistanis or Indonesians or Span-
iards.'

'Good, good,' said Short.

Vaux wanted to leave the matter there. It was dangerous
territory.

Short took a deep breath. 'I have to tell you that the
Americans want a full internal inquiry into the episode. They
have a bee in their bonnet and I think you ought to know what
it entails. They have raised the possibility that in fact you knew
the documents were phony and that to help Kadri and his Syrian masters you colluded in the fraudulent misrepresentation
of the Russian-Syrian arms deal.' Short's eyes were focused
closely on Vaux to detect his reaction.

'That's total baloney,' said Vaux as he stood up to close the
french windows. Several clouds of gnats had suddenly invaded
the garden and he didn't want to play host to them along with
the other flying insects. And the practical, nonchalant act
seemed a fitting accompaniment to his casual dismissal of the
Americans' outrageous charge.

Short adopted the pose of an English gentleman. 'Not to
worry. I'm sure you'll be exonerated from any such allega-
tions. We of course don't agree with the Americans. But sometimes we have to accede to their requests. If we don't, you
understand, they get quite uptight and threaten to withhold
cooperation in other security matters which could be vital to
us.'

'I understand,' said Vaux.

Vaux felt relieved. He could not have foreseen Major
Short's next question.

'You know a woman named Veronica Belmont, I believe?'

Vaux suddenly had to think hard about what they knew
of his association with the beautiful Arab exile and what
he must conceal to protect her. He took a Camel out of its

yellow and white pack and wondered whether the depiction of
the burdened camel in front of the Egyptian pyramids marked
him in the major's eyes as an Arab lover. He didn't offer Short
one because he had learned at Davis's place that he was a non-
smoker. He lit the cigarette with a match from a big box of
Swan Vestas. It had given him time to think.

'Yes, indeed. Met her right here at the pub opposite Davis's house. It's a sort of b&b and I stayed there when I first
came over. Before I finally bought the house.' He knew he had
to block all the other painful facts he had learned about her
sad life except what she had initially told him when they first
met and later when she suddenly showed up in Geneva. Nothing else.

'She was staying there too?'

'No, no. She was just having a drink at the bar. She was
working at St. Alban's Cathedral. An archivist. PhD and all
that. Anyway, she was doing some sort of study on medieval
manuscripts for a research outfit.'

'Did the first meeting lead to what one would call a relationship?'

'Sort of. But what's all this got to do with Operation Helvetia?'

'She was seen with you in Geneva. We are curious people.
We wondered why.'

'That's easy. Her research took her to some monastery in
Vevey. The old abbot there had given her permission to look
at some ancient parchments that hadn't seen the light of day
since 1300 or something like that.' (Vaux had forgotten Veronica's actual but phony pretext: to look at a diary kept by St.
Alban about his eighth-century travels across Europe to Switzerland.) 'So she looked me up, having learned that I was on a
freelance assignment covering the Geneva peace conference.
My official cover, if you recall.'

Major Short looked down at his polished brogues. He
was no actor and couldn't hide his skepticism. He was on the
brink of telling Vaux that they had discovered she was a mole

but then remembered that Vaux had never learned of her undercover work for MI6. And, of course, Vaux still presumably
counted her among the living. The shock of B.B.'s real job, her
betrayal and subsequent demise, could wait for the appropriate moment.

After a pause, Short said, 'Well, that about wraps it up,
old chap. Thanks for seeing me. All the luck in the world with
the new house. I can see you've spent a lot of money on it. I'll
be in touch.'

With that he walked through the living room to the front
door. He had parked a white Volvo 960 on the curb in front of
the bungalow. Vaux waved him goodbye from the porch and
couldn't believe how quiet the place was without the usual
shouts, bangs, and crashes of the construction gang.

* * *

At about 7 a.m. the next day Vaux lay in his new bed,
listening to the excited morning birdsong. He felt a coolish
breeze come in from the open top windows. His first thought
was of the Short inquisition. And then of Veronica. What had
become of her? Why hadn't she contacted him? He couldn't
call her at Century House because he wasn't supposed to know
she worked for the firm. And what was behind Short's questions about her? Had she sent that postcard from Newquay?
Forster's literary edict made the sort of subtle, encouraging
point she would want to make.

Then he heard cars and vans driving up as some of the
contractors arrived early. Doors slammed and heavy construction boots thumped on wooden floors. His eyes were still
closed when he felt a sudden light punch on the stomach, followed by three or four on the chest, a whining, complaining
sort of moan and then wet, spongy licks on his nose, eyelids,
and lips. It was Rex, the Goodchild dog, who had scampered
in ahead of Patrick to wake him up. Rex was eager to sample

the meaty leftovers Vaux usually gave him before Mrs. Parker turned up for work. The reasons for Vaux's generosity were twofold: Mrs. P couldn't accuse him of eating too little or not liking her one-pot creations. And he liked young Rex.

Patrick Goodchild had recently showed up for odd jobs around the bungalow, usually applying white glossy paint to the new doors and wood paneling that were being installed. His father had got him the job in the hope that it would last a good six months or so. Patrick's worthy plan to marry Betty, the mother-to-be of his child, necessitated a fatter bank account than he'd been able to accumulate to date.

Vaux had asked John if he'd like to tidy up the overgrown garden, but John had declined. He had said that Davis's big spread was all he could manage and suggested Patrick could cut a fine hedge, tend to a flower bed, and mow the grass as good as anyone. But Vaux sensed that it was their boyhood friendship that prevented John from volunteering his services. He was too proud to come and do manual work for his old friend. Vaux understood.

27

By late July, Vaux had heard nothing more from Major Short. He had been waiting for the call to summon him to Century House, and he had given the pending 'internal inquiry' a lot of thought. After hours that became days and weeks, he had finally decided to make a clean breast of everything. He would admit that his close friendship with his old college friend had made him particularly vulnerable. He had agreed to his leading role in Operation Helvetia partly out of a basic loyalty to Britain and indeed what he acknowledged he owed the British state. But he had never been a patriot in the Colonel Blimp sense—*My country, right or wrong!* And so it wasn't too difficult for the Syrians to lure him into their scheme of deception.

He particularly saw their point in the sad, seemingly eternal Palestinian-Israeli conflict. What other nation in modern times had been allowed to keep territory seized in war? What other nation, except Israel, could defy umpteen U.N. resolutions with impunity? Also mitigating his error of judgment, in his view, was the fact that the Russian arms deal didn't seem to him to presage another Middle East war. The Russians had a long history of giving (or selling) military aid to the Syrians, and he was convinced there was no grand plan to launch a war of liberation against Israel. It was also indisputable that Israel was the strongest military power in the region and that the Jewish state had the full military and financial support of the United States. All the Syrians wanted was to replenish their severely depleted and antiquated armed forces.

So, he would argue, it wasn't as if he was doing a 'Fuchs'—
by which he meant passing on top-secret blueprints for the
atomic bomb to the Soviets or, in this case, their allies. His tac-
tic would be to underplay the importance of the $4.5 billion
arms pact in terms of geopolitical significance and to claim
that the British had all along deceived themselves about the
gravity of the new Russian-Syrian alliance.

However, he would admit he had made a grave error of
judgment. He had been seduced by Kadri's and Hakki's brain-
washing marathons into seeing Britain as the enemy of the
Arabs. And, to some extent, he would plead *mea culpa* to the
charge that financial reward played an unduly large part in his
decision to go along with the ruse to snare the Syrians. He
wanted to buy his dream home, and every time he turned his
back, he was outbid by rival, even phantom, punters. Thus, he
would contend, that perhaps he had entered into the whole
enterprise with too little seriousness, in somewhat cavalier
mode, a character defect often detected by former bosses and
editors.

He would have to tell them what had really happened
that night. Except, of course, for Veronica's role. He would
not endanger her by exposing her part in the drama of that
evening—let alone his discovery that she was all along working for the Syrians. In his more self-confident, ambitious moments, Vaux had fancied he might even be able to persuade
her to go over to the other side—physically, that is, do a bunk,
and let her hero Yasser Arafat find her gainful employment at
his HQ in Libya.

For he couldn't suppress a recurring fear that she, perhaps
her very life, could be in danger. Yes, he was resolute on that
score: he would not betray her, he would leave her name out
of it. He would tell them how he was drugged, virtually kidnapped, and then ferried to the Russian consulate and about
the long sessions with Hakki (they now had access to him—he
would confirm his story) and the veiled threat that if he didn't
do what they asked him to do the consequences could be dire.

He had been totally in their hands and there was even talk of a Russian tramp freighter waiting to ship him from Marseilles to the Syrian port of Latakia. An anti-British show trial would have been scheduled. But of course, the firm's position would be to claim that once he had been sprung from captivity and come back to them, there was no reason why he shouldn't have told them the truth. They would have protected him (if necessary for years) from any further attempt to shanghai or otherwise harm him. Then, he decided, he would shrug his shoulders and rest his case.

* * *

Having determined this course of action, Vaux walked with a lighter step. The renovations to the bungalow were almost finished. Bill Grainger, the building contractor, had known what he was talking about. In fact, it looked as if the final touches would be done well before September 1. He wouldn't be surprised if Grainger asked for a bonus for early completion.

As he passed No. 7 Willow Drive, he heard Rex's raucous barking and John's commanding voice ordering him for Christ's sake to shut the fuck up. He quickened his pace. He was headed for the Pig & Whistle and a light lunch. Sandwiches had replaced the bangers and mash ever since Mrs. Parker had started to cook the one-pot dinners. The summer had been quiet socially, but he liked it that way. It had also been hot and dry, which had helped when gaping holes temporarily replaced windows and tarpaulins covered jagged gaps in some of the external walls. The kitchen was transformed into something out of *House and Garden,* and the new white- tiled bathroom had been enlarged by knocking down the wall to the adjoining, separate W.C. There was now room for a shower stall and a bidet (Vaux wondered dreamily who would be the first guest to use it—Veronica, he hoped), and the old re-enameled

1930s tub had been adorned with a brass Continental-style hand shower. Above all, he loved the terrace and, of course, the treasured view of parkland and meadows.

Pete was wiping down the bar. He had a long face and it looked as if he had been crying. He didn't look Vaux in the eye but sniffled as he held the tankard under the tap.

'Anything wrong?' asked Vaux. Pete was usually such a cheerful young man, and Vaux immediately knew he'd asked a silly question.

'Nah—I'll be all right.' He wiped his eyes and nose with a Kleenex and Vaux could see that his eyes were brimming with tears.

'You don't look so good. If there's anything I can do—'

Pete tried a feeble laugh. 'You can find me a new lover, if you like.'

Vaux hadn't expected this. Pete and Harry must have broken up. 'Oh dear. I'm sorry. You and Harry had words?'

'Yeah. More than just words, though. He's found someone else. He's the boss—the landlord, like. So it's marching orders for me, innit?'

Vaux tried to draw on his life experience. It seemed wanting. So he said, 'A bright, good-looking guy like you will find someone very soon. Just make sure Harry does right by you—severance pay and all that.'

'Thanks, Mr. Vaux.' The telephone rang and Pete turned to answer it. 'It's for you, sir.' He passed the heavy white phone to Vaux.

'Vaux.' He recognized Arthur Davis's voice.

'Arthur. How did you know I was here?'

'Not spying on you, if that's what you think. Happened to see you crossing the road, that's all. Look, I've just had a call from you know who. Urgent. I'm to get in touch with you at once. Can't think what it's all about. But you'd better pop over, old chum.'

'After I've finished my beer.'

Vaux slid the phone back to within Pete's grasp. So Pete's life was about to change. It now looked as if his was also. After his confession, would they charge him for breaching the Official Secrets Act? Put him on trial for taking part in a conspiracy to deceive HM government? Would the firm demand the crown's money back? He couldn't begin to guess how they would react. Or how they would expect him to make amends. But to be realistic, he had to expect what to him would be the ultimate, ironic punishment: the loss of the house he now cherished and the life he had once figured he'd live out there.

* * *

The uneasy sensation in the pit of his stomach reminded Vaux of exam day at his old school. He thought back to those untroubled days. Then, of course, he had taken his Englishness for granted. Now he was about to reaffirm that latent patriotism. He was now sure he was doing the right thing. There were certain immutable laws that man had to live by—and as an Englishman, some unique honor code, deference to which conferred the rights of kinship. He was to put his fate in the hands of the Establishment that he once despised. They had hired him for his services and he had betrayed them.

But they had won the day. They seemed to possess some intangible, superior force that had kept them in control for a thousand years. So be it. He wasn't King Canute. Who was he to try to turn the tide?

These gloomy thoughts were crowding in on him when he saw Alan Craw's thin, drawn face loom up over the newspaper he had been pretending to read. He was sitting on a hard, wooden straight-backed chair in the tiny reception area at the Gower Street offices. Ms. Dimbleby had set a mug of coffee down on the side table where Vaux had found the morning edition of the *Daily Mail*.

'Vaux, old chap. Come on in.' Craw sounded uncharac-
teristically cheerful. They clearly had no idea of the bombshell
Vaux was about to ignite in the inner sanctum of Section B3.
He wondered if he would be permitted to walk out of the
offices that day alone and free. Or whether he'd be asked to
wait while they organized the theatrics of a perp walk, a handcuffed arrest and transportation to some high-security deten-
tion center.

* * *

Behind the chipped, varnished brown door from which
the pleasingly familiar figure of Craw had emerged, an earnest
and sometimes heated discussion had taken place between Sir
Walter Mason, Alan Craw, and Major Eric Short. Short had
advocated a quick but thorough internal inquiry to establish
the validity of the CIA's suspicions. Craw had hedged his bets
as his powers of intellect worked on overdrive to discern Sir
Walter's thinking. In truth, of course, Sir Walter's mind had
been made up following the lengthy discussions with Col. Sir
John Blakeley, the director-general. That decision, taken over
breakfast at Playfair Castle, Sir Walter's country seat in Dorset, would be often cited by the cognoscenti as one of the last
glorious examples of British self-assertion and independence
in the dying years of the twentieth century.

* * *

'These kidneys are the best I've had for a very long time,'
said Sir John, scooping up three more of the delectable mor-
sels from the silver chafing dish. He moved back from the long
mahogany sideboard to the table. They were alone. At 6 a.m.
none of the other guests had yet attempted to rouse themselves for the Sunday morning hunt.

'Sybil always insists on lamb kidneys. No comparison with calf's kidneys. Fennel and red wine recipe. She knows her offal, does Sybil. In fact she's damn good with food in general. Never cooks herself but knows about the best ingredients and recipes. Must have at least forty cookery books in the kitchen.'

Sir John thought about his late wife, Shirley. She was never any good in the kitchen. But she made up for it in other ways, bless her heart. This sentimental train of thought was halted by Sir Walter's sudden insistence that they get down to business now before anybody else appeared for breakfast.

'Yes, of course.'

'Have you slept on it?'

'Yes,' said Sir John. 'I heartily agree with your position as stated late last night. It seems inconceivable to me that Freeman's suspicions are justified by the facts as we know them. You know Vaux, of course, and I have to rely on your judgment. I do think, however, that this time we are fully justified in rejecting this bloody man's theories. He has no proof whatsoever on which to base these charges—charges that would reflect badly on our own judgments and assessments of the situation.'

'The clincher, as far as I'm concerned,' said Sir Walter, 'is that this Arab defector—what's his name, Hacker or something—has said nothing whatsoever to prompt the Yanks' suspicions. Yes, we caught that wretched girl Barbara Boyd and, yes it seems that we were hoodwinked by Kadri and his cohorts, but there's no evidence whatsoever to think Vaux was in on it.'

'Do you know whether the Americans asked this Arab asylum-seeker point-blank whether he could definitely confirm or deny that Vaux conspired with Kadri?' asked Sir John.

'Freeman has never said anything on that point—which suggests to me again that they've got very little to back up their suspicions,' said Sir Walter.

'Yes, indeed. So we tell the Americans—to use one of their delightful expressions—to go jump in the lake and leave it to us. We've got other fish to fry, according to your latest information regarding this bloody Kadri fellow.'

The information to which Sir John referred was a sudden and unexpected putsch in Damascus by a close circle of President Al-Assad's supporters. The aim of this faction, as far as field intelligence had discerned, was to cleanse the top echelons of government of all non-Alawis. The president himself was a member of the Alawi sect, a minority within Syria's Shiite Moslem minority. It was the latest power-play in an unending struggle between the more secular Alawi sect, who dominated the ruling elite, and the orthodox Sunnis, who favored a more religious regime based on the laws of Islam.

Many good and capable public servants, diplomats, and top administrators of Syrian state corporations were purged in what became known as the Palmyra massacre. Only half a misnomer: no blood had been shed. But the plot had certainly been hatched at the luxurious Cham Palace hotel, close to the magnificent ruins of the ancient Greco-Roman city. Assad loyalists to a man, the non-Alawis woke up one bright Monday morning to learn that their services to the Syrian state would no longer be required. Pension arrangements and dismissal bonuses would be negotiated in due course.

Sir John heard the footfalls and chatter of a couple who were descending the wide, sweeping staircase to the breakfast room. He wanted to get in one more quick question.

'By the way, Walter, any untoward repercussions from the Boyd business?'

'Whole thing's blown over, thank God. The local coroner's verdict was clear-cut: death by misadventure—namely an unfortunate head-on collision with a twenty-ton truck while attempting to overtake another vehicle. She was in the wrong lane. End of story.'

Sir Peter Urquhart, a former M.P. and now editor of the *The Beacon,* a recently-launched, far right conservative weekly, entered the room with Ann Kolter, whom Sir John remembered from the previous day's introduction, as one of the magazine's new writers recruited directly from the Conservative Party Research Department. He hoped her brains matched her dashingly good looks.

* * *

In the fetid atmosphere of Sir Walter's office, only a tall fan in the corner, whose noisy motor earlier had been switched to HIGH by Ms. Dimbleby, mitigated the fug generated by three men in a cramped office on a hot summer's morning. The sash windows had been opened by only an inch in deference to Sir Walter's fears that any eavesdropper in one of the offices overlooking the internal well might hear bits and pieces of his top-secret discussions.

The three men, with jackets draped at the back of their chairs, had just finished debating Vaux's fate. It was Sir Walter's gentlemanly gesture to let his two deputies believe their opinions really mattered. But in truth, Sir Walter told himself, it really didn't make a ha'pe'th of difference what either of them said: the decision had been made. Vaux was to go back to work.

Short had advised against it. He had said that instinct, or what kids these days called 'vibrations,' told him that Vaux was hiding something. He had been downright shifty when Short questioned him at his new home. He believed that the Americans could be on to something. Craw, on the other hand, was quite fond of the old journalist. He had done his best under difficult circumstances, as he himself had. How were they to know the Syrians were that smart? He should be given the benefit of the doubt.

So Mason put an end to the pointless chatter. 'Go get him,' he told Craw.

Vaux was invited to sit down in a wooden armchair directly opposite Sir Walter. Craw and Short flanked him on either side. Mason invited Vaux to take off his jacket. He folded his blue blazer on his lap. The atmosphere was heavy—literally and psychologically. Vaux was now sweating, his white shirt uncomfortably damp under the armpits. Sir Walter had a good look at him. He wanted to see if Short's 'shifty' description was borne out by the reality. He had to admit Vaux looked worried and uncomfortable. But, of course, he had been led to believe that he would be in for a thorough grilling this morning—the first preliminary step to a full-scale official inquiry into the fiasco of Operation Helvetia. Naturally the man was anxious.

'Please relax, Mr. Vaux,' said Sir Walter, who felt uncomfortable himself when he saw a sensitive man suffering unnecessarily. 'We're not going to eat you.'

Vaux laughed on cue. He wiped his forehead with a polkadot handkerchief Mrs. Parker had that morning washed and ironed and placed in the top pocket of his blazer.

'You've met us all—Craw and Short, I mean.'

'Yes sir.'

'Well then, let's start.'

Vaux sat up straight and was about to launch into his wellrehearsed statement of confession. But Sir Walter spoke before Vaux could find his voice.

'I suppose we could tell you that there's good news and bad news.' Sir Walter looked first at Craw and then at Short for a nod of approval. Craw nodded but Short kept a steely look in his eyes as though to suggest he had not changed his view about Vaux. Sir Walter continued: 'The good news is that we have wound up the investigation into the Geneva shambles. I'm being blunt, as I want you to be in all your dealings with me, Vaux. It *was* a shambles, no mistake. And as I'm sure Major Short told you, the Americans have informed us that we were hoodwinked—hook, line, and sinker.

'Their evidence comes from one Amin Hakki, a defector and now resident in Washington. He gave the Americans the goods—the real arms deal. And of course, they passed it on to us.' Sir Walter paused and took a sip of black coffee from a Styrofoam cup.

'This chap Hakki gave the Americans additional top secret stuff, of course—some of which Section B3 has already acted upon.'

Vaux thought that this was it. He had been exposed by Hakki. Mason was now playing the cat and he was the cornered mouse.

'So let us go on from there. The Americans have made us look silly. But if they'd had the same ace up their sleeve—an old friend of Kadri's that could be used as a lever to pry open the details of that arms deal—believe you me, they would have dealt it. The Syrians saw us coming for one reason only: there was a traitor in MI6 who passed on everything we were planning to the Syrians at the very outset of the operation. They were waiting for us. Simple as that. The mole has of course now been eradicated. In this business, you live and learn. Treachery's no stranger to us—it just comes unexpectedly and in the most illusory disguises.'

Vaux's heart was beating even faster now. What did the old boy mean by 'eradicated'? What had they done to Veronica? He couldn't be referring to anyone else. No wonder he hadn't heard a word for all these months. Was she incarcerated in a place where they put traitors who had been tried in secret?

But no names were given. He couldn't ask. If he revealed that he knew Veronica Belmont, a.k.a Barbara Boyd, worked for them, he would only complicate his prepared and straightforward confession. He remained silent as Sir Walter Mason resumed.

'I don't know why I said I'd start with good news. Maybe the fact that we caught the mole is good news. But the rest is hardly very cheering. What I mean by the bad news, however, may not seem bad at all to you.

'It hasn't yet hit the newspapers or even the BBC, thank God. But there's been a sort of intra coup d'etat in old Damascus. The upshot of which, old chum, is that your friend

Kadri has gone into self-exile. He fled Damascus after a palace putsch and as far as we can make out, headed for Morocco where some aunt of his lives. Don't know all the details. But we intend to find out. That's where you come in, eh, Craw?'

Craw preened himself at being brought into Sir Walter's verbal ambit. 'Yes, indeed, sir.' He looked intently at Vaux who by this time had slumped low in the chair, his clammy hands gripping the wooden varnished arms tightly.

'It'll be like old times, Vaux. I want you to get back in contact with Kadri and see how the land lies,' said Craw.

'And before you reject the idea out of hand,' added Sir Walter, 'you must remember that essentially your old chum's been fired. All those years of dedication and hard work for bloody Assad down the drain. He's got to be bitter. And bitter, disillusioned men talk. Get my drift?'

Vaux started to compose a sentence. 'Well, sir—'

Sir Walter put his hand out like a traffic cop ordering a driver to stop. 'You will receive the usual stipend as a temporary NOC—non-official-cover officer. That's fifty grand minimum—more if it takes an inordinate amount of time. Your job is simple: you get into contact—we'll supply the whys and wherefores—and then you embark on a comprehensive debriefing exercise. Kadri knows everything there is to know about the inner workings of Assad's regime: military, political, social, economic—you name it. He worked as deputy governor of the central bank for twenty-five years and then he was transferred to the defense ministry as the chief procurement officer. As far as we are concerned, the man's a walking encyclopedia of facts and figures about the Syrian state, eh, Craw?'

Major Short drew up his outstretched legs as if to remind Sir Walter of his presence. A slight cough to clear his throat was audible.

Craw beamed with optimism. 'It will all be made very easy for you, Vaux. You'll probably go to Morocco on vacation—perhaps having got into contact with him earlier. You'll have a good old laugh about Geneva. He'll probably be apologetic. But we feel confident that one more gamble on his good nature and friendship toward you will pay off. We are convinced, as we think you are, that he meant no ill-will toward you by the big scam he played. He was simply protecting his country from us interlopers. Now he has no incentive to do that. He'll be a mine of information.'

Vaux had been listening to everything Sir Walter and Craw had been saying. But his concentration had been diverted by the mental re-rehearsal of his confessional. Despite their new plans for him he was determined not to betray himself.

'Before we go any further on this,' he said, 'I think there's something you all should know.' He looked sideways at Craw and then at Short. Sir Walter's eyes widened and he made a hand gesture that invited Vaux to proceed.

Vaux then launched into his memorized litany of betrayal. Sir Walter's mouth seemed to droop further at each shattering detail. Craw's eyes were firmly fixed on the brogues at the ends of his long, outstretched legs. Short looked straight at the traitor in their midst, his lips betraying a small smirk of justification. Sir Walter suddenly got up and closed the one-inch gap at the bottom of the grimy sash window. The room was hot and stifling and all three listeners loosened their neckties and opened their collars. Vaux's forehead showed little beads of sweat. His damp shirt clung to his skin. He felt as if he was holding forth in some Arab *hammam*.

Then silence. They heard the muffled taps of Ms. Dimbleby's typewriter as she serenely pursued her secretarial chores. Sir Walter shuffled some convenient papers on his desk. He looked over his wire-framed glasses at both his colleagues, then at Vaux. By some sort of collegial telepathy, they had agreed that a discussion was in order—without the presence of Vaux.

'Step outside for a minute or two, would you, Vaux,' said Sir Walter in a calm, almost friendly tone.

Ms. Dimbleby looked up from her typewriter, a little surprised that Vaux had decided to return to sit again on the uncomfortable upright chair. He felt like an errant schoolboy sent outside the headmaster's study while his tutors debated whether to expel him or give him another chance. In the sanctum, Sir Walter appeared somewhat dumbstruck. In the circumstances, thought Craw, this was hardly surprising.

'So the bloody Yanks were right all along,' said Sir Walter. 'Vaux got seduced into going along with the ruse.'

Short couldn't resist the reminder that, along with the Americans, his suspicions had also proved accurate. 'I told you both that I came away from that one-on-one interrogation with the feeling that he was hiding something.'

'Nothing about B.B. playing any role, though,' observed Craw. 'Perhaps she stayed in the background and never showed herself as working for the other side.'

'Enough of post-mortems, gentlemen. We have to come to a critical decision. Do we still use him or do we hand him over to the director of Public Prosecutions?'

'I say he should get his just desserts,' said Short. 'Probably about twenty years.'

'It's important to keep focused on our prime needs,' suggested Craw. 'Pumping this character Kadri for every piece of information about Syria and Assad's regime would be a big feather in our caps.'

'And the only man in the whole bloody universe who can do that for us is Vaux. Kadri wouldn't open up to anyone else. 'Course, we don't know what his attitude toward Vaux will be, but at least he's got a fighting chance to carry off the mission,' said Sir Walter.

He then betrayed a slight smile of satisfaction. He had just thought the obvious—which in the heat of the post-confession discussion the three men had overlooked.

'We have to remember that now we've got something on him. I plan to use that leverage to our very good advantage, gentlemen. This is a critical time in the Middle East. Just this morning, the D-G informed me that the region could be on the brink of a big breakthrough—hopefully toward peace and not war. Secret talks between Arafat's PLO and the Israelis have been going on since April. C says they are preparing the agenda—with American backing, of course, for full-scale negotiations next year. The aim: to set up a viable Palestinian state. Of course, Israel will have to give up some of its settlements, but they could be prepared to do that if Palestine offers them real security from terrorism.

'So the timing of this operation of ours could be critical. Who knows what Arafat has told Assad and other Arab leaders about the secret talks? Who knows whether it's all just a feint by the Palestinians who in their heart of hearts probably don't want to sit down with the Israelis and work out a joint security pact? Who, for that matter, knows whether the Israelis are going along just to please Washington, their indispensable bankers whose billions keep them afloat? I think the talk at the highest levels of the various Arab regimes could answer some of those questions.'

Sir Walter had convinced himself, if no one else, of the course of action that had to be taken. 'Craw, get him back in, please.'

Craw got up and opened the door. He nodded to Vaux, who rose heavily, straightened up, and walked back into the office. He knew that within a few seconds he would learn his fate. Prosecution, a *sub rosa* trial, and a long retirement at Wormwood Scrubs rather than No. 32 Willow Drive? Demands to reimburse crown money within thirty days? He was convinced they would never let him leave today as a free man with a valid passport.

But Sir Walter looked reasonably benign. He had the look of a weary father about to reprimand a wayward son. He took off his eyeglasses and placed them gently on the desk.

'Look here, Vaux. This is a very serious business. This could mean twenty to twenty-five years, you know. You have

betrayed queen and country. If you had told us the truth as
soon as you returned to that hotel in Geneva after your incarceration you would have been treated as a hero. Even if
you didn't get the real goods on Syria's arms purchases, at
least you would have got an A-plus for trying. Plus probably
a big financial thank you from us for your best efforts, not
to mention compensation for your week-long incarceration at
the hands of those thugs.

'However, let's not dwell on the past. We still need you.
What I outlined to you earlier remains a No. 1 priority. We
have a big opportunity here—far more significant even than
what we might have learned from Operation Helvetia had it
been a success. You are the only person our friend Kadri will
talk to—we're convinced of that. What's more, now he sees
you as an Arab ally and co-conspirator, I think he's all the more
likely to spill the beans on a lot of things that to us are vitally
important. He'll throw some bright lights into some very dark
corners. Craw.'

Craw had been listening closely to Sir Walter's new rea-
soning. He had now been asked to contribute to and to support Sir Walter's apparent unilateral decision to turn Vaux
once again into an MI6 asset.

'Absolutely, sir. Vaux, you are his great friend, probably
his best friend—that's obvious. He would never have given
you the chance to escape from the grip of the Syrian security
services had you been just a Joe Bloggs off the street. You are
even, may I suggest, one of his few really intimate friends. And
this is your opportunity to atone for your earlier, shall we say,
wayward behaviour.'

'That's putting it mildly,' said Short, who now realized his
distaste for Vaux represented a minority opinion.

A further discussion ensued, a reiteration of the logistics of the Tangier mission, the broad agenda of questions that
should be put to the former senior Syrian official, and Vaux's
vital and indispensable role. Finally Sir Walter, now showing

distinct signs of fatigue, asked Vaux if he seriously wanted to make amends and complete the mission or whether he preferred to face the potentially dire consequences of his unfortunate dereliction of duty. Vaux realized they were offering him propitiation for his confessed sins. They were also offering him an easy choice. If he accepted the assignment, life would go on. His new and cherished home would be there for him when he returned. Yes, he said, he was available to undertake the task they had planned for him. And he was grateful to Sir Walter for giving him the opportunity to serve his country one more time. He did remind Sir Walter and his two colleagues that although the initial act of deception constituted willful betrayal, his subsequent if belated confession surely would have modified any penalties he may have had to pay. Short snorted at this last plea of mitigation and left the room.

Then Vaux asked: 'Should my cover be the same—a freelance journalist roaming the world?'

'What do you think, Craw?' asked Sir Walter, who had already decided that Craw should again be Vaux's case officer for Operation Couscous.

'That's something worth pondering, sir. Don't forget there's no real need for cover here. Kadri's out of the government and he's more likely to talk frankly to an old friend than to a reporter who's hungry for a scoop.'

Sir Walter smiled at Vaux. 'I think Craw has a point. By the way, did you see that article in the *Evening Standard* some months back on the Geneva peace talks under your Derek Westropp byline?'

Vaux's eyes widened. 'No, sir. I didn't.'

'Brilliant. Written by one of our Arabists at the Foreign Office. He'd been an observer at the conference. Nobody knew any different.'

'I suppose I'd better find out what I "wrote" before Kadri asks me any questions about it.'

'Oh, I shouldn't worry about that. He knew that was only a cover—your working for the *Standard* and all that.'

'Yes, I suppose he did,' agreed Vaux.

* * *

Vaux was dismissed. Outside, he began to relax. He was beginning to believe in miracles. He indulged in the unfamiliar luxury of not thinking ahead, not planning what to say to an interrogator, not rehearsing his pleas for understanding and human weakness.

He heard someone mutter his name. A tall young man was walking beside him. He looked vaguely familiar but Vaux couldn't place him.

'We haven't officially met. My name's Chris Greene. I work in Section B3. Look, can I buy you a pint?' Greene pointed to a corner pub.

Greene and Vaux headed for a booth at the back of the pub, now unusually quiet after the exodus of the lunchtime crowd. Greene had placed two large glasses of draught Heineken down on the table and then walked over to the jukebox. He put some coins in and selected three Everley Brothers classics. Even though he was barely out of his twenties he was no aficionado of high-decibel pop. But now it suited his purpose.

Vaux took a long draft. 'I needed that,' he said. 'Thanks very much. Is this an official meeting?'

'God no,' exclaimed Greene. He sat where he could watch the front entrance. 'In fact, if I suddenly leave for the little boys' room you'll know someone from the firm has come in.'

'Mystery and intrigue,' sighed Vaux. 'I'm getting quite used to it by now.'

'Look, I'll be quick about this. It's strictly confidential. You don't know me, let alone have ever talked to me. Okay?'

'Agreed,' said Vaux. He took out a packet of Camels and offered one to Greene, who shook his head.

'It's about the girl you knew as Veronica Belmont?' His statement ended in an interrogative lilt that reminded Vaux of the way he'd heard many young Americans talk. One more import from the States that's caught on. He remembered what Mason had said about the eradication of the mole. Perhaps he would now find out. His memory's eye suddenly saw her beautiful face, the sultry eyes, the deep bevel of that Arabian nose.

'Go on,' he said, barely audibly.

'Vaux, she's dead.'

He looked up into the young man's blue eyes. They were watery and he appeared to be genuinely moved. Vaux said nothing.

'Look, I don't know what they told you in there, but her real name was Barbara Boyd. She worked for us—the firm. But it turned out she was all the time working for the Syrians. She was born here and brought up here, but she was an Arab at heart. Her mother was English, her father a Palestinian refugee.'

Vaux knew now that the young man was telling the truth. But he still wondered about his motivation. Was this another ploy by Sir Walter and Co. to try and pry more information from him? Perhaps everything today was a sham—to lower his defenses. In their minds, no doubt, concealing his knowledge about an active mole in their midst rose to the level of high treason. Veronica was the one subject that had never come up in the negotiations to save his skin. He had presumed of course that Veronica was still in place.

Greene took a deep breath and another long pull at his beer. 'You'll be wondering why I'm telling you all this. It's simply because I knew you had a fling with her. I was a watcher in Geneva and my job was to look after you, essentially. I didn't do my job very well when you decamped to Vevey—but old Craw let me off lightly. The point is B.B., as we called her, worked sometimes in tandem with me. We got quite close in Geneva and, believe it or not, I fell in love.'

'Oh God,' murmured Vaux.

'When she was exposed by that bastard Hakki, all hell let loose. You can imagine. Mason can't stand the Americans and to be told by them that the Arabs had a mole in place right within Section B3, well, he just went ballistic. There was never any question of an inquiry or trial. She was never questioned, let alone charged.'

'So what in hell happened to her?' asked Vaux, sensing the answer before Greene could reply.

'It's what in spy books they call XPD, expedient demise. Professionals like us just use one word—elimination. She was killed while doing a job for the Syrian intelligence service. And if it makes you feel any better, she had just murdered a key CIA man.'

Greene got up and bought two more pints. Vaux sat there in dumbfounded silence. He crushed the cigarette butt in the ashtray slowly and with extreme pressure, as if it were the perpetrator of the evil act that had obliterated a good woman from the face of the earth.

'I just thought you ought to know,' said Greene. 'You must have wondered what had happened to her.'

'I did. But I couldn't get in touch with her until she contacted me.'

'Why—you didn't try?'

Vaux knew he was again on dangerous ground here. Perhaps this really was all planned. He was about to tell Greene that he and Veronica had agreed on a discreet period of silence. But what sense would that make if all he knew about her was that she was some bluestocking PhD doing arcane research projects for an obscure think tank? Only if he had known she worked within MI6 as a double agent did all the hugger-mugger stuff make sense.

'I did try—but unsuccessfully. I couldn't find that outfit she said she worked for in the London telephone book. She said she'd call me when we both got back to England. I never heard a word.'

Vaux asked Greene how and where it had happened. Then he left him in the pub. As Vaux walked to the Goodge Street tube station he knew that his life, after all, would never be the same again. He had hoped something serious could develop between them and he was sure those feelings were shared. But perhaps she was just a good secret agent and a good actor. She had, according to Greene, killed a CIA man whom she had entrapped in a sexual relationship. Before she was killed she must have sent that morale-boosting postcard to him. And she had died working for her cause. Not a bad epitaph.

28

'I hate flying,' said Vaux.

Chris Greene had just called him from a public phone booth in the circular concourse of the Piccadilly tube station about the planned trip to Morocco and whether he preferred any particular airline. He had suggested various alternatives: Air France via Paris and on to Casablanca perhaps, or Iberia via Madrid and directly to Tangier.

'You mean in the Erica Jong sense, or literally—you really hate flying in an airplane?' asked Greene in an attempt to be amusingly disingenuous.

Vaux had to think for a few seconds. 'Erica Jong? My goodness, you're a bit young to remember her, aren't you? She wrote *Fear of Flying* thirty years ago.'

Greene had achieved his object. He liked impressing older people. 'It was required reading for my sister's women's lib history course. I borrowed it one evening when I was bored.'

Vaux had forgotten what the book was about. He recalled vaguely that it was a feminist tract imploring women to go out and shake off male-imposed inhibitions and sanctions and live a little.

'Looking back, I guess she helped a lot of women and confused a lot of men into the bargain. Anyway, yes, it's flying high up in the bright blue sky that I don't like. And the traveling strangers that force conversation on you. So forget it. I'll go over land to Spain and then get a ferry. I can arrange the trip myself.'

'No, that's my remit, mate. Specific instructions from Craw. I'm in charge of the logistics and all that. Leave it to me. I'll see what I can do.'

'Craw's actually delegated some simple tasks to a lowly junior?' asked Vaux mockingly.

'He's a changed man since Sir Walter put him in charge of Operation Couscous. Says he's won back the old guy's faith in him and put the major in the back seat.'

'Short, you mean?' said Vaux, remembering Major Eric Short's rather cold demeanor that morning in Sir Walter's office and the stiff military debriefing on the newly built terrace a few months back.

'Yeah. Sir Walter seems to think that tension between his two deputies creates better long-term results or something like that.'

'So your job isn't to watch over me in Tangiers, I take it.'

'No. They seem to have assumed that you know my face. Didn't tell them about our meeting, I hope.'

'Of course not. Unless I was followed from the Gower Street office after I last saw Sir Walter. In which case your accosting me and inviting me for a drink would have been duly reported.'

'No chance. I was looking out for that.'

Vaux put his new mobile phone back on the glass-topped table. So they had given his new project a code name—Operation Couscous. The brilliance of Section B3's original thinking had once again astounded him. He looked beyond the garden to the gently rolling hills. It was an early-August afternoon. It had been a long, hot summer and some of the fields and meadows that spread before him had lost their early bright green freshness. His lawn was cracked in places and the sun-baked grass had turned the color of straw—despite Patrick's constant watering. The leaves on the trees had also lost their luster; they had paled beneath the long hours of strong sunshine and drooped sadly as if crying out for a heavy downpour.

* * *

In the days that followed the supposedly clandestine meeting with Greene he had made a conscious effort to put Veronica Belmont out of his mind. Perhaps he was just another victim of her talent to deceive. He tried to convince himself that he was really in the same category as the CIA lover whom she had ruthlessly wiped out. He was beginning to get over her, even though he could never accept the cold-blooded way the firm had decided to deal with her. Surely to God there were more civilized ways to eliminate spies; in another decade, perhaps before the big scandals of the 1950s and '60s, she might have been sentenced to twenty years. Then within a year or so, some prisoner exchange would have been worked out—just as they used to do in the old Cold War days when spies were often exchanged over the Glienicke Bridge that connects Berlin with Potsdam.

Construction on No. 32 continued. Most of the radical renovations had been completed: the kitchen, with its granite counters, stainless steel appliances, and ceramic tiled floors; the large bathroom with glistening new fixtures, the renovated tub and shower stall with the new brass fittings; and the main living area that looked out to the deep, flagged terrace, the garden, and the countryside beyond. A single bed and dog basket for Rex had been installed in the small 'box' room that had been the first of the bedrooms to be repainted.

Patrick Goodchild sometimes stayed overnight; he said he slept better there than at his own house—no kid brothers to wake him up, no nocturnal bumps and sworn oaths as his father groped in darkness from bedroom to refrigerator for a drink. And Rex, always exhausted by nightfall, slept quietly— except when, in his canine dream-world (betrayed by jerky muscular spasms, grunts ,and subdued yelps), he found himself chasing a squirrel to the bottom of the garden.

Vaux had thought little about his new assignment. He saw
it as a laid-back, leisurely seven-day debriefing exercise—with
Ahmed, his old friend, oblivious to any suspicions that Vaux
would report back word-for-word what he would hopefully
reveal about the inner workings, the secrets and geopolitical
ambitions of the Assad regime. He tried to recall Sir Walter
Mason's shopping list of key questions: what lay behind the so-
called Palmyra putsch—what it meant in terms of any changes
in foreign and domestic policies. What were the international
ramifications—a change in Syria's alliances, a new, perhaps
more conciliatory, attitude toward the old enemy, Israel? And
how extensive were the personnel changes at the top of the
Assad regime? Had the kitchen cabinet been reshuffled? And
something Sir Walter had failed to mention but which occupied
much of his own thoughts: what had forced Ahmed's own premature retirement? Why had he chosen self-imposed exile?

Chris Greene's sudden call wasn't all that unexpected. Sir
Walter Mason, once he had come to a decision, wanted everything done yesterday. But Vaux needed a little more time.
He could hardly, just suddenly, appear in Tangier, knock on
Ahmed's door, and claim to be an innocent tourist who had
learned by pure chance of Kadri's decamping to Morocco. No,
there had to be a more sophisticated strategy. And it would no
doubt call for some sort of conference with Sir Walter, Craw,
and various other minions at Section B3.

He sat at the large kitchen table with a strong cup of Ty-
phoo tea in one hand while the other held the tabloid paper
Mrs. Parker brought in every morning. She moved the new
chrome Dualit toaster toward him then turned her attention
to whipping the scrambled eggs Vaux had said he rather fancied.

'Card came for you this mornin', Mr. Vaux. It's on the 'all
table. One of 'em foreign scenes, looks like,' she said.

Vaux's eyebrows rose slightly but he went on reading: a
short, snappy story about one of Sir Elton John's bodyguard's
plans to write a revelatory 'tell-all' book about the pop idol's

private life. It was a front-page story with a three-inch tall headline. Vaux sighed as he remembered the old *Daily Mail*—a serious, conservative broadsheet, now no doubt forced to compete with the likes of the *Sun* and the old, racy *Mirror*. Then he heard the clatter and banging and scampering of small paws on new pinewood floors that heralded the arrival of Patrick and Rex. They hadn't stayed overnight, so Rex was particularly enthusiastic about greeting Vaux with salivary licks to his legs, bare under the dressing gown, and the snaps and appreciative growls that indicated his delight at seeing his second master for another day. Patrick calmed the dog down with a few judicious pats on the back and head, Vaux fed him a slice of brown toast, and amid whimpers of protest, Mrs. Parker whisked him gently out of the kitchen door and onto the concrete path that led to the back garden. The odors of wildlife and the scents from the garden helped Rex instantly forget the undignified expulsion.

Patrick sat down and without a word handed Vaux the postcard. It showed an ancient white-roofed, cubic medina on a steep hill that descended to a crescent-shaped beach. Tangier, the storied city of mystery and intrigue—that now, from what Vaux had learned, had cast off its old, mystic character to become just another North African port on the lines of Algiers and Tunis. Even so, the exotic flavor of these coastal towns of the Maghreb still possessed the power to stir the imagination and quicken the beat of any adventurer's heart. Vaux's own pulse beat faster as he read the message:

Now enjoying a much-deserved retirement—as, I
hope, you are. This place is magical—a paradise! You
must come as soon as possible. I promise you
that this time I shall behave as a true and proper
Arab host. My phone number is 039 92 14 75. A.K.

'Good God,' said Vaux to himself.
'Friend of yours, then?' asked Patrick.

'None of your business, young man,' said Mrs. Parker as she poured Vaux another cup of tea.

'Paradise' seemed a bit of a stretch from what he'd read about Tangier and Morocco. But then again he recalled that the Paul Bowles' novel he had read earlier that summer had been written in the '50s. He thought back to his days in Cairo and wondered if he'd find similarities. The idea of being shown around by Ahmed excited him—interpreter, guide, and host combined. It would make a pleasant break. And perhaps he'd have a chance to rebuild their friendship.

But what was he saying? He would be going there to pump Kadri for every fact, military and economic, and every political trend and nuance that related to the current governance of a sovereign country, Assad's Syria. He felt a hand squeeze his arm.

'You all right, Mr. Vaux?' Patrick had pulled him out of his reverie.

'What? Oh yes, sorry. Yes, it's from an old friend of mine. Retired to Morocco. Wants me to go there for a vacation, see his new house and all that.'

'Sounds cool. Lots of good, cheap hash there, I hear,' said Patrick, suddenly the sophisticated traveler. 'Bring back some plants and we could have a bumper crop at the bottom of the garden.'

'Now young man, none of that. I'm sure Mr. Vaux isn't interested in that sort of thing—and nor should you be. Hash, indeed. Never heard anything so outrageous. And you about to be a father.' Mrs. Parker, face flushed, left the kitchen. Vaux was mildly surprised she knew what Patrick was talking about but thought she'd admonished him appropriately.

'You've offended Mrs. P's sense of propriety,' said Vaux.

'Yer what?' answered Patrick with a grin. 'Whatever, she'll get over it. What's on tap for today, then?' It was his usual request for marching orders.

'I hadn't thought about it,' said Vaux. 'It seems awfully quiet today.'

'Demolition makes more noise than reconstruction. Pulling down brick walls is a loud, noisy job. Laying bricks, one on top of another, and plastering and that, are quiet, almost silent jobs, aren't they,' mused Patrick.

'I guess you're right. What about finishing off the painting. I noticed some of the base or skirting boards still show only the flat undercoat.'

'Okay, will do,' said Patrick enthusiastically. That's what Vaux liked about him—his enthusiasm. Where did he get it from? Certainly not his dad. Which reminded him of something he'd been meaning to bring up.

'By the way, what's up with your father? I get the distinct impression that he's avoiding me. He walked out of the Pig & Whistle the other day with just a nod of recognition. And he's never in the front garden where I used to see him and stop for a chat.'

'Oh, he's just embarrassed, that's all. He'll get over it.'

'Embarrassed? What about?'

'He says he owes you some money and he feels bad because he can't afford to pay you, or something. Says he touched you up for quite a big loan just after you arrived here.'

Vaux recalled the 'loan' of two grand. 'Oh, I didn't expect him to pay it back. I wrote it off as soon as I gave him the check. I know he's got his problems—bringing up all you kids, financing his old lady's travels, and so on. I'll have a few words with him, make him feel better about it.'

'Thanks, Mr. Vaux.'

'He's also got your wedding to consider. That's going to cost him.'

'Yeah, but it's only going to be in the registry office. Then a few people back at the house. Nothing too fancy.'

* * *

Kadri's postcard meant that Vaux did not have to think
up any excuse to 'suddenly discover' that his old friend now
lived in Tangier. He would have to inform Section B3 so that
they wouldn't waste their awesome brain power in concocting
complex, labyrinthine plots to help Vaux establish some sort
of cover. It was an amazing coincidence.

So astonishing that Vaux's creative imagination went on
overdrive. He began to wonder whether the whole thing could
be another set-up. Was this a deliberate ruse to lure him to
Morocco—where just about anything could happen to him—
and arrange his disappearance without trace? Could the Syrians (in collusion with the Russians) have decided to dispose of
him to preempt his revealing the details of his abduction and
the tacit—and politically embarrassing—cooperation of the
Russians in whose stately lakeside villa he had been incarcerated? Could they know about his ultimate decision to confess
his collusion with the Syrians? Was it possible that somehow
they had learned of his change of heart thanks to some contact within B3? Was Greene a mole? Had Craw betrayed him?
Then again, perhaps the Syrians and/or the Russians believed
in preemptive strikes—shut him up before his resolve to remain silent collapsed.

Later he began to think more positively: surely, he figured, the other side must still see him as an asset. After all,
he had been a key player in confirming Barbara Boyd's (a.k.a
Veronica Belmont's) intelligence on Operation Helvetia. He
had confessed to and confirmed the British plot. They had rewarded him financially, and unless there was some new su-
per-paranoid chief of intelligence directing strategy, he, Vaux,
must surely be standing in their good graces.

It would be interesting to hear Sir Walter Mason's view of
the sudden development. Maybe B3 would cancel the mission
because it simply baffled them that Kadri would actually *invite*
Vaux to his own critical debriefing. Unless, of course, they
theorized that Kadri had 'turned.' Perhaps the Palmyra coup

had pissed him off enough to persuade him to betray his old masters and look for some remunerative deal with the Brits.

* * *

Chris Greene had placed a dog-eared manila folder on Craw's desk. He sat down and examined his boss's face as he riffled through the various travel documents. He noticed a slight tan, a furrowed forehead, and deep circles under the blue eyes. He seemed to have lost some weight and he wondered if the office talk about a pending divorce had any substance. If so, it could be giving Craw some sleepless nights. He had married money and perhaps he now looked forward to long years of living on a modest civil servant's salary. As always, Craw was immaculately turned out: dark blue suit, a blue and white striped shirt with cut-away white collar, his old Oxford college (Worcester) tie, and square gold cufflinks that were exposed by periodic tugs to the jacket sleeves.

'Why on earth can't Vaux just hop a plane in London and fly straight to Tangier? There are direct flights, I believe,' said Craw with a look of total bafflement at people's strange travel preferences.

'He was absolutely determined to go by boat and train, sir. Hates flying, he says, and points out, with some justification, that there is hardly any urgency at this point. I mean, he's got to meet up with Kadri by some sort of accident or coincidence—which we haven't worked out yet—and this time at least time is *not* of the essence.'

Craw looked up at his assistant. A bright, attractive young man, so far unencumbered by domestic problems, his whole life ahead of him, probably a passable career, not over-ambitious but conscientious enough. A tinge of envy entered his soul. He sighed, then sat up straight and turned over the various tickets and confirmation slips.

'Let's see now. Dover to Calais by boat train, then on to Paris. Thirty-six hours in Paris, staying at the very expensive five-star Intercontinental on Rue Castiglione. Near Les Jardins de Tuileries, if I recall. Vaux will be able to luxuriate in the amenities of the hotel and then enjoy his constitutional within the historic gardens. Know your Paris, Greene?'

'Fairly well, sir. Haven't been there since my college days, though. Usually went Newhaven–Dieppe. Took about eight harrowing hours. Can't wait for the Eurostar to start up.'

'Where did you stay in the City of Light?' asked Craw, feeling that probably Greene was right: there was no particular urgency to any of this.

'Oh, some fleapit near the Place de la Republique. Close to the Arab quarter.'

'Good grounding for this job, then.'

'Yes sir, I suppose so.'

'Lots of kebabs and couscous.'

'Coincidentally, sir, Operation Couscous is what we have to discuss here and now. Sir Walter is expecting us to come up with a Plan A and Plan B plus a contingency back-up in the case of an emergency.'

Craw gave Greene a look that mingled distaste with utter contempt. 'I haven't forgotten, Greene. That's next on this morning's agenda. Meanwhile, I want to check Vaux's itinerary.

'Let's see. From Paris he takes the night train to Madrid. What's this supplementary charge attached to the SNCF reservation slip?'

'It's a 30 percent mark-up to ensure he has the two-berth sleeping compartment to himself. No unwelcome strangers with whom to share the night.'

'That's hardly necessary, is it? He won't be carrying any classified documents or anything. He's going under his real name. He's strictly a non-official-cover officer traveling to what could be a highly revealing and useful assignment—the logistical details of which he is carrying in his head, etcetera. Why shouldn't he share the compartment?'

'A matter of personal taste, I should imagine. He told me he'd pay any extra costs his special requests may entail.' Greene in fact had never discussed with Vaux the possibility of any extra charges for a custom-designed travel program. But he felt he knew the man well enough to assume he'd agree after the fact.

'Oh, well that's all right then. After all, we're paying him enough for this little enterprise. Now, let's see. So he's in Madrid for a day and a night. Booked in at La Reine Vittoria. Ah, that's better—a two-star. Know it well. On the Plaza de Santa Ana, a favorite hostelry of Hemingway's and still popular among the bull fighting aficionados. Also very close to the Prada. Vaux will no doubt have a great afternoon looking at the Goya and Valasquez masterpieces.'

He turned over another piece of paper. 'Okay. Then the RENFE Madrid-Algeciras night-train—another sleeper— from Atochia central station to La Linea, where he gets a taxi into Gibraltar. Why the devil doesn't he stay on the train to Algeciras? That's where the ferries leave for Tangier.'

'Says he has some personal business to attend to in Gib, sir.'

'I see. Let's get on with it, shall we. Plan A, please.'

Chris Greene wasn't all that surprised that Craw had passed the buck. He knew that if Craw adopted his ideas they'd be dressed up a bit and presented to Sir Walter as an example of Craw's original thinking. But he could do little about it unless in the future some opportunity presented itself to put the record straight. He doubted that this would be the case, but he went ahead anyway.

'I've been thinking about this for some time. It won't be easy to fabricate a chance meeting between the two old friends. On the other hand, sir, it's clearly not an impossible task. I've been looking at the street map of Tangier and, of course, I've been liaising with our man in Rabat—'

'What's he got to do with anything? And what's his name, anyway?' asked Craw sharply.

'He's the MI6 man at the embassy in Rabat. He's been seconded to B3 to be our point man for Operation Couscous. His name's George Greaves.'

'How old is he?'

'No idea, sir. Never met him—just exchanged coded messages.'

'Go on then, man.'

'My plan, sir, would entail a minor car accident in the center of the city—probably at Place de France, a sort of large roundabout just outside the French consulate. Kadri would be in his car and a taxi driver could be paid off to do the dirty work. It would be a fender-bender but, as you might expect in a busy part of an Arab town, there'd be a hell of a fracas: excited crowds would mill around the scene, the cops would eventually arrive, and the local rag would have to report the affair.

'The next morning, Vaux is sitting in one of the sidewalk cafes sipping his mint tea and reading the *Tangier Courier.* He reads about the unfortunate mishap that held up vital rush-hour traffic—donkey carts and all—for an hour or so, and to his great surprise discovers that Ahmed Kadri is one of the crash victims and is living right there in Tangier where Vaux had by sheer coincidence decided to take a holiday. He'd come through Spain and had decided to see Morocco and indulge himself once again in the Arab milieu of which he's so fond. Of course, he then made inquiries and proceeded to contact his old friend.'

Silence descended on the putative architects of Operation Couscous. Greene couldn't tell whether Craw was impressed with the plan or not. Throughout his presentation, his boss had been doodling on his blotter, drawing stick-people with big heads, long outstretched arms, and short legs. Craw took a deep breath.

'Won't do. Won't do at all, Greene. I've been in this racket a long time. And if there's one thing I've learned it's to keep things simple. Simplicity is my watchword. Your plan, Plan A, is far too complicated. The timing would be damned difficult, for one thing. We'd need someone to observe Kadri's movements, we'd need a reliable Moroccan taxi-driver—if such a species exists at all—and then there'd be the fall-out to contend with. Why, the poor bloody Arab could lose his taxi license or something. Then he'd spill the beans and we'd really be in the shit.'

Greene tried to kill a nascent smile. He sensed that his departmental chief had fallen into his well-prepared trap.

Craw said: 'So, as I say, let's keep it very simple. Vaux takes the evening promenade—they call it by its Spanish name there—the *paseo*—along the main street, and believe it or not, he bumps into his old friend who, like all good Tangerines, is doing the same. Perhaps accompanied by a wife or girl friend, who knows? They both express complete surprise, shake hands, make introductions to any third parties in their midst, and walk away together to the nearest bar or restaurant. A celebratory reunion transpires. They renew their friendship, Vaux is invited to stay with Kadri at the villa, and Bob's your uncle. Vaux, of course, would have been tipped off about Kadri's exact movements by an agent in place.'

As if to suggest 'end of discussion,' Craw obliterated his etchings with half a dozen bold crisscross strokes from his old, gold-nibbed Conway Stewart fountain pen. He looked up at Greene, who seemed to be stammering a little.

'There's one problem there, sir.'

'And what might that be, dear boy?'

'Greaves reports that Kadri never leaves his villa unless in his Mercedes. He's usually chauffeured by some old retainer, an Arab. Sometimes a young man lanes him. But the point is he has never been observed to go for a walk outside the walled gardens—let alone into the town for the evening *paseo*. His everyday shopping is done by his servants.'

'Quite a life he seems to have made for himself, what? Mercedes, servants, big villa overlooking the sea, etcetera.'

At the point of this profound observation two gentle taps were heard from the direction of the closed door.

'Come!'

Major Eric Short, in a brown tweed suit, brogues, and a regimental tie, hovered uncertainly. 'Sir Walter thinks I should brief you on the Couscous contingency plan. Plus I may be useful for some input into Plans A and B,' he said.

'Ah yes, indeed, Eric. Do sit down. Your timing is perfect. Please brief us.'

'Well, the contingency plan will only be brought into commission if and when an emergency arises...'

'Such as?' asked Craw in a tone to suggest any emergency that could possibly spring from such a simple, uncomplicated operation could only be figments of rich, over-fertile imaginations.

'Vaux has to be protected. We don't know what his reception will be. Perhaps Kadri will be mad as hell and suspect that Vaux has followed him there with the express purposes of badgering him for vital and secret information. Kadri has spent his whole life working for the Assad regime. He knows a lot, and he knows that we know he knows a lot.'

'Which wouldn't be far off the mark, would it?' said Craw.

Short went on: 'There are two assumptions we have to make: one, he moves into the villa with Kadri; two, he stays in whatever hotel we've chosen for him. If he stays in the hotel it will be easy to watch him, protect him. If he is invited to stay with Kadri, it will be more difficult. But there will be twenty-four-hour surveillance of the house, the comings and goings. We don't want him abducted and pumped for information about us, for example. And above all, we don't know, until Vaux finds out for us, whether Kadri is disillusioned with the Assad regime or whether Damascus still commands his loyalty. All these contingencies have to be considered.'

Craw looked at Greene, who had managed to retrieve the battered, bulging file from Craw's desk while Short delivered his thoughts on the dangers that could possibly confront their man in Tangier. For the umpteenth time Greene riffled through Vaux's travel tickets and reservation slips.

'Yes, well, I presume you are looking into all that, Eric. You'll touch base with Greene, of course. And now I think we're ready to go and see Sir Walter.'

'What about Plans A and B? Don't you want to bounce them off me—see perhaps if I can't contribute some constructive ideas?' asked Short, anxious to learn what the collective brains' trust had produced before he went in with both men to face Sir Walter.

'No time,' said Craw. 'Greene, we won't need you. Get a profile on this cove George Greaves in Rabat, will you. I'll want to know whom I'm dealing with over there.'

Greene was not going to be a complete pushover, but he knew Craw had successfully sidelined him. 'Are we going for Plan A or B, sir?' He thought that his chances of getting an honest answer were greater if he didn't identify the respective authors in front of Short.

'Oh, some compromise between the two, I should think. Our world is full of compromises, what, Short?' He watched Greene disappear into the crepuscular gloom of the narrow corridor that led to his small back office. Then he put his arm around Short's shoulder and accompanied him to Sir Walter's sanctum.

Ms. Doris Dimbleby stood by the door whose top half featured a frosted-glass window. They could see the darkened image of Sir Walter as he stood in front of the grimy window that looked out on to the well of the building. She tapped the glass lightly and opened the door. Sir Walter turned round and smiled at his visitors.

'Shall I get some coffee?' asked Ms. Dimbleby as she bustled into the room, making for Sir Walter's desk. She orchestrated a lightning rearrangement of various folders, pens, rubber bands, paper clips of assorted sizes, and antique paperweights.

'Yes, Doris, that would be very nice. Gentlemen, sit you down,' said Sir Walter.

Craw thought his boss looked unusually benign, even ebullient this morning. What had got into Mason? Perhaps Ms. Dimbleby, that dear old spinster, had at long last decided to retire and the old man was contemplating hiring that young girl in the accountants' office he was always looking at through those dirty sash windows. Or maybe he was at last contemplating with some optimism his own final retirement—expected, according to the office grapevine, at the end of the year.

'Well, gentlemen, have you prepared your plans for Operation Couscous?' asked Sir Walter, still beaming.

'Yes sir,' said Craw. He prepared to deliver Plan A, Greene's rather too sophisticated concoction that would bring their man into contact with the quarry. But before he could say a word, he observed Sir Walter's hands raised in what looked like a plea for silence. He was having second thoughts, perhaps. Maybe his own infallible plan—Plan C.

'Don't waste your breath, Craw.'

'Sir?'

'I've just heard from my old friend Davis who, lucky bugger, continues to enjoy his retirement in Hertfordshire. He lives close to Vaux, of course, and they sometimes meet up. I am happy to tell you that all our agonizing about how we are going to manufacture a meeting or get-together between the two men in Tangier is now quite unnecessary. Vaux has been invited to visit Kadri by Kadri himself. He received a postcard a day or so ago and he, Vaux, that is, plans to leave for Morocco within ten days.'

* * *

Vaux was sitting at the bar of the Pig & Whistle. It was about noon and he was on his first pint of Watney's. The substitute manager, or bartender—Vaux could never quite figure out the man's duties—was in attendance. Customers called him Mr. King. He was a retired caretaker at the local comprehensive school. But he had defied the years: he had jet-black hair and a smooth, wrinkle-free face. His movements were erratic: he'd be standing at the bar one moment, then suddenly disappear into the kitchen and beyond, only to quickly reappear to pull a pint.

'Harry around?' asked Vaux as Mr. King put the glass tankard before him on the wet beer mat.

'Upstairs. Be down in a jiffy, I shouldn't wonder,' said Mr. King.

'Having a lie-in, I expect,' said Vaux to no one. King had gone through to the kitchen. He perused the narrow columns of the *Telegraph*. A front-page story reported that in a Belfast pub the IRA had murdered four suspected informers in cold blood. Vaux quickly looked around the bar for any possible assassins. Then he heard the clatter of heavy boots jumping down the staircase. The master had awakened. But in strode Patrick Goodchild whom Vaux hadn't seen for a couple of days. He looked disheveled and tired.

'Oh, hello, Mike. I was just coming round to your place. Finish off that paint job.'

Vaux then heard the more gentle and careful steps of Harry as he descended the staircase. He went past the barroom door and straight into the kitchen.

'Want a quick one first?' asked Vaux, hoping he didn't look too startled. Mr. King was back, busy polishing glasses and looking through the bar to the back patio.

'Nah, don't think so, if you don't mind. Got to look into Dad's place first.' He was still struggling to put on a leather bomber jacket as he left the pub and ran across Watford Lane.

Fifteen minutes later, not by coincidence, thought Vaux, John Goodchild came in, greeted a few customers who were sitting at the back of the bar, and sat down next to Vaux. He asked Mr. King for a pint of Double Diamond.

'Haven't seen you for ages,' said Vaux.

'I know you had a few words with my son the other day.
And I'm much obliged. Also, grateful. I've been feeling guilty
about that money and to be honest, yeah, I've been avoiding
you. But I want to tell you something: no way you're going to
let me off the hook. I'll pay you back just as soon as I can see
a way to do it. Please trust me on that. Otherwise you're no
friend.'

Vaux was moved. He hadn't wanted Patrick to say anything to his dad. But he supposed he should have told him
that.

'Okay, John. Let's put it behind us—'

'No mate. You haven't been listening,' ave yer?' He empha-
sized each word: 'I-will-pay-you-back—just as soon as I can.'

'Very well. Another pint?'

'Don't mind if I do. How's the house going?'

'Your son's been very helpful, putting the finishing touches
on and all that sort of thing. He's quite a worker when he gets
down to it.'

'I know that. A good cook too.'

'How are the wedding plans going?'

Goodchild stared into his big glass and looked as if he was
composing his best diplomatic answer. 'I honestly can't say. He
says everything's on schedule for nuptials in early September.
But there's been, shall we say, a development. Come and sit
down.'

Vaux looked at his watch. But he was in no hurry. They
walked out on to the patio and sat at the usual round bistro
table.

'Pat says he met you this morning already.'

'Yes. I was here when—'

'I'll finish for you—when he come downstairs from the
bedroom.'

'So he stayed the night. Probably washing glasses until the
early hours,' suggested Vaux.

'Yeah, right,' said Goodchild, the skeptic.

'Look, you said yourself that Patrick's going ahead with
the wedding. Have you seen him with—who is it, Betty? —
recently?'

'No, no mate. You don't understand. I've had it out with
'im. Says he's been having it on with Harry ever since young
Pete left. Admits he swings both ways. Even says it's quite fash-
ionable among his age group. I can tell you, Mike, I'm worried
as hell. What's going to become of him?'

They both took long pulls of ale.

'Look, John. Your son's right. It's not that unusual these
days. All this gay liberation stuff has opened up people's lives. I
don't agree with everything they do, but the net effect seems to
be a more casual attitude toward this sort of thing. No big deal,
old son. These days everyone is more open and more frank
about sex. Don't make too big a thing of it. And for God's sake
don't disown your own son or do anything dramatic.'

Goodchild gave no reply. He got up and bought another
round. Vaux lit a Camel and left one on the table for Goodchild.

'No thanks. Can't stand that toasted shit.' He fished in his
pocket and produced a blue plastic tobacco pouch. He put a
ball of loose tobacco on the table and then went through the
theatrics of rolling his own cigarette with deft twists and turns
of his hands. He licked the adhesive seal, put the stringy object
in his mouth, and lit up with a transparent plastic lighter. He
took a deep drag. Powerful twin plumes of smoke exited his
nostrils as Goodchild exhaled with an audible sigh of pleasure.

'No, you're right, I suppose. Can't fight that sort of thing.
If it's in 'im, there's bugger-all anyone can do about it, if you'll
excuse the pun.'

Vaux offered some instant solace. 'He's a good worker.
I'm very happy with the work he's done at No. 32. I guess he
doesn't like conventional office hours, likes to call his own
shots.'

Both men sat in silence for a while; they were enjoying
the smokes and the midday beer. Birds twittered and chirped,

and they could hear the roar and clatter of heavy trucks on Watford Lane.

Goodchild decided to change the subject. 'Anyway, when are you going to have the grand reopening of No. 32? Big garden party and all that. I can see it now: large marquee on the lawn, a real big spread, barbecue, long trestle tables laden with booze—punch, the beers of the world, and champagne. Hey, maybe you could have a joint "do" with Pat—*his* wedding party, *your* house-warming. What d'ya think? September would be a great month. Can't put it off too long, you know. Autumn's coming. Gets chilly hereabouts then.'

'I've got to go over to the Continent again, John. So I'll think about it when I get back. Meanwhile, I was wondering if you'd be prepared to act as caretaker while I'm away.'

'What's wrong with Mrs. P?'

'Nothing at all. But she says she needs a few weeks off herself to catch up on her own housekeeping and other chores.'

'Catch up with the neighborhood gossip more like. Wait till she cottons on to what's going down with my son and Harry. She'll have a bleedin' field day.'

'I'm sure they'll both be discreet.'

'Yeah, right. Like with you this morning.' They both watched a pigeon land heavily on the flagstones, then the fluttering, skyward mass-evacuation of sparrows and finches.

'Anyway,' said Goodchild, 'what about Patrick? He's skint—he could do with the extra cash.' Goodchild now preened himself to signify the adoption of a stagey refined accent. 'I assume, of course, you intend to pay for these home-minding services.'

'Of course. No, it's just that I thought Pat might be preoccupied, what with the wedding and that sort of thing.'

'I'll personally see to it that he stays at your place like he used to—with Rex and all. I'll walk down the road to see how things are going every other day or so. How's that?'

'How about a hundred a week for your trouble.'

'Done,' said Goodchild.

29

Vaux opened his eyes. Shafts of bright sunshine were reflected on the ceiling. The wooden venetian blinds stirred slightly as a gentle breeze came through the open windows. He looked at his new Timex watch and swore. It was 10:30 a.m. and he had meant to get up early and join Ahmed for breakfast. They had had a late evening, drinking into the early hours while Vaux talked about his leisurely five-day overland journey through Europe and across the Straits to Morocco. Ahmed for his part was mostly silent, listening intently and playing the perfect host.

He had arrived at around 10 p.m., after a long day in Gibraltar where he met up with George Greaves who, on instructions from Alan Craw, had flown in from Rabat via Malaga. Greaves had rented a car at the airport where he made contact with Len Powell, chief scientist/technician at MI6's Century House headquarters. They both drove to Gibraltar where they had arranged to meet Vaux at an out-of-the-way hostelry in Caleta, a small fishing village about ten miles from the old British bastion town.

Powell, of course, had shadowed Vaux in Operation Helvetia, but he chose not to tell him that he possessed tapes of his pillow talks with Barbara Boyd as well as the tediously long and useless recordings of clinking glasses, tinkling ice, and pouring liquids that provided the background sound effects to Vaux's lone drinking bouts.

George Greaves was over six feet tall, had a big girth, grizzled short hair, and a round, reddish face. He smoked

small Dutch cigars and shared Vaux's taste for whisky. He had
served three years in Rabat following six years in Tunis. He
was usually designated an assistant cultural attaché. He was a
respected agent-runner, spoke passable Arabic, good French,
and had a working knowledge of Dutch thanks to a long post-
ing in Jakarta. Vaux liked the man at first sight and felt a little
more secure knowing that he hovered in the wings with his
helpers. A hasty but well-prepared evacuation was always the
final option should things go awry.

'This is Mr. Powell,' said Greaves. 'I think you two should
be alone for as long as it takes. Get the technical stuff over with
and then come down to the bar. I'm going to have a bloody
Mary to get over that nerve-shattering trip from Malaga. All
those blind hairpin bends made me dizzy and Powell was no
bloody help—the quintessential back-seat driver that he is.'

Vaux sat at the base of the large double bed while Powell
sorted through a leather attaché case. He read a few documents and handled several packages.

'I got carpeted for not wiring you in Geneva, old boy. So
this time I'm not going to lay myself open to Craw's castiga-
tions. I've thought a lot about this mission. And as I understand it, it's quite straightforward. You'll be the guest of the
target party. You intend to milk him for everything he knows
over the course of a few days. Right?'

'That's about it,' said Vaux. He shivered at the thought
of perhaps being required to place miniature microphones in
hidden places all over Ahmed's villa.

'So here's the situation. I'm not going to ask you to wear
a body mike plus the attendant recording equipment. The
system is very effective but a bit cumbersome—looks like an
armored-vest or a flak jacket. It can be a bit dodgy, especially
when you go to bed at night in an unsecured house. Plus you
can get careless, leaving the bloody thing on a bedroom chair
while you're having a bath only to have an undercover maid
come in and find it.'

'You do have dark thoughts, don't you.'

'That's the business, sir. Anyway, so what I suggest is our latest little gizmo, designed and developed by our scientific department with a lot of input from yours truly.' Powell opened up what appeared to be a small velveteen jewel box. Inside was an oversized stainless steel wristwatch with a black leather strap. He took it out and opened the back. Vaux thought he was going to insert the usual cell battery, but the round metallic disk looked bigger than that.

'This, believe it or not, contains what we call a micro-digital memory bank—a micro-miniature CD-ROM if you like, designed to record for twenty-four hours. It's best to replace it every morning, really, because it can stop recording without warning, of course. I'll give you loads of spare disks that you can stash somewhere in your luggage. They look like ordinary watch batteries, but a bit larger.'

He handed Vaux the watch. It had the Timex brand name emblazoned on a white face with black Roman numerals. There were two buttons on either side of the watch.

'The top right-hand button is an on/off switch for the recorder. Remember—you press to start. The top left-hand button is your usual hand-changing winder. The two lower buttons are nonfunctional. Of course, the time mechanism works off the same cell battery as the CD recorder—life span about three months. When you have to take out the old recording disk and replace it with a new one, you open the back of the watch by pulling out the on/off button. Same when renewing the battery.'

Vaux examined the watch. He observed a sort of mesh grill around the steel rim. He pointed to it. 'The tiny mike, I presume.'

Powell nodded.

'Remarkable. What will they think of next? Just as well I came away forgetting to put on my old Accurist.'

'You have one of them?' said Powell, fascinated. 'Used to get one every Christmas when I was a kid. Gone up market since those far-off days, but still reasonably priced.'

'Anything else I should have or that I should know about?'

'Not really. That should be enough. Just flip it on when you get down to one of your long conversations with the target party. Or when you are sitting down to dinner with him. It's a marvelous invention, if I say so myself. And impossible to detect.'

* * *

Greaves had retired from the bar into the deep luxury of an over-stuffed rattan chair by the tall windows that looked out over the Strait of Gibraltar. There were three sets of opened french windows that gave on to the large terrace. The day was calm and sunny, the sea as flat as glass, and big plump seagulls constantly swooped down to the balustrade that marked the boundary of the terrace. A few aged guests sat in deck chairs under parasols and threw peanuts at the squawking white gulls. Small birds—sandpipers and yellow wagtails—waited patiently for a gull's sudden take-off to get their share in the feast. Vaux had left Powell in his room. Whether by design or not, Powell had signified his need of a siesta. His business, in any case, was done.

'Beautiful location, what?' said Greaves as Vaux sat down opposite him. 'This is the Admiralty brass's favored place. They send the submarine crews here for their forty-eight-hour leaves while the subs are being fixed up in the dockyards. First thing the chaps do of course is decamp to Gib where at least they can relax and find some women. Some of those Spanish girls are pretty stunning. Nothing here but a bunch of old married retirees—and a few spooks.'

Vaux looked around as if to reaffirm Greaves' observation. 'Well, I seem to have finished with Powell. I take it you know about my little piece of wizardry,' he said as he pulled up his sleeve to show off the watch.

'Oh, yes. We call it the eavesdropper's chronometer. Very effective. But remember that the range is limited. No good for recording beyond ten feet. Ideal for cozy tête-à-têtes or taping a dinner companion, but useless for anything else.'

'I'll remember that,' said Vaux.

Greaves signaled to a white-jacketed young waiter for another drink. 'I'll have a vodka martini this time, please. And my friend——'

'I'll have a Cutty Sark.'

'Now down to business,' said Greaves, suddenly serious. 'I assume my brief from Craw of B3 is accurate: you intend to pump a Syrian defector for all the info he can give you. In exchange for his eventual asylum in the U.K...'

'I'm afraid your B3 brief is *in*accurate,' said Vaux. He waited while the waiter served the drinks. A bowl of olives and pearl onions was placed in the center of the table between them.

Vaux then related the history of his relationship with Ahmed Kadri and the more recent anecdotes concerning Operation Helvetia and the CIA'S discovery——thanks to Hakki's defection——that MI6, in particular the Section B3 team, had been duped.

'Taken to the bloody cleaners, if you ask me,' laughed Greaves as he shoveled three green olives into his mouth. 'But what about your old friend Kadri. *Is* he seeking asylum?'

'No, not as far as we know. He's living in his aunt's house in Tangier. A big villa, apparently, on the mountain——or what they call the mountain.'

'Yes, I know Tangier well. The so-called "mountain" is a hill on a promontory with a great view overlooking both the Med and the Atlantic. Very exclusive, of course. A smattering

of old European money and a handful of millionaires including
that old American reprobate Forbes, owner of the successful
eponymous financial magazine. Plus King Hassan's mother, or
the Queen Mother as they choose to call her. About as old as
our own Queen Mum, I believe.'
  'I understand that Kadri's aunt is away, so we'll be by ourselves. Should be a fruitful few days,' said Vaux.
  'I don't have to remind you of our main needs: who's in
favor, who's out. Who are Assad's serious rivals? How does
Assad lean toward the Israeli problem? Is he using the Golan
Heights as an excuse to bash Israel, or as a bargaining chip? We
understand that he didn't like Egypt's peace deal with Israel
one bit, and our sources tell us he's totally against Jordan's
tentative moves to wrap up a similar agreement. Therefore we
have to assume he remains intent on pursuing a hard line to-
wards Israel.
  'Presumably he still needs to build up his armed forces,
so is he drawing up an even longer shopping list to submit
to the Russians? Why did he side with Iran in the Iraq-Iran
war? What's his position now vis-à-vis Iraq and Saddam Hussein? His air force is in a shambles and needs modernizing.
So where's he going to get the money? A drive to find more
oil perhaps? They have a bit already, but nothing like Iraq. The
longer-term: how is his relationship with the new Russia developing? Is the new détente for real? And don't forget, these
Arab dictators love their guided missile systems—most aimed
at Israeli airfields—in an attempt to make up for Israel's air
superiority. Assad's got most of the missile specialists based
in Aleppo—see if anything's changed and whether the under-
ground production facilities are still in Hamah and Aleppo.
  'We especially have to know more about the dozen or
so men who form his kitchen cabinet. Most of these jokers
belong to the same Alawi tribe as Assad. But even after this
latest purge, there are still some non-Alawis that are close to
him—Sunnis like Major-General Muhammad Khawli, chief
of air force intelligence and head of the National Security

Council. Assad believes in divide and rule, and a lot of non-Alawis and non-Muslims support him including minorities like the Druze and the Kurds. He's also strong among the old Sunni elite in Damascus.

'But was that Palmyra purge perhaps the first step in some ethnic cleansing game to rid the regime of non-Alawis? If so, we're in real trouble because practically all of our most well-connected agents in place are non-Alawi officials. So, old boy, we want to know which way the wind's blowing. Your exiled friend should be able to fill you in—and in spades. He was right up there, perhaps not intimate with Assad, but certainly one of the top officials in the defense ministry...'

By the time they both went to their rooms to clean up for dinner, Vaux's head was reeling. He wondered how Ahmed would react to the sort of marathon interrogation B3 expected him to conduct. Mason would demand results; Greaves would want data, facts, figures. They totally ignored one human factor: his respect for Ahmed, his old friendship stretching back to their youth. How could he grill Kadri as if he were tied up like a hog and some MI6 hireling poured water down his throat until he revealed all? Mason, Craw, and Co. simply assumed he had no respect for the man. He did. They also wrongly assumed he knew nothing about the cold-blooded and brutal murder of Veronica, a civilized, affectionate woman who happened to have other fish to fry, deep loyalties that could not be reconciled with British foreign policy interests.

Over dinner in the Caleta Palace's white-on-white art deco dining room, talk focused on the on-site security measures that would be taken as soon as Vaux arrived in Tangier. There would be a twenty-four-hour watch over the house, comers and goers scrutinized, car registration numbers checked, and constant surveillance of Kadri whenever he left the residence. Powell, who had joined them, gave him a heavy, chunky mobile phone. 'It's really a semi-walkie-talkie. We can hear you but you can't hear us. Take no notice of the Nokia emblem, it's as phony as a three-dollar bill. Should you need urgent help, just punch 666. The surveillance crew will be there in seconds,' he said.

'But let's hope it never comes to that,' added Greaves.

* * *

He heard the thump of a car door closing, the start-up of an engine, and the crunch of gravel as the vehicle moved away from the house down the long, palm-lined drive. He got up and walked over to the window. Prying open the wooden slats he saw the rear of a black Mercedes 190E sedan as it headed toward the tall black iron gates that opened slowly and presumably electronically. He couldn't see who was in the car or whether the driver was alone. He went into the bathroom and saw that the towels, soaps, and various toiletries had been set out as if the place was a five-star hotel.

When he got downstairs the house was quiet and deserted. He remembered where the kitchen was so he walked through the large 'European' living room to the swing doors through which he had seen the old woman Ahmed had called Fatimah emerge the previous evening with sandwiches, pastries, and coffee. It was a wide, white-tiled kitchen with an old range, a big white American refrigerator, circa 1930, and a tall copper boiler in one corner. The low windows looked out on to the pine and eucalyptus woods that scaled the 'mountain' to its peak.

Vaux helped himself to some orange juice he found in the fridge. Behind him he heard a shuffle. A youth in a long striped jellaba stood in front of him. He was lean and tall with dark curly hair, deep brown eyes, and bright white teeth. He smiled a good morning.

'Salaam.'

Vaux acknowledged the greeting with a nod. He wasn't sure whether the boy understood English.

He tried anyway. 'Is Ahmed, Mr. Kadri, about or has he left the house?' he asked.

'Mister Ahmed, he gave me this to give you,' said the boy in near- perfect English, producing a note he had been concealing under his jellaba.

Had to go into town to do some errands.
Hope you had a good night's rest. Please
help yourself to some breakfast. Fatimah will be
in to prepare lunch at about 11.30. I
should be back by then. Ahmed.
P.S. If you need anything, just ask the boy (Salim).

'*Choukrain,*' said Vaux, quickly recalling the Arabic for thank you. 'You know perhaps where the bread is?'

'I bring, sir,' said Salim.

Vaux took that as a hint he should get out of the kitchen. He walked over to the big picture windows. Here the vista was even better than he had imagined before setting foot in the house: a green lush garden dotted with umbrella pines, cedars of Lebanon, white-flowered jacaranda, and purple bougainvillea. Several small fishponds surrounded with statuary dotted the grounds, and, as the lawn sloped down to the distant cliffs, a large rectangular mosaic-tiled swimming pool. Around the pool were several tables shaded by parasols. Sun loungers were scattered at random at the water's edge. Beyond the far-off cliffs was the azure expanse of the Atlantic with white caps dotting the surface. On the horizon, an oil tanker slowly headed northwards.

Salim came in with a plate of croissants and a small cube of butter. 'You want drink, mister?'

'No thank you. I've had some juice.'

The boy bowed and retreated to the kitchen.

The house was a stucco cubic arrangement with two stories above the main floor. On his arrival, Ahmed had given him a quick tour: there were four bedrooms on each of the upper

floors, all with their own bathrooms; two large living rooms
on the main floor; a dining room, most of whose space was
taken up by a chunky long oak table that sat twelve people; a
study; and the big kitchen in the rear.

Vaux heard a car engine. Doors slammed and within a few
seconds Ahmed strode in. Behind him was an old Arab in an
incongruous black business suit that seemed too small for him
and an open-necked white shirt. He shouted for Salim, who
was given instructions to unload the car and take the provisions in via the kitchen door.

Ahmed Kadri gave Vaux a long hug. 'As-salama laikoum—
peace be with you, Michael. This is Abdullah. You didn't see
him last night—it was his night off. He is my dear friend and
general factotum, as I think you say in English. If you want
anything, just ask him. He runs this establishment, knows
where everything is, knows Tangier like the back of his hand,
and can get you out of all sorts of scrapes whether with the
traffic police or officious bureaucrats. And when you go sight-
seeing, an unequalled guide.'

The two men shook hands. Abdullah had a weak, warm
grip and his expression was suspicious. Vaux thought that perhaps the old retainer had a visceral dislike for strange house-
guests.

'Come into my study, Michael. We have much to discuss,'
said Ahmed. He was wearing a white linen suit, open blue
shirt, and brown loafers. He was comfortable here, thought
Vaux. And there was none of the stress or tension he had
sensed in his friend during their Geneva reunion.

They walked through the 'Moroccan' lounge, furnished
predictably with filigreed octagonal side tables, leather chairs
draped by Bedouin blankets, scattered poufs and ottomans,
and, in the center, a large brass tray supported by a square
table of mother-of-pearl and wood marquetry. An incongruous GE air conditioner was attached to one of the large arched
Moorish windows.

On each side of the door that led into the study two carved chests with shiny leather sides and hooked clasps were placed. The study was lined with bound books, and a big rosewood desk sat in front of the long windows that looked out onto a balcony from which wide stone steps led to the garden. Beyond the bushes and shrubbery he could see the driveway, so Vaux figured his bedroom was directly overhead.

Kadri sat down in a high-backed leather chair and pointed out a low-lying armchair covered by a small Persian rug that was positioned close to a deal escritoire.

'Did you rest well, my brother?' asked Kadri, in the sort of stilted, precise English he now seemed to have adopted.

'Very well. Overslept, in fact.'

'You probably needed it. All that travel. You said you got the hydrofoil from Gibraltar. I was curious. Why wouldn't you go to Algeciras? There you have the choice of a hydrofoil or a first-class ferry.'

'Oh, I had some personal banking business,' said Vaux, half honestly. He had opened an account at Barclays where he planned to transfer some of his Swiss money. But he wondered why Kadri chose to question him on his itinerary.

'Ah, I see.'

'You have a delightful house—'

'Not mine, old boy. My aunt's, actually. She was married to a Moroccan heart surgeon and this was their summer home. He worked in Casablanca, and they used to come here to get away from that hot and teeming city. Not at all like the Bogart film, you know.'

'So I heard,' said Vaux.

'She's a widow now and, alas, in a nursing home out on Cap Malabata. Alzheimer's, I'm afraid. She's quite happy for me to stay here, of course. Old Abdullah looks after the place, and there's nothing he won't do for me.'

Both men looked at each other in a kind of awe or wonderment, perhaps hardly believing that once again fate had brought them together. Vaux broke a long silence.

'So what happened, Ahmed? Why on earth did you have to retire? Is it a sort of self-exile?' he asked as he played with his watch and gently pressed the on/off switch.

'Don't let's discuss it now, Michael. We have so much time. I hope you plan to stay a few weeks at least.'

'I'd love to.'

'So now I propose a morning swim. Come, I'll take you to the pool.'

Vaux stood up. 'I'd better get my swimming gear.'

'Don't bother. Salim will provide everything. He'll be at the pool now.'

30

Ten days later George Greaves was bent over an ancient portable Remington in his room at the ornate El Minzah Hotel on the Rue de la Liberte in the center of Tangier. He was transcribing the latest batch of miniature CDs dropped off by Vaux at the American Express offices on the Boulevard Pasteur. The local facilitator was a veteran employee of Amex who worked occasionally for the firm in return for a modest retainer, regularly augmented by fictional but unquestioned expense accounts. Greaves adjusted his headphones on his large head and pressed the forward button on the specially designed miniature CD player.

The transcript would be delivered to the British embassy in Rabat via a courier, an English schoolteacher at the American School in Tangier, who was happy to freelance for the home team whenever the opportunity arose.

Transcript begins:

Kadri has told Vaux that the Palmyra coup was not, as our field agents had previously reported, purely a takeover by the Alawis and the ouster of the Sunnis.

Kadri: No, Michael, that's not at all accurate. The regime is still a mixed-bag. Assad, an Alawi, of course favors his own sect and tribe. But he is a shrewd leader. He is not called 'the Sphinx' for nothing. When he was confronted by six of the most powerful men in the regime and told he must reshuffle some of the senior posts and at the same time weed out a few lesser officials—including me—he never indicated whether he approved or didn't approve of the dirty half-dozen's demands. I enjoyed that film, by the way, so let's call the putsch *leaders that, so we are clear who we are talking about.*

So Assad made sure that the men directly under him still represented a mixture of Alawis and Sunnis. He doesn't want a Sunni revolt on his hands or Sunnis going around disgruntled and discontented. I can tell you, for instance, that some of the vice-presidents—the most important men after Assad himself—are Sunnis. The foreign minister, Abdul Mashariqa, is a Sunni. Other Sunnis include the prime minister, old Kassim who's from a respected Damascene Sunni family. And then there's Bashir Zuhayr, the Baath Party's secretary-general, another Sunni.

(Here the quality of the recording is poor. Kadri and Vaux seem to be in a car and the engine noise along with open windows and the clamor of traffic, crowds out the sound of their voices. Perhaps Powell can look into this: a more sensitive or redesigned mike?)

* * *

Transcript continues. (The parties appear to be at the swimming pool. Splashing water tends to muffle their voices, but skillful filling in of the blanks (by yours truly) gets to the general sense of the conversation.)

Kadri: You see, Michael, Assad is very shrewd. Members of what you might like to call the 'power elite' are constantly in a state of flux, with people rising to power, some falling from grace, others being rehabilitated—this goes on all the time. So the Palmyra thing was nothing very new. It just seemed more dramatic because the dirty half-dozen had the gall to present Assad with a fait accompli. *And he had the foresight to accept their proposed changes. I suspect he's biding his time.*

Vaux: What about you, Ahmed? I know you're a Sunni, even if not a particularly religious one. Where does all this lead for you? And why did they want to see the back of you?

Kadri: It has very little to do with my religion. Some bastard high up in the GSD——that's the General Security Directorate, similar to the CIA, really——took it upon himself to investigate the death of Barbara Boyd, our dear, departed agent at MI6, as you well know. This was, I believe, a chap named Shawcat Al-Shara. Anyway, he asked me to explain the near-disaster in Geneva. He completely ignored the fact that I saved the day by persuading you to work for our side. Without your contribution, how could we have deceived the Brits about the size of the arms deal?

But for some reason, he smelled something fishy about our friendship. He was one of these self-educated types who despised anyone who'd gone to a foreign university. He specially didn't like friendships forged abroad with foreigners or non-Arabs. He had it in for me and argued that I was unreliable. He knew some influential people at the GSD and out I went. There was no interview, no questions and no appeal. I'm still waiting to see what they have decided to give me as a pension. (A triumphant yell and a loud splash of water as presumably Kadri dives into the pool to forget his problems and give things a rest.)

* * *

The transcript continues:

Vaux:You're always saying that our friend Hafez Assad is a shrewd old bugger. Give me some examples, Ahmed.

Kadri:Well, for instance, remember I told you about his recruitment of Sunni Moslems as an insurance against insurrection. He's gone even further than that. There are non-Muslim minorities like the Druze and even Christians in his kitchen cabinet. Also, the non-orthodox Ismailis are represented. Then think about his wooing the Russians. Even in the Cold War days there was a tremendous armaments trade between the two countries. He was a key player in getting the Soviets to back the Arabs against Israeli expansionism and, in fact, there was even a secret treaty that stipulated the Russians would come to the aid of Syria should the Israelis launch an attack. In return for that deal, Assad agreed to give the SCP, the Syrian Communist Party, more freedom. At one point the SCP were the most vocal domestic critics of the regime.

Vaux: But cozying up to the Russians didn't do you much good in the wars of 1967 and 1973.

Kadri: The treaty was signed in 1980 and was to last for twenty years. But before that, the Russians backed Kissinger's efforts in '74 to get a ceasefire. And in those negotiations, don't forget, we got back parts of the Golan Heights that had been occupied by Israel since 1967. But again, Assad's very canny: he's always resisted too close a relationship with the Russian bear. Despite a lot of pressure from the Soviets he has always ignored their pleas to cooperate more with the Palestinians. Also, Moscow could never understand Assad's reluctance to form some sort of alliance with the Iraqis. After all, both leaders are members of the Baath Party, supposedly a pan-Arab nationalist-socialist union. The Russians think in terms of the old Politburo, you know—the international overseer and guide for national communist parties throughout the world. They don't get it, they don't understand Arab rivalries, least of all the Sunni / Shia divide. Don't forget Iraq's Saddam Hussein's a Sunni. Assad's Alawi sect are Shiites.

Assad thought, and I think he was right, that the Iran-Iraq war was the wrong war at the wrong time and against the wrong enemy, and two years after that useless war ended, Saddam Hussein decides— mistakenly—that he has the U.S. go-ahead to invade Kuwait! So Assad in this case backs the U.S. coalition. You can hardly say the man's not a shrewd pragmatist.

(At this point, a female voice intervenes, apparently asking the two men to come to the terrace for dinner. The voice presumably belongs to the young woman who arrived about three days after Vaux and who, as far as we have discovered, is the daughter of one of Kadri's sisters. Our linguist experts say she has a Syrian accent, unlike the cook-housekeeper, an older Moroccan woman. But she also speaks perfect English with a Home Counties accent. Her name is Safa. After a brief interval, Vaux put the mike back on. Clinking of glasses and the sound of pouring liquids suggest pre-dinner drinks.)

Transcript continues:

Vaux: So, Ahmed, do you think there's a chance that you will ever go back? Or are you enjoying your exile too much to even think about it?

Kadri: I think about it all the time. I love my country. And I have no bitterness toward Assad. Perhaps when he goes through all the personnel changes that the dirty half-dozen demanded he'll have second thoughts and exercise his veto power. He has a sort of Praetorian guard, you know, who in the final analysis would protect him. Not that I think any of the rebels have the guts to really stand up to him.

Vaux: So you'd go back like a shot if all was forgiven.

Kadri: Yes, I would. Now let's have some fun this evening. Safa, what would you like to do after dinner? Hit the bars, perhaps? Or a nightclub? They say the beach bars are humming. The tourist season is still in full swing, so there's plenty of nightlife. Perhaps a few drinks at the Rif Hotel and then over to the Miami—I think that's the best beach bar. Not so many rowdy Englishmen, if you forgive my saying so, Michael.

Vaux: It's up to Safa. Her wish is my command.

Safa: Oh my God! Michael, I'm flattered. No, you're the real guest here. I'm semi-permanent now I'm done with Durham. Ahmed said I could stay while I consider what I'm going to do with the rest of my life, didn't you Ahmed?

Kadri: Yes, my dear. The Miami it is then. Let's party.

(Laughter. Vaux switches off the recorder.)

* * *

The transcript continues:

Vaux: So you think this friendship with the Russians will continue under Yeltsin?'

Kadri: Oh yes. Russia sees itself as a sort of broker to counteract America's increasing assertiveness around the globe. The Russians haven't yet got to grips with the fact that they're no longer a super-power. They can't accept that. So there's a sort of natural antagonism, perhaps a jealousy, toward the U.S., and they know that the Israelis rely totally on the Americans for arms and money. So they feel they have a genuine counterbalancing role to play in the Middle East power play.

Vaux: So we can expect more arms deals like the one you brokered in Geneva...

Kadri: Sure. Hakki played a useful role too, remember.

Vaux: I thought you'd want to forget. Did you expect him to defect?

Kadri: How did you know he defected?

Vaux: They told me at the end of my official debriefing in London.

Kadri: Oh. Did they also inform you about the assassination of Barbara Boyd?

Vaux: No, they did not.

Kadri: A tragedy. She was a lovely person and a loyal colleague. Anyway, yes, Hakki's defection came as a complete surprise. He gave no hint at all that he was unhappy. You know, he left his wife and two young kids in Aleppo.

Vaux: I didn't know that. Will they let them join him in the U.S.?

Kadri: They could. Assad's not completely heartless. But I've a feeling that air force intelligence will try and take him out before too long. They're pretty ruthless and unforgiving. Don't forget Hakki betrayed Barbara Boyd. She'd still be alive if he hadn't sung like a sparrow.

Vaux: What's the air force got to do with it?

Kadri: Accident of history. Muhammad al-Khouli, one of Asaad's old and trusted advisors, succeeded Assad as commander of the air force after Assad was elected president in 1971. They have agents in Syrian embassies and at Syrian Airlines offices all over the world. Their job at home is to keep track of extremists like the Muslim Brotherhood. Abroad, they hunt down defectors, troublemakers, and assorted dis-

sidents. By the way, have you ever wondered why Hakki never...(Here Vaux seems to have inadvertently pushed the off button.)

* * *

The night they went to the Miami beach bar, Vaux felt long dormant libidinal stirrings. Safa, Ahmed's young niece, was an attractive girl who had just graduated from Durham University with a degree in modern history. When she was five years old, her father, a civil engineer, took her to England where he had landed a job with an international construction company. When he left Aleppo in 1975, he was a widower. Her mother, one of Ahmed's two sisters, had died of breast cancer at the age of thirty-five.

Safa had olive-tinged skin, big, brown, almond-shaped eyes, a thin, aquiline nose, and full, sensual lips. She wore her black hair long, sometimes drawn back in a ponytail. She was, her uncle thought, perhaps a little too slim and a fanatic for exercise and healthy, diet-conscious eating. Vaux had taken to her immediately. In a way, she reminded him of Veronica, a younger, less mature version, but the same expansive, happy personality, the extrovert, perhaps, to balance his tendency to retreat into his shell.

* * *

Earlier that evening, when they were having cocktails on the terrace, Vaux's quick action—pressing the off button on his miniature CD recorder—was prompted by his suspicion that Ahmed was about to ask him if he ever wondered why Amin Hakki had not exposed him along with Barbara Boyd, a.k.a. Veronica Belmont. Vaux thought that what he had decided to call 'the Hakki conundrum' was best left unsolved. To remind the listeners at MI6 about Hakki's mysterious

reluctance to implicate him in the Syrian deception would,
he considered, be counter-productive. Why stir muddy waters? Why give enemies like Short another bone to chew on?
And Ahmed, of course, must believe that this lurking threat
of exposure still bothered him. As for Kadri's 'revelation' that
Veronica had been taken out by B3's thugs—probably Special
Forces—Vaux felt good that perhaps this could only embar-
rass Sir Walter and his team. They would surely regret not
having informed him earlier. How, they would now be wondering, would knowledge of their ruthless solution to their
mole problem affect his critical morale?

Kadri had voiced the expected question.

'Yes, I did wonder why Hakki protected me. Do you think
it's a ticking bomb? Hakki just biding his time, then expose me
when it best suits him?'

'Could be. In which case you'd better watch out. But I
really don't think so. All I can guess is that for some strange
reason he feels he has to protect you. I've thought a lot about
this, Michael. He's a devout Christian, you know, Greek Orthodox, as a matter of fact. One of the very few who work for
the regime, or did work. I think it could be a gesture of compassion. I know he liked you. He told me so. He always said
he couldn't stand Barbara Boyd/Veronica Belmont because he
had a visceral hatred for spooks. Once he even told me he
sometimes had suspicions about her being a *triple* agent! In
other words, he thought she could all along have been really
working for the Brits, not us. He was a cautious, suspicious
man. But he saw you as an ingénue, if you like. A man who had
stumbled into a dirty business involuntarily and reluctantly.
You are lucky, perhaps, to give that impression to people who
could turn out to be dangerous enemies.'

Salim had brought a bottle of Coke for Safa. He picked up
an old-fashioned silver cocktail shaker from the drinks trolley
and shook it violently. Then he poured the clear, cool liquid
into two martini glasses. He served Ahmed first, then Vaux.
He made a small bow and retreated through the french win-

dows. Abdullah emerged with a tray of baklava and *assabiyya,* fingers of pastry and crunched hazel nuts.

Vaux looked over at Safa. 'To your future career, whatever you decide on,' he said, raising his glass.

Kadri said, 'Yes, indeed. To you, my pretty niece! Did you know she got a first, Michael?'

'No, I didn't. Congratulations again.'

'Thanks,' said Safa, her eyes now focused on the far distance. It was dusk, and beyond the trees and the cliffs a cobalt sea looked calm and quiet. Abdullah still hovered. He said something to Ahmed in Arabic.

'Abdullah is asking whether you would like *bisara* soup— that's pea soup— followed by a plate of *tanjia,* which is lamb stewed to perfection. Or would you prefer European, a *bifteck,* perhaps.'

'No, I'll go native. Thank you, Abdullah.' The old man, now dressed in a long brown jellaba and a pair of pointy, gold-braided red babouches, bowed slightly and went into the house.

Vaux had known that Ahmed's westernization, begun all those years ago in England, had never extended to any inclination to talk about his wife, Nadia, and their family. It seemed to him that, to most Arabs, a wife was a necessity, a fixture, and their children a natural extension of their domestic arrangements. There often seemed little romance involved— and, of course, many marriages were arranged by the families concerned. Even though he had never met her, he was curious about Nadia's fate. It seemed only polite to ask.

'Is your wife joining you here, Ahmed?'

'I'm not planning a long exile, Michael. She wanted to stay to be near our children, even though all three are now old enough to look after themselves.'

Vaux sensed Kadri didn't want to pursue the subject any further—perhaps because his young niece was present.

* * *

Abdullah drove them home from the beach club at about 2 a.m. Both men had been drinking and talking all night. Safa had sipped red Moroccan wine and smoked a few joints of *kif,* proffered by a stream of admiring, mainly European, young men. Ahmed put his arm around Vaux's shoulders as they walked into the house. They saw Safa go straight to her room. Vaux remembered hearing Ahmed say that his niece had the right idea and that he was going to bed too. Old Abdullah would see to anything he wanted if he chose to stay up a while. But Vaux was tired, too, and a little drunk.

He fell asleep quickly. He had put his wristwatch on the bedside table, a precaution against lint and fluff from the bedclothes that could clog up the mike's grill. The click of a door opening woke him up suddenly. He saw someone move toward the bed and was about to reach for the watch when he realized it was Safa—in the same blue jeans and white shirt she'd been wearing all evening. She put her forefinger to her mouth as if to suggest discreet silence, tugged her jeans off, and climbed into the bed.

Nothing was said. Vaux could remember thinking that he'd blown the opportunity before it had begun: he was too tired and drunk to enjoy what she had decided to offer. But he was wrong. Her warm, smooth body clung to him like a child. Her gentle hands began to stroke his torso as she kissed and tongued his chest, his neck, and at last his lips.

She felt his warmth and response and there was now no doubt in her mind that her attraction to him was reciprocated. But she could feel that he was tense, and he seemed to be straining for something. He wasn't totally comfortable. She worked her way down and decided she would resurrect his desire. Her kissing turned to slow-tongued caresses, and Vaux gradually came to life. He was just coming down from the high of the strong orgasm when he realized she was leaving. She pulled on her jeans and waved her arms into her shirt and she was gone.

Vaux got up and opened the door slightly to see her walk away down the corridor. He thought she may have turned and waved a goodnight kiss. But she was gone.

A door opened and Vaux saw Salim in a long white night-shirt and bare feet tiptoe down the long staircase. He had been in Ahmed's room, probably, Vaux thought, to deliver some mineral water to last through the night.

* * *

Transcript continues:

Vaux:You said yesterday that Assad wasn't completely heartless—he'd be inclined perhaps to leave Hakki to rot in the U.S. under some squealer's protection program. But where was Assad's compassion when it came to making those decisions that led to the bloodbaths at Hamah and Homs when his security forces killed hundreds of women and children in an operation to wipe out his political opponents?

Kadri: If I didn't know you were a journalist and loved your history I'd say you had really done your homework. What's this, an official debriefing?

Vaux: Call it a debate between friends. You said your man, the leader of your country, whom you still respect, is not heartless. But the massacre in Homs was an international scandal and many saw it as a desperate act of a tyrant trying to cling to power.

Kadri:You have to go behind the story—I shouldn't have to tell you that. The Moslem Brotherhood ambushed government troops sent to Homs to look for dissidents and terrorists. This is 1982.What's a government supposed to do? Maintain law and order. So our troops moved in and fighting continued with the rebels for about two weeks. At the end of the pacification, some 10,000 civilians had been killed and about 1,000 Syrian troops. Call it overkill, if you like. The collateral damage was unfortunate but couldn't be avoided in a crowded, cramped city.War is war, Michael. How do you justify the killing of women and children at Dresden?

*Vaux: The justification usually given by my fellow countrymen is
that they bloody well did it to us first.'*

* * *

Here Greaves stopped typing, took a swig of J&B, and
shouted at the top of his voice: 'Halle-bloody-lujah!! Right on,
dear boy. You deserve a flamin' gong for that!'

At that very moment there was a knock on his door.
He took his headphones off, slid the CD player under some
papers, and went to see who it was. Two of the four British
army personnel sent over by the DIS—the Defence Intelligence Service—to monitor Kadri's villa and if necessary ensure Vaux's physical safety, stood before him. He'd met them
briefly a few days earlier but had forgotten their names. They
were dressed like a couple of English backpackers.

'What the bloody hell are you two doing here? You should
be on the Mountain Road.'

'That's just it, sir. Impossible task. We keep getting moved
on by the local constabulary. We've even offered bribes, English fags, a flask of gin. Doesn't make any difference. They're
adamant. We can't loiter in that area where all the toffs live,
that's what it is.'

Greaves looked up and down the ill-lit corridor and then
closed the door behind the two watchers. They were both in
their twenties and he guessed they had been seconded from
some army outfit.

'Okay, now let's go slowly here. Your names, first.'

'I'm Sergeant Binkley. This is Corporal Smyth, sir.'

'Spelt with a "y," sir,' said Smyth.

Binkley was tall, very thin with short, dark hair. His partner was what the English call 'thick-set'—solid and compact.
He had a crew cut and the bush of hair was straw-blond.

'There's not a lot of room here so just sit on the bed while
I think, would you?' The two men looked at each other and sat
on the bed.

'First off, if you want to smooth the way with a Moroccan traffic cop don't just offer fags. Roll some hashish joints—*kif* they call it here. And I don't care if it is against army regulations. Nobody's around to question your possession of the ancient weed. And you can buy the stuff anywhere. They all smoke it. Put it on the expense chit. And another thing— forget about gin or any other alcohol. These chaps just don't drink it. Against their religion. All right? Now, where are you from?'

'Aldershot, sir.'

'No, I mean what regiment or outfit. Special Forces?'

'No sir. Royal Corps of Transport.'

'Transport Corps? Christ, this is a specialists' job.'

'The Special-ops boys are all tied up with the IRA, sir,' said Smyth.

'Yes, I suppose so. Where are your colleagues?'

'They're kipping. We do twelve-hour shifts, it's their time off.'

Greaves picked up the phone on his desk. He dialed for an outside line and began to talk Arabic. To Smyth and Binkley, he sounded as if he were strongly protesting some terrible injustice. On the other end of the line, the accused shouted back so loudly that Greaves had to hold the receiver away from his ear. Binkley looked doubtfully at his comrade. Then suddenly Greaves adopted a soothing, conciliatory tone. It seemed to have worked. Turbulent waters were calmed. The other man had seemed to surrender and talked quietly and unexcitedly. Then Greaves gave an effusive goodbye and put down the phone. He looked over at the young watchers. His confident smile indicated a happy resolution of the problem.

'Well, that's cleared up. That was the local *Sûreté's* Chief Inspector Hamid Al-Zubaidi. I know him. I had arranged everything, paid him off a few thousand dirhams. He says he assumed that was for a week only. So I've got to get him some more dosh. Can't be helped. Once this is done you can resume your duties. What are you chaps driving?'

'A Jeep, sir. Jeep Wrangler,' said Binkley.

'Okay, you can take me up to Jew's River—it's at the base of the mountain. I'm meeting Hamid there after I pay a visit to the Banque du Maroc over the road. You can wait for me down in the lobby.'

'Right, sir,' said Binkley.

Greaves rummaged through his papers, shoveled some into his briefcase along with the CD player, put on a cotton safari jacket, and left the room with the two NCOs.

31

Vaux was happy. He was delighted with the unexpected revival of his sex life—dormant since his separation from Veronica—and with the rekindled intimacy and warmth he shared with Ahmed so many years ago. It felt almost as if Ahmed was right when he responded to Vaux's expressed surprise that their paths should have crossed once again: '*Mektoub!*'—it is written. Perhaps it really was in the stars. But there was also something romantic and ineffable about the very milieu of this outpost of southern Europe: a modern villa perched on a hill, fragrant with the scents of lavender and rosemary, the warm, gentle breezes from the Mediterranean, the peaceful, languid nights of love-making. He did not question and in fact relished the conspiratorial pact with Safa—which was that neither of them should speak of what Safa chose to call their 'liaison.' Was there something in his and the Kadri family's genes that encouraged secrecy and clandestine relationships?

But he had flashes of regret: he was not being honorable toward his friend. He had wistfully felt that he would have found a more embittered and disillusioned man in Ahmed, the sort of disenchanted informer that old Sir Walter thought he would discover. If Ahmed had become a real and convinced Assad foe, they could have had fun composing a story—part fiction, part fact—to deliver to the insatiably curious and hungry boys at Section B3. They could have conjured up more secret arms deals, speculated on Syria's strategic pan-Arab goals, highlighted Assad's love life, named probable presidential successors, not to mention the identity of various pro-western

conspirators who could now be planning an imminent coup
d'etat. But it was not to be.

* * *

Vaux had discovered an old, rusty Hercules bicycle in a
decrepit two-car garage that was hidden away behind a cluster
of palm trees. It solved one of his early problems: how to get
the CDs to the American Express office in the center of town.
He asked Abdullah for some oil and sandpaper, checked the
brakes, and tested the old three-speed Sturmy Archer gears.
Within twenty-four hours, Abdullah had produced an old tire
pump and the good news was that there were no punctures in
the inner tubes. He told Ahmed he needed some exercise other than a few laps in the pool and would take a ride now and
again around the mountain. He also discovered a dusty white
1976 Triumph TR6 under a tarpaulin. It had been cannibalized
by, according to Ahmed, mysterious plunderers.

Another discovery in his early days at the villa was the
flat roof above the top floor. He went up out of curiosity. Old
plastic bags and yellowed newspapers were lying in the gaps
between several small wooden shacks that housed electrical
equipment and tools. A large, oval, rusted steel tank contained
the house's supply of water. A solitary slatted folding chair was
placed close to the edge of the roof on the southeast corner.
Perhaps Abdullah or Salim came here for some peace and quiet, a solitary smoke—and a prayer. (He had observed a straw
prayer mat on the Mecca-facing east side of the roof.)

He sat down to enjoy the view and discovered the chair
had been strategically placed to offer a 360-degree panorama
of the surrounding gardens and the sea. Then he saw it: just
behind a line of beech trees close to the Mountain Road, a
military green Jeep was parked. A young man with cropped
blond hair had got out and was stretching his arms and walking
around the vehicle.

The watchers, without a doubt. For Christ's sake! He'd demand that Greaves remove them. They stuck out as obviously as whores in a monastery.

* * *

Breakfast was usually brought to him in his room by Fatimah.

She was portly but compact with graying black hair. She wore a black cotton outfit that hung loosely from her broad shoulders down to her thick ankles. She spoke no English but communicated with smiles and gestures. She usually came up with croissants and a bowl of *café crème*. Later, Salim would knock gently, enter the room with fresh towels and linen, and pick up discarded shirts and underwear for the daily laundry. Vaux wondered if he had finished school. He seemed a bright boy and his English was passable. Perhaps Ahmed had coached him. It was the sort of thing his old friend would want to do.

'Mister Ahmed, he says he like a meeting with you at ten o'clock, sir, in the European lounge,' said Salim as he draped Vaux's terrycloth dressing gown over the bed.

'Oh, really? All right Salim, thank you.' He was somewhat surprised. Ahmed usually disappeared in the mornings, along with Abdullah who drove the Mercedes. He never inquired about their errands but guessed Ahmed had business to attend to in town. And then there was the aunt out near Cap Spartel, a rocky promontory he had seen one day with Safa on their way to visit the Caves of Hercules and the spectacular Atlantic beaches beyond.

The 'European' lounge was furnished with bulky art deco pieces, over-stuffed armchairs with blue and white floral covers, a long walnut sideboard decked out with traditional silver platters, entrée dishes, and cocktail shakers, a large, low-lying couch, and mahogany side tables that could be stacked one upon the other. A thick Moroccan carpet and scatter rugs covered the parquet floor.

Ahmed was sitting in one of the armchairs. Safa sat on the sofa reading an old European edition of *Newsweek*. Vaux's first thought was that Safa had decided to tell her uncle about their relationship and that perhaps Ahmed had objected on the grounds of the age gap and the abuse of his hospitality. His conscience had already dealt with such questions, but he prepared for the worst.

'Ah, Michael. Did you sleep well?' Vaux looked at Safa, whose eyes were glued to the magazine.

'Yes, Ahmed. There's something about the air here that helps me sleep like a log. I drop off as soon as my head hits the pillow.' *Why do lies and half-lies fall off my lips so readily? But the bit about the air is genuine.*

'Good, good.' Ahmed gestured to the armchair next to his. Vaux sat down. 'I have asked Safa to tell her story. I think you will find it interesting. It's highly political and I know you are interested in this sort of thing. It has a bearing on the Arab-Israeli problem. I am aware that you have thought a lot about this and I also believe, at least I hope I know where your sympathies lie in this matter. Safa, would you put that magazine down, darling?'

Safa raised her head, placed the magazine beside her on the couch, and looked at Kadri as if for prompting.

Kadri said: 'Safa was born in an old Syrian town named Qunaitra in the governerate of the same name. It's situated in the Golan Heights, which, as you know, is still, after all these years, occupied by Israel. So my little niece was born in occupied territory. I want you to go on from there, Safa.'

Vaux fiddled with his ersatz Timex.

* * *

The transcript continues:

Safa:We lost the Golan in the Arab-Israeli war of 1967. It's a part of the world that's belonged to Syria since time immemorial. Qunaitra was an ancient and quite beautiful town and I was born there in 1970. The population had shrunk to about 100,000 by then—in other words, in thirteen years of Israeli occupation, some 400,000 Arabs had left the town for greater Syria. Most of them went to the bigger cities like Damascus and Aleppo. These refugees were banned by Israel from returning to their homes once they decided to leave. My father worked for the Israelis for a time but refused to cooperate when they asked him to help in the construction of their illegal settlements.

My father and mother had left Qunaitra (with me, of course) in 1972. They went to Aleppo where my father lectured at one of the polytechnics. My mother died three years later. That tragedy helped my father decide finally to move to Europe. He had studied in England and that helped him land a three-year contract with an international construction firm. The authorities thought he was coming back after his contract ran out but he never had any intention. He's a Sunni and had always resented a government dominated by the Alawis, a Shia sect. Besides, after five years studying civil engineering in Liverpool, he'd become quite an anglophile.

Vaux: That's gratifying, at least.

Kadri: Meanwhile, the United Nations had declared the Golan occupation, like that of the West Bank and Gaza, as totally illegal under international law. U.N. resolutions 242 called for the withdrawal of Israeli troops to their 1967 borders. Later, the U.N. also passed resolution 338, which called specifically for the return of the Golan Heights. Continue, Safa.

Safa: Anyway, then came the 1973 war. We wanted our land back. Egypt attacked Israeli forces from the west, Syria from the east.

Kadri: This war was not the Arab fiasco some think. Syria overwhelmed the Israelis in Golan and the Egyptians pushed over the Suez Canal. The Israelis, despite their brilliant intelligence services and the help of the CIA, were taken by complete surprise. They took several days to regroup. But of course when they did, they succeeded in pushing both armies back. The war was a stalemate and the ceasefire was negotiated by Henry Kissinger, then the U.S. Secretary of State. The Egyptians held on to the canal and a few months later, after a lot of Israeli haggling, we did regain parts but not all of the Golan. One liberated town was Qunaitra.

Safa: Ah, Qunaitra! When we returned, what did we find? The total destruction of the city. The Israelis had bulldozed and torn down every standing building—houses, homes, office blocks, shops, even the souks—the lot. Of course, the small house where I was born was gone too. They had also destroyed the region around the ancient town.

Kadri: The U.N. condemned the barbaric act—which was also probably a breach of the Geneva Convention.

Vaux: But why did they do that? What was their motive?

Safa: Revenge, perhaps. Bloody-mindedness born out of the sort of hatred that engenders more hatred. How can we be expected to like them and accept them when they bully us, destroy our ancient heritage, and stubbornly occupy our lands despite the illegality and the world-wide condemnation?

Vaux: They would say you brought it on yourselves—by launching the attacks in the first place.

Safa: In the first place, they shouldn't have been on our land.

Vaux: It's always so difficult to criticize Israel because you're immediately charged with anti-semitism.

Kadri: Yes, the Israelis are good at that—blurring the lines between a genuine political argument and outright racism. It's something that very few people—fair-minded people—in the West have been able to overcome. Again it's all the guilt, the legacy of the holocaust.

Anyway, Michael, I wanted you to hear Safa's story because very few people from the West are fully aware of what happened at Qunaitra. Sometimes small facts on the ground illustrate the nature of the conflict better than hundreds of words about political and military strategies and tactics. (A pause) So, my loved ones, enough of this. Come, let us go with Abdullah and Salim to the souk. We have provisions to get in, and I want Safa, who has been to far too many

Sainsbury's and Tesco's, to see how people have shopped and haggled for their everyday needs for eons.

* * *

Vaux's bicycle ride to the town center was all downhill. From the villa—down the Rue de la Montagne and on to the long, mottled plane tree-lined Rue de Belgique and finally to the narrow alleyway where he padlocked the old Hercules behind the Place de France—the trip took about fifteen minutes of effortless cruising. But his attention to road conditions could never waver. The grizzled drivers of the small yellow taxis (what the citizens of Tangier call the 'petit taxis') recognized no speed limits and no highway code. The more dignified chauffeurs of the stately 'grand taxis'—usually an ancient Mercedes—were more inclined to recognize the vulnerability of two-wheeled transportation while wizened old Arab men and women on donkey carts went about their everyday excursions totally aloof from any modern modes of transport.

He had arranged to meet Greaves at the always crowded and bustling Café de Paris directly opposite the stately French consulate on the Place de France. French colonial influences seemed to be highly resilient. Even the wicker chairs and marble-topped tables placed on the street outside the café were reminiscent of Paris. In the center of the square was a grassy traffic island that some days boasted a working, ornate fountain and on dysfunctional days played host to a gaggle of strutting pigeons. Palm trees lined the square, and the scents from the shrubbery and plants of the consulate's manicured gardens mingled weakly with the exhaust fumes of the heavy roundabout traffic.

Vaux sat down at a table that seemed to balance precariously between the raised stone floor of the café and the outside pavement. There was a stone pillar on the right-hand side so that they were at least half-hidden from passers-by. He found

Greaves dressed in a seersucker suit, white shirt, and Panama hat. Vaux wore a blue tracksuit, recently brought in by Kadri from one of his shopping expeditions.

'Totally secure, old boy. Meeting place of the whole world. Well, Tangier's world, anyway. Two Englishmen having a morning drink together—what could be more natural? What'll you have—some mint tea?'

'Do they serve beer here?' Vaux felt thirsty after the bicycle ride.

'Yes, indeed. Have the local brew, it's quite good. Me, I'm going to have my usual morning Pernod.'

The old Moroccan waiter, in white apron and black trousers, sported a small black moustache on a pale face and looked appropriately French. He wrote the short order down on a writing pad. Then he wiped off the table, cleaned the ashtray, and put down two paper mats. The two men sat in silent anticipation. Vaux, for reasons that baffled him, had a sudden pang of homesickness. He felt he would rather enjoy having a pint of Watney's at the Pig & Whistle right now. The drinks were quickly served along with a carafe of water. A piece of paper was tucked under the ashtray.

'Look, I asked to see you for only one reason. Those bloody watchers are sitting in their Jeep outside Kadri's villa looking for all the world like, well, what they are. If I saw them, then I'm sure old Abdullah has noticed them. He's a suspicious old guy and very close to Kadri. Anything he sees that he finds unusual, suspicious, or curious would go straight back to his master. You have to think of an alternative plan.'

'They're there primarily to protect you, old boy. They can't sit with me at the Minzah, for heaven's sake. What alternative is there?'

'I don't know—perhaps you could see if a nearby house is for rent or something. Some of the scattered villas that dot the mountain look pretty neglected and I wouldn't be surprised if they're unoccupied.'

'That's a thought. Many of the better-off European residents have gone back home, some unable to sell their villas at any price. Tangier's not the magical city for expats it once was. Maybe we could plant the boys as squatters in a strategic location, without going through all the rigmarole of renting the place. Kadri's place is about halfway up the mountain, isn't it?'

'Yes. And there's no time to lose. I have a feeling that old Abdullah is already working on it.'

'What makes you think that?'

'Just that he's one of these old loyal retainers who misses nothing. He's probably gone through my things with a fine-tooth comb already.'

'Hope not. What will he think of all those tiny little silvery disks?'

'God knows. Batteries for the watch, I hope.'

'What, all fifty of them? And with the total steadily declining as you deliver them to old Faud at the Amex office.'

'I'll cross that bridge when I come to it.'

'I've just had another brilliant, thought.'

'What's that?'

'You reported an old broken-down TR6 in the garage. What if you hire our handy team of sports car specialists to come and do it up—repair the bloody thing and make it roadworthy.'

'But the watchers are English, George. How the hell would I explain that?'

Greaves thought for a moment and drained the last of the cloudy yellow liquid from his glass. 'They could be a mobile team sent out by Leyland Motors or whoever the hell owns the Triumph brand name these days. British experts, available at a cost of course, who travel the world looking for old sports car aficionados—just like you.'

'I see two disadvantages. First, what do these Special Forces fellows know about cars?'

'They're not SAS, that's for sure. They're transport wallahs—RASC types. Call themselves something different now. Know all about the internal combustion engine. What's the second objection?'

'Abdullah could recognize them. He's probably already cycled past the idiots to have a good look at them.'

'You're right. Forget it. I'll stick with the squatter plan.'

Greaves signaled for two more drinks. Vaux lit up a Camel.

Greaves said, 'How are things going apart from this particular problem?'

'You're doing the transcripts. You tell me.'

'It all looks pretty good. Nothing earth-shattering or likely to spark a new war in the Middle East. But plenty of fodder for Section B3 and Sir Walter's voluminous files at Gower Street.'

32

It was to go down in the verbal annals, the classic apocrypha of Section B3, the subsection of the British Secret Service devoted to Near and Middle East affairs. Just two minutes would have made the difference between success and failure, between fiasco and a satisfying conclusion to what had seemed a brilliant enterprise. The story was filed under the sad rubric of 'what might have been...*if only*.'

Just after saying goodbye to Vaux, Greaves, as was his usual morning habit, turned right outside the Café de Paris and walked down La Rue de la Liberte past his hotel and on to the Grand Socco, a busy, tourist-clogged square that led to Tangier's ancient medina. The cobblestoned square, a two-minute walk from the Place de France, is lined by small shops and boutiques that sell Moroccan carpets, wooden cabinets, and boxes of inlaid marquetry; stuffed leather poufs; leather camels, baby elephants, and rhinos; brass lanterns, trays, and sconces; Berber daggers in Arabesque sheaths; Bedouin swords; and a thousand and one other pieces of bric-a-brac from the Maghreb and farther east. Every morning, Greaves bought some item here to add to his collection of exotic mementoes—something to remember his peripatetic diplomatic career when he finally retired to that dreamed-of thatched cottage in the English countryside.

On this particular morning, Greaves made for the Café Central, a few steps down in the social scale from the Café de Paris, but all the more interesting for that. There was no rush to get back to the Minzah; his transcripts were up to date.

A waiter brought him a glass of *anis* along with a small ceramic jug of water. He had forgotten to bring something to read so he casually looked around at the customers who sat at the small wicker tables on the raised terrace. It was the usual crowd: middle-aged and older men in brown or white jellabas, some hooded or wearing a red fez, others in tight-fitting, shabby European suits and scuffed shoes. A quiet group at one table concentrated on a game of backgammon. Two overweight men who both sported long white beards deliberated over elaborate chess moves. In the square, veiled women and girls passed by in couples. Then he saw old Faud from the American Express office with a friend of about the same age. They were sharing a long-stemmed nargileh pipe.

What Greaves couldn't know is that the two men shared a typical Tangerine upbringing: they had both seen the good old easy money days when the town was an international zone governed by a tripartite colonial regime comprising the British, French, and Spanish. As young men they had witnessed the Independence Day celebrations when in 1956 Rabat took over from the colonial powers and integrated the city into the new post-colonial self-governing nation. Life was never the same again. But the two men soldiered on, grabbing jobs when they could, bringing up large families, providing for their wives and children.

Faud's father, Muhammad Al-Mallah, had worked for the Deuxieme Bureau, the French intelligence organization, during the Second World War. He never discovered how the Moroccan secret police found out about his wartime activities. But to save himself from torture or worse, he agreed to transfer his loyalties to Morroco's new intelligence service. His son willingly inherited his connections. As an American Express employee, he was well positioned to pass on both useful and useless information regarding U.S. and European expatriates and particulars, mainly financial and sex-related, about the annual crop of tourists to a town known for easy drugs and commercial sex.

Meanwhile, his old friend Abdullah al-Mawada pursued a more modest career. His talents lay in serving the wealthier members of society, particularly in their domestic arrangements. He was an accomplished chef, an unrivaled procurer of provisions (at the *souk,* he could haggle over the price of a chicken for an hour), a gentleman's gentleman, caretaker and general factotum to the privileged. Dr. Solemein Cherqui, the renowned cardiologist, had been among his many employers. When the master had died of a heart attack, he was happy to continue to serve his elegant, elderly widow, Madame Sharazad, Ahmed Kadri's aunt.

The two men, now in their early sixties, had had different lives. But they had both been born in Dradeb, a poor and neglected settlement about ten miles outside the city, whose citizens had for generations somehow managed to eke out a hardscrabble existence. The two old Moroccans had attended the only elementary school in that poor town, and ever since those early, testing days of boyhood, they had remained good and loyal friends.

Greaves was to recall that fateful morning many times— at official debriefings and when reminiscing with his more intimate colleagues: *if only*...Vaux had not hurried away to pick up his bloody bike and pedal up the mountain to his pining fucking mistress. *If only*...he had thought to invite Vaux for a short walk, a look around the medieval medina following a companionable drink at the shabby Café Central. *If only*... the two secret agents had been together, so that Vaux and Greaves could have seen both those old residents of Tangier sitting and talking together—*and instantly connecting the dots.*

The alarm would then have been quietly but decisively raised, so that the helpers and the watchers could quickly prepare for coordinated action. Greaves would have been the anchor man: he would have sent all four RASC wallahs to their staging posts, ready to pounce as soon as Vaux pressed the 666 panic button for urgent help and assistance.

But the brutal truth was that Greaves, a loner on one of his habitual solitary walks, had never seen old Abdullah in his life. And the collective thinking was that on that fateful morning, Faud was well aware of this. So after a quick check to see if Greaves had any companions, he had clearly decided to ignore the man to whom he delivered every few days the mysterious, rattling envelope. Any thoughts of polite and friendly introductions had been quickly dismissed, thus destroying any chance that Greaves could by one brilliant stroke have made the connection between the two men.

Faud, of course, also knew Vaux—the man who played for time by looking at tourist brochures in the Amex office while waiting for Faud to finish up cashing travelers' checks for some customer. He had put two and two together a few days earlier when he had seen the sender's return address printed on the top left side of the white rectangular envelope: Villa Mauresque, the big, white house where he knew his friend Abdullah had worked for several years. That was an unforgivable breach of tradecraft by Vaux who presumably considered Faud's longtime connections with British intelligence as tantamount to complete trustworthiness. But the nexus linking Vaux, Greaves and the Villa Mauresque was now established beyond doubt. All that remained was for Faud to suggest that Abdullah begin to make some discreet inquiries.

* * *

'What a smasher! She's a bloody knockout,' said Corporal Smyth as he looked through his army-issue binoculars toward the distant swimming pool.

'Here, let's 'ave a dekko. Christ almighty, I wouldn't kick her out of bed. She's a looker, all right,' agreed Sergeant Binkley.

They were standing at the top of the narrow circular tower that had been built as an eccentric add-on to a rambling, cren-

ellated faux Moorish castle in the early '40s. The 'architect'
of what the Mountain's residents called 'Loew's folly' was an
equally eccentric American movie director named Ben Loew.
He had died in the late '70s and his two Hollywood-based sons
had been trying to sell the place ever since. It stood strategically about a quarter of a mile uphill from the Villa Mauresque and now sat uninhabited and dilapidated in overgrown
and neglected grounds. The watchers forced an easy entry and
moved in. They concealed the Jeep behind a stand of umbrella
pines and a wild, unkempt clump of oleander and yuccas.

'Tanned and very sexy, that's what she is. I wonder who's
banging her?'

Smyth was fatalistic. 'Who cares? We've got no chance.'

'And there's the wog we're supposed to look out for. He's
all dressed up and walking around as if he's about to leave.
Get down to the Jeep, Corporal. Follow him. Let's do the job
proper for a change. Then we can report everything back to
old Greaves.'

'Will do, Sarge.'

Smyth trundled down the narrow spiral staircase. Pigeons,
scared by his sudden and unfamiliar movements, fluttered
quickly from the tower's narrow embasures into airspace.

'And make sure the two-way radio's working this time.
I want you to tell me what's happening. Okay?' shouted Binkley.

He adjusted the binoculars slightly to maximize the clar-
ity and magnification of Safa's image. She was lying on a sun
lounger reading a book. She looked as close as three feet away.
Then he saw Vaux (recognized as the cyclist who had slipped
the message for Greaves to them as he was bicycling down the
mountain) approach her. He was wearing a t-shirt and shorts.
They exchanged some words and Vaux bent down to kiss her.

'So that's the bloody scene, is it?' muttered Binkley. He
didn't know all the ins and outs of their mission. But their CO
had told them it was top secret and that their primary task
would be to respond to any emergency call the party whom

they were protecting—one Michael Vaux—might make, and their secondary task was to watch the comings and goings at the villa and notify one George Greaves of the British embassy in Rabat, residing at the El Minzah Hotel, if anything 'untoward' occurred.

Quite what Major Peter Barclay had meant by 'untoward' Binkley didn't know. But he knew one thing: there was something queer and unforeseen about Vaux's apparent fondness for the beautiful guest who had arrived out of the blue about ten days ago. He had told Greaves of her sudden appearance via a phone call and he had replied that he already knew who she was—a niece of Kadri's, the fat cat who occupied the villa. But this luvvy-duvvy stuff, he reckoned, was a new development, and he'd have to call Greaves again from the small bar of his billet at the Atlas pension on the Boulevard Mohammed V.

He swept the binoculars to the far right and just caught sight of the black Mercedes going through the electronic gates. The car turned left toward the city. A few seconds later, Smyth's Jeep appeared. 'Smyth has two favorite pastimes: chasing a piece of tail and tailing a suspicious customer,' murmured an amused Binkley as he refocused his Zhumell on Kadri's beautiful houseguest.

Half an hour later, his radio crackled. 'Come in, Smyth, over.'

'They parked the Mercedes outside the American Express office on the Rue Pasteur, Sarge. Kadri and the old fellow went in together. I hovered around a bit outside then went in to look at the travel brochures. They'd gone into some back office with one of the clerks or travel agents. Shall I wait around? Over.'

'Just hang about a bit and continue to tail them. See what else happens, over.'

'Message received and understood—sir! Over and out,' said Smyth. He knew Binkers hated being called 'sir.'

* * *

Transcript continues:

Vaux: Assad must be getting on, Ahmed. What's going to happen when he leaves the scene, do you think?

Kadri: There are occasional reports about his health. But I think he's good for a few years yet. If he were do drop dead tomorrow, there'd undoubtedly be a power struggle. Myself, I think Abdul Khaddam would be the ultimate winner. He's what the Americans would call a 'tough cookie,' a hardliner who's been close to Assad for nearly thirty years. He's vice-president now and a former foreign minister. One of the chief architects of our involvement in Lebanon. He'd be a tough guy to beat in any big fight over succession.

Vaux: I read somewhere that there are two sons hovering in the background and that, like a lot of strongmen, Assad is perhaps grooming one of his own offspring to succeed him.

Kadri: Yes, there's a younger son, Rifaat, and Bashar, who's probably his favorite. Bashar's studying in Britain——he wants to be an eye surgeon, or so they say. But I think——and I could be wrong——that the old 'lion'——that's what Assad means in Arabic—— is a bit too shrewd to arrange a succession within the family. I've never seen Assad as a builder of a dynasty, but then again you never know with these autocrats.

Vaux: Any other candidates for the top job when the old lion goes to his maker?

Kadri: If I were a betting man, I'd say an outside favorite is a chap called Mustafa Tias. He's an old friend of Assad's and he's been defense minister for some time. My boss, in fact, when I moved over to defense from the central bank. He's been our key man in the final negotiations to procure arms and equipment from Russia. The only thing against him is that he's a Sunni——and no matter how pragmatic the post-Assad team might be, I don't see them giving supreme power to the Sunnis.

Vaux: Presumably, thanks to Tias, the Syrian forces are in much better shape than they were in the early '70s in the wake of the Arab-Israeli war.

Kadri: No comparison.

Vaux: I suppose the key question now is whether you could beat the Israelis if and when war breaks out again.

Kadri: The short answer is no. But Tias' main argument was always that you didn't have to win a war. You merely had to make a few harsh blows against Israel to extract real concessions when the ceasefire was arranged. That's what happened after the Yom Kippur war of '73. As Safa told you, we won back Quneitra on the Golan Heights despite losing the war.

I can tell you, Michael, that we've built up massive strike capabilities in recent years. We have missile production factories in Aleppo and Hamah, we have a joint facility with Iran to build SCUDs. We'd throw everything at Israel in the first few days of fighting, including— if the situation were dire enough—possibly WMDs. By which I mean biological and chemical weapons like sarin nerve gas and anthrax.

Vaux; Sounds like Armageddon.

Kadri: We wouldn't have started it.

Vaux : Where the hell would you produce that sort of thing?

Kadri: All over the country, Damascus, Homs—the big population centers.

Here there is a shuffling noise, some shouting and laughter. A female voice, probably Safa, challenges Vaux to a lap race. A big overwhelming splash of water drowns out all other noises. The on/off stud is activated and the recording ends.

33

Vaux was taking a siesta, a habit he had adopted more to conform to the habit of his host than any real need for sleep. Someone knocked gently on his door. Ahmed Kadri stood before him in traditional Arab dress—resplendent in a long white burnoose embroidered with gold braid.

'Michael, we are having a feast tonight to celebrate Safa's decision to continue her studies in England next year. I trust you like lamb and goat couscous, it's one of Abdullah's specialties. We will sit at the low table in the Moroccan lounge and there are no house rules against wine or *kif*. Please be down by seven o'clock. I have some errands in town. Safa has gone with a few new friends to Ceuta to replenish the bar with tax-free booze.'

Vaux thought the announcement oddly formal. Ahmed hadn't waited for a reply before quickly but quietly closing the door. And Safa hadn't mentioned going on any trip to Ceuta, the Spanish coastal enclave about three hours' drive east of Tangier. Nor had she shared with Vaux her apparent decision to go back to university rather than embark on some new career. Earlier, they'd had a light lunch at the pool. After a lap race won by Safa they picnicked out of a hamper. Kadri had mused some more about likely successors to President Assad, but Vaux had stuffed the wristwatch into his shorts. He tried to memorize what his friend had said. He would dictate an addendum to the latest recording. But he wondered why Safa had never said a word about Ceuta, let alone invite him to come along.

He put his head back on the big pillow. His blissful stay at the Villa Mauresque would soon be coming to an end. He had squeezed every ounce of information he could out of his dear friend (without making the whole process look like a prolonged interrogation) and the only satisfaction he felt was that the job was approaching completion. Could he now pretend to himself that nothing at all sinister had really happened? Could he still maintain his friendship with Ahmed after all the deceit and dishonesty? He knew that he still loved him. And he told himself that the surreptitious exercise would, in the final analysis, do little harm. So Section B3's archives would be fatter, perhaps more comprehensive. But he doubted that he had reported anything that could harm the Assad regime or Ahmed's own interests.

Yet, if the truth ever came out, how could he face this man who had put so much trust in him, had behaved like the excellent Arab host he had always been. He knew Ahmed deeply regretted what had happened in Geneva. And he knew that Ahmed would have done anything to prevent his friend from suffering the logical fate of a spy in their midst. He still shuddered at the thought of that Russian tramp freighter waiting in Marseilles to spirit him off to a Syrian port. He heard the faint distant chants of a muezzin calling the faithful to prayer. Then he fell asleep.

* * *

The transcript continues:

Vaux: After discussing the likely power struggle for the top job when and if Assad dies, Kadri came up with an afterthought, not directly recorded. But here's the gist of what he said:

Kadri: A wild card in all the maneuverings that Assad's death would cause is a very rich and powerful man named Rami Makhluf.

He happens to be the president's nephew. The Makhluf family is probably the richest in Syria. They own a bank, duty-free zones at the border, and several high technology outfits. The CIA has apparently estimated the family's worth at some $3 billion. Makhluf's still in his thirties, but his money could sway a lot of minds...So I'd have to put him in a list of possible contenders for Assad's crown.

* * *

Ahmed was bent over a low walnut cabinet, and it wasn't until Vaux saw him juggling with some old gramophone records that he realized the bulky piece of furniture was an ancient radiogram. They had finished eating and Abdullah was busy clearing the table while supervising Salim's efforts to serve sweet mint tea and Moroccan coffee. Suddenly Ahmed stood up and turned toward Vaux.

'You will remember this, I hope.'

Vaux heard the unforgettable opening notes of George Shearing's *Lullaby of Birdland*. Instantly he was transported back to the graduation ball in Bristol's old city hall. It was the late '50s and the popular swing number was on the hit parade, a favorite among students and professors alike. He remembered his dancing partner: Professor Margaret Longfellow, their lecturer in French literature, a tall, slim, no-nonsense bluestocking whose enthusiasm for her subject was contagious.

'God, yes. Wonderful. That night is etched into my memory forever. I couldn't believe Maggie Longlegs would accept my invitation to dance. But she did—and I got an unusual A-minus in the French intermediate exam.'

'I think she saw you as a typical, wan, stringy, vulnerable young man in need of a strong woman,' laughed Ahmed. 'You were very slim in those days, Michael.'

Then Kadri raised his arms as if inviting Vaux for a bear hug. 'Come, brother. Let's dance together tonight.'

Vaux advanced toward his friend. They hugged each other and Ahmed started to move with the music. After staggering a little, they both froze.

'You lead, Michael. I'll follow.'

To the rhythm and cadences of Duke Ellington's orchestra, they danced around the room. Safa, dressed in a silky blue kaftan for the occasion, had been quietly reading a blurb on a vinyl record sleeve. She now looked wide-eyed at the two men as they navigated around the bulky furniture. Abdullah was suspicious and watchful and his grim face, Vaux thought, seemed to belie the joyousness of the event.

Ahmed held him closely. 'I watched you both foxtrot around that ballroom that memorable night. I was wildly jealous, you know. Ah, youth! We all do things, feel things, that perhaps should be forgotten.'

Vaux was trying to decipher the cryptic remark when Kadri suddenly pushed him away. The music continued but both men stood facing one another in silence.

Then Kadri said: 'Come. We have some business to discuss.'

He led the way to the study. Abdullah followed them, and Vaux felt a sudden pang of apprehension. Abdullah shut the door behind him and Kadri sat down in his leather swivel chair. Vaux drew up a hard-bottomed wooden armchair so that he was facing his friend. Abdullah stood at the door.

'First, I want to continue our discussion about where my beloved country, the cradle of civilization, stands in today's anxious world. I don't feel we've exhausted the subject.'

Vaux was surprised. The party was apparently over. And Kadri wanted to talk of serious matters of state. He was alert, however, and adroitly moved his hand to cover his watch and push the on/off button. It was more a knee-jerk reaction, he later convinced himself, than any conscientious move to do his duty for England.

'Also, in discussing Syria's defense situation, I completely forget to tell you about our Special Forces outfit. Have you ever heard of *Al-Saiqa?*'

'No,' said Vaux, his mind in turmoil. There was something incongruous about this sudden briefing, perhaps even bizarre—like Ahmed's sudden urge to dance with him. Why couldn't Kadri leave this afterthought or postscript to tomorrow?

'Some have called them terrorists. But in fact they are like America's Navy Seals, or your SAS, if you like. Their enthusiasm is unlimited. They are trained in all the usual special operations techniques—hostage rescues, anti-hijacking, clandestine operations, the occasional tactical kidnapping, as well as long-range reconnaissance and intelligence gathering. You may be interested to know that Russia's ruthless Spetsnaz squads have helped train them. Like most clandestine forces, they represent a motley but loyal crew—some former East Germans, some non-Israeli Jews. The unit has penetrated into several neighboring countries including Israel, often posing there as Druze residents. A lot of their arms and equipment are bought in the black market. You will find them with American M-16 automatic rifles, Israeli UZI machine guns, Italian Berettas, and German MP-43 silenced machine guns.'

'May I?' asked Vaux as he fished for a Camel.

Kadri ignored him. After a pause he said: 'In fact, the situation that now confronts us may require that Ahmed Kadri, a temporary Syrian exile, request an *Al Saiqa* team here within twelve hours.'

Vaux exhaled a blue-gray cloud through the side of his mouth. *What the hell was Kadri talking about?*

'You've lost me, Ahmed.'

A long pause. Then Ahmed said: 'How could you? In school we learned all about the perfidious English and the treacherous French. And now I'm witnessing perfidy in action. You have betrayed me, Michael.'

Kadri was calm. His color perhaps had heightened. But he sat comfortably at the desk, his arms spread out before him, his hands clasped. Vaux's mind had suddenly shut down. For a moment he wondered if he was dreaming—perhaps this was a horrible nightmare brought on by the heavy eating and drinking and an evening over-freighted with emotion.

'Well, what have you to say?' demanded Kadri.

Vaux instinctively knew he had to play for time. But beyond that his mind was a blank.

'I don't know what you're talking about, Ahmed. Is this one of your party games? Will Safa soon appear as a witness to my treachery?' Vaux clung tenuously to the slight hope that Ahmed's blunt accusations were related to his still undisclosed affair with Safa.

'I see. Then we shall have to show you. Abdullah, please come.'

Abdullah shuffled toward them. From his ample, billowy cloak he produced a handful of silvery disks. They suddenly reminded Vaux of the silver six-penny coins of his childhood. They tinkled as Abdullah spilled them on the desk.

'Would you care to tell us, Michael, what these dazzling little pieces of metal represent or are used for?' asked Ahmed, his voice betraying a strong effort to remain controlled.

Vaux quickly answered. 'They're batteries, that's all. For my watch. I like to keep a reserve. These old Timex pieces are known for their short-lived cell batteries. Didn't you know that?'

'Good try, Michael. You were always good at rapid responses. Perhaps you would be a good recruit for *Al-Saiqa*.'

Vaux smiled but was too familiar with Ahmed's penchant for sarcasm to be taken in. He decided to go on the offensive. 'Where did you find these, Abdullah?'

Abdullah looked at his employer to answer.

'Abdullah is a faithful servant. His job is to protect this house from trespassers and other evildoers. There is nothing he won't do to protect the family.'

'Including breaking into my briefcase, it seems,' said Vaux. He had kept the CD disks along with his emergency mobile phone in his briefcase. It was secured with a combination lock.

'Nothing was broken into, Michael. Abdullah has street smarts among other instinctive skills. He merely looked at the passport you carelessly left lying on your dressing table and guessed you did what millions of people do—use the first three or four sequential numerals of the day, month, and year of your birth so that you could easily remember your combination without having to write it down. The briefcase is undamaged.'

They had come to an impasse. For a moment Vaux thought that perhaps his explanation would be accepted.

'So anyway, what's the problem, Ahmed? Some spare batteries and a defunct mobile phone. Aren't we getting a bit paranoid here?'

'Another good try, Michael. But not good enough. I would ask Abdullah to explain but his English is not that great. So I will put to you this very simple question: why do you feel it necessary to deliver, oh, perhaps a dozen or so of these watch batteries every few days to the American Express office?'

'That's ridiculous. I've been popping in and out of that place to cash travelers' checks and change money, that's all.'

Kadri smiled. He had the look of a triumphant cat that had cornered a defiant mouse. 'I believe you know Faud Al-Mallah—who works there, of course.'

'I don't really know him, but he often handles my business when I'm there.'

Kadri looked at Abdullah, who had shuffled back to stand in front of the door. 'What would you say if I told you that Faud regularly takes the envelope that you leave with him to the El Minzah Hotel, where he hands it over to a Mr. George Greaves who, I gather, works for the British embassy in Rabat? What's more, the same envelope rattles like an envelope full of coins—or little cell batteries, if you like?'

'I know nothing about that,' said Vaux.

The ensuing silence may have indicated to an optimist that a truce had been called. But Kadri quickly crushed any such hopes. 'May I have a look at your hungry battery-powered watch, Michael?'

Vaux couldn't know that for Kadri this was a shot in the dark. For he still entertained a scintilla of hope that there was perhaps nothing sinister about the damn cell batteries. In any case, Vaux had been cornered. He took off the watch and hoped that Kadri would make only a superficial examination. He looked at the oversized wristwatch closely. He played with the two buttons. The back sprung open and Kadri seemed fascinated with what he saw.

'Two batteries—one extra large and one normal size. How totally amazing.' He twirled the watch around in his fingers and brought the gauzed rim closer to his eyes.

'Everything they make these days gets smaller and smaller, doesn't it. Miniaturization, I think they call it.' He closed the watch and placed it on the desk. 'What is it, Michael? It's clearly no ordinary wristwatch.'

Vaux bent over, his elbows on the desk, his head resting in his hands. He said nothing. He had been impressed with Ahmed's handling of the situation. He had been caught red-handed—once again—but his old friend had adopted what seemed a conciliatory tone. He had used his first name, he had not exploded in indignation when he had had every right to do so. He had remained calm. He had not threatened violence.

Finally he raised his head. 'It's the latest, state-of-the-art, cutting edge recording equipment produced by the backroom boys at Century House,' said Vaux in a flat, matter-of-fact voice.

Then he began to tell Ahmed Kadri about Operation Couscous.

* * *

Faud had always known that he had leverage—even if his English wasn't proficient enough to know the meaning of the word outside its relevance to mechanics. The intelligence agencies that sought his services had recognized that he possessed potentially valuable assets and that he could avail himself of opportunities that they could use to their own advantage. His work for the firm came spasmodically, so that the major source of his income after the puny wages from American Express was the monthly stipend from the Direction de la Surveillance du Terretoire, or DST, the Moroccan intelligence service. It was a stand-by retainer more than reward for work done: he had to be on immediate call to investigate suspect tourists and sundry longer-term visitors who had entered Morocco possibly for nefarious purposes through the port of Tangier and via the airports and the country's long land borders. Suspects these days were usually aspiring drug dealers who sought a fortune from selling the potent hashish grown in the Rif Mountains. Nowhere in the world was it easier to 'buy low' from the destitute Berbers of the Rif and 'sell high' to the insatiable potheads in the West.

In the old days, the non-desirables would have covered the gamut of human foibles from pedophiles and Spanish prostitutes to smugglers bent on spiriting out Morocco's antiquities to eager collectors in Europe and North America. Occasionally Faud was called upon to tail a suspected would-be assassin of King Hassan. Since the '70s, when two attempts on the king's life had miraculously failed, there had been many such alarms. As a consequence of all this, Faud's compensation, supplemented by overtime pay, grew at a gratifying, if erratic, pace.

Faud had told Abdullah about Vaux's mysterious envelopes and about the Brit who gratefully received them at the Hotel El Minzah. He had told him partly out of loyalty to an old friend, but also perhaps to impress him on how closely he kept tabs on everything that went on in his particular bailiwick. But he hadn't made any money from this confidence. Abdullah was always broke. When he got his weekly cash wage it would go straight into his wife's hands. But the Syrian whose aunt was in a nursing home, and to whom Abdullah owed allegiance, could perhaps benefit from the information Faud had passed on to Abdullah. If so, he could eventually present a bill for his efforts. But the proposition was iffy. There was no way Faud could yet know whether the intelligence relayed to Abdullah was of benefit to the master of the house or not.

But one thing he did know: Greaves would almost certainly want to know that the head of the household would soon be made fully aware of the mysterious traffic in 'Private & Confidential' packages between the Villa Mauresque and the El Minzah Hotel. Such information always carried a price tag.

George Greaves was duly informed. Faud told Greaves he couldn't reveal his sources. But the nephew of Madame Sherazad Cherqi was, as he spoke, receiving information with regard to the 'matter of the mysterious envelopes.' There was nothing he, Faud, could do to stop such revelations, the source of which remained a dark mystery.

Greaves didn't waste time in further questioning. He went over to the writing desk. Out of the slim top drawer he grabbed a wad of dirhams.

'I think you'll find that's 40,000 dirhams. Thank you, Faud.'

Faud's quick mental arithmetic told him that the thick brick of paper notes was the equivalent of $5,000. He divided the money into four wads and stuffed them into four different pockets. He bowed slightly and left Greaves' room.

* * *

Vaux saw wisps of white clouds through the tall windows. It was the dawn of another hot, sunny day in this elusive paradise. Now, in his mind's eye, he saw No. 32 Willow Drive just as it had been when he left: tarps covering a mound of red roof tiles, piles of sand in the front garden, the builders' trucks parked along the curbside and on the new macadam driveway, Rex running around chasing a squirrel, and Patrick lying on his stomach in the hallway, finishing off a skirting board with high-gloss white paint.

They were still in the study. Abdullah had disappeared.

They had been talking now for three hours and both men were scrambling for some solution to their shared dilemma. Kadri had engaged in a habit Vaux remembered from their student days—snapping his intertwined knuckles, a sort of accompaniment to his thought processes.

Vaux had put it to his old friend that 'in the final analysis' what he had done had really harmed no one. What's more, he pointed out, he wasn't to know when he accepted the assignment that Ahmed hadn't nursed bitterness and resentment toward the Assad regime. Who knows how London would have rewarded him for his total cooperation? Asylum, perhaps. And possibly employment as an Arabist at the Foreign Office. But, yes, he readily admitted that by recording their conversations he had betrayed Ahmed's confidence. It was what a politico would call a dirty trick, not worthy of him. He asked for forgiveness.

Kadri was not yet ready to forgive. But he did recognize that the farcically named Operation Couscous had been thought up by the deviants at Century House, those narrow-visioned civil servants who could never see the world situation from Arab eyes. He understood, too, that by agreeing to go along with the enterprise, Vaux was atoning for his guilt in the deception of his British employers over the phony intelligence he had produced on the winding up of Operation Helvetia.

But he also pointed out that what Vaux had done was tantamount to outright treachery, the total betrayal of an old friend who, it should be recalled, had transformed what was to become a fiasco for Vaux into a virtual triumph. It was he, Kadri pointed out, who had devised the scheme whereby Vaux would come out of his bungled efforts at espionage untouched and uninjured. It was he, Kadri, who had saved him from abduction to Syria and in effect acting against the real interests of Syria, the country that, despite his temporary exile, still commanded his loyalty.

But then Kadri conceded that perhaps he had used Vaux and that Vaux had used him—they had in fact used each other, pressured by forces and influences that had always worked against and were inimical to what he called their cherished 'brotherhood.'

They had talked until their throats were parched. Kadri banged rapidly on a small brass gong on a nearby side table. Salim, who to Vaux's surprise had apparently waited up all night in the kitchen, was asked to bring bottled water and some ice.

Finally Kadri said, 'There is one way you can now redeem this sad situation, Michael.'

'Tell me,' said Vaux wearily. In his total fatigue, he had come to the irreversible decision to propitiate his guilt, to atone for his disloyalty and deceit, by acceding to anything his old friend demanded.

'You will write me a memo. You will reveal the identities of two senior officials—one at the defense ministry, the other in the PSD, the Political Security Directorate—who you will say you know are working for the British Secret Service, MI6. These are the two men I have since learned were instrumental in my removal from the government. Yes, we will finger them as agents of the British Intelligence Service working at the very heart of Assad's regime. I don't have to tell you how I was treated. But revenge would be sweet. It would also open the door for my return.'

Vaux looked at his old friend across the desk. He was tired too, he told himself, and probably not thinking straight.

'Ahmed, with all due respect to the regime that still commands your loyalty, wouldn't they be put straight in front of a firing squad? No trial, no inquiry, period. Could you live with that? I don't think I could.'

'Ah, you Brits. Always a conscience when it suits you. What about the brutal assassination of Barbara Boyd? Look, if it makes you happier, there's a solution to that problem. Somehow or other they are forewarned. We'll give them time to get out of the country. They can enjoy an unexpected and unplanned exile.'

'How would you let them know?'

'I still have contacts in Damascus, Michael. Don't underestimate me.'

When Vaux finally got up to his room, Safa wasn't there and nor was his briefcase.

* * *

Sergeant Binkley swept over his visual domain with the powerful Zhumell binoculars. He saw a slight movement from behind the stand of palm trees that hid the tall, rusted gates that opened on to the driveway to Loew's folly. He twirled the focus lock a little and zoomed into an old Arab astride a slow-moving mule. He was headed toward the tower.

'Blow me down. We've got a visitor. Corporal—go see what he wants. And be polite.'

'Sir!' Corporal Smyth trundled down the narrow spiral staircase.

Binkley saw Smyth talking to the old white-bearded man who wore a flat, white *pakol* on his head. Despite the rising heat of the day, he was dressed in a heavy brown woolen jellaba. A piece of paper was exchanged and Smyth seemed to be reading it. The old man bowed slightly and turned the mule around to head out of the property. Smyth ran back to the tower.

'What's this then?' asked Binkley as he grabbed the note from Smyth's hand.

This could be an emergency. I believe our man is in danger but has somehow lost access to the alarm. I want you to go to the villa a.s.a.p. Pose as backpackers, old friends of Vaux from the U.K. Do a thorough recce and don't try to be clever. No arms unless concealed. Verify his status and act accordingly. Report soonest. G.

'Jesus Christ. Let's go, Corporal.'

They scrambled down the staircase and ran out of the tower toward the parked Jeep. Suddenly Binkley stopped in his tracks.

'Wait a minute, mate. More haste less speed. Go back up and take out two of the revolvers stashed along with the rest of our vast armory. That's all we're going to need. Plus a couple of coshes. Oh, and a couple of knives. Okay?'

Smyth said nothing as he turned and ran back to the tower. Binkley reread the note and walked calmly over to the Jeep. He saw that it was parked at some sort of angle as if one of the wheels had got stuck in a deep rut. But then he realized what had happened: all four tires had been slashed. The vehicle, even with two spare wheels attached at the rear, had been immobilized. He sighed, opened the driver's door, and sat sideways on the seat waiting for Smyth to return.

'Take it easy, Corporal, no rush,' he shouted as Smyth began to trot toward him. He'd put the weapons in an old army haversack.

'Oh shit,' said Smyth on seeing what had happened.

'Yeah, oh shit, mate. We're going to have to walk down there, effect an entry, and see what the bloody hell's going on.'

It was nearly noon and the day was going to be another scorcher. Binkley wiped his forehead with his shirtsleeve and sorted through the haversack. He took out a Smith & Wesson .38 and dug it into the back pocket of his jeans. He withdrew a long-bladed knife and stuffed it into his thick army-issue woolen sock. Smyth did the same but left the coshes in the haversack.

'Who d'ya think did it?' asked Smyth.

'Whoever's down in that posh villa and wants to sabotage our efforts to rescue the guy we're supposed to be watching out for.'

'Who is?'

'The guy who's all luvvy-duvvy with that gorgeous bird, that's who. Take a dekko.' From his khaki shirt's breast pocket, Binkley produced the crumpled photo of Michael Vaux given him by Major Peter Barclay at his initial briefing. 'Do you think you'll be able to recognize him if you see him?'

'That's the guy who stopped by and gave us the note for Greaves, isn't it, Sarge?'

'Right on, Corporal. So here's what we'll do.'

34

Vaux stands at the tall windows overlooking Cairo's Midan el Tahrir, the frenetic traffic junction by the side of the wide, turbid River Nile. The square is a maelstrom of overcrowded buses whose desperate passengers often clamber onto the roofs, speeding yellow taxis, donkey carts, motor scooters, and cyclists wearing flowing robes and jaunty *keffiyahs*. Nothing has changed since his three-year stint in the teeming city in the '60s. In those days, he had stayed as a paying guest at a doctor's apartment on the east side of the square. On the south side now, he can see the french windows that opened onto the balcony of the room that had been his home so many years ago.

Nearby is the landmark Hilton Hotel, perched on the banks of the mud-colored Nile. It's nearly noon, and despite the oppressive heat, Vaux has poured himself an *arak* that he slowly savors as much as the anticipation of his appointment with Chris Greene. The doorbell chimes at precisely 12 p.m.

Greene, in a dark blue lightweight suit, open-necked white shirt, and black wingtips, stands before him. Vaux had always thought him handsome, and now the Egyptian sunshine has given him a golden tan and bleached his light brown hair. He still has that youthful smile—despite all that has happened. Vaux puts out his hand but Greene ignores it. Instead he puts both arms around Vaux's shoulders and gives him a hug.

'First things first,' says Vaux. 'What will you have? I have a very small but adequate bar. Unfortunately no chilled beer.'

'When in Rome. I'll have what you're having.'

Vaux hands Greene a small, stemmed glass of the color-
less drink. They sit down in deep leather armchairs.

'It's good to see you,' says Vaux. 'I really never expected
you to be in Cairo.'

'Craw wanted rid of me for some reason. I think Sir Walter was tiring of Craw's byzantine office politics and was beginning to see me as a possible successor—once he'd engineered
Craw's transfer. But the wily bastard—Craw, I mean—came
up with the brilliant idea that I needed some experience in
the field. So Cairo it was. I don't think old Sir Walt knew I'd
gone until I didn't show up for the staff meeting one Monday
morning.'

Vaux has an incredulous look on his face. 'And they gave
you the go-ahead to see me?'

'Not exactly, Mike. I'm here on my own volition, if you
like. They'd go ballistic if they knew I had met you.'

'I appreciate it. You're not wired, are you?'

'Don't be ridiculous. You're a friend. That's why I'm
here.'

'I don't deserve you.'

'You know there's an arrest warrant out, don't you?'

'I guessed there could be.'

'There was mayhem at Gower Street when they realized
what you'd done. Sir Walt wanted your guts for garters—all
that sort of thing.'

'That's not surprising.'

'Did you know that Kadri gave you a total bill of goods?
That neither Khateb nor Abdul Khundkar were British agents.
It was a trumped-up charge. Fortunately they got out of
Syria in time. Or did you think that Kadri was telling the
truth?'

Vaux hesitates. Greene doesn't need to know what he
thought. 'What's happened to them?'

'Khateb got a job at Sciences Po in Paris. He's a lecturer
on Middle East affairs. And Khundkar apparently retired in
Switzerland. He had loads of money stashed there. But what I

can't understand is why, after we had denied any knowledge of these two alleged spies, Assad wouldn't let them return. They could have come back and destroyed your friend Kadri. Then where would you both have been?'

'That's obvious, Chris. Once an assertion like that has been made against you, why should anyone believe your story? In other words, Assad figured the Brits would deny all knowledge of the two alleged moles anyway. So no matter how strong the men's denials, how powerful their pleas of innocence, Assad simply would never believe them. He wouldn't take the chance. He believed that I had told Kadri the truth—simple as that. Assad and his advisers figured where there's smoke there's probably fire.'

'I suppose you're right. Proving a negative is practically impossible.'

'And what about George Greaves? I rather liked the old rogue.'

'He blamed the fiasco on Special Forces. They should never have seconded the task to the transport grunts. He said the real guys would have had you out of there in a jiffy—whether you wanted to go or not.'

'That's probably true.'

'What happened when they came knocking on Kadri's door?' asked Greene.

'It was a pantomime. They said they were old friends of mine—both of them under thirty and not a very likely story. But they couldn't gain any entry unless they had a plausible tale. Old Abdullah handled them politely. He showed them into one of the lounges and I was summoned. By that time, of course, I had made up my mind. I didn't want to go back. So I told them I was safe and unthreatened and to report the facts back to Greaves as soon as possible. I didn't want Greaves calling in the cavalry and whisking me away. It was all over as far as I was concerned.'

'Greaves says the girl seduced you—that it wasn't a political decision on your part.'

'Safa? Yes, she played a part. But I could have resumed our relationship in England. She was going back to college, she would have been there.'

'Then Ahmed? You couldn't betray your friend?'

Vaux gets up and pours another two drinks. 'I think the Arabs need all the help they can get, Chris. I've thought about it these past months more than anything else in my life. It somehow fills a void. I was empty before—looking forward to a lazy, meaningless retirement in the Home Counties. I was just too comfortable.'

Greene sips his *arak*. He crosses his long legs. Behind Vaux, through the tall windows, he sees the ancient feluccas plying the dusky brown river. He thinks of this unending scene across the centuries.

'I respect you for your decision, Mike. But I wouldn't be a friend if I didn't say I think you're wrong. If you're referring to the Israeli-Palestinian problem, I believe that slowly but surely we are breaking the impasse. Last year's Madrid conference, the Geneva talks earlier this year—we know all about them!—have helped the West to make progress toward a just settlement—for the Arabs and the Israelis. They're talking about a road map now, a step-by-step process of building confidence and eventually working out a compromise.'

Vaux shakes his head. 'The Israelis are experts at prevaricating, playing for time. I don't think they'll ever come to terms with the Arabs until the Arabs themselves present a cogent, articulate argument. I want to help them make that argument so that the West collectively decides to pressure the tough little bully of the neighborhood to comply with international law. Do you really think the Israelis have changed as a result of these interminable conferences?'

Greene doesn't reply. Instead, being the romantic he is, he asks: 'Will Safa join you?'

'I hope so,' says Vaux. Quickly, he suggests lunch. 'The Hilton's got a nice coffee shop.'

'We could be seen. Rather not risk it, thanks all the same.'

Then Greene produces a long manila envelope from the inside pocket of his jacket. 'This is what you asked Susan Appleby to send you. It's a deed of transfer, I believe.'

'Correct. I'm transferring ownership of No. 32 Willow Drive to John Goodchild. I can't thank you enough for arranging this with Susan and the solicitors. Perhaps you'll be good enough to witness my signature. The lawyer at the Syrian embassy will notarize the documents later.'

The two men bend down over a marble-topped coffee table and scribble their signatures in triplicate.

Greene stands up and stretches his arms. 'When are you leaving for Damascus?'

'Tomorrow or the next day. Ahmed has arranged some sort of job and has already rented an apartment for me. I'll soon be working as a sub-editor for the *Syrian Times*, an English-language newspaper—with promises of bigger and better things ahead.'

'That's government-owned isn't it?'

'Probably.'

'I'll make sure the embassy people put it on our subscription list.'

They both laugh. Vaux stays at the door while the rickety lift makes its uncertain ascent. Then Greene, ever hopeful, turns to face him. He decides to throw out the ultimate lifeline.

'Look, old boy. If you change your mind and want to come back, just go to the British Council offices in Damascus. It's on Maysaloun Street. Ask for the chief librarian and give him your business card. We'll make quick contact.'

The grilled doors shudder as they close and Greene waves goodbye.

* * *

Vaux goes over to the tall windows and touches the silky surface of the heavy chintz curtain. He looks out on to the bustling square. Now past noon, the frenetic pace of Cairo life seems to quicken as the blazing sun and still air push up the mercury to over 45 centigrade. He turns to go to the drinks table when he hears a light tapping. He walks over and opens the gilt-paneled double doors.

For a moment he thinks he has lost his mind. Perhaps the heat… But no, she is real. The woman takes off her headscarf, her dark, lustrous hair falls over her forehead, she smiles and stretches out her hand to clasp his.

'Perhaps you'd better sit down, Michael,' she says.

His heart is pounding as he holds her, both his arms around her shoulders almost as if he wants to reaffirm that she is real. He beckons her into the ornate paneled living room.

'Don't say anything,' she says. 'I'll get you a drink.'

'I'm drinking the *arak*.'

He watches as she carefully pours the drink. She brings the glass over to him and sits down at his side on the red plush sofa. Her eyes invite his questions.

'What on earth happened? They told me you were dead.'

'I'm very much alive, darling. Let me explain.'

Vaux holds his breath, takes a sip of his drink. Had it all been another hoax, a trap set to push him into an emotional abyss?

But Barbara Boyd reassures him. She tells him what happened the day they planned to kill her. After 'disposing' (her word) of Alex Simonds, the CIA agent, she sat quietly in the guest lounge of Highcliffe House. She knew she had been followed: she had spotted the tail on her as soon as she drove out of the Newquay hotel. She knew an Army Range Rover when she saw one, and when it carefully followed her onto the B3276 any slight doubt was removed. She was planning her exit strategy when she heard a movement and looked up to see a young girl, probably about nineteen, wriggle out of her backpack, sit down at a writing desk and study a road map.

They got into a conversation. She realized that this young lady could be her savior. She told Betty Bowen that she had been followed to the hotel by a crazy ex-husband (it had been an acrimonious divorce) and she feared the worst in terms of harassment and even physical violence. Could Betty drive?

Yes, indeed, said Betty, who lived in Brisbane, Australia, and was currently hiking around the West Country where her grandparents had originally come from. But she didn't carry a driving license since she never expected to be driving on what, for economic reasons, had to be a walking/hitch-hiking holiday. But Betty Bowen was happy to rescue a beautiful young English woman from a horrible and obsessive 'ex,' and so she agreed to drive the rental car back to Newquay where in any case she had been headed. She was relieved not to have to hitchhike and again face some fresh, pushy driver whose mind and hands were often on something other than the road. Barbara Boyd gave her her own driving license, plus the rental documents and car keys.

Later, she caught a train to London and headed straight for a GSD safe house in Camden Town. Two days later she was in Paris where she took a flight to Damascus. A complete security blanket enveloped her on her arrival. Her GSD bosses decided to keep everything under wraps until they were convinced that she was safe from any further attempts by British or CIA operatives to take her out. No one outside the closely knit Syrian intelligence service was informed of her survival and return. And that, of course, included his friend, Ahmed Kadri.

Vaux looks up and into her dark eyes. She sees a face contorted by bewilderment, perhaps even horror.

'But you sent an innocent young girl to her death!' he protests.

'No, Michael. I couldn't know they meant to kill me. I feared detection, that's all. They were obviously on to me by then. So I had to elude them. I had no idea then that MI6 had arranged for my imminent elimination.'

'So some innocent's parents have been put through un-
told agonies since the disappearance of their daughter…'

Barbara holds his hand again. 'Another tragic victim of
terrorism, perhaps,' she says.

'Yes.'

'And now I must go, Michael. A car will come tomorrow
morning at 10 a.m. and the flight leaves at noon. I shall accompany you. I hope you like that idea.'

'Of course I do. But must you go? Can't you stay
awhile?'

'No, darling. I have a long "to do" list. I will see you in the
morning. Until tomorrow, then'

'Yes, until tomorrow.'

The lift's door closes with a metallic clang and the tiny
cubicle shudders as it starts to go down to the dim, marbled
lobby. She blows a goodbye kiss as once again she drops out
of sight.

End

Acknowledgements

Heartfelt thanks go to John Johnson (Nova Scotia) for his diligent research into Middle East politics and the Arab-Israeli conflict; and to Adam McCrum (East Anglia) for his invaluable suggestions and observations throughout the process.

Roger Croft is a former journalist whose articles have appeared in major publications including The Economist, The Sunday Telegraph and the Toronto Star. He has also worked in Egypt where he freelanced and wrote editorials for the Egyptian Gazette.

Made in the USA
Coppell, TX
04 April 2020